# A WAR AROUND US

## THE MORETTI CRIME FAMILY

### K DOSAL

A War Around Us
© Copyright 2023 by K. Dosal

First Edition
Publication Date: July 25, 2023
ISBN: 978-1-7358845-5-4

Cover Art: Mitch Green

**K . D O S A L**

SWEET & DANGEROUS ROMANCE

# KATIA

Our last names made us enemies.

Both tied to the East Coast but torn by years of vendetta.

We weren't meant to coexist.

That was until I received a call that pulled me deeper into the life of sin.

I was a Vitelli. A woman. A pawn in a man's world.

I was first and center of the board for an arranged marriage.

Then I saw him. A calloused heart and soulless eyes that toyed mine with a game.

My devil wore a suit and tie.

*But when you're a Vitelli, you can't be a pawn if you're a part of the sin.*

# LUCCA

I started a war.

A decision I didn't hesitate after seeing her. The Vitelli principessa.

A decision made by hatred.

It was my turn to take from the Vitellis.

Even after knowing she'd been promised to another.

Because in this game, I was the one who moved the pieces.

*Yet, I didn't know my biggest opponent would be her.*

# WARNING

A War Around Us is book two of an interconnected series. While this book can be read as a standalone, it is recommended to read books in the order they are published for the best reading experience.

-

Some scenes in this story contain graphic sex scenes, gun violence, torture, gore, mature language and situations that may discomfort or trigger an emotional response.

Reader discretion is advised.

A War Around Us inspired soundtrack
Available on Spotify:
https://spoti.fi/3Q7MJpP

# THE FIVE CRIME FAMILIES
## *Character Ranking Glossary*

### MIAMI
The Moretti Family
**Lucca Moretti:** *Boss*
**Salvatore Mancini (Sal):** *Consigliere, former boss*
**Arlo Gerardi:** *Underboss*
**Viktor Novak:** *Soldier*
**Ilias Novak:** *Soldier*

### NEW YORK
The Vitelli Family
**Mario Vitelli:** *Boss*
**Lorenzo Vitelli (Enzo):** *Underboss*
**Leonardo Vitelli (Leo):** *Capo*

### LOS ANGELES
The Borrelli Family
**Pietro Borrelli:** *Boss*
**Tino Borrelli (son):** *Underboss*

### LAS VEGAS
The Costa Family
**Alonzo Costa:** *Boss*

### CHICAGO
The Russo Family
**Stefano Russo:** *Boss*
**Mateo Russo (son):** *Capo*

# THE MORETTI CRIME FAMILY CREST

*For those who have been underestimated;*
*Give them hell with a smile.*

# I

## LUCCA

**ONE DAY BEFORE HIS FOURTEENTH BIRTHDAY**

HEAVY RAINDROPS BOUNCED AGAINST THE METAL ROOF OF THE CAR. The silence of the eleven-hour drive was interrupted by the deafening rumbles and roars from above. My eyes flew to the clock on the dash: five minutes left.

In five minutes, we should be under the shelter of our new home. She'd promise we would be able to stay longer than the two months from the place before. *"A couple of months. Who knows, figlio, maybe even a year!"* I knew better. With a small smile and a nod, I had given her the peace her stress-filled eyes had grown desperate for.

Anything for *Mamma.*

As the car rolled slower, more broken streetlamps passed by. Darkness consumed the wet streets. The only source of light against the storm was weak headlights and fickle lightning.

*"Grazie Dio."* My mother thanked God and continued, "We're here."

I couldn't see anything from the passenger seat. Then, the car turned, and light shone against the structure.

I scanned the quaint one-story, two-bedroom home. Even while the windshield wipers sped against the glass and the rain obscured my vision, I couldn't miss the state of the house. From the overgrown grass and the broken rail on the front steps to the fallen gutter that had cracked a window in its path, I understood. Mamma had lied.

We were in trouble, and we didn't leave Wisconsin for a better place.

"It needs a lot of love, but together, we can make it ours." Her voice broke for a split second, the same way it did when she was hiding something from me. Lately, it happened more than once a day.

"It's perfect," I uttered and stared into my exhausted mother's eyes. Small wrinkles decorated the corners of her round hazels, and her dark hair rested just below her shoulders, framing her petite features. A dim smokescreen of a smile appeared, but like an hourglass, I saw right through the surface. She has been marked by the signs of a lifetime of running through life.

"Maybe even a year, huh?" I echoed her words.

She chuckled, and her eyes softened. "Maybe even more."

In order to not break her hope, I omitted my thoughts.

"Now, stay here. I'm going to check it out and turn some lights on."

"No, Mamma. I'm coming with you."

Her gaze snapped toward the house, and her hand paused against the door handle. The only sound between us was the unforgiving rain.

A smile spread across her face as if she hadn't fallen silent at all. "No reason for us both to get drenched while I fumble with the lock."

I wanted to push, but instead, I gave in to my mother's stern glare.

"Fine, but I'm not waiting for all the lights."

"As if you've ever done so."

I almost smiled.

She fought her way through the weeds and rain until she stood underneath the poor roofline that was taking more water from the sky than preventing it from getting in. By the time she opened the door, the back of her clothes had stuck to her body.

I waited.

And waited.

It had been a few minutes since she'd entered, and the first light had never lit. Neither did the second.

Fear quickly settled, and danger knocked on my chest.

Each swipe of water I watched run down the windshield meant another wasted moment. I had hesitated, and Mamma had taught me that hesitation was our biggest enemy. Our instinct, our ally.

Running was another lesson I ignored.

It felt like that was all we had ever done, but I couldn't run, not now. Not without her.

Shutting the door quickly without a sound, I moved toward the tree line and away from the glare of the headlights. Rain kept my eyes from fully opening, and its pour prevented me from hearing anything other than heavy drops and thunder. My shoes sank into the muddy puddles of grass as I hurried closer. Lowering my body to the front of the house, I quietly moved and ducked past the windows until the open front door creaked in the wind.

Before I took the first step, I heard it. My mother's struggles.

Without hesitation, I slid past the front door. I didn't make it far before my feet stumbled. My hands shot out quickly, catching my body before it could hit the floor. But I didn't feel the solid touch of hardwood, the sticky sensation of vinyl, or the rough texture of worn carpet. It was warm against my cold hands, rigid and yet soft.

My eyesight adjusted to the dim room created by the car lights, and my eyes fell.

With eyes wide open and a knife by his left shoulder blade, a lifeless body lay beneath my palms. Bile rose as my bottom hit the floor while I scurried away from the dark puddle that continued to grow.

My soaked and soiled shoes slipped against the floor, and the more I kicked to get away from the mud-mixed blood, the more I fought to gain space.

Thump.

*Mamma.*

Her struggles continued, but they shortened, then weakened. Frantically, I rose from the floor, wiped the feeling of the body my hands had touched, and followed the trail of my mother's gasps. Each step I took, messy imprints of brown and red stalked my path.

She was pinned down, thrashing against the hand that covered her face as the man reached for his back. He reached for his gun, distracted. Prickled short hair, olive skin covered in colored ink, and blaring teeth. His mass tripled the size of my almost fourteen-year-old body, and yet, he didn't hear me until it was too late.

Surprise, adrenaline, and anger couldn't suppress the wicked demon I'd been born with any longer. I rushed toward him. His body hit the ground in a heap. Without wasting any time, I delivered a blow to his temple. Pain shot through my hand. Burning knuckles and sin, I punched again with blinding rage, but he wasn't any kid or man I'd brawled with before. He was powerful, skillful. Trained. As his body twisted, he carried his right fist down my stomach in anger.

I bent in pain and gasped for the breath taken from my lungs. Dazed by the ache and loss of air, I had no time to react to the agonizing drag of his fist on my face. Again and again. I held on to the throbbing anguish of his hands and blocked his last punch. Its force drove my back to the ground. His body rushed over mine, and I shot my knee into his groin. At last, I saw shock and pain sweep through his hardened eyes. It was quickly forgotten as his scowl threatened death. His heavy hands and fingers wrapped around my throat. I couldn't smell the rain, blood, or the rotting house. Not while my windpipe burned in misery.

Letting go of his deadly eyes, I scanned the floor for a weapon. I didn't have long before my body would pass out or accept the afterlife.

Mamma's footfall distracted me, and his hands slacked slightly. He'd heard her too.

I didn't face her gurgling sounds, the anguish that bounced off her body, or the slaps her small hands achieved on his skin. It was impossible for me to face her in defeat.

Then, I felt it.

The cool metal against the tips of my fingers. The handgun that mocked life at its distance.

With the little strength I had left, I inched further to my right. It was such a small movement that he didn't feel my body slithering below.

Battered knuckles gripped its power. Index finger curled, weakening the fearful void. My palm was the one to answer the lifeline call.

I could now face my mother's frightful gaze. It was bloodshot and filled with unshed tears. She scratched his arm over and over, but it only forced him to apply even greater pressure to her thin neck. He loosened his grip on me as he concentrated on her. With his hand seconds away from crushing her windpipe, Mamma's eyes held an apology. They held long conversations and years of love.

And yet, her eyes only saw me.

Trapped by them, my chest bounced in burning heaps of silent pleas for her to hold on.

*You can't leave me.*

I knew what had to be done. With no hesitation or remorse, I raised my right hand. His foul smile that was aimed at Mamma vanished as he felt the Grim Reaper's icy touch under his jaw.

His head fell.

His eyes widened.

And I pulled the trigger.

I was the last thing he saw before the bullet penetrated his head. Blood splattered the ceiling in vivid red. The sight of it made it my new favorite color.

The color laced with life and twisted with death.

The blast echoed along with the thunder as his head bowed and his body slumped forward.

I let his weight drown me in the quiet.

I allowed his dead figure to numb my exhausted and beaten body as a reminder to never embrace any weaknesses.

And as I lay beneath him with his blood on me, I failed to feel any remorse.

The rain had washed off the gore, but I kept the sin nearby. Mamma and I didn't speak a word. We just walked out and didn't look back. I should have talked to her. Asked for the truth. Hugged her tight. Or watched her love-ridden eyes for a while longer. Instead, I passed out in the passenger seat and woke up with a bitter future under a flickering streetlamp.

# ITALY

# II

## KATIA

THE EARLY MORNING SKY CAME ALIVE WITH PEAKING SUN RAYS. THE DARK corners were slowly losing ground to the bright beginning of the day. A farewell whisper of the night vanished as I watched the fight end. A fight that could never be won because, after darkness, light always shone. It was inevitable, time.

I hadn't missed a sunrise since I'd left the States as a child, knowing it could be my last in peace. I knew this day would come. I had wished I could have been forgotten, but the more years passed, the more I understood duty wasn't something I could avoid.

I was a Vitelli.

Duty ran through my veins, as did the countless deaths my last name carried.

Fully dressed, I sat at the foot of my bed staring out the window, taking in the last peaceful Italian sunrise with a pounding heart. Each beat tallied the seconds, the minutes, I had left.

The ringing of an incoming call broke the bitter silence inside my room. The two men that stood by my door shifted, but I paid them no attention.

It didn't matter if my guards allowed them in. I wouldn't follow them without hearing the order from my grandfather or another family member first. I wasn't naïve; I was born into an unconventional lifestyle that demanded caution.

My grandfather lived on the outskirts of Salerno, quietly and heavily guarded. A port city just southeast of Naples, Italy. Built on the ruins of a Roman temple where the calm waves of clear blue water promised to soothe out your troubles. A place I left shortly after receiving my first structural job. I should've never left Nonno's house, even for the sense of independence.

Because after all the years of being him and I, their presence meant my time with Nonno was over.

With my palm stretched, I waited for the weight of his phone while my attention remained out the window. The ringing grew closer until I silenced its shrieking sound.

No hello, no pleasantries.

I knew who placed the order. Lorenzo. My eldest brother. The next in line to the New York Mafia.

"It's been years, Enzo," I spat with the weight of my future. "And yet, you sent two goons to infiltrate my home. This is not the way to get my attention."

"I'm not looking for your attention." Dark and detached, he voiced, "Duty calls."

"Who is he?"

"You have two hours before your flight leaves."

"Wait, Lorenzo!"

"See you soon."

The line disconnected, and my time to stall was over. I took one last look toward the golden rays, a farewell to the shimmer of freedom as the weight of my duty rolled through my mind with thundering clouds. I stood ready to face my fate: an arranged marriage.

# MIAMI

# III
## KATIA

C OULD YOU LOOK LESS MISERABLE?" I IGNORED ENZO'S QUESTION AND watched the dark clouds as they hovered over the full moon.

*Three days.*

That was how long it'd been since I'd left Italy without a goodbye and stepped on American soil.

I hadn't had the chance to get answers or bring up my career before the call ended, asking to pack my life. Duty called.

No, not asked, ordered. It only served as a reminder that even as a successful twenty-six-year-old woman with a career, clients, a future, and plans, my life had never been mine.

In two hours, I'd packed eighteen years into a suitcase.

*Ten years.*

That was how long it'd been since I last saw my eldest brother, Enzo.

*Eleven years* since I'd last spoken to Leo, my second-oldest brother.

This was after he bled a poor bastard with the blade of his knife for whistling in my direction as we walked down the streets of Venice.

No one *saw* anything. No one *said* anything.

Today proved it didn't matter how far or long I'd been pushed away from this family. I still carried the weight of blood and power only a *principessa* of La Cosa Nostra could.

For me, it meant a loveless marriage.

Because that was all we had ever been in their eyes as a woman, a bargaining chip.

The large blacked-out sedan reduced its speed at the sight of the large gates that hid my future den. That was if everything went according to Enzo's plan. The size of the home didn't surprise or intimidate me. Money never did, not when I'd been showered with it to do what was asked of me, as if happiness had a price.

"Don't ignore me," Enzo sneered, and the feel of his dark gaze slid over me. "This is not the time for your games, Katia."

Leo was entertained in the back as his dark chuckle traveled inside the cab.

I gave Enzo my full attention. His stern brown eyes demanded an answer.

Without regard to his men at the front, I spat, "My apologies, *brother*. I'd forgotten it's *just* marriage."

His lips curled in distaste before he shot back, "Say the word, and California it is."

My head snapped forward, and my breathing sped up as my shoulders stood back. I didn't speak a word.

"Didn't think so," Enzo replied coldly.

The urge to feel the cool touch of my brass knuckles caused my hand to twitch, a desperate tic. Curling my hand around my small clutch where I kept it safely inside, I brought it closer. But it wasn't enough, and instead, I ran my fingers over my right thigh. My eyes closed to the hint of the thin holster strap where my push dagger hid beneath my dress.

*Hurt him.*

*Hurt him as much as he is hurting you. Show him how his parting gift can be put to use after ten years.*

I took a calming breath, easing the fire that burned through my veins, while the car rolled to a complete stop next to the stone front steps of the mansion. This was it, the bit of freedom I once possessed would be taken tonight. All due to ego and a sloppy murder.

Enzo pulled the door handle, stopped, and uttered, "Don't fuck this up, Katia. I won't blink twice before I deliver you to Los Angeles." He exited the car, and I waited for his threat to vanish from my mind. Instead, it sank deeper into my soul.

My door opened, revealing Enzo's inked hand stretched out for me. I took it without choice before wrapping my hand around his arm. The same arm that helped me up as a child after scraping my knees, only to be told that pain and blood were no reasons to cry. They were meant to teach a lesson.

Two steps later, Leo stood to my left, and with each footfall closer to the front door, the more I struggled to keep my legs from giving in.

It angered me to see my own body failing me. I was stronger than this.

Hell, I'd been molded from afar for this role in a country miles away.

"Trust me when I say I am looking out for your best interests, *piccola*," he murmured without looking away from the door, his jaw clenched tightly.

I'd always been *"little one"* in his eyes. It didn't feel right anymore, not now. In spite of our broken family, I knew he believed he was doing me a good deed.

Seeing how far his judgment had strayed left a bitter taste in my mouth.

"My name is Katia," I gritted out.

The front door opened, exposing the money that spilled within its walls. I wondered how many ounces, bundles, lies, and blood it had taken for such details. Marble floors spread through the main floor until meeting the inside terrace, and the crystal-cut grand chandelier sparkled past the dim lighting. Pillars decorated the inside structure, and I couldn't help but admire its structural design.

Hundreds of white roses adorned the room, giving no chance to the endless perfumes and colognes worn by the bodies that lingered as the rose scent triumphed over. Breathing deeply, I bathed in their purity before they could wilt due to the corruption that stood in just one house.

Some would call this a charity gala, a fundraiser for a cause. I called it a fraud. Not one person would be standing here unless they had something to gain.

Leo soon slipped away from our side and into darkness. The place he loved most.

"Do you need a drink?" Enzo asked.

I didn't, but I wanted a minute alone, so I nodded. Knowing Enzo, he didn't care for one either, at least not now. What he cared about was learning his surroundings, ensuring the two men that came with us had infiltrated the home and our car was ready for a quick exit.

*Father would be proud.* I almost chuckled at my own thoughts. He wouldn't give us a second thought even if we all died. In his eyes, we were all too much like our mother. However, *I* mirrored her sage green gaze. For him, it was enough. I *was* her, and I continued to pay the price. After her passing, his hatred only grew. That was until I couldn't move from the pain he'd inflicted, and I was shipped overseas at the age of eight.

Freedom, at least that was what I saw it as. The rules, my grandfather's scrutiny, and the feeling of captivity were welcome compared to his wrath.

I glanced around before straightening my brown hair over my shoulders. I urged my hands to stop fidgeting and held on to my clutch a bit tighter. My long, deep red dress stabbed my ribcage, and I allowed the uncomfortable feeling to ground me in reality.

Then, I saw her. It was impossible not to pick her apart from this crowd as her eyes shined with hope and dread. Davina. I tried not to let myself fill with hatred knowing I was here, standing in the same room because of her. On the contrary, I almost smiled when her eyes snapped at mine. The smile would have been filled with praise. One tiny girl had rattled the ego of many, got away with it, and showcased the scar Leo had left on her neck with pride, as if it was a middle finger for La Cosa Nostra.

And yet, I couldn't help but pity her. She had no idea what this life meant, and she still chose it—blindly. When the tall blond man who walked protectively by her side whispered, her attention shifted away from me as her eyes glimmered for him, and I understood.

*Love.*

The death sentence in our world.

An illusion of happiness and a set of shackles meant to prevent you from flying free.

I was so intrigued by the girl who was almost killed at the hands of my siblings that I missed the speech given from afar. Not giving it any importance, or the people that swayed in place, I searched for Enzo as he'd taken longer than anticipated. Instead, I found Leo in the far corner. Only the left side of his face remained out of the shadows. The side that intimidated many by the size of the scar that decorated his left brow and the corner of his eye.

We both kept quiet and away from view as claps and chatter erupted in loud echoes. Leo murmured something under his breath that was not clear for me to understand. As the claps died, classical music replaced the chatter from the live duo nearby. The crowd thinned little by little.

The aura changed within seconds. Dark violence silently swarmed inside, and as I felt its fierce pull, my eyes swung to its call.

Three men walked in our direction with purpose. My feet took a small step back, deeper into the shadows as I stared blankly at the trio. My mind dismissed the two that walked a few feet behind, only focusing on him.

*"Lucca."* His name slipped through my parted lips, and my body stilled.

Lucca's powerful footfalls never faltered, but his dark gaze narrowed as his head inclined slightly and he continued down the hall.

*You are not hearing voices.*

Lucca's fingers reached the tie of his three-piece black suit, leaving his tattooed neckline exposed as he adjusted himself. His sight turned toward the remaining people inside his home before he gripped the doorknob to his right and disappeared from view. While he took the violent aura along with him, the pull still tugged me tightly to follow. A dangerous pull that was wise to ignore.

A blond-haired man followed quickly behind. His resemblance to the one who'd escorted Davina earlier only brought more questions. As the last guy traced their steps, his wicked eyes caught mine. Dark hair and an even darker gaze trained on me. He stopped, craned his head, and pursed his lips in disgust as Leo moved forward at my side. His eyes assessed me carefully.

They weren't supposed to know about me...yet.

With a quick grip on my brother's arm in so-called fear, I'd deceived the man into believing I was no one to care about. Just an ordinary woman lost in this made world who sought the thrill of being with a mafioso.

Of course, he fell for it.

He took one last look at Leo before closing the door behind him.

I let Leo go. "Who was that?"

"Your future brother-in-law, Arlo. Lucca's righthand man and Miami's underboss," he replied with distaste.

*Brother-in-law?* Aside from their olive skin and Italian features, Arlo and Lucca bear no resemblance to one another.

"Enough talk, it's time." Enzo's voice traveled faster than my body could find him.

I wasn't surprised to see his hands missing our drinks. Even our small conversations contained lies. Little white lies we've told each other for years. The lies we hide behind.

Arlo adjusted his tailored suit before he leaned over to Leo.

With a nod, I watched as Leo walked closer toward the door but waited as Enzo stood before me.

"Stay here, and away from view. Only step inside if Leo is the one holding the door open. You hear a gunshot —"

"I know. Find our men and get in the car," I finished.

"Don't forget what you are here for."

"I won't."

Enzo gave me a small nod and walked past me, and I was left alone.

We were the enemy.

Invited, yet unwelcome in this city.

A small prayer should have fallen from my lips. A prayer for Enzo's plan to come through tonight. A prayer for the moment Lucca realized he'd been one step behind. A prayer for what was to come.

But the prayer never reached my lips.

Now, all I could do was watch the pieces fall and the chaos unravel.

LEO HELD THE DOOR OPEN, AND THE ROOM FELL SILENT AS I STEPPED INSIDE the room.

"A marriage," Enzo proposed.

With each step I took closer to Enzo, the tension grew thicker.

I couldn't look around to catch anyone's reactions or pay attention to the built-in bookcases on the walls. Not when his eyes were on me.

With my head held high, I kept my pace steady while my lungs filled with the smell of oak and bourbon.

Lucca's eyes were cold, but as his dark gaze held mine captive, they swirled with menace. As if a game had begun. It was a game only he knew the rules to. A game I was bound to lose. And the longer I kept my eyes on him, the more I believed my ways of deceit would be put to the test.

I wanted to leave this room, take this dress off, and spar until my body gave in. I wanted to say, *"The hell to Lucca,"* and board the next plane back to Italy. To the New York Syndicate, that was a treacherous dream. With the end of my time in Italy, all I knew was the Mafia life.

And in this life, I knew how to fight.

Lucca scoffed. My thoughts weren't safe around him.

"Katia Vitelli." My name rolled effortlessly from his tongue with his faint Italian accent. "I thought you were a myth. Guess they just kept you well hidden."

The game had started.

"They did for years in the old country. That is until you are needed to fulfill your duty," I spat.

Enzo wanted me to sell this union, and this was *my* way. With my voice loud and clear. To a man like Lucca, he would see my spirit as a challenge. He will say yes, if only to banish it.

I was baiting him, and as he chuckled darkly, I knew I had.

"Does your boss know about this?" he asked Enzo without releasing his gaze from mine.

Lucca was toying with him as he pushed lines no other man dared to cross. Even with one question, he had reminded Enzo he wasn't the Boss of New York. Our father was, making him unable to make such agreements without permission.

Without looking at my eldest brother, I knew he envisioned every way he could gut the man before him. After all, that was what our family did best. Cut, carve, and butcher. But unlike Lucca, Enzo was born into this world and tailored to the role. It was only a matter of time before New York would answer to him.

"My orders are to fix the problem and solidify the family. I am only following orders. I don't make them *yet.*"

I've been around made-men all my life. I was a *principessa*. But this…this was different. My future was hanging at the hands of a ruthless bastard. A killer with a brutal reputation.

Even then, I was here to get the answer I needed.

As I stood across his desk, my eyes traveled over Lucca's jaw. The shadow of his beard didn't let a reaction slip by, but I kept looking for the tells. My gaze slid down his neck. Portions of his tanned skin were covered in tattoos, piquing my interest in their meaning, if they had any at all. By the amount of ink on his neck, I knew there was more underneath his crisp suit. My eyes were distracted by them, so I looked for his hands instead. I hunted for a twitch, a habit. Instead, his large, inked hands rested on his desk without a single movement.

I could feel his eyes on me while he raised his left hand to his jaw. Lucca ran his hand along his raspy beard, getting what he wanted when my eyes halted on his lips.

Damn him. I'd done it unconsciously.

Indeed, this *was* a dangerous game.

I didn't hide when our eyes met again. Once they locked, he gave me the answer I was looking for.

An ominous smile spread across his face as he said it.

"Deal."

# NEW YORK

*D*<sup>EAL.</sup>"

My eyes tore open, snapping me away from the vivid dream of Lucca's piercing dark eyes on me as his one word sealed a vow.

Laying still underneath the covers of my bed, I felt the racing pace of my heartbeat. The rise and fall of my chest as I looked into the dark room. I clenched my fists to release the prickling sensation in my fingertips and tried shaking away the vision of *him*.

It was useless.

I couldn't even call it a nightmare. It was a memory filled with mistrust and uncertainty that kept me on edge.

Frustrated, I left my bed and stepped toward the large windows and slid the black-out curtains open. As I looked out to the manicured lawn I'd roamed aimlessly as a child, I was surprised to see Enzo's car parked on the drive.

I'd called him for three days, asking him to please get me out of my father's home. To forget about masochist traditions and mafia etiquette and just drop me off at a hotel. There were no answers to each call or text message.

But he was here now, and I couldn't stay cooped up in this room anymore.

This home reminded me of the scared child I'd once been, and the longer I stayed here, the more my mind reacted to old memories and fears.

Quickly, I rushed away from the window and past the four-post bed my father replaced the day after my mother's death.

He had removed any details she had left behind.

The bathroom lights were merciless as they pronounced my lack of sleep. I knew it would take some time for me to conceal the dark circles under my eyes. I sped through my morning routine in hopes of catching Enzo, and once my face showed no weaknesses, I left the bathroom in search of a fitted dress.

Ignoring the sprawled suitcase at the foot of the bed, I reached the closet door where my garment bag hung heavily. I hadn't bothered placing my belongings inside a home I had no desire to ever step foot in again. It will all remain unpacked, longing for each passing day to be the last in this never-ending jar of memories.

After picking a suitable white and black dress, I stared at my reflection and strapped my push dagger under the skirt of the dress. For ten years, it'd brought me comfort. It'd been me and *her*. With threats looming, I wasn't about to stop wearing it. Especially here in this home.

*"You can never let your guard down, Katia."* My grandfather's scolding voice passed through my mind.

The thought of spending more time on my hair vanished as something inside me shouted to search for Enzo. After I slipped on a pair of designer heels, I did just that.

As soon as I stepped into the corridor, I was greeted with silence.

No guards at my door.

Not one soldier was in the hall.

The silence stretched the further I walked toward the staircase, and with each step I took, the heavier my heart felt.

Not one staff member roamed the main floor.

*Where was everyone?*

The last time I remembered the house being this empty was the day my mother passed.

My father's shout was muffled by our thick walls, and my body turned toward the sound.

*Enzo.*

I had no business following my father's roars, and yet, I found myself taking a step closer and closer to the mahogany door of his study. His voice was loud and yet indecipherable, but his wrath was clear. The need to retreat back to my room grew, and when I heard the tone from Enzo, I knew it would be best.

I'd done everything to stay off my father's radar since arriving. Getting caught by his study wasn't the attention I wanted. Enzo would have to wait.

Frustrated, I took a deep breath and stepped back.

Then, my body froze. My heart pounded, and my eyes shot back to the door as the distinctive sound of metal locked and caught. It was the sound of the slide pulling back as the hammer pushed a bullet into the barrel, ready to be fired. The only thing left was to pull the trigger.

I've learned not to react before thinking. To not be led by emotions. To control impulsive behaviors as it was necessary to stay alive in this world.

And yet, I did the opposite.

I flung the door open, and now, I stared at the end of the barrel as the door echoed shut.

I stood still, watching my father's finger wrap around the trigger as his face morphed into pure ire. A quick look around and the only other gaze I found was Enzo's troubled and furious eyes.

My father lowered the weapon as he stared at me, repulsed. He took a step forward. I took one back. He drew another, and I stood my ground until his hand gripped my cheeks forcefully pushing my body against the door.

Pain shot through the back of my head, and the hollows of my cheeks burned as his hold tightened. Fear swarmed inside, and I fell back in time. A time of tears and a sense of helplessness.

Petrified, I stared at the human who was a part of me. The man I should look up to and the one who should protect me. But Mario Vitelli was nothing more than a demon I had run away from in my past.

I wasn't the child who couldn't meet his eyes. I was the woman who could see him clearly for who he was.

*Hurt him.*

*Hurt him as much as he has hurt you.*

My hand slid down my thigh as his thumb and index finger jabbed deeper, nudging my mouth apart. Then, I felt the outline of my dagger, and I was myself again.

It had taken me a second to push back the young and fearful child that screamed for help away. Now that I had, my green eyes looked up at his dark brown.

He saw the change. He felt it.

My strength.

It had been futile and reckless. A reaction that I had chosen based on feelings. I had gained nothing but a brief moment of satisfaction before it all went black.

# V

## KATIA

A THRASHING ACHE IN MY HEAD WEAKENED MY SENSES IN A THICK cloud. I pushed through it and concealed its hammering pain to prevent slipping back into the peaceful sleep I'd been forced into.

My nose twitched as the stench of alcohol filled my lungs. I opened my eyes and swung my hand over my nose to ease the strong scent. I came in contact with an arm and a cotton ball flew away from the long and calloused fingers. I looked up at the person whose hand I'd stroked.

Lorenzo's.

He stood before me, and I lifted my head off the pillow. I'd made it to a sitting position before his hand held my shoulder firmly, keeping me off my feet and in my bed.

I hated him for it, and my heart repelled the touch. I didn't like hands on me, but my body welcomed the childish gesture as my hasty move caused a hazy rush of unsteadiness.

I pulled away from his touch.

"Look at me," Enzo ordered.

I did.

"Stay down, Katia. You got enough unwanted attention for the day." His blank expression inched closer, and after a few seconds, he spoke. "I'll have someone check on you every two hours." Enzo tried to reach for my shoulder again, but I evaded the contact. He closed his palm instead and turned toward the door.

No.

"Wait, Enzo!"

He didn't stop as he said, "I'll be back after you rest."

"No." I stood strong and watched his hand pull away from the doorknob. "Now."

With a clenched jaw, he turned and retreated back into my room until he sat comfortably in the boudoir.

"Fine."

"I can't stay here," I blurted and took a deep breath.

Enzo watched me in silence. The silence grew as he carefully chose his words.

"You'll be leaving tomorrow."

"Thank you." I sighed.

"Lucca will be here first thing in the morning."

"What?" Shock mingled in my eyes.

With a shrug, Enzo said, "My guess, Lucca found out about Father's deal."

"You are keeping something from me."

"You are a woman."

"And yet, you needed me to fix *your* fuck up," I dared.

He didn't react, he almost seemed…tired?

"Unless I know what's needed, whatever you are planning, Enzo, will fall apart." He took my words, thought them through, and I pushed. "You still need me, don't you?"

"Father had promised *you* to California."

As in Pietro Borelli, the Boss of Los Angeles?

My heart clawed at the idea. The thought of sharing a life with Borelli, a man almost triple my age, caused a cold shiver through me. I didn't dwell on who would be more gentle and tentative, and the idea of love never crossed my mind. No man in our world was capable of such things, and after meeting Lucca in person, I'd been right.

"And yet, you went against him?"

"I did what had to be done," he said, unconcerned. "And I wasn't going to allow you to go to Los Angeles."

"Don't act as if your decision wasn't to save yourself. As if my well-being crossed your mind." A dry chuckle slipped.

"Believe what you wish, Katia. Either way, it means keeping you away from Los Angeles and New York standing." Ice-cold truth.

"Broken vows could lead to war." My voice broke at the idea of the lives it would claim.

"So be it." He gritted his teeth, and as he flickered his eyes away from mine, I saw the battle in them. In the end, he chose to give me a piece of information I was missing. "All because of the girl."

*Davina.* "What about her?"

"It's not that she witnessed a murder, but whose death it was."

"Tell me."

"The more you know…" He trailed off. "Let's just say he was a very powerful politician, and the authorities recovered enough evidence to connect him to us. I thought Leo killed her. Now, I have to fix his fuck up since she took something from the crime scene that connects it all."

"What did she take, Enzo?" My heart raced.

"*The* bullet casing."

It all started to make sense. I had been told it was vital for me to catch Lucca's interest. To secure the marriage deal as Miami held all the cards for our downfall. We had no trust between our families, a long feud fixed for years and created by my father. By marrying into Miami's crime family, it meant Enzo had a way to bind both families. A way to separate the old ways and bond them to new ones for his time to come. Connecting the pieces, the girl, Davina, had not only shaken the hierarchy of New York. She spread bloodshed and rattled an entire syndicate. Taking advantage of this, my brother weakened my father's position and gained ties.

I shook my head with a reeling mind as I said, "If earlier was a fraction of Father's response, he won't allow it."

"He's old and lost in old times. He'll have to go through with it." Enzo stood, done answering me. "Miami is stronger than California will ever be, and we can't trust Miami's word without a tie binding us."

"Is there a chance I might still be California's?" I asked. A lot can happen in one night. Empires can crumble, and words can be bent.

Enzo stopped in front of my door with a chuckle, turned, and smirked.

"Knowing Lucca will be here tomorrow should answer your question." Holding the doorknob, he quipped, "As long as you step foot in Miami by Lucca's side and have a diamond on your finger..." He trailed off.

It was unsettling.

Enzo's relationship with Father was filled with hatred, as it always had been. But as he tried to be nothing like Mario Vitelli, I recognized how calloused and vicious he'd become. The more Enzo's plan was seen through, the more he mirrored the man we detested. Our father.

There was nothing more I could say as he stepped out of the room, leaving me with nothing but an increasing pounding in my head and the threat of collapsing powers soon to come.

# MIAMI

# VI

## LUCCA

I WAS A PRISONER OF MY OWN MIND. ENDLESS SCENARIOS, THOUGHTS, and echoes played in the constant rhythm of puzzles. Each piece held a purpose, and all carried power. A daring labyrinth without gateways and peace. Only turns and moves to stay alive and ahead of those who posed threats to me and the expanding empire I've built.

No room for hesitation.

No room for unthoughtful deals.

But I had taken a counter move. One driven by retribution and emotion. Feelings that were buried in a time of memories that left me confused. It was disturbing to have committed myself to a marriage I had no clear vision of. Even while I tried to justify it as the most effective way to keep my younger brother, Ilias, alive, my motives were far from innocent.

The Vitellis had taken something from me. Now, I was taking *her*.

And she had been offered as a peace treaty. Enzo was clueless as to who he had entrusted his sister's future with. It was laughable.

He thought he was one step ahead of me, but I'd heard rumors of her father's deal with California. Enzo's motives to act at such lengths to defy his father had to be deeper than his sister's, and New York's, interests. I had to find out what they were.

Meanwhile, I would parade my prize in front of Mario Vitelli.

"This could start a war, Lucca." Salvatore Mancini, Miami's former Boss, coughed out his reasoning.

"It's done. I accepted the deal."

My eyes followed the swirling bourbon in the glass I held. It whirled restlessly, as did my mind pondering this countermove. The pieces I needed to move to keep Miami safe, and her as mine.

But what sweeter vengeance could I achieve than by having her in my bed, and her father submitting to the arrangement? Handing over his only daughter to *me*.

Nothing.

Now, I will see through it.

"Your *mothe*—"

"Do not," I snapped.

With my attention fixed on Sal's frail features, I shook my head. If anyone knew the truth, it was him. I didn't have to explain myself to Sal or any man. Not when I was now the head of our organization. He may be Miami's consigliere, but he answered to me.

We both knew this as we stared at one another from across my desk, but Sal was more than that. He was the only man who shared my blood, and the only piece I had left of my mother. The one who took me in and groomed me for what was my birthright.

Sal's body trembled at the painful cough he let out. I watched as cancer masked his lungs, slowly dwindling his strength. The fit stopped, and he lowered his fedora over his head until his thinning hair was hidden beneath. He took a long-labored breath and met my eyes again.

He didn't try to explain his reasoning. He just sat patiently.

For the respect I held for my *zio,* I said, "I won't back out on my word. That's all we have."

*Honor.*

"I know." He breathed tiredly.

"You have said it yourself. I need to marry soon."

"Not her, and not for the reason you've agreed to."

"That's where we disagree." My lips twitched. "It's the perfect reason. *Her.*"

Sal remained quiet. Nothing he could say or do would change the outcome of my decision. Even if it led to a war. I wasn't blind. I saw the danger it opposed, the tension that could expand within our syndicate. While I continued to be watched carefully as the new Boss, cowardice was not a word that would be whispered near my name. And I wasn't one to fail.

"It's late. You should be resting."

"I'll rest soon enough." I didn't miss the underlying meaning of his words. I ignored them, and he asked, "Who will you take with you tomorrow?"

Arlo was out of the question as my right hand and underboss. His duty was the *famiglia* when I wasn't around. As my brother, he was the only one I trusted with such a task with Sal by his side.

Viktor couldn't be pulled too much into this world. I couldn't risk my brother's cover with the DEA for this.

As for the youngest of us four, Ilias had been warned to never step foot in New York. It'd been part of the arrangement we'd set the night of the gala.

All four people I trusted had to stay. Leaving me with Rio and Sergio as my answer. They were loyal and had proven themselves to me from time to time.

My eyes found the bourbon-filled glass I hadn't yet tasted. I concealed my smile with one last swirl of my cup as tomorrow promised her emerald-colored eyes, and I gulped down the liquid to pacify my thirst for vengeance.

THE PRIVATE JET LANDED SMOOTHLY AGAINST THE LATE FEBRUARY SNOW. I hadn't taken a step out into the cold weather, and I already looked forward to my return to Miami's sun and warm weather. I stood once the cabin door opened. A gust of wind traveled inside, cooling my warm skin. I buttoned my coat and stepped into enemy territory.

Our Italian Outfit consisted of five families: Miami, New York, Las Vegas, Chicago, and Los Angeles. All united by our own territories. As in every family, conflicts arose, and feuds were never forgotten. To keep us strong against our enemies, we came together as one. If an issue emerged that could break or harm our syndicate, it would be taken to the council. Each boss would vote, and a decision would be made.

Our closest tie had always been Las Vegas and its boss, Alonzo Costa. New York's had been Chicago, whose ruler, Stefano Russo, was near death in age, but his heart still pumped. Marrying a Vitelli not only favored my ill desires, but our allegiance would weigh heavily in council.

Even then, this was New York. Not my city, my streets, or my men. Since it did not answer to me, I treated it as an enemy.

"Boss."

I turned and gripped the waiting car door. Rio had stayed behind to speak to the captain but had made it back to me.

With a nod, I acknowledged Rio while I kept my eyes on Sergio's task. Sergio held one of Viktor's gadgets he had snatched from the DEA. It traced anything from wires to explosives, as well as GPS signals. He made a quick lap around the car before he got into the driver's seat.

It was clean.

"Our pilot advised us to return by noon," Rio said. "The radar shows unsafe flights any time after that. It'll clear by morning."

I glanced at my watch. I had three hours.

"Let's go." I opened the door and slid inside the warm vehicle. As soon as the car rolled, so did my mind.

Three hours.

# NEW YORK

# VII

## KATIA

ISTARED AT THE BRUISES LEFT ON MY CHEEKS. THE DARK STAINS LEFT BY FINGERTIPS that paraded with the morning's light, along with the busted skin by my hairline from the strike it had taken by the butt of my father's gun. The amount of makeup I had used to fade them wasn't enough. Their shadows remained unhidden.

I straightened my fitted black sleeved dress as a soft knock announced my time was up. Tommaso, my guard since childhood, stood in front of me. A crown of thin hair rested on his head, and tired round cheeks sagged to his jaw. His eyes wandered to the corner of my forehead, and he gave me a curt nod. I guess my hair concealed as terribly as my makeup did.

"You've been asked to join your father's study."

This was it.

The trade of one cage for another.

Fucking men. Too proud to recognize our power but quick to shove us to amend their mistakes for their own gain.

I felt like cattle as I walked through the corridor. The slaughter may have been a better outcome than the humiliation to be traded as one. The closer I got, the harder it was to tell my feelings apart.

Humiliation. Dread. *Suffocation.*

They all blended into one, settling deeper with every *click, clack* sound created by my heels.

*Click, clack.*

There it was, the grotesque mahogany door. One last touch to my hidden best friend on my thigh and I rolled my shoulders to reveal the men that hid behind the door.

While I had no respect for my father, it was customary to address him first in his home until he allowed my gaze to shift to a man who didn't share my blood.

I swallowed my pride with a nod. "Father."

His lips twitched as his gaze revolted against my presence. I ignored his glare and faced Enzo and Leo as they stood together on the right side of the room. I tipped my head down, and they both returned the gesture.

"Katia." My head snapped. I hadn't heard my father's voice speak my name since he'd shipped me to Italy. I was eight. "You've met Lucca Moretti." His hand extended to my left.

Deterring my attention away from my father, I found Lucca. His eyes fell down and roamed up my body before they settled on my face. He was an extremely difficult man to read, but his dangerous aura clung to him like a veil.

Lucca wore all black, from his dress shoes to the tall coat that hung from his broad shoulders. And his eyes—his eyes preyed over mine violently. It was a shrill warning mixed with thrill, but the longer we stared at one another, the more I recognized their punishment.

He'd found out about my previous engagement; he knew my intentions the night we met, and I felt their danger with his gaze aimed at me.

There were seven made-men in one room, including the two that stood next to Lucca. All waiting for a breach of this unity. Ready if the time came for their guns to be drawn. With blood cravings and happy triggers all around, I fought for composure as I tried to keep my breathing steady.

"Mr. Moretti." I acknowledged him in a polite manner. Now was the time to ease the demon, not provoke it. I needed Lucca by my side and a ring on my finger to keep the promise until the wedding.

His eyes attentively held mine, gripping each breath I took in depraved pleasure.

"Now that you have met properly." Father dug into the deal made by Lucca and Enzo without his presence as if it had no value. "We should discuss this so-called arrangement."

A slight twitch in Lucca's jaw was the only indication of displeasure he gave. I was sure I was the only one who caught such a detail as Lucca let go of my eyes to face him.

The room chilled as the aura was stifled with a cry, and a shudder ran over my body.

"I wasn't aware a discussion was needed." Silence trembled with an edge as Lucca spoke. "I wouldn't have flown to your city if I had known Lorenzo's word wasn't one to be honored." Father's face morphed with indignation. "Or is Katia not *mine?*"

*His.*

Lucca didn't leave any room for miscommunication. Each word he spoke delivered a blow Father couldn't sway or bend. It was clear Mario Vitelli didn't want this union with Miami, but to say so out loud meant discrediting his heir's word.

He had given me to Los Angeles, but it didn't hold the strengths of Miami's arrangement when they had Davina and the evidence to bring New York to the ground. A mistake so severe and unforgiving for someone in Leo's position.

He'd left a witness of a crime breathing, and she did what no one else in our world had done. Get away with it.

New York was exposed.

Enzo had to fix the problem.

I had to follow orders.

And Mario Vitelli had to submit.

*"She is."*

Lucca's lips curled. He was *enjoying* this.

"Now, before we leave, I would like a word with my *fiancée* in private."

Father forced a smile and gestured for Enzo and Leo to follow. With a glance, he dismissed me and said to Lucca, "Safe travels. I heard a storm is forming."

That's it. My father just walked out, and his farewell had no regard for our well-being.

"Grab her belongings, and wait by the car," Lucca instructed his men, and we were left alone.

I faced him and the dangerous pull I felt the night I met him spread over my heart. Cold, dark eyes gazed down on me, and he took a step forward. I was careful not to let my eyes fall. I wouldn't cower under him, but they lured me as his body neared.

*Don't speak until you're spoken to,* my mind warned me. I wouldn't have listened if it wasn't for my loss of words.

"Your ring," he stated.

Following his movements, I watched as his coat pulled back and his hand retrieved a small box from the inside pocket. Distant and impersonal, he opened the box and offered me the ring to take.

It was beautiful and elegant. At any other moment, I would have gushed about its antique and unique style. The gold band crossed in gentle loops. The small diamonds crossed the openings, leading to a stunning oval diamond set into a gorgeous setting. Its size didn't surprise me. After all, I was to become the boss of Miami's wife, but the detail and refined piece to pick instead of taking a more generic route, did.

"You can pick out a different one." Lucca had taken my silence of appreciation for displeasure.

"No." I looked up at his eyes before they returned to the ring. "It's beautiful. Thank you." I caught the honesty in my voice, amazed that I was being sincere. Vulnerable even. My fists balled.

He noticed, and his hand stretched between our bodies. Palm up, it challenged.

Opening my left fist, I fought its trembling, and I hated every second of it. It showed weakness, but I couldn't stop it. My body acted on its own, failing to heed my commands.

Lucca stood unbothered as he grasped my cold hand, gliding the gold band securely onto my finger. I dared to look up. His eyes swarmed in sadistic triumph as he memorized my ringed hand. *His.*

"You should change into warm clothes before we leave." His offer caught me off guard.

A dress in this weather wasn't my first choice, but it was the easiest to conceal and retrieve my push dagger.

"I'm not cold."

"Your body's temperature says otherwise." Lucca squeezed my fingers. The tell of my lie.

I pulled my hand away. "Do you care?"

He smiled. It was the first time I'd seen it, and while it reached his eyes, I didn't trust it.

"I care to leave the city before the storm arrives." He waved his hands. "So, if you need to get comfortable and warm, do so now. I won't be stuck in New York for longer than I need to be."

It was the longest Lucca had ever spoken to me, but it was clear he didn't care as he ignored my statement. There was no reason to say I, too, shared his hatred for New York. How I've been waiting for the last night I would sleep under my father's roof. A house that haunted me to the point of fleeing thoughts.

He. Wouldn't. Care.

"I'll grab my coat."

"Wait."

I froze, and his hand startled me as it applied pressure to my arm. Lucca then twisted his hand, bringing me back to face him once more. I had promised I wouldn't cower under his stare, but his eyes sought violence. With his hand tightening and causing pain, my heart could almost weep at the life I would have as his wife.

I wasn't expecting trust, respect, or love out of our marriage. I was no fool.

But I had wished for a life without physical abuse. A life I never wanted to return to. Because I would *always* fight back, and it would only hurt more.

Lucca's free hand tipped my chin. Defiant, I searched for his eyes, but they weren't on mine. They were focused on the bruise my father had gifted me by my hairline. His gaze then scrutinized every inch of my face. My arm muscles ached, and I swung my arm.

He held both my face and my body tight.

"Let go." I seethed, but my next words caught his attention. "You are hurting me."

He dropped his hands automatically, without an apology, as if he had lost his cool.

"Who?"

In one word, he ordered an answer.

"Do you care?" I asked again, but this time my tone had grown bitter. I could easily have said *my father, but* after the way he had hurt me himself, he had no right to ask.

"Don't be bold, Katia. I torture answers with a smile."

An icy chill settled over me. A whip of warning to stay quiet. A lash I didn't listen to.

"You would torture your future wife?"

"Yes." His detached voice answered. My breath hitched as my mouth parted, and I wanted to scream out the trapping shackle on my finger. Lucca closed any space left between us. His hand trailed to my chin. "I will have you begging." His thumb dragged my lip while his eyes trailed with the swipe of his thumb.

Quick, labored breaths filled my lungs as I reeled in his words. With his hands on me, it was a difficult task to accomplish. I tore away his heavy fingers.

"Now, answer *me*."

Exasperated, I blurted, "Mario Vitelli."

Lucca didn't seem shocked to hear my father's name, but he turned away from my gaze. When I found his eyes again, they were empty and out of my reach.

"I'm not used to being gentle," he said quietly. "But if I leave a mark on your arm, it will be the last."

"If you leave a mark, I'll be sure to leave you one."

My emotions won over the years of practicing deception, but I wasn't mentally capable of fretting over my tongue.

Humor shimmered through his eyes so quickly that it could have been an illusion.

I heard the whispers of Lucca Moretti. The youngest mob boss to have ever taken over a syndicate. The ruthless and cold killer. How quiet and yet lethal his mind worked to his gain. Most importantly, how he was a man of few words. That when he spoke, each word was deliberately thought-out and purposefully said. Perhaps I should have paid them more attention.

"Stay cold then." I'd forgotten where this conversation had started. "After you."

Tired of mind games, I walked. While his steps were silent, his presence was loud behind me. Lucca's strong hand shot out in front of my body before I had the chance to open the door. Inked fingers gripped the copper doorknob, and I saw my brothers waiting as he pulled the door open. Both Enzo and Leo were far enough for privacy but close enough to hear a cry for help.

The weight of Lucca's hand connected with my lower back as he stood beside me. A jolt of warmth and possessiveness followed his hand gesture.

It wasn't the kind that would make your toes curl up from feeling wanted. It was the kind of possession that slowly suffocated. As he showed it in front of my blood, I knew that for men like Lucca, the word possessive was nowhere near the depth described in textbooks.

Leo's lips twisted, and for once, he kept his volatile actions restrained. When Lucca's hand pressed forward, I took a step with him in tow. Leo held on to a ledge so thin, with features flaring in displeasure. Meanwhile, Enzo's eyes watched me carefully.

I almost laughed. A belly and ear-splitting laugh at the absurdity of the play before me. A charade showcasing ego and control. The bubbling humor, however, faded when I crossed a sober reflection.

Not one cared for *me*.

It wasn't fully their fault. They were never taught to protect me. Never taught to look out for me, and the only way they did was by causing others pain or treating me as they would a boy of their age. Mother was the only voice for me, but even then, it was minimal. After she was gone, they only had a slight idea of what wasn't right. Shortly after, I never saw them again as I was shipped out of the country. The times I did see them, they had changed with time into vicious and overprotective brothers.

Leo didn't like other men speaking to me. If they did, it always ended with his knives drawn and a fight. So when I received the whistle that caused the end of someone's life, I knew I couldn't handle the idea of someone dying for *nothing*. We had argued that day in Italy.

We'd yelled and cursed so harshly that it was the last time he visited. I said things, and he said things out of spite. But Leo never accepted his fault. He believed *that* meant being a brother.

Enzo, on the other hand, often talked to me. He didn't treat me like the kid I was. On the contrary, he chided me and spoke to me the same way my father did to him. Stern and emotionless.

Our broken relationship wasn't all on them. I too had issues. I too fought back and lashed out with words I knew would wound. I picked their weaknesses and learned their scars to keep them bleeding and open. It wasn't until I was older that I realized my faults.

It was too late then.

It was too late now.

Our wedge was too unstable to repair.

Us Vitellis were known for our blades, and while we hadn't bled each other, we stabbed one another. Too bad, even as siblings, we'd lived up to our last name.

It was all about power.

Money.

Fear.

Lucca didn't miss my weakening spark, and his palm flattened. Was I so easy to see through? It was rare when someone could see my inner struggles. I excelled at concealing emotions. Most times better than my own father. I was off my game.

Today, I was *weak*.

"Mario couldn't stay. Business demanded his attention." Enzo explained our father's absence, but the disrespect wasn't lost on Lucca.

"Expect a summer wedding," Lucca's cold voice announced. "I'll let Katia decide the date." Enzo stretched his hand out. Lucca shook and held it. "No harm is to come to Ilias or Davina."

At the mention of the woman's name, his eyes shot toward Leo, who wore a cruel smile. Lucca's fingers curled over my skin, catching his reaction.

"As long as my sister is protected, I don't see why we wouldn't hold our end of this deal."

Lucca pulled away from their shake and slid his hand over my waist. His hand wrapped so effortlessly.

"Tell me, Vitelli. Who protected her from the bruises on her face?"

Enzo's lips twitched as his eyes slid to me. He was bothered by Lucca's accusation.

"She'll become my wife as promised, but what occurs under my city and roof is not part of the arrangement."

Enzo searched my eyes, but we'd become strangers and anything he wanted to share got lost in broken communication.

Drained from this made-men meeting, its politics, the unsaid threats, and warnings, I drew away from the present. I only heard the distant, *"I'll be waiting for the decided date,"* from Enzo.

We walked out of my childhood home without my acknowledgment of my family. In spite of wearing a long coat, the low temperatures of New York, and my feelings, numbed my heart with a bitter blow.

Lucca's warm hand left my back as I slid inside the back cabin of their black car. Keeping my eyes on the headrest in front of me as we rode in silence.

I never looked back. Not even when the airplane took off into the air and away from the city I'd been born in.

An hour had passed with the low humming of the engine circulating in the bleak atmosphere. It was hard to keep busy when I was seated in front of Lucca. Difficult even to refrain from asking questions or keep my eyes from wandering toward him.

Of course, nothing bothered Lucca. He just sat comfortably, with a tablet in one hand and a drink in the other.

A second hour passed. This time, I spent my time entertained by the straight lines and angles of my drawing. I was lucky the moment I spotted my large carry-on where I kept my sketchbook. I didn't ask. I stood and picked it up, taking out my pencil and drawing book. Lucca's attention never flickered away from his tablet. I sketched, erased, drew again, and erased some more.

Not even my design worked in my favor.

I gave up on my model and closed the book.

I stared at him.

Stared at the sharp lines of his face. The light scruff that helped hide his reactions but added a distinctive appeal to him. His hair was lightly styled, enough to know he took his time in the morning to run his fingers over the longer strands but not enough to seem preoccupied with such detail. His thick hair almost seemed naturally shaped as it waved back on his head and an inch to his right. Only the top was long enough for my fingers to grip. I shook away the thought and lowered my gaze to his neck, but the tattoos peeking out of his tailored collar shirt were more difficult to shake.

Any turn my gaze took of him wasn't safe. I chose his chest instead. Before he had taken his seat, he had discarded his coat and blazer, leaving only his tie and shirt safely tucked underneath his vest. While I couldn't see his skin, my choice wasn't the best because now I could see the outline of his muscles under his fitted black shirt. The lean, yet strong cut chest and shoulders.

I couldn't deny it, Lucca Moretti was appealing to the eye. Luring even, with his hard and quiet demeanor.

I stared back at his eyes.

He was staring back at mine.

# MIAMI

# VIII

## LUCCA

I READ THE NUMBERS AND STATISTICS OF THE LEGITIMATE BUSINESS
I OWNED and compared their data with the figures from offshore
accounts my tablet displayed. A distraction I needed to keep the
demon away from seeing my favorite color painted on the streets of
New York.

Mario Vitelli tested my patience with his disrespect. As an old and
proud man stuck in the old ways of the Mafia, I had expected it. Even
looked forward to it. To see him yield as I forced his proud hand to what
I wanted.

The safety of those I looked after and his daughter.

But the sight of her bruised face, the cut above her temple, and her
slightly dilated pupils wasn't something I'd anticipated.

I don't like surprises. While men in our world often turned their
wrath to our women, he had lost any right from the moment she had
been promised to *me*. His words and absence to finish the meeting were

a mere insult compared to the insolence of presenting her in such a state.

He'd mocked me with the fingertips that marked what was now mine.

His marks meant so much more, and he knew it. I refused to take his disrespect lightly.

Each glance at her reminded me that this was just the beginning.

Katia was the perfect example of poise. She masked her emotions and yet, let her voice escape loudly. I saw glimpses of vulnerability only so often, and each time it was evident she loathed the slips.

My plan to break her and parade her in front of her father hadn't changed. But now that I had her so close, I saw the threat and danger she posed. Her beauty was sinful, and her will was powerful. I couldn't trust her. After all, she was a Vitelli.

I ignored her peeping eyes. They only lasted a few seconds during the time we sat quietly. The hints of her stare spread throughout the second hour in the air. Through that time, I gathered a few burning interests about her. Like the constant touch to her thigh. A tic that seemed to calm her for a short while before she would run her fingertips all over again. She was hiding something underneath the fabric of her dress, and she did so terribly. At some point, she stood and returned with a sketchbook. When the first swipe of her pencil scratched the paper, Katia drifted away. The sight of her concentration raised questions about the stranger who had left Italy, since I had not expected her to be a painter or an artist.

At some point, she loudly exhaled. Frustrated and unhappy.

Good.

Then I sensed her eyes again. This time, they'd meant to stay.

I watched as they moved over my face and neck before they landed on my torso with a blend of distinctive reactions that all worked in my favor. Whether her mind disapproved of this marriage, her body and her eyes spoke a different tale.

Katia looked up, but my eyes were already waiting for hers.

Our eyes declared wars of hatred and punishment. In this war, white flags and surrender didn't exist. Freedom could only be granted after death, but soon after, the fire pits of hell will claim such a gift.

"If I asked you a question, would you answer it?" I savored her raspy and thick Italian accent. The years she'd spent away had made her more of a foreigner to the country she had been born in.

"Yes."

"Honestly?"

"I don't lie. I find them tasteless." I contemplated my next words. "I will tell you if I can't share something, but I must warn you that some answers can be painful."

"But you would." Disbelief marked her tone.

"That's what I said."

"Why did you agree?" Her thin fingers wiggled between us. "To this?"

"New York would never take our word as a promise. It was the logical answer to keep my brother safe and his..." Girlfriend didn't seem the right word. "His woman, Davina, out of danger."

"Was that it?"

"You want a list?" I asked as her jade greens waited. "I needed to marry for the position I've been titled. I've held off by using Salvatore as an excuse. But my time is running out, and I don't need my own Outfit breathing down my throat because I'm unmarried. It also helps with numbers during a council vote—"

"I got it."

I hid my annoyance at her interruption and focused on her disrespect. She'd asked for honesty, and in return, she'd snapped.

It wasn't worth my time trying to decipher her mood swings. Picking up my tablet, I dismissed her.

Katia didn't have to like the idea of an arranged marriage, but it could quickly turn into hell if she didn't give in soon. A challenge I gladly accepted.

"Will we share a room?"

That caught my attention, and the corners of my mouth lifted.

"Yes."

"We aren't married."

"I'm condemned to hell either way, aren't *you?*"

It was a particular way to ask about her sins, but there was one sin I particularly cared about.

Women in our world were often promised and married at the age of eighteen to twenty-two, but she had been tucked away and far from temptation by men like me. While I had ten years over her, she'd stayed unmarried for far longer than the traditional time frame for a *principessa*. Making her encounters with the opposite sex more likely, but still tricky to manage as she'd been under the protection and guard of her grandfather. A tenacious bastard who'd created who Mario Vitelli now was.

How many times had her fingers counted the beads of her rosary and uttered Hail Marys as her penance? Was she a good Catholic girl who walked to God's home every Sunday? Was she even a believer? Or had she given up religion?

"Probably," she answered.

"You ask for honesty from me, but your answers are half-truths." It wasn't a question.

"Aren't you worried about what would be said if I'm seen sharing a bed with you before the wedding?"

I covered my chuckle with a scoff, and her eyes popped open.

"Anyone smart wouldn't allow even a whisper."

Her lashes fanned as her eyes lowered to her hand. She caught the direction it had taken to her thigh and brought it back, tucking them together.

Definitely hiding something.

"You *will* sleep in my bed."

Her eyes flamed.

*Test me,* the demon begged.

Katia didn't utter another word, and for the first time, she looked out the window. The weather had changed so quickly in the sky as brightness filtered through, promising Miami's heat soon.

I didn't offer the idea of her changing out of her form-fitting winter dress. The black color would attract the sun, and the long sleeves would soon stick over her arms once we landed. This time, I let it go.

Let Miami give her the warm welcome her eyes showed.

Hell.

Home. That was what the streets of Miami were to me. My brothers, the reason I bathed in blood and corruption. The Moretti Crime, my claim to this city and empire I'd rebuilt.

Salvatore had given me the keys to the syndicate long before he'd stepped down. As his health deteriorated, he became more of a background to business encounters. Entrusting me to step up to my birthright. He still operated as the boss in front of the *famiglia.* We couldn't look weak, even to our men. When it became evident the boss of Miami was terminally ill, moves had to be made. Shifts to be waived until the Mancini name was taken and replaced by mine.

I'd built something unorthodox within our Outfit. A syndicate where trust and honor ran thicker than blood and made up by now four men who'd once left Miami's Home for Boys. Each one is a crucial key to running Miami as I saw fit.

I took the last step off the plane and waited for Katia's descent. Her eyes squinted, looking ahead, and she let out a brash exhale against the humidity and high temperatures.

*Welcome home.*

With a concealed smirk, I said, "After you."

*"Such a gentleman."*

Her fucking mouth. Her will excited me and yet filled me with ire. With her, patience was not one of my strengths.

In one swift movement, I faced her with my hand wrapped around the back of her hairline. Shock glistened from her green gems as she tried to draw away. My face inched closer in wild darkness. There was no escape. My hand covered most of her neck as her hair entwined with my fingers. A small, delicious taste I wanted to explore further, but first, she needed a tug.

"Listen carefully. I will not repeat myself."

A shimmer of fear flew past her features. Good. This game she wanted to play risked high stakes.

I had to make her understand, and this was the only way I could do it without causing her physical pain, even while my demon begged for it.

"This is Miami, Katia. My city. Therefore, soon yours." Her eyes swayed, and I applied pressure to keep them on me. "Inside the doors of my home and my bed, be my guest. Feed my twisted mind. But I won't allow your disrespect in public." Her hand gripped my forearm tightly.

"Are we clear?"

There it was, the igniting fire in her eyes.

"Don't treat me like a child." Her head tilted defiantly. "*I* was born into this world."

Her weak jab didn't faze me. She didn't know who I was, or my past.

"Then act like it." I released my grip and rolled my shoulders back.

Katia's head tilted, her lips curled, and she gritted her teeth.

"I was aware we were too far to be heard. Even on the plane, my voice never reached your man." She spoke quickly, but now, it was she who wanted to make things clear. "I won't cower to you, Lucca." It was the second time she'd spoken my name. It fell from her lips just as alluringly as it had in front of her father.

"I know the rules of this world of ours and what it means to become your wife. Which is why I never spoke out loud. Whispers can become threats. If a boss's *mere* wife can disrespect him, what will keep others from doing so?"

Hm.

"Don't look surprised. I'm a woman, not an imbecile. After all, I am here because others could not have done what I could." I pushed her to continue. "A treaty between families."

"Your brother did that."

"But it's me who is marrying *you*."

With a smirk, I said, "Good, then we are clear."

Katia walked past me, and I watched her go straight to the waiting car. Her hand gently touched her neck, rubbing the back of her neck gently. A gesture that could have been taken due to the discomfort I'd caused, and I couldn't remove my eyes away from her. The confidence she displayed even with her back facing me.

I was right. Katia posed a threat. She knew more than I had given her credit for. That was my mistake, underestimating her. But she'd overshared, and glimpses of this deceitful creature were revealed.

That gesture was nothing more than a clever line to lure me into her cunning agenda.

As I followed behind her, I thought of our brief conversations, and the brief glimpse of fear she'd shown.

What had been real, and what had been a game?

# IX

## KATIA

I WAS LOSING CONTROL. A FEELING THAT LEFT ME DESPERATE AND RECKLESS. Placing blame on the drastic changes in my life would have been easier than the thought that *he* was the reason for my outbursts, but I knew the truth. It *was* him.

I never had an issue with self-control. But when he was around, all I managed to do was spit my thoughts out loud.

Nonno would be disappointed if he could see my actions, my inability to maintain composure and poise. After all, my grandfather had guided me for this life. The person who empowered me from a young age to be strong. Not by the force of his fist, but by showing me the ugly of our world. He didn't shield me from its cruelty or what it meant to be a woman of the underworld. Instead, he taught me how to rise above. He taught me to survive.

Then why was I feeling *everything?*

We rode in silence while crushing tension gripped and squeezed my chest. My dress felt tight, and a cold sweat broke through with rolling chills. The car's motion added to the smothering air that traveled with us with each bump and sway in my body. I refused to look out the window. Miami would have to wait; I wouldn't face it in such a state.

Minutes passed, and the outline of my dagger against my fingertips didn't offer the air I so desperately craved. Instead, my fingers became numb and damp. The longer I waited, the more my hair stuck to the back of my neck.

*Breathe.*

But all I smelled was him. All I felt was his warmth. All I sensed was his darkness.

Distant gates announced our arrival, and they opened, revealing the grand and beautiful fortress that hid killers. A few men stepped away from the shadows as their boss rolled inside, and where my eyes turned, hidden cameras I'd grown accustomed to flooded my view. Not one inch of the perimeter was left unseen by the eyes of surveillance.

I'd passed the same gates, stepped into the same circular stone drive, and listened to the spurts of water from the fountain under the pending light of the moon a few nights ago.

But the sun now exposed the cruel reality.

My future.

The magnificent custom-built manor was nothing more than a beautiful, detailed façade.

"Katia?" Lucca's voice drifted. I shifted my head away from his view and closed my eyes. The weight on my chest increased. "Katia." His voice grew stronger.

Lucca traveled with no shadows in his city, and he parked the car, leaving the engine running. It was just us and the punishing suffocation.

"*Sì.*" Italian flew from my lips in longing for familiarity. Since arriving in the States, the times I have communicated with others have all been in English. The simple *yes* brought back a piece I'd missed.

"*Che succede?*" Lucca's English was no match for his dominant Italian tongue. It was captivating and dangerous. But his question meant nothing, even if it had been asked, *what's wrong?*

The switch of language brought more of myself back than the sharp dagger had done on the ride. Now that I had the chance to use it, I didn't switch to English. I wanted to use it, listen to it, and bathe in it until I felt whole again.

"Your Italian is flawless."

Lucca, too, spoke back in Italian. "It's my first language. I only spoke English as a child when needed. The day I turned fourteen was the day it became my main form of communication."

He'd said more than I'd expected. Even his tone had relaxed. *Did he too feel the ease of its poetry?*

I crushed the idea. All men in our world spoke the language. He couldn't possibly feel the comfort and solace like I did.

"Now, answer me," he demanded.

I spun and stared into his dark eyes with the same judgment he carried.

The tremors of my fingers had slowed but remained, as did the pressure of my chest. I had asked for honesty, but how could I offer such a thing when the questions asked were too raw to admit?

I settled for half the truth. "The flight left me feeling unwell."

His eyes narrowed, my answer wasn't appreciated, and silence stretched.

"Then let me walk you to *our* room to rest." Lucca opened his door and exited the car.

I didn't flinch as the car door shut loudly. I flinched when he spoke back in bitter English.

BODIES SWARMED IN AND OUT OF VIEW. TOO MANY FOR ME TO KEEP UP WITH AND become familiar with their features. The walk up to the house, following behind him, felt inferior. I was already out of my comfort zone with a floor plan I had no knowledge of. A city I wasn't familiar with, and a mansion with an exit without an escape. The clicking sound of the door closing behind me finalized who I used to be.

We continued walking in silence until he veered to the left. There, two large staircases met in the middle of the grand room that overlooked the inside of the courtyard and entry. He swayed to the one on the left.

"Wait." I hummed.

Lucca stopped but didn't face me. I was thankful because I wasn't even sure why I stopped him. Maybe I just wanted a minute to think. A second to gather my composure and courage to grasp my future. Or maybe I wasn't ready to see the bed we would share, or the room where my things would blend with his.

"I'm thirsty." That was what I managed to utter.

*Jesus.*

Lucca didn't reply. He only took a slight left and continued walking away from the stairs. Trailing behind him, I reencountered the same path I had once taken. His study.

Leaving the door wide open, Lucca walked deeper into the darkened room. I halted near the doorway while his footfalls continued until they ceased and drapes opened, allowing natural light to filter through the sheer curtains of the tall windows at the end. Somehow, his frame had remained away from the sun's rays, but I saw the shadow of his hands reaching his front. He unbuttoned his blazer and draped it on a coat hanger as if he'd shed a layer of his disguise. Lucca's eyes fell to his wrists, and mine followed his fingers as they effortlessly removed his cufflinks and softly placed them neatly on his desk.

The silence, the shadows, and his movements were too much. Too effortless and indifferent. All while I stood behind by an open door with the compressing feeling of confinement.

He then began creasing the ends of his sleeves, slowly rolling them and exposing his strong inked forearms. When he finished, he had revealed more skin, ink, and veins than I'd seen from him. I stood appalled, eyes fixed on him.

His tie was next as his thumb tugged, and the sound of silk slipping loose shrilled through the smothering room. With another layer shed, it left behind his vest, which quickly met the hanging suit jacket. I finally removed my gaze when his fingertips touched the first button of his dress shirt, unwilling to watch his neck free and exposed for my gaze.

I looked away and tried to make sense of the spines of the books on the bookcases. Their titles and letters were difficult to follow, but I made out a few. They were mostly different volumes on law, medicine and anatomy. Leather, broken spines, and no signs of dust lingering. My fingers touched their worn, yet unique spines, realizing they were in alphabetical order.

"You have a preference?"

I nearly said, *"Not* non-fiction,*"* but I spotted the title *The Laws of Architecture.* I faced him.

Lucca was standing by a corner bar with two crystal-cut glasses resting before him.

He meant alcohol.

I'd said I was thirsty after all, but I had envisioned a glass of water. Drinking something stronger was a risk with my low alcohol tolerance and current state of disarray. But after thinking of the next stop I would take after his study, I replied, "I'll have whatever you have."

Lucca's eyes hesitated, and after mine fell to his open shirt, I led mine back to the safety of the bookshelves.

I heard the sound of liquid pouring, the pause before it began again, and the moment the clink of a heavy glass canister sat back to its resting spot. His footfalls were next. The closer he got, the louder they became, and when I turned, I'd left the timid gaze on the bookshelf and looked up at him.

He held a glass of brown liquor. It seemed small in his grip.

I took it and looked up. "Thank you."

Lucca gazed over my lips, up my eyes, and moved to the corner of my hairline. They remained there for a moment longer before he turned around without a word.

He was maddening, the way he gave no tells, no signs, nothing.

It was impossible to read him, to know how to act according to his slips for my gain. No matter who I faced, I had managed to be stout and understand their ways. It's how I lived life and came out on top of *every fucking encounter*. But he never granted even a faint crack.

*Make him trust you.*

There had to be another way that didn't leave me vulnerable. There's *always* another way.

I just needed to find it before I could lose myself in the house of an unemotional mafioso.

The drink disappeared between my lips, burning with its choking taste as I turned to face his broad back, in one sip.

"I have work," Lucca's nonchalant tone announced when he stood behind his desk.

Dismissed.

I chuckled, and he looked up at me. Bringing the hand that held my cup, I wiped the bourbon left on my lips with the side of my thumb. Uncaring of how unladylike it may seem or how he would interpret such a gesture.

His gaze followed my steps as I walked through his study, and I picked up the first brown crystal container I touched and poured another drink. After all, he had work.

With my hair back and my head held high, I walked toward the bookshelf, picked up *The Law of Architecture* level one book, and continued to the door.

"Your eyes have been dilated since New York."

I stopped by the cracked door.

"My guess, the gash against your hairline."

My hand gripped the glass a bit tighter.

"You said the flight left you feeling unwell."

My eyes remained fixed on the heavy door.

"It's a concussion. One that should be monitored for the first forty-eight hours."

Having experienced cuts, bruises, and injuries firsthand, he knew it was during that time period, but he has yet to address the point of his speech. All he'd done was stir the memory of my father.

"You shouldn't have another glass, *Katia*."

*Yet, you gave me my first.*

I let the door open enough for my frame to slip, but before I got the chance, he cut even deeper.

"Was it the butt of his gun?" I heard curiosity in his tone, but it did so much more.

Taking a deep breath, I quieted the need to lash out. I couldn't show any more weakness. Not here. Not to him.

I faced him and his untouched glass as he remained standing in the same place he'd dismissed me from. But there he was, *still* acknowledging me. Without letting go of his stormy eyes, I placed my own glass on my lips. They flared when my mouth parted, and in one gulp, I drained it and set it on a table nearby.

"It was. But not before I stared at the end of his barrel." I licked my lips and breathed in, cooling my burning throat. His jaw twitched, and instead of contemplating its meaning, I turned and left.

This time, *I* dismissed him.

LUCCA HAD SAID A CONCUSSION, I'D SAID THE FLIGHT, BUT THE ALCOHOL SAID otherwise. I needed a bed, and fast. Could be the mind games, the change of weather, the unfamiliarity, or the weight of my ring finger, but whatever it was, it was catching up on me.

Men filtered through my vision, and voices carried all around. This home was too loud, too crowded, too foreign. I retreated to where we had detoured from. The path to his room. *Our* room now. Once I stood in front of the same staircase on the left, I climbed each step eagerly to get out of the black, sleeved dress and find solace in an empty room.

A long hallway displayed three doors. The last one stood before me at the end. The master bedroom. I opened the door, and his scent hit my face.

Possessive, powerful, and cruel with a hint of smoke.

Asphyxiating.

And yet, I inhaled its danger. Allowing the sick part of me to long for what it craves.

Want.

I closed my eyes, accepting my fault, but the second I opened them, it had become a distant memory.

Instead, I focused on the layout of the bedroom. Like his scent, the black and brown tones of the darkened bedroom reflected him in the same way. Elegant and dangerous. Inviting.

A brown cashmere throw blanket, shades of black, and granite-colored pillows drowned out the white bedding's glow. Dark walls spread all around, so dark the shade of color mixed with black was unknown. I followed the walls, and the higher I looked up to the tall, vaulted ceiling, the more the illusion of a void played in my mind. The lighting wasn't strong. There were two mounted structures that acted as lamps on each side of the bed, shining their light up the walls and creating a calming atmosphere. But what I could fall asleep looking at was the long, hanging, crystal-pendant chandelier. As if large diamonds rained at different speeds. Only bright enough to showcase their beauty.

A mix of modern and classic blended flawlessly into something stunning.

Ready to discard my dress, slip inside the bed, and drain the day off my body, I searched for my bags. With no luck, I found the walk-in closet. Rows of Lucca's dress shirts, suits, and shoes lay immaculately on built-in cabinets. Nothing stood out.

A desire to find a flaw lured me closer. That's how I found a few dark jeans, workout pants, shorts, and plain tees in drawers. Neatly folded and in perfect condition. I headed to the drawer on the island, only to discover his watches and cufflinks.

Picture-fucking-perfect.

Running my finger over a detailed *M* cufflink, I twisted it.

There.

Before my smile widened, I looked up. It turned out, all I had to do was look to my left.

My leather suitcases stood out along with the empty and broad space they rested before. Not one was missing, but I specifically only cared for the one that held my most prized possessions, my knives. In long strides, I met what I had left of my life, opened it, and found comfort. As I walked out of the closet, I stepped out of my heels, leaving them behind near my bags, and headed toward the bathroom.

The amount of water that poured over my body was unable to wash off the unsteady feeling of today. In the darkness, I drifted off to sleep with wet hair, questions, and fleeting feelings.

A faint rustling sound drifted me away from sleep. Slowly, my hand slipped under the pillow without a sound. Ready for a threat, I opened my eyes. They found Lucca stepping out of the bathroom with only a white towel wrapped around his hips. Under so much ink, his strong back muscles were hidden, even most of his legs. My eyes followed the leftover water that ran down his hair, neck, and arms. Lucca walked unbothered and unconcerned until the ink, his tan skin, and cut body disappeared out of view into the closet.

Relaxing once again, I peeked through the covered windows. Sunlight had not slipped through, but a ray of hope to catch sunrise did. It may have been the same sun, but it wouldn't be the same Italian morning.

The closet door cracked open, and Lucca stepped out in another full suit. It was blue. White shirt, matching vest, no tie.

*No tie.* Why did I notice such a detail?

Not once did he turn my way, or acknowledge I'd slept in his room, his space. He just made his way to the bedroom door and stopped once it opened.

"Breakfast will be served in an hour." His head inclined to his left, and I saw his clenched jaw. "Don't ever sleep with a weapon in my bed again."

The door shut, leaving his threat behind.

*Fuck.*

I stood up and tossed my pillow. My chest rose and fell with the fast beat of my heart.

It was empty.

My butterfly knife was missing.

A burning rage and blinding ire demanded its return. With a quick glance at the door, I knew the only way to get it back was through him.

The sunrise would have to wait. I had a part of me taken, and I was bound to get it back. But first, I had to dress for the façade.

Another dress and another flawless face later, I walked out of the room with my heels pronouncing each step I took. With my push dagger securely strapped to my leg, I was ready for him.

I had no clear vision of where I was headed, and after I took the last step down the stairwell, I wandered to the back of the house. The trail of plate clatters and the aroma of freshly baked pastries led my feet. Ignoring the grandly structured rooms and the detailed décor, I shadowed the path to Lucca. Two double doors were opened, and the glimpse of a chair announced my destination.

I took a deep breath before exposing my lust for pain and walked inside.

He wasn't alone.

I paid the second figure no attention, even as it stood by Lucca's side with a phone in his hand talking to him. Meanwhile, I remained by the entrance with emotions that grew stronger as I saw *him*.

Cruel and calculating bastard.

He sat composed and relaxed with an untouched plate of fruit at the end of the table.

My eyes never veered away from him. Instead, I watched his every move in detail.

Lucca wasn't paying attention to the figure anymore.

No. He'd heard me, I was sure of it. I wore heels for a reason. And *still*, his head remained angled toward the other man.

Yesterday was in the past. I had left any frail thoughts and slips behind. Today, I missed my sunset and woke up without something that belonged to me.

There was no sane Vitelli alive. I guess he'd forgotten the blood that ran through my veins.

Finally, silence.

With finger-styled dark hair and a locked jaw, I was acknowledged.

Lucca's eyes flared.

*Oh, he's displeased? I'm glad.* That made two of us.

"Arlo, this is Katia." Our eyes spoke of war. "Katia, Arlo." I didn't take my eyes away from him. "My brother." *And underboss*. His stare was clear. I was in front of one of his men. Brother or not, I had to play the part.

I smiled. "We've met before. Pleasure, Katia *Vitelli*."

Arlo was built like a heavyweight fighter. Tall, and over muscular for my taste. He was all dark skin and ink, but on him, it screamed mafioso. I was sure he had been an enforcer at one point, but his snake eyes claimed he still held the title of punisher. Only a few had the same empty look, but his remained vacant even in broad daylight. Thirsty for pain and blood.

A dark huff and a foul smirk erupted from Arlo. "Same."

Arlo's guarded hazel eyes scrutinized me carefully. They landed on my hairline before they glanced back down.

You've underestimated me before, Arlo.

I slid my eyes to Lucca's, and my smile tightened. Pushing my feet forward, I held the back of the chair to his left but remained standing.

"Lucca," Arlo called out for him, but Lucca watched me instead.

This was the dining room. Not a place for meetings. Did they miss the lavish food displayed on fine glass trays?

I wasn't planning to leave or apologize for interrupting. After all, it was breakfast.

"Are you joining us for breakfast, Arlo?"

"No."

Observing him from across the table, I stood behind the wooden groves of my own chair and pulled it back.

"Well, I'm famished. And if you are done, you may leave now."

With his lips curled, Arlo's face transformed. His head tilted back, and his breathing changed.

I smiled.

"Wait in my study. I'll meet you shortly," Lucca ordered.

Arlo didn't move.

*Ohh.* I'd really bothered him.

"Arlo," Lucca's tone warned.

Arlo gritted his teeth and slowly withdrew his gaze from me. He walked away in silence.

I dropped my smile and sat.

"Do not provoke Arlo," Lucca's curt voice warned.

I couldn't care less.

"Where is it?" I asked.

"How many more?" he countered.

Concentrating on my empty plate, I asked again.

*"Where is it?"*

The sound of his chair scraping the floor below put me on high alert. Our distance shortened, and I was left vulnerable as he towered over my sitting position. Menace echoed in silence as neither of us backed down.

A string of dread arrived with his footsteps. It didn't compare to the chain of fright as his hand clasped my jaw. Or the alarm of my stretched and exposed neck as he pulled my head back. Deep breaths calmed my fear. His fingers tightened until I looked at his eyes.

With Lucca standing behind me and his hand wrapped around my jawline, he challenged.

"Don't test me."

"I want it back," I gritted.

"No." He let me go.

I stood, and as I took a step, my body collided with his. Hard and unmovable.

"What are *you* going to do, Katia?"

Lost between my next move and his body. My lips parted, and heat spread.

There were a few things I could do. They all required physical strength and my push dagger. But that fight was lost long before I entered this house.

Powerless in this made-man realm.

It has been this way for years. Nothing could change it, but neither could I.

"I *need* it back." My voice changed. It wasn't demanding, it was stating a fact.

"How many?" His head dipped while my eyes watched the detailed lines of a cross that marked his neck.

It was easier this way. For my words to flee truthfully, if I focused on anything else then what another could gain by my answers.

But answering how many I had with me was a hard answer to give. How could I answer when it meant they could all disappear?

It would mean leaving me bare and defenseless.

"How many weapons do you own, Lucca?"

"It's not the same. You hardly had any luggage."

"Knives are easier to conceal."

"Which is why I'm asking."

With our short, curt questions and terse answers came a sliver of communication. It was low, nothing friendly or gentle as we discussed arms. Another mark tallied to our fucked-up arrangement.

"Over thirty."

He stayed quiet for a minute, and his cross wasn't offering the same distraction as his scent bounced over my body.

"I'll be sure to have a case for them before tonight ends."

Surprised, my head lifted. I shouldn't have; my hatred returned while his icy demeanor never left.

"Pick any room you would like them stored in." Quickly he added, "But I won't allow a knife inside my room."

This was worse.

A void swept my chest, draining out the control and promise my blades offered.

Knowing I wasn't able to fully comply, I had to think quickly.

"Your study," I answered.

It was the room with the least access to others. If I was intending to leave them in a case, they had to be safe.

"I'll let you know when it's ready."

I didn't look up when he took a step back, or glance as he stepped out of the room. I waited a few more minutes in silence before I too left the space.

Numbed.

It was for the best. Because if I allowed myself to feel how I'd been robbed of my life and future, it would anger me, but if I allowed the feeling of giving up my blades, I would be beaten. I would be left broken.

Numbness was my conscious best friend, therefore mine.

# X

## LUCCA

TIRED OF PEOPLE TESTING ME TODAY, I FLUNG MY OFFICE DOOR OPEN. I took a deep breath and stopped at the sight of a wood and glass casing. It was designed to hold different-sized blades and made to blend with the same tint of the aged bookcases. An addition to my personalized space I wasn't expecting. Until today.

The long and narrow table sat on the corner right behind my desk. As if it had always belonged there.

It reminded me of the first person who tested me today. And the only one who remained alive.

Knowing she was near, my mind snapped glimpses of her green eyes and thick bourbon hair. The way her thin structure and delicate neck could easily snap if my hand had the chance to be wrapped around it again. Or the way her jugular popped when her pulse raced, taunting for a knife to slit and free its life source.

A chuckle fell from my lips from my dark thoughts. The ones that have kept me alive.

My demon was still awake and unsafe to be around after taking a life just a few short hours ago. Yet, I fished my phone out of my pocket and called her.

"Hello?" Katia's sleep-laced voice asked. Confused from the unknown number she had answered to.

A quick look at the clock, I realized I had awakened her. It was past eleven.

"It's here. Bring your phone and laptop down too."

I ended the call and walked over to the bar. After pouring and drinking the first glass in one sip, I refilled it once more. This one won't be drained to ease my thoughts.

Taking the furthest seat from the new cabinet, I closed my eyes and waited.

The door creaked, and I saw her searching for me.

White was a nice color against her golden skin. A thin satin slip dress hung low on her back, showcasing a few faint and small scars scattered far in between. Alluring me to count each one, to feel the softness of her skin against my blood-filled hands. Lace decorated the edges of her chest and teased just below her ass. It left her long legs bare, drawing attention to their defined form and strength. I could see the hint of her nipples peeking as her hair swayed in thick curtains while she sought out for me.

Katia's posture remained tall, but when her eyes didn't find me, she hesitated.

Making my presence known, I said, "That's what you chose to wear around the house at night?"

Her head snapped, and her eyes scanned all of me. When they landed by my collar, they turned careful.

Katia's lips parted and quickly shut.

"I'll make sure to wear a robe next time," she replied softly, too quickly and too perfectly.

"Now, say what you stopped yourself from saying."

Her eyes landed again on my collar, and mine narrowed.

"I thought your men were better trained." That sounded more like the spiteful creature I've acquired.

Was she insinuating...

"I didn't really think. I've just been used to wearing what I pleased." Now that was a truth. "After the flight, you'd said *Inside the doors of my home and bed, be my guest—*"

"*—Feed my twisted mind,*" I finished and let a sip of bourbon wash the thirst. "Is that what you are doing?"

Katia's round eyes widened, and her grip tightened around the brown bag she'd carried inside. As fast as her disbelief flashed through, it left without a sound, but her eyes stormed.

"Then you lied."

*I lied?*

Her tongue accused, her eyes believed it, and her body agreed.

I rose leaving my drink behind. My demon demanded blood for such insolence. For such a loose tongue, and confidence to utter such words. With each blinding step, control slipped, reasoning failed, and wrath begged to be set loose. Not once did she cower.

She should be *pleading*.

The split second I was in reach, my hand rose. Her eyes closed. She didn't flinch, they just accepted what was to come. It quieted the demon, the need for red, and caused the wrath to settle. I wasn't a liar. I had given her my word that I wouldn't mark her skin, and a bruised woman wasn't what I wanted under my roof.

I didn't care if she didn't believe it then, or even now. There were different ways of breaking her.

My hand connected to her jawline, fingers spreading to her nape and cheekbone. Powering over her small frame. I caught the glimpse of her eyes opening, but I watched the pressure my thumb applied as it ran over her lipstick-free and round lips.

"I've killed many for less," my voice warned. "So, explain to me, Katia." Setting her lips free, I looked down on her. "How am I a liar?"

Katia didn't hesitate. "When you said Miami was your city, and soon mine. It meant this house too. It meant I could at least roam freely, just as you do, in the walls of this fortress you've made." Her teeth captured her bottom lip, and when she continued, teeth marks imprinted for my gaze to follow. "Without the worry of your men or of what I wore to bed."

"*Soon* yours," I corrected. "We aren't married, nor have I fucked you yet."

"You and I both know, the moment I left New York, we might as well have been. The wedding is just a symbol for the *famiglia*."

"And yet, you don't bear the name Moretti." I let go of her face.

I could see the lost battle in her gaze, and with a small crease between her brows, her head inched away.

"Then why take my blades?"

There was a part of me that knew they were her false blanket of security while there was another part that knew it and did it regardless. The other part recognized that she was a Vitelli.

"I didn't. They have just relocated."

Reason remained weak in me, and I turned before her mouth could revive the demon.

"Leave your electronics on my desk. They'll be replaced with new ones by lunch tomorrow with our firewalls. Your cabinet is in the far right," I instructed, and fell back to the chair where my glass rested nearby.

I watched as she did what I'd asked in nothing more but mere lingerie. It shouldn't be called sleepwear, not when the slightest bending of her frame taunted my dick with the crease of her ass.

Katia worked quietly by the corner. She adjusted the inside of the casing in a particular manner. Fully invested and precisely to her liking. When she had finished, she took a step back to admire the bands before she did something I hadn't expected. She took a seat behind *my* desk.

No one had ever sat there besides *me*.

It was a sight that I didn't like, a sight that bothered me as the head of this syndicate. But as she pulled two rags and the knives out of her bag and spread them above my desk with her hair cascading over her features, bottom lip fixed between her teeth, and tits in display with lace trim, I didn't mind it enough to ask her to get off my chair.

Taking her time with each knife and dagger, Katia wielded the weapons with ease. Effortlessly, she manipulated the handle to the blade with both hands covered in cloth without dropping one, and her not drawing blood made me wonder how far her expertise reached.

Katia gave up so much in just one night. Their importance to her. Because no one cared this deeply for anything unless it was of value to them. I had taken the hint this morning. And it was just one, a simple butterfly knife. *This* was hurting her, and she demonstrated it as she polished every single one as if each swipe was a caress, and a goodbye.

One of Katia's greatest weaknesses were her blades.

I brought my cup to my lips and tasted my smile.

Katia then stood and began placing the knives on the straps she'd tailored to fit. Surprisingly, it had taken the least of her time as only a few remained on my desk, and she broke the silence.

"They didn't pose any harm in the room."

Katia didn't glance my way, and my smile broke. Fully entertained.

"It's hard enough for me to sleep."

"Afraid of a tiny knife?"

Katia stepped away from the cabinet, her attention landing on me. And while her words weren't an insult, her mocking tone was. She wanted them back. This was the weakest attempt to get them. It cried with desperation, and its cry told me I had accomplished the beginning of breaking a part of her.

"No, I just don't trust a Vitelli with one."

Katia picked up her bag, and in slow steps, she made it to the door.

She was already struggling to walk out. With a quick glimpse, her eyes lowered to my collar.

"You should burn it. There's blood on your collar."

Katia walked away, and I walked to my desk chair near my new pride collection of pain—hers.

I welcomed the silence with her departure, even if my mind wasn't. New threats had surfaced with Katia's presence in Miami. Whispers of California's rage had reached. My men saw the power of the arrangement. Not one had voiced anything but their loyalty and eagerness to have the *principessa* of New York as the queen of Miami. They understood the danger and the war that would come, and they were ready for it.

*I* was ready for it.

My phone rang, and I closed my eyes.

*"Si."*

*"Abbiamo un problema,"* Arlo spoke through the speaker.

When we had a problem, Arlo took care of it before it reached me. Unless it was important, or I had to be known. By his tone, it meant our problem was someone. Someone who I had to agree and order to be taken for a swim.

"Where?"

"Same place. See you shortly."

With fresh images of Katia's silky dress, her unsaid pain that caused the hard-on that didn't get taken care of by her lips, and the wrath's need to still punish someone, it was best I left. If not, how long would I last before I sought my ill desire for her pain as I used her underneath me? In this state, my cruel hands would leave marks in every inch that would painfully bruise.

I left. After all, I didn't lie.

# XI

## KATIA

*G*ET READY, WE'LL BE LATE FOR MASS," LUCCA'S DETACHED AND EVEN voice ordered before he disappeared from view as quickly as he'd made his presence known.

In Italy, Nonno expected my presence with a smile on my face every Sunday morning. I couldn't fail to show, even in sickness. I guess something in the Mafia never changed, the faith of the made-man.

I wore all black. It seemed fitting.

The church was quite a drive after the road construction delay. However, once we arrived, I took one last peaceful breath inside the quiet and uncomfortable mood of the car. We both hadn't spoken a word, and as people piled around the main double wood doors, the car rolled to a stop in front of the entrance. Two men waited by our closed doors, and I turned to Lucca.

He too wore all black, and he sat patiently as the parked car ran with his eyes forward. He had something to say, and I watched as his mind played with the right words as he remained composed. His profile showed his strong jaw and the clean trimmed beard that hid so much beneath. Then he turned to face me, and the coldhearted man stared deeply into my eyes.

"I don't miss a Sunday, but I'm afraid that will soon change, so I am introducing you to the church now while time allows it."

Taken aback, I repeated his words in my head. The underlying meaning of his admission and the importance he gave to the Catholic Church. There was no misunderstanding how this man was a follower of God, and surprise wasn't what I had expected.

Did Lucca confess his dirty and cruel heart, his deep sins? Or did he walk into the house of God guilt-free and with the same power as he did everywhere else?

Did he kill, torture, steal, cheat, and commit mortal sins with the weight of the afterlife?

In Italy, I used to roam around the city searching for churches. They were my favorite architectural structures, and each new church I found was like a sweet surprise. My love for them started long before Italy. It had been my mother's refuge. While we hardly left our home, that was the one place she did take us. Until one day, it was just her and I taking a ride to the same stone cross building.

She wept. I sat with a coloring book and pencils.

She prayed. I drew.

And once her chest and tears settled, we left. Every time I walked out, I wished for the next time I could stare at its high ceiling and colorful windows even if the big church made her cry.

Until one day she was gone, and I never returned to the same church again. With time, I learned the meaning of depression, sorrow, and void. My mother was a victim of all three, and with Father by her side, there was no escaping the cause.

She died in a car wreck, but by the looks of how her room missed many of her belongings, it never felt like an accident.

Now, I stood inside the stained-glass windows of Lucca's church. It brought me no peace, not this way. I watched as the clock ran while I stood with my arm wrapped around his while the eyes of the congregation took in the outsider, me.

"Smile," Lucca murmured as people swarmed in our direction.

I did as he asked and let go of his arm to stand tall with an imitation of content smeared on my lips. Lucca's hand swept below, grazing and resting his long fingers against my back.

Abruptly, his hand disappeared and was replaced by tiny hands that pushed us away. A ray of dirty blond curls and giggles flew between us, and my surprise was replaced with a smile. The little girl glanced back with a beaming toothless smile, running and laughing as her dusted freckled nose pinched together. She was so fast that only glimpses of her pink daisy flowered dress and bright yellow shoes peeked through the roaming bodies.

"My apologies."

I turned to the voice and found a tall man with warm brown eyes and dark golden hair. His eyes couldn't make eye contact for long before they were searching behind us.

"No need, Rana." Lucca pulled me back, placing his hand where it had once rested. A small smile played on his lips, amused. "Katia, this is Rana, and *that* is his daughter Milly."

"A pleasure meeting you both." I held my chuckle.

Rana's brows furrowed, and he shook his head.

"This wasn't how I envisioned meeting the boss's fiancée, but..." Broad shoulders shrugged. "Welcome to the family."

"Thank you," I replied, but I was most welcome for the glint of sunshine that lightened my heart for a moment in quick speeds and yellow shoes.

"I don't mean to be rude..." Rana trailed off, and his eyes moved along with his head past us.

"Go, Rana," Lucca ordered, and the man rushed away.

My gaze followed his trail, and I asked, "Rana?"

It meant frog in Italian, but I couldn't piece together how he'd taken such a nickname.

"He sings to stay awake, but others call it croaking." Our eyes met, and he said, "Come, there's a few people you should meet."

Introductions were made one after another. Countless names and bodies flowed continuously, many of which were affiliated with the Moretti Mafia. His men spoke to me with respect as their wives gushed and promised a visit to get to know each other further.

Congratulations for our union were endless, and I noticed the way he was treated with regard. Something not easily obtained in our world. Lucca had earned their trust and having me by his side was something his own capos and soldiers approved of for their boss and city.

I nodded, smiled, and chimed in the conversation when required. The doting and perfect example of his future wife and queen. All while we walked and stood under the house of God. This was the hardest thing for me to understand, the way Mafia men were able to follow the church and their faith so closely and still cause havoc in the streets with sin.

"Would you like a glass of water before mass begins?" Lucca brought me closer as he whispered.

In response, I nodded, my mouth dry after playing my part.

He dipped his chin, and his hand pressed for me to walk farther away from the crowd to the side of the church.

Arlo met us by the corner, a bottle of water in his hand, and a face that didn't match any of the men I'd met from their *famiglia*. Dark, and bothered to see me *here*.

"So thoughtful," I provoked with a grin and took the water from his hand. Arlo's lips twisted, annoyed.

Arlo didn't wait another second to leave us alone, and I unscrewed the cap to take a small sip.

"You will meet the priest after mass is over," Lucca murmured, his eyes away from me and out to the mingling conversations around.

I took his wrist and checked the time, fifteen till eleven. Mass should be starting soon.

Lucca turned and watched as I let go of his wrist, surprised.

I held his eyes, waiting for his reaction. His demeanor calmed, and I met a man I hadn't yet met until now. A man of the church, and something about the way he carried himself inside sacred grounds gave me an inch of comfort. An inch of understanding of who he was.

"Is something wrong?" Lucca asked without an ounce of care.

"No." I took one last sip of water and handed the bottle back to him.

My eyes veered from him and roamed through the wooded rows and rows of pews. Many began taking their seats and the loud chatter dimmed, but I found a pair of eyes that were particularly intriguing. They watched Lucca from afar, desperately seeking his attention.

Instead, she found me staring unapologetically at her. She didn't cower under my gaze or remove her intrusive glare.

I didn't know who she was, but her bleached hair and immaculate hourglass figure was clear for the eyes of the men even while clothed. I wouldn't have given her any attention if it wasn't for the way her eyes had locked on Lucca. Almost longing.

I shifted my gaze from her to him. As he stared at me, oblivious to the leering eyes on him, I observed him closely.

It was evident she wanted to be in my spot. She wanted to walk through the church doors and have his hand by her side while he introduced her as *his*. Not me. She made it clear.

"We should take our seat," I managed to say while my mind reeled to the short-haired blonde, and without meaning to, my fingers slipped up his chest to his tie. Fixing the already perfect knot under his gaze.

It wasn't until we were seated in the second row that I realized what I had done unconsciously.

Placed a claim on a man whose soul and body wasn't mine.

*Could it be jealousy?*

I should've never cared about who she was, or what relationship she had to him. Yet, as I caught a glimpse of his bowing head as he prayed,

I did. A part of me longed for a man who treated the church as a sacred space. A man whose beliefs mirrored mine. A mafioso who followed the rules of the church and the word of God as closely as he seemed to.

A part of me knew he did. The other part felt the pull that drew me closer to him. It was impossible not to as I witnessed his devotion to more than just himself. Because it gave me hope for my future. *Our* future.

And I felt peace again. The peace of the church, and I turned my attention to the sermon.

Lucca didn't pray, sing, or recite out loud. Instead, I heard the gentle *amen* that tumbled from his lips. The words he whispered, knowing every verse of the Lord's Prayer.

When the tithes followed, I hadn't been prepared to toss anything into the golden canister. A mistake I never made, and knowing how I'd failed to prepare made me uneasy. I had only carried my credit cards inside my small clutch, no cash, not one blank check.

His hand lowered to my thigh, and his head sank to whisper close enough for only me to hear. "I will take care of it. It's now my duty."

Our eyes connected, and I shook my head slightly, alarmed at the thought as I recognized what he was implying. What he had truly done by bringing me here. He had not only introduced me to the church where we would be wed on this sacred ground. We were now seen as one in his eyes, and those in the church, even before marriage.

"Lucca," I murmured with alarm.

He didn't reply, only his hand disappeared from my thigh as it reached inside his suit. His hand returned with a thin envelope that I was sure had a check enclosed. He handed it to me.

I watched the striking white envelope and bounced my eyes from it then back to him.

"I can't." He heard my hushed tone as his jaw tightened.

What was happening? This was too real, and all because we had both stepped into the house of God. Opening new fears and closing doors I hadn't been ready to give up. But as the canister reached our pew and Lucca's gaze remained straight ahead, I picked up the envelope and dropped in inside while I felt the eyes of everyone on me.

I sat for the remainder of the mass in a daze. Waiting for a minute alone with him without the watchful eyes or the priest's voice echoing throughout, when I heard, "The mass has ended. You may now go in peace." I breathed deeply, hoping I could do as he'd said.

Go in peace.

We stood, he shook a few hands, smiled and nodded a few more times, and then he pulled us away from the main room. Taking us toward the left side corridor where we waited *alone*.

"Was any of that real?" I voiced my thoughts.

Lucca's inked fingers held his wrist together in front of his relaxed body, and all I could focus on was the black ink rose on his hand.

"What was real, Katia?"

"You, here? Your devotion?" I spat quickly, with my back avoiding any chance of being seen. "Was it real, or was it just for your need to place your claim?"

Lucca took a step away from our distance and pulled my gaze away from his black rose to his eyes with his fingers on my chin.

"Don't question my faith." His low tone warned with displeasure. "And if you must know, all I tried to do was calm your worry by stating it wasn't your duty to pay tithes anymore. It's mine. It's very simple, Katia."

He dropped his hand from my face, along with the connection.

"It's for the best," he replied coldly. "Now turn around and smile, the priest is coming."

Right, the lie. The lie I had to tell even in front of a priest. It felt wrong, so instead, I turned, took one step back to Lucca, and faced the priest with a slight but genuine smile.

"Mr. Moretti, a pleasure as always. Do you mind introducing me to the woman who filled the seat next to you this morning?" Big brown eyes and a wide smile turned to me.

The priest appeared to be in his late fifties to early sixties, and welcoming. The wrinkles on his face showed the joy and sincerity he'd given over time. With ease, his aura soothed me, and I relaxed in his presence. I wouldn't offer that easily to anyone, even to a priest, but it came almost naturally.

"Father, this is Katia, my fiancée."

"A pleasure," I said.

"The pleasure is all mine. Welcome to the church." His hands stretched by his sides in offer. "Now, Lucca, what's this rash engagement you haven't mentioned to me? I must remind you there's an order you must follow to vow this union before God."

I glanced up to Lucca, eager to see how much truth he would reveal.

"It was quite sudden, but I brought her here as soon as I could, Father." Not a lie. "I am aware of the order, and I will be sure to be here for the marriage class. Although, unfortunately, we will both be taking a step back from Sunday mass. Please understand, I wouldn't be missing it if it wasn't necessary."

"I believe you, son." I stared at his black cassock robe and his white Roman collar as he reached his hand out for Lucca. Lucca shook his hand, and the priest wrapped his free hand over Lucca's inked fingers. "I know you are the faithful man your mother raised you to be."

Lucca tensed behind me, and with a curt nod, their hands fell apart.

"Now, as for you, Miss Katia, may God be with you, and it was a pleasure meeting you."

We left the church in silence and took each step down the small stairs until we met his running car. One of his men exited the driver's side while Lucca opened the door for me. Our hand met as he helped me inside, and the door quickly shut. I watched him from the window as he spoke to his men before he walked in front of the car until he sat inside with the doors locked.

We sat in silence for a few long minutes before I asked, "How do you do it?"

"Be specific."

"Walk into the church with the sins you carry?"

"How do you?" Lucca asked instead. He didn't have to elaborate.

"I guess we do have something in common."

He dropped the shift in gear but kept the car from moving forward, and he turned. "What's that?"

"Both our mothers introduced us to the church."

I shouldn't have uttered a word because now I could see the hatred in his whiskey browns directed at me.

"Don't speak of my mother."

Simple and grim, his tone warned, and my chest tightened as I brought back the man I knew.

Heartless and brutal.

# XII

## KATIA

EVERY MORNING, I FOUGHT TO GET OUT OF BED. EVERY AFTERNOON, THE energy to eat. Every night, the understanding I would be alone. I should be happy Lucca was avoiding me as much as I was him. But loneliness can bend the mind into craving a simple glance. Even from the enemy.

Today, the routine changed. My brand-new phone rang for the first time. Twisting the covers, I shifted to the nightstand and Lorenzo's name flashed across the screen of my phone.

"Enzo," I answered.

"I'm sorry, did I wake you?" He didn't sound concerned.

"No. What do you need?"

I heard him pacing through the phone. It was unlike him.

"I was just…" He paused. "How are you?"

"Living my dream life." I sat up on the bed. "What do you think, *Lorenzo?!*"

"*Merda.*"

Yeah, shit.

"Look, Enzo, it's too early for whatever scheme you are—"

"I just called to see how you were. To assure that you were safe."
Enzo meant it.

*Safe?* Did he forget who I was to marry?

"You know where I live, right?" I asked in disbelief.

"I know, I know. You are safer at Lucca's than out on your own right
now."

*What?*

"What do you mean?"

Silence.

"Just stay inside, and when you rebel, don't do it alone. Okay?"

"Do not hang up." I seethed.

The call ended.

*Stronzo!* I tossed my phone and left the comfort of the bed to face
the day even if the house was wide awake.

Our conversation was short, and his warning slipped even in the
short time we spoke. Enzo was rattled, and it settled heavily, as not
many could manage such a reaction from my brother. Something had
to happen. Something he hadn't expected, something so abhorrent that
he felt the need to hear my voice. Even then, it had been a reminder
of the ways of a Vitelli. Our resistance, and the terrible job I've been
doing to uphold our name. Lying in bed, taking long baths twice a day,
and reading *The Laws of Architecture* until sleep claimed me, wasn't
it. Now, my body had grown weak from the lack of movement and
exercise. Weakened by a poor diet. Weakened by feelings of pity, and
I'd done so at a critical time.

The threat had been loud, and I wanted answers. First, I needed
Lucca's trust, and even if my ways hadn't worked on him, a shift had to
happen. For once, I had no plan, just a goal.

To not live in misery for the rest of my life.

I needed my knives back, a way to keep myself busy with work,
exercise, and a ray of freedom. Just a ray, that was all I've ever known.

Slipping on my favorite black heels, I grabbed a hanger and hooked the zipper of my dress and slid it up. I checked my lipstick one last time inside the closet's mirror and inspected the fading bruises that time had healed. I bent down to the floor. My hand slipped underneath the mirror, and when I felt the piece of metal that hid my holster and knife, I pulled it free. While low on the floor, I pushed my leg through its opening, and as I rose, so did the leather strap.

With Enzo's warning, I wasn't going anywhere without it. Not even in this room. I'll deal with the consequences *if* he ever finds out.

I made my way out of the room and down the stairs, enjoying the sound of my heels. The only warning of my presence I was willing to give. Still unfamiliar with every inch of the house, I started with the kitchen.

"Morning," I greeted, and three pairs of eyes shot up.

The noise seized inside the chef's grand kitchen. Clean steel lines with the same marble flooring and brown furniture stretched inside, making it not only equipped with the finest tools for a cook but also refined.

"Good morning, Ms. Katia," a tall older woman with kind eyes and caramel and gray streaks of hair said. "I'm Mrs. Greco. Head of staff." She wiped her hands on her apron with a nod.

"Pleasure." I stared at her bluntly. She was being genuine, but there was an underlying air about her that I couldn't grasp.

"How long have you worked here?"

Her brows raised, and her lips thinned, confused by my question. "Years."

Hmm. *Years.*

"My apologies for taking so long before meeting you all." I smiled.

"Oh, don't apologize!" A round brown-eyed and bright-smiled girl chuckled. She appeared young, maybe eighteen? Too young and too sweet to work in a house whose door welcomed killers. "I'm Talia, and this grumpy boomer is my dad, Carlo."

Talia's dirty-blonde ponytail whipped quickly to face her father. I followed her playful grin to the man whose mouth was stuffed with a hand full of a half-eaten croissant. Carlo appeared to be in his late fifties, but life had not been kind to him. His eyes were the same color as Talia's, but they were tired and jaded. With short, peppered hair and scattered sun marks across his face, Carlo quickly chewed as he lowered his head to the floor.

"It's all true. However, I am no grump, Ms. Katia." He defended himself, and his eyes narrowed to his daughter.

"Nice meeting you, Carlo."

"Likewise."

My grin was filled with amusement. "How many others am I missing to meet?" I asked and faced Mrs. Greco.

Talia beat her reply. "Chef Diego, but he only shows up when big meals need to be prepared. He's little." She whispered at the end, and she made sure Mrs. Greco wasn't watching before she placed her palm down to her shoulder, advising his height.

I chuckled.

"And my dad has someone who helps him with the grounds and small house repairs. Tiago, he's super skinny and tall."

I liked her. Her energy was contagious.

"Well, I would love to come back and chat about some dishes. Maybe I can help in the kitchen one night." That caught Mrs. Greco by surprise.

"You cook?" Talia's voice raised.

"Yes, when I lived in Italy for a few years alone, I had to learn to cook my meals. I quickly realized I enjoyed doing it."

"If that's what you wish." Mrs. Greco's timid grin agreed.

"Can't wait," I said, eager to feel the familiarity of cooking, and the touch of normalcy of preparing a meal. "I also wanted to ask for someone's time to show me around the house and the grounds, if possible."

"Of course," Mrs. Greco rushed, wiping her hands again before looking down at the dough before her. "I just—"

"Oh, there's no need to waste the thirty minutes of kneading you've done. I can do it," Talia offered with a shrug.

Mrs. Greco hesitated, but the thought of disrespecting the boss's future wife wasn't something in her nature. Even while the dough had gained the perfect amount of volume and bounce to form and bake. It meant she had to not only toss but also restart her hard work.

I helped her make the decision. "Great, where should we start?"

Talia's face lightened as she rushed away from the counter. Her hands cupped around the pastry, and she nudged it as she gave her father a quick kiss. "Finish eating," Talia's hushed tone warned before she twirled and walked toward me.

"We'll start with the boring places and save the best for last." She laughed.

"Perfect, lead the way." My hand extended for her to walk ahead of me, and with a nod, I said, "It was a pleasure meeting you all."

"You as well," Mrs. Greco added, and Carlo's head dipped respectfully.

When I followed Talia's black flats, she began telling me which switches worked for certain lights and which plants weren't real. It was a difficult task to keep my composure, as she flipped and flopped between things she found significant to share. Mrs. Greco's tour would've definitely been a dull experience compared to Talia's description of the rooms and the names she gave to certain decorations.

The more I explored inside the house, I saw similar themed bedrooms. These bedrooms had warm tones, marble, and detailed furniture that matched the entire interior of the home, and his bedroom became my favorite room in the house. It was different, darker. As if he had transformed the rest of the house into this refined, elegant space for others to enjoy. But Lucca didn't seem to be one to do anything to please others. He'd done it to his taste, and his room was a part of him others wouldn't be able to see.

As we walked around the house, men came and went in all directions. Their eyes always found me before quickly looking away with a curt nod. As soldiers, they were at the bottom of the ranks. All they were meant to do was follow orders and enjoy the money of their sins.

I didn't nod or talk to any of them. Not only was it not my place but also, as a *principessa*, there were certain etiquettes that were taught to me at an early age. Now, as the future queen of Miami's underworld, the stakes had risen, and new unsaid manners had to be followed.

Thankfully, this was the easiest part for me.

There was one particular place where men emerged before leaving through the front door. "Where does that lead to?" The long corridor had a few doors to its left, but only two on its right.

Talia's chatter stopped, following the direction my eyes had landed.

"Um. That's the training room." Her explanation was clear to me, but the hint of question in her tone gave her a sense of uncertainty about what really occurred behind that door. It was best if she didn't know, and I didn't pique her interest any further.

"You should show me the outside areas before the sun rises too high."

Talia laughed and forgot her doubts as she turned toward the back of the house. "It's not even summer yet, Ms. Katia."

*"Expect a summer wedding."*

I forced a snicker. "I'm in no rush."

No rush at all, Talia.

We found Talia's dad, Carlo, on the other side of the pool. He was pulling a few weeds and sweating underneath a beige colored floppy hat. Carlo gave us a small wave and continued working in the garden.

A few yards to the far left, a full-sized home rested inside the perimeter of the property. A small grass road connected a trail to the front of the house. It would be quite a walk to make, but a golf cart by its entrance explained how the path had been created.

"Does everyone live on the property?" I asked.

"Oh, no. Well, yes, we do. But ours is hidden behind Mr. Mancini's."

"Salvatore Mancini?"

Talia struggled with her reply. Uneasy, her fingers wiggled, rubbing against each other.

"Yes. After it was built, Mr. Moretti moved him in a few years ago."

*Moved him in?*

As if Salvatore had no choice? I've been aware of Salvatore's ill condition. Hell, it was the reason Lucca had taken the seat before his time. Right?

I wanted to keep her talking, ask about Salvatore. To piece together the memories of the man I remembered as a child and put the missing pieces together. The godfather of not just one of my brothers but both, until one day I never saw him again. Instead, I left it alone. Talia was just too pure for me to use for information, and my questions will be answered with time.

As we walked back inside and the tour neared its end, there was one thing I wanted to know. Something that wouldn't compromise her by saying too much.

"How did you end up working here? You don't *have* to answer me." I gave her the option.

We paused near the courtyard, and she looked at the flowers inside, but her attention wasn't fully on them. For a second, I thought she wouldn't reply, but then she began.

"There's not much to it, really. My father had known Mr. Moretti for a *long* time. He used to landscape the home Mr. Moretti lived in. Then one day, dad came home and announced he had gotten another job with better pay." Talia shrugged. "Nothing really changed except for the size of our pantry." She chuckled, but it quickly faded. "Then my grandmother passed away a few years ago. I didn't cope with her death too well. I wasn't my best, but now I am here, better, and with my dad."

There was certainly much more to it.

"I'm sorry for your grandmother's passing."

Talia smiled faintly with fondness in her eyes. "Thank you."

I FOUND MYSELF INSIDE LUCCA'S STUDY. NOT ONCE HAD HE HINTED THAT I couldn't come in without his presence. After all, this room housed my prized belongings. It was hard to grasp Lucca's limits and difficult to understand his unsaid boundaries when mistrust was the root of our arrangement. I'll push until there is no room left to give. Even as we shared the same roof, we were still strangers who communicated as well to remain so.

A part of me had hoped he would be inside. To play the game and start scheming for my future. Wrap him in a craft of beliefs until achieving my goals. But the only thing inside was his lingering scent.

I glanced at my case before I dragged a chair near and sat with my tablet in hand. In silence, I sketched with the peace of my blades next to me and allowed the straight lines and angles to distract me from the shackles I'd been given.

The door busted open in a rush, and my eyes were drawn to a different hair color than what belonged in this room. Ready for whomever felt comfortable enough to rip the door open with such haste. My posture automatically tensed, alert.

Fair blonde hair and icy blue eyes hesitated when they caught me watching from the corner. I'd met them once on the same night Enzo had sealed my fate. However, since that night, his eyes had hardened along with his appearance.

*He* was the selfish bastard that had trapped an innocent life into this world with the belief of love, but I guess, in his eyes, it was a better outcome than death at the hands of my family.

Ilias Novak.

To my understanding, the youngest of the four brothers whose blood were all apart from another but maintained a bond stronger than kin.

He was also one of the few that had infiltrated the Cosa Nostra with no Italian lineage. His Russian blood ruined what many stood for as an Italian Mafia and what the word *mafioso* meant for many. But I couldn't care less. In the end, we all bleed the same color.

In a way, I agreed with Lucca about something. How the old ways of this world didn't always work for the best. How modifying a few laws could mean greater strength. *I wonder how far he would risk breaking them.*

Now, I remained silent before one of those changes. Neither one of us broke the silence. While I saw him as a possibility of trust, I caught his indecision and resentment.

Ilias perceived me as a Vitelli, and what it meant. The scars, pain, and wounds left on his lover's skin by my brothers. And yet, he struggled as my presence meant her safety. *Their* safety. The traded cage and the power I held for balance.

"Don't stop because of me. You seemed in a hurry," I said, disturbing the silence with my words.

His broad shoulders ticked while he pondered.

"Sorry if I startled you, I wasn't expecting you to be here." There was a glimpse of guilt inside him.

I took it as a win.

"No need to apologize," I replied and wagered my next words. Lowering my gaze, I did what I did best: deceit. "I hope Davina is doing well."

His body tensed as I uttered her name, and I watched as his eyes calmed. My tone had been convincing, my body language sincere, and my eyes portrayed care, and Ilias had believed them all.

He wasn't Lucca. He wasn't immune to my illusions, and now I had infiltrated one of his closest men. Slowly he would stop seeing me as a Vitelli, and trust will slither through the gaps. And the longer I remained trapped inside this hoax, the more I would earn my way in.

"She is." Ilias nodded politely and aimed his attention at Lucca's desk. "I must get going," he explained and walked deeper inside.

With determined steps and avoiding eye contact, he stood behind Lucca's desk. Ilias opened the top drawer and fumbled through its contents before retrieving a letter-sized envelope. An echo cut through the thick tension of unease as the drawer closed shut.

The height of his frame had grown by its proximity, and I kept my eyes fixed on him as he approached. After all, I didn't trust anyone. As he stood there without taking the initiative to leave, I grew weary of his next move. Weary of our distance and the negative thoughts that could be running through his head.

With his height and weight, it wouldn't be an easy fight. And yet, I was only one step away from my knives.

But I didn't feel threatened in his presence. *No.* Because as he stood rooted in a battle with himself, all I felt was his confusion and uncanny mistrust. His body struggled with his movements and actions, uncertain of how to proceed.

He glanced back at me and explained, "Lucca asked for it." The envelope wiggled between his fingers.

I shook my head, playing along with my ruse. "You don't answer to me." It had been true but saying it out loud gave me a vulnerable approach.

"I'm aware, but you're still the woman of this house."

Fuck.

*Was that respect?*

I almost felt guilty for...no I didn't. I remained silent and waited until he left the room. He was part of this world; therefore, a part of the game.

# XIII

## KATIA

I STARED AT THE SUNRISE. THE PROMISE OF A NEW DAY, AND A FRESH beginning. But that promise fell short in my life. A lost cause I learned as a child. Yet, I always sought its peace, and the desire of possibility. I wouldn't say hope; that died the day my mother did. My father made sure no trace was left of it.

The sunrise fought against the dark skies that guaranteed chaos. Soon, thunder will reach, and rain will descend from the sky, obscuring any light. It would allow the shadows to stay while streams of water and filth would run through the streets.

I waited for the sun to lose its fight and left the room before breakfast could be served. The house was quieter than usual, and today, my steps were silent as I had traded my heels for tennis shoes. Thunder cracked and the vases shook as I walked through the house in search of Lucca. His car was parked on the circular drive, but his study and dining room were empty. I had nowhere left to search as the skies rumbled from above. Lights flickered, and I saw his shadow through the back paneled glass doors.

Lucca stood outside and far away from the shelter of the roof's overhang, but the wind had picked up, causing the ends of his styled hair to wave. I watched him for a moment longer behind the safety of the glass before I pulled the door open. His head turned, our eyes met, and his back remained to me.

"This is the last time I ask, Ernesto. Call it in or do it yourself, but get that streetlamp fixed." He ordered through the phone and ended the call.

His dark mood hadn't changed much since that night I'd seen him before the church, but it wasn't as bleak as the immediate warning I felt after seeing the red stain on the collar of his shirt. Rather than a white shirt, he wore all black today. There was only one difference between that night and now; black hid blood splatters.

My ponytail swayed with the breeze, and the temperature had lowered with the upcoming storm. It was loud even though we stayed quiet.

I picked my rehearsed words in my head, ready to initiate the first conversation we had in days. But Lucca fully turned, his gaze roamed over my body, and I was rendered into silence. Heat surged and warmed every inch his eyes landed on my body. From my high waisted yoga pants that were skintight, the uncovered skin between my middle. To the distinguished appreciation shining over my matching black sports bra.

This man was capable of silencing any room with ease. And now, with just me out in the open, I was another casualty of his gaze.

Slowly his eyes lifted, and I closed the gap between my lips. With each exchange, it was becoming difficult to resist my desires. For my heart to beat in calm cadence and to keep my legs from squirming by just his stare. As much as I wanted to hate him, Lucca's dangerous lure kept holding me tighter, closer, and more aware of my needs as a woman.

He may have been a man of few words who lacked emotion, but

right now, his eyes didn't hide the hunger that swirled in his irises. Right now, he wanted me to see it.

I was no fool of the wants of a man, and I wondered how long before he would lose his control and demand what he could've had since the first night I lay in his bed. But Lucca hadn't acted, pushed, or insinuated anything out of me. It was evident that he found me desirable.

Any man in our world would've taken it long ago. Why wasn't he?

In a way, I was thankful. I wouldn't have been ready then, but now my body has sparked curiosity. Longing. But in our unorthodox arrangement, it meant a lethal mix of hate, sex, and blood. A hysteria that not only tempted but also warned.

"Do you have a minute?" My voice hitched.

Lucca walked closer. The few wrinkles scattered over his black shirt and rolled sleeves caught my attention. He hadn't changed. He had just arrived home. Somehow, his rugged appearance and the fullness of his beard from an extra day added to his appeal.

Lucca made it difficult even after a long night's look, and I struggled to remember why I looked for him in the first place. Struggled surrounded by his presence.

As we both stood on the covered stone patio while thunder neared and the wind whistled between us, I had his full attention.

A disturbing concern of knowing where he'd been all night left me perplexed by such interest. I would be a fool to ignore its meaning, and yet I did.

"There are a few things I need." I hesitated. If he'd been in such a foul mood over a streetlamp, my timing could have been better than starting this conversation.

"Go on." But the hunger that continued to fail to hide behind his eyes gave me the go ahead.

"Some stuff I can order online, others I prefer to pick up in person." I started with the easiest subject. Security, and how far I could push the limits he wouldn't voice about my freedom.

Nothing. Lucca gave up on nothing.

"Define *things*."

"I traveled light, Lucca."

He waited.

"Clothes and essentials."

"Order what you can. I can take you for what you can't tomorrow."

What?

"I can drive myself."

"You're not traveling alone."

"I never said alone." Lucca's brow rose, so I clarified. "I don't remember a time when I didn't travel without a shadow. I just meant *I* could take myself."

Amusement twitched the corner of his lips. "And how many times did you *lose* such a shadow?"

I didn't answer. He would see right through the lies.

"Like I said, I can take you tomorrow."

Fine. I gave up and moved on to the real topic I wanted to win.

I opened my mouth, ready to strike my next bargain, but I was interrupted by the ringing of his phone. His jaw locked, and he let go of my eyes as he looked down at the screen. It rang three times more before he silenced it. Lucca didn't return his attention to me. Instead, his gaze passed through the glass doors behind me. I saw his mind reeling. Far from our conversation with the stress of his day to day and something else I couldn't grasp. It was unsettling. How much he carried and imprisoned inside. The way he hid it all, showing no emotion.

The first drops of water splattered against the stones while others splashed loudly into the pool. More followed, faster, heavier. Awakening the petrichor scent from the earth I loved so much. I closed my eyes briefly, taking a deep breath and allowing the calming smell to wash over me. I shouldn't have because it soothed my thoughts, pacified my heart, and eased my will.

Then I was back in the trance of his gaze while I felt vulnerable and exposed. Lucca combed his fingers through his hair, and took another step closer, then another. Even with the twists of the wind, my breathing shortened.

"What do you want, Katia?"

My name sounded powerful on his lips. My name sounded tempting on his tongue.

I wanted so much, but for now, I wanted to make a deal.

"Access to downstairs."

His unconcealed displeasure was bare. "Why?" he asked cautiously.

Lucca already knew my answer. The workout clothes I was wearing said enough, but his mistrust was clear and always nearby.

*I will make you trust me, Moretti.*

"I haven't exercised since I arrived." I kept my explanation short. Less for him to read and pick.

"Don't play me for a fool."

"I'm not, but I figured it would be the safest place. Within your walls and eyes, among your men, than finding a gym where new people come and go." I meant it, but I hadn't kept my reply short.

Lucca shook his head, but he didn't say a word. His mind processed and thought out all scenarios to keep control from my request.

At last, he gave *me* something. It could be taken as power and patience. The ability to think through all outcomes and loopholes. I could see it as a possible weakness. His need for control.

Every strength could be a weakness when put into a different perspective.

Ruling over his thoughts, *I* took a step closer. A move that risked but could also gain.

A gamble.

My chest now bounced against his while my head leaned back to not miss a sign. But his lips were near, and his scent was unforgiving, and I found myself in *his* web. Tangled by all of him, trapped in his appeal.

I had meant to cloud his judgment, and instead, I had done it to myself.

"Careful." He warned, but I was lost between the details of the inked lines that slipped through his collar. Lucca's warmth brought me back as his hand securely gripped my nape and his fingers curled behind my ear. My scalp grew sensitive to his hold, and a shiver ran through my body like the wind.

"I will ruin you." Was it a warning or a promise?

In a daze, and taken by desire as the skies roared, I dared to taunt him as he did me.

"You can't ruin me." The pressure in my chest ached, and heat burned my skin as if the tip of a blade had broken through it.

Lucca's body closed any distance left. His eyes flared out of control, and when my smile broke, his thumb wiped over its feeling.

"You should listen. It will hurt less."

"Pain is not something I fear, Lucca."

Lucca scoffed, "Don't feed my twisted mind, Katia." His lips lowered, and my heart raced. "It's sick when it's let loose."

Mint, bourbon, and a hint of smoke feathered my lips. I stood still, waiting for his mouth to collide and for me to take and relish on what could've been. Even if it was for a moment.

But his lips never reached mine, and he stole any suggestion as his hand untangled my hair and his body spread distance.

"I said I would have you begging in torture before, and I *will* ruin you. The moment I fuck you, you will learn I never lie."

Lucca's dark eyes released me and left. All while my legs shook and my body expelled the pent-up desire he'd built. And I won *nothing*.

# XIV

## LUCCA

KATIA HAD FINALLY MET ME IN THE MATCH OF WANT. I HAD WANTED her since the moment she first stepped into my study. It had been a difficult feature to hide from so many eyes on us. I wanted to take her and brand her with my name to spite the Vitelli. To take her as they've foolishly taken from me. But her poise and the fire in her irises had turned me on as easily as her looks had. She had been a woman created just for my tainted soul.

I wanted her to trust me. I wanted her to believe there was love in me to give. I wanted her to think of a fulfilling future in this hell of a world.

I wanted to *own* her heart.

That was my initial plan. To give an inch and take so much more until her body and soul could only see *me*. And when all her walls were broken, and her spirit seared with hope, shatter each piece slowly. But each day, new barriers got in the way. All of them took time away from my intention to make it happen.

I had to find the balance, but for now, my men needed me. Tomorrow, I will focus on her.

Running on nicotine, bourbon, and a fresh clean suit, I sped through the streets of Miami. A deadly mix as my body couldn't take much more in its sleep deprived state.

The storm outside mirrored my control, and I rode in silence, feeding off its roars. Traffic was light for a late morning, making my time to the shipping dock quick. After ignoring Arlo's call earlier, I'd received his coded text message for urgency. I was ready for the worst. I just hadn't expected it to be to such a degree.

"What do you want to do?" Arlo asked.

I stared at the dead body as his echo traveled through the empty shipyard building. The smell of rusting metal and wet muck filled my lungs with each short breath I took. It didn't matter how potent the scent was, nothing could take my attention away from the body.

*Breathe.*

*Think.*

But how could I do such things and remain calm with such a message?

It was clear the war had started, and I wasn't the target.

Katia was.

And I saw *red*.

"Lucca?"

I bent down, and in between my knuckles, I caught the tarp and lowered it down the innocent body.

It was a woman. Her hair, skin, and height matched Katia's, but her build was slightly different, and her bloodless features were off. She'd worn a yellow summer dress that now filled her torso and abdomen with bullet holes. A whole clip had been unloaded onto her frame. With each entry wound, the yellow was replaced with shades of deep red and burnt orange, creating an ombre of death. One of her strapped sandals was missing, and her toes showed raw gashes and chipped nails from her weight being dragged across the ground.

She'd been killed and left to bleed, only to later be disposed of near one of my abandoned docks. Only a few knew it was mine. It was the only explanation for the missing blood puddles and the discoloration of her body. She may have been found today, but the old rope marks on her wrists spoke of days of misery.

"Glove?"

I couldn't leave a trail behind. Fingerprints could be left on any solid surface, including the human body.

When I felt the latex over my outstretched hand, I slid my fingers through it as I looked at her face. So young, so *incorrupt*, her only sin was the hair and skin tone she'd been born with. My hand inched closer, and my thumb ran over her closed eyes. I had to check. I pulled her eyelid open and met the color green.

I breathed in through my mouth as my jaw locked painfully at the color.

*Again.*

This was the second dead body with similar characteristics and eye color as *hers*. I knew from the first victim it was meant for me, but I never acted out of emotion. Instead, my moves were strictly strategies that would eventually outsmart and slowly kill my target. I had to confirm it wasn't a hoax before making my move.

The first could have been mistaken for a deal gone wrong. The junkie was too desperate for her next fix at the cost of her own life. If it hadn't been for how similarly she'd been left. Moved from the place of the murder. Dried blood and dropped off to one of my properties.

By the looks of this new body, her yellow dress, and designer sandals, she was far from a junkie.

I didn't believe in coincidences. There was no such thing. They were warnings, some others were signs of a bigger play in motion. I had been right.

I stood, pulled the tarp over her body, and tucked my discarded glove inside my pocket.

Adrenaline rushed through me, hammering my heart in rage. This was my city, and a civilian had been picked based on looks, for a *message*.

It's been received.

"I know what you are thinking, but would he really risk going against *La Cosa Nostra?*" Arlo's low timbre tried to ease me. It failed miserably.

The answer was in front of us. Pietro Borrelli had violated code, but he'd done so quietly and indirectly to remain clean. Anything would be based on speculation unless proven in council. My enemy was one of my own, California.

La Cosa Nostra ran on codes. One of them: we didn't touch made-man women or kids. Not *ours*. Internal affairs were fought between men, businesses, and territories. Even then, I would've taken precautions. But now, with her head as the endgame, stakes have been raised, and codes will be broken within our *famiglia*.

Borrelli was too old to win, too stubborn and dumbfounded in ego to see straight. Even if Mario Vitelli was the one who broke his word, I knew there would be consequences for taking her under their deal. But Borrelli made a mistake by starting a war I would finish. If he wanted to do it on the sidelines, so be it. It'll be dirtier this way. In the end, I had more power in the council and streets. I couldn't lose to either side.

"I failed to act when the first body popped. I'm not willing to risk the third one being Katia."

She was mine. Mine to torture, mine to protect. *My queen.*

Borrelli knew what he'd done. Now was the time to pay.

"I need your orders."

I ran my hand over my face before it settled over the bridge of my nose. I couldn't slow down my mind enough to pick the first order to give. I needed a minute, a drink and a fuck to clear my mind. I didn't have any of them, but the thought of Katia's lifeless green eyes snapped me back.

"I need Ilias at my house until Rio returns tomorrow. Make sure Wex and Vino are with him but not inside. The following day I want him investigating all new and future money transactions made in our waters for any irregularities." Sharp orders fired rapidly from my lips. "Sergio and Mimmo should set up a crew to watch the ports." With Katia as the main target, her safety was first. I faced him. "And you, up the security in our clubs and establishments."

Arlo agreed with a nod before he dipped his head toward the body in question.

"Make sure her family is taken care of by the end of the day. Cash, nothing to be traced back to us."

"Already working on that." Arlo flicked his wrist, and after a quick glance at his watch, he added, "The cleaners will be here in five."

Good.

"Now." The craving to lose control intensified, and I could almost hear their cries. "Have we identified who dropped her off?"

I had surveillance in every corner of the properties I owned, and if I didn't own them, Salvatore did. Nothing happened in this city without the Moretti family knowing. It was a death wish, and one I delivered with pleasure.

Arlo's attire of black jeans and a tee answered before he even nodded. "Yes. Two males, they are in their early thirties and not affiliated." Poor bastards, they had no clue. "They reside in Model City and are usually together at night."

"Perfect."

Miami was the definition of beauty in disguise. Cruel at night and unforgiving if unknown. Filled with street gangs, murderers, and the homeless who would do anything for a white line. A combination of chaos, money, crime, and tourism. An exquisite disaster.

Model City housed the finest criminals at night. Usually skittish, and with the confidence of a wolf but the composure of a rat. Even then, they all knew the Moretti name. Not one neighborhood stepped out of line. It's how they survived.

I guess a reminder has to be made.

"Let's go," I announced, and while adrenaline continued to plow through me in waves, we left the body behind.

Sleep would have to wait. I had to take care of business. I had made Katia a promise to take her to the city tomorrow. I couldn't break it, and that meant I had to ensure her safety.

Sergio leaned outside Arlo's vehicle with his arms crossed in all black. When we neared, he straightened, and I tossed him my keys.

"Follow us back to the city."

Sergio nodded. In silence, he walked over to my car while Arlo and I cornered his. I climbed inside Arlo's blacked out SUV and closed my eyes, but peace wasn't something I had the pleasure of in this life. My phone rang inside the cab. Lately, that was all my phone did, and it was unusual, as anything related to the family came to Arlo first. The only people who contacted me directly were my brothers and those who had my private number.

"Are you planning to answer?" Arlo grumbled, annoyed by the phone's chime.

"I need a drink," I mumbled, rubbed my face, and picked up my phone.

LV flashed on the screen. A person I had no drive to speak to, but I needed to.

"Lorenzo," I answered Katia's brother.

"I heard a few whispers."

"Do tell," I deadpanned.

"Another hit. Soon."

The whispers had just reached him and were delayed. They were a fact.

"You're a bit late, Vitelli."

"So they are true."

"Yes."

"And Katia?"

"Safe."

Silence.

This time, I filled him in. It wasn't about liking him; it was about numbers. And a dead Enzo did me no good. Because soon, he *would* take his father's seat.

"It has started." The shifts of power and old alliances breaking. The roots of all wars. "I suggest you huddle up," I dug.

"I'm not hiding." His tone deepened.

"It doesn't seem like you will need to. Miami will be taking the hits."

"What do you mean?"

I contemplated on how much I should share. He already knew about the first body, the resemblance to his blood, and the suspicions I had. This second body confirmed it.

"Your sister is the target."

A gutting pressure rose as my words were spoken out loud. No longer a thought but a statement. One that rattled my demon and my emotions to trigger madness.

"Should Katia—"

"Don't," I cut him off.

"It's a smart move, Moretti." I heard his frustration, but I couldn't care less.

"She will not be leaving the city." Not for New York, not for another country, state, or home. Katia would still be hunted, and the possibility of being found without me wasn't something I was willing to entertain.

"Fine."

"I must go," I said and hung up. There was nothing else to say.

"Lucca?" Arlo snapped my attention, and I caught the small twitch of his jawline.

"Yes."

He stayed silent, surprising me. Arlo didn't hide from me, not his thoughts, his actions, or his unwanted advice. Even as his boss, Arlo had always been the least afraid of repercussions. As a brother, he was the most vocal to express his displeasure even if he knew it would cause a reaction from me. Our brotherhood was unconventional. We would kill for one another, but we wouldn't speak of our bond. None of us four did. It wasn't needed when trust and respect were our language. Show over tell.

But I had been keeping him in the dark since I made the vow to marry a Vitelli. Only Salvatore could see right through it.

I didn't speak of the past. Never allowed it to resurface. Why would I? I was past the point of breaking, I was numb, and all I ever felt was rage. I fed off the power, fed off the chaos I caused. Fed in the pain and the feeling of control.

The past created who I was.

"You know I detest hesitation." I fucking did. "Speak freely."

His grip tightened around the steering wheel. Not once did he glance my way. Annoyed, he shook his head.

"I hope she's fucking worth it, *fratello*." His disgust was made known.

"Careful," I warned. Katia was a subject that was well mixed with the past. "Don't forget our brother was in the line."

"And yet, I know that's not all the truth there is."

I trusted Arlo with my life, but could I trust Katia's to him?

"She will be my wife, Arlo. Soon your queen, I need to know she will be safe with you."

Arlo scoffed, "Don't question my loyalty."

Good.

I could tell him to give her time. Talk about how great she is. How I care about her. Maybe then, he would see more of her than her last name. But I couldn't because *I* didn't.

"PLEASE!" I RELISHED THE CRIES OF THE MAN BEFORE ME AND WONDERED HOW loud they could reach.

Sweat and blood poured down his beaten face. One of his eyes had grown shut as his nose bled in its bent position. His buddy next to him had passed out from the pain Arlo had inflicted long ago, and the cries of one man were no longer enough to pacify my need.

I wanted to hear them both until I grew tired enough to silence them all at once.

A pool of their blood mixed below them as they sat bound in tight ropes. The kind that would bruise and mark their wrists from their struggles. The same way the body of the dead women bore.

"We didn't know she was yours. Please! I beg you!"

I shot his knee cap.

"Ahhhrr!" He sobbed and thrashed in pain, causing the feeble chair to wobble.

"I don't think you are understanding." I lit a cigarette, took a long drag, and put it out on his body before I placed the bloody butt in my pocket. "Don't beg."

The smell of burning flesh filled the tiny square kitchen. Its foul smell matched the filth they lived in. Empty cups of instant noodle soup were scattered throughout the floor. Trash overflowed over the can, and not one single dish had been washed. The rodents had grown accustomed to our presence, to the screams, and now waited patiently for the food we were preparing.

Blood decorated the aged lace curtains in red polka dots over the sink. Grimy vinyl floors bathed in warm blood, and as I looked around the space painted in my favorite color with a smile, I liked the new updates to the home. It had become one of the messiest jobs in a while. They would be left here, nothing would be cleaned, and I still wouldn't be tied to it. There was always a risk, which was why we didn't work this way anymore. Why we left with no trace, but this was meant for a message.

The passed-out body had grown pale, relaxed, and immobile. Perhaps he finally bled out. With a quick stare at Arlo and a nod to the ash-colored body, Arlo inched closer and pressed his gloved fingers to his neck.

*One second, two seconds, three seconds...*

His name was Connor. Born and raised by a mother who cared more for a needle than the endless children she birthed. Like many of his siblings, he'd run straight for the life on the streets. Quick cash, endless highs, sexual diseases, and crime.

*Four seconds, five seconds, six seconds...*

Life wasn't meant to be easy. Yet, no one taught you that.

*Seven seconds, eight seconds...*

That was how his curly, strawberry-blonde hair ended up hanging down his face without a bounce. His sunless skin ashy of color, and his silver-dipped chains doused with his own blood.

*Nine seconds...*

Arlo shook his head.

*Ten seconds.*

That's how long it took to reassure his life had left his body, but that was never enough, not for me. Unlike New York, I *made sure* their souls were banished.

Arlo stepped aside, and I raised my gun, enjoying the weight of the six bullets I had left in the clip, and pulled the trigger.

"Ahh! No, Con!"

Huh, I guess they were friends.

Taking a step closer to whose heart was still beating, I placed my gun in its holster and looked down on him. Agwe, a boy of Jamaican descent whose family worked hard and had tried time after time to keep him off the streets. Instead, America made it simple, cool to fall into the gutters. To steal even from his blood. A life he took joy in.

"I'm feeling merciful." I stretched my cracked knuckles, and Arlo smirked behind him.

"Please, anything. I would do *anything*!" Slobber, tears, and snot ran uncontrollably. Pathetic.

"I have a question."

His head shook vigorously, and his cry intensified.

"Man, I don't know anything!"

Yeah, I'd gathered that much, but his sin would still be punished.

"Answer me, and I'll make your death quick."

The grown man wept for the miserable life he wanted to live.

Sergio's steps neared from behind and stopped. Standing close, he leaned on the open doorway. His eyes found mine, and his head dipped. Sergio was done with his task.

I returned to the wails of Agwe as he continued to mourn the life of his friend.

"Do we have a deal?"

His mouth opened, singing a vowel of grief. I took it as a yes.

"Why her?"

Sniffing, his large brown eyes looked up, and his shoulders rose. "She was the girl in the picture, man. We just took the job and followed the instructions."

A picture.

My blood cooled, and my body shook with force. My pulse tugged with strings of madness, colliding in outrage at his words. I had to see it. Touch it and bear the image in my head for me to believe the captured silhouette was *mine*.

But first, "*Who* gave you the order?" I had to know.

"I swear I didn't know she was yours!" Spit dribbled down his lips.

"Don't make me ask again."

"He didn't give his name, just promised good cash," he cried, but as I took a step closer, he blurted, "Midthirties, and had burn marks on his hands!"

I could think of a few, but one in particular stood out in my mind.

"Where is the picture?" Even and calm, I asked.

In violent wails, he muttered, "Under the lamp."

In a quick spin, I scanned behind Sergio. Sergio moved aside, not bothering to get the picture himself. He fucking knew not to get in my way. Not when I could see death. Not when I felt the sting in my fingertips, and my hands itched for answers.

There was only one lamp. Gray with a film of dust over a box that served as a table in the far corner.

With each step, I saw Sergio's work. The two bundles of unmarked cocaine on the couch. The peppered dime sized bags on the floor and the broken scale by the center table. All serving the purpose of the fabrication created for the law, but enough for the myth to travel across states until Borrelli caught the gossip of the poor bastards he'd hired.

Finger marks covered the lamp's vase, indicating the amount of times it had been touched to show what hid underneath. With the force of the back of my hand, it was flung and shattered, causing a glass blast of tiny pieces.

I saw the image, and the demon broke free.

I picked it up. Watched Katia's grace through the pixels, unaware as she sat inside a café. Open laptop, coffee mug to her right, bold emeralds looking up at what had caught her attention.

My jaw shut painfully as my teeth gritted. It hadn't been a similar characteristic kill, it was a one human hunt.

Grooves in the left bottom corner tarnished the picture, and when I flipped it, I only felt the need for torture.

It was dated a year ago with one word.

*Italy.*

Borrelli has kept an eye on Katia for over a year now. Waiting, obsessing, and *I* stole his trophy. Now, he wanted her blood.

I laughed. There was no humor to it, and yet, I laughed. I folded the picture, turned and placed it inside my pocket, keeping the bloody and unfinished cigarette company.

I passed by Sergio and stood in front of Agwe's terrified spirit while Arlo's body straightened knowing his brother was nowhere near.

My body lowered to the bound man. His body paralyzed in terror the closer I got to his head. Silent tears poured down until I couldn't see his eyes anymore.

"I don't feel merciful anymore," I whispered in his ear.

The man wailed.

I pulled back, watching from above as he lost all hope. My hand reached back, but instead of my gun, I grabbed Katia's favorite—a knife.

And the demon prevailed. Ruling over my senses. Taking the crown and delivering every wound. Butchering all life as blood stained and soaked my hands in red. I watched him as he soon would meet death's realm. And I searched for a feeling. *Any* feeling that might emerge from my consciousness. I did so involuntarily, like a ritual.

Yet, regardless if they were young, old, good or evil, any sense of emotion was always the same. Absent. Tonight was no different.

Tonight, the demon and I smiled through the pain of the man's prayers.

Silence followed after the slaughter. The body was unrecognizable, and I still felt nothing but wicked satisfaction.

I never looked back. I had no reason to when you owned the city. In a neighborhood where no one kept an outside light on. The kind that didn't leave home after dark. The kind that death hunted. The same death that swirled inside me now.

Once the humid air struck my face, I followed the open door Sergio had ready for me. I sat inside the blacked-out windows of Arlo's car, wiped my hands clean, and unlocked my phone's screen.

I had an unread message. I opened it as Arlo's door shut and the car rolled away from the curve.

**ILIAS: Did you know she walks non-stop during the night? I**

**need extra compensation for the lack of sleep.**

I should have left it unread. Instead, my mind reeled while I felt Arlo's glance bounce from the windshield to me.

"You shouldn't be the one with gashed knuckles."

"Upset you missed the fun?" I deadpanned.

"No," Arlo's deep voice replied. "But you're the boss now."

"And as one, I will continue to get my hands dirty when needed."

I snapped my head toward him. Tired of words and ready to wash the filthy blood that soaked my shirt clinging to my chest.

"And indeed you did." His lips twitched with humor.

I felt none. Not while my pocket burned with Katia's picture and her lifeless green eyes haunted me. And I felt a violent need to have her near.

"Now, take me home."

"Yes, boss."

"And one more thing, find out where Tino Borelli is."

# XV

## KATIA

I WOKE UP STARTLED BY AN EERIE PRESENCE. A DARKNESS THAT ENTERED THE room and was now trapped by the clicking sound of the door shutting. The large crystal drops from above were on the lowest setting I'd left them on, making it hard for its light to reveal who it was.

But I knew.

Lucca.

As he stepped deeper inside, light caught his state.

I sat up quickly, wide awake and stunned by the massacre his white shirt exposed. So much red, some dried, some remained wet. Alarms set off, worried about his well-being and warning me to remain quiet, pleading for me to ignore his state. Because if his shirt showed such carnage, he was still lost and taken by its bloodbath.

Lucca was at its merciless point. Depraved and immoral.

I've seen it many times but on him. On him it was petrifying.

"Are you hurt?" I asked in a mere whisper.

The response was cold and hard.

"No."

"Was anyone killed?"

Lucca abruptly stopped midway through the room. My heart bounced; then it yelled for my body to awaken to the threat of his eyes on mine.

"I meant one of *ours*."

*Ours?* His eyes narrowed.

"Go to bed," Lucca ordered and continued on the path to the bathroom.

Enzo had warned me, but the truth was smeared and smoldered in Lucca's eyes.

The war had begun, and a part of me worried for his safety.

Fast streams of water hit the shower tile, revealing Lucca's movements, and as I lay back on the bed, my heart stung anxiously with an unsettling weight in my chest.

I had to fight Lucca harder. I had to find a way to win small battles between us because I was running out of time, and I felt powerless in this home as danger roared behind its doors. It seemed vulnerability was the only move I had left to regain the ability to protect myself from such. It meant I had to be honest and open when he was around. To show a part of me even *I* was a stranger to. It could work, but I struggled because vulnerability was the opposite of power. Yet, I lied to myself.

Because the moment I left myself exposed, he would break me.

He'd warned me himself.

It was a risk I had to take. A risk that promised knives, training, and the sliver of freedom. Now, without any of them, I have learned my weaknesses.

*"Weaknesses are the door to death."*

My grandfather's words recited in my head. Without them, I was weak.

The bathroom door opened, and Lucca slipped through silently. His mood hadn't changed, and I carefully watched him. The strong lines of his muscles, to the towel that wrapped around his hips. Too soon, his strong inked back disappeared into the closet but quickly returned in only a black pair of boxers covering his taunting body.

I gripped the covers a bit tighter, rolling their soft texture against my fingertips. He wasn't fully dressed. In fact, it didn't seem as if he had any plans for leaving the room.

The dim light disappeared, and my body stilled beneath the sheets. My eardrums thudded as they followed each tap his bare feet made against the floor. As my bottled nerves melted through my body with the unfamiliarity of his actions, quick breaths escaped silently, and my eyes remained open in the darkness as if I could see through the night.

The bed shifted, dipping inches away from me. His scent wrapped around our short distance as the covers bunched in ruffles and the weight of his body spread evenly.

I couldn't move.

Instead, our bodies lay in silence.

We were so close, sharing the same bed, and yet we were divided.

Only the falls and rises of my chest and our breathing blended in one.

There was something about the darkness. The kind that allowed you to hide behind it. The kind that eased. The kind that enticed you to relax. A veil so thin and yet too obscure to resist. Just like Lucca's darkness, it compelled me to it. As much as I fought darkness, the urge never left, and I wanted all its kinds.

I knew sleep hadn't claimed him, and I wanted a glimpse of his thoughts. Lucca had once promised he would always be honest when it came to my questions, but he had also warned me of his answers.

But as he'd walked bathed in blood, and a spring of concern for him had appeared, it made my decision to allow glimpses of vulnerability to slip easier.

So I asked in Italian, disrupting the silence in a soft murmur and allowing our tongue to take away the bitterness of words.

"What's on your mind?"

"You really want to know?"

His Italian attracted my body to turn, even as his slow and rough tone warned. I shouldn't want to. I knew that. At least not while death grasped him tightly.

"Yes."

I waited and waited, and when I realized he wouldn't reply, Lucca spoke in raw honesty.

"Your jade greens." My mouth shut as he paused, and his voice deepened. "Opened. Lifeless." I held onto the cover. "Dead."

My eyes closed, defeated. There was a burst of emotion inside me bubbling up. Quickly, I suppressed it. It was one thing for him to detest me, hate me even, but did he really wish me dead?

"Is that what you wish?"

Lucca took too long to reply. With every second that passed, the deeper my heart sank.

I would be married to a man who longed for my cold body.

Eventually a reserved, "No," fell from his lips. My eyes opened as if I could see his reaction, and instead, I met the murderous timbre of his words. "It's what others wish."

"And yet, it's not a new threat."

It wasn't. A title in the Mafia came with a bounty. Even before being given to Lucca, I was aware of who I was. A *principessa*, a daughter of a mob boss. If anything, my head had much more value as a wife of one. A curse I was born with. One that kept me attentive to threats, and one that reminded me why I had to learn to protect myself.

"Perhaps." He too knew. There was more he didn't say. More he wouldn't disclose.

A thought swept through our conversation. An opportunity I couldn't waste as I spoke in the darkness. It was a wild thought to his menacing aura, and it could break the sensitive and slim composure he held.

But I took the chance with a fickle heart.

"If you could just allow my—"

"Not now, Katia," Venom spat, cutting out any ideas and possibilities.

I ignored his wrathful tone, a dumb decision, but now that I could practically feel the cold blade of my missing knives, I dared.

"You know it's safer for me to carry."

"Sleep, Katia."

"I won't bring it to our bed."

Silence.

"Just. One."

The stiff air held me in a chokehold, and my chest heaved as it fought from its bitter smother. Losing control and urging for a win.

"*Please*, Lucca." Vulnerable. Raw.

And I felt gutted by my own blades.

"Don't make me regret it."

I could practically cry in screams of triumph. I swallowed them all, and instead bit my smile as my shoulders caved in victory.

Without thinking, my arm stretched blindly until it met his stiff body. His muscles tensed beneath my fingers, but I allowed his warmth to resist from pulling back. A reaction so unintentional and yet so sincere.

"Thank you," I whispered.

As his rigid body eased from my touch without rejecting me by moving away, I stayed. And I allowed the moment to linger.

Under the darkness, between death, wrath, and Italian words, I saw the possibility of a future with a killer.

For a moment, I allowed it.

For a moment, I grew weak.

For him.

I SWEAR I'D LOST MY MIND. I WOKE UP WITH A SMILE, EVEN IN AN EMPTY BED. Today I got ready without hiding, and with a strapped knife underneath my white dress, I enjoyed each click and clack of my red bottoms. I knew, soon, they would be replaced by workout wear. Because Lucca gave in once, the second time would be easier. Or so I hoped.

There was an extra bounce of determination with each step I took downstairs. Because the high of getting my way was a feeling I could get used to. One I enjoyed, even if it felt naive.

Lucca had promised to take me into the city, and I looked forward to leaving the house. Perhaps I could get my way again under the sun instead of a veil of darkness. At this point, I would never stop trying. Addicted to the possibilities, the risks, and the chances for another moment of treaty.

Breakfast should be served soon, but I had left the coziness of the bedroom to catch him before the presence of others. To measure his mood; maybe it had lifted as mine had.

The door to his study was shut, the house was quiet without his men running in and out, and I stood still in front of the heavy wood frame.

Where was everyone?

I didn't bother to knock. I just pushed the door open and took a step inside.

My feet failed me, and my body froze at the sight.

Forget about Lucca and his mood. I was petrified by two bears that sat on each side of him.

With wide eyes, a bouncing chest, and a hammering heart, my foot slid backward.

"Don't," Lucca's calm tone assured.

Yet, nothing in me eased.

I knew their breed. Knew their protective line and their long wolf-like teeth that could tear and kill when trained. They weren't dogs. They were weapons.

Caucasian Shepherds.

One white as fresh snow, the other midnight black. Opposites in appearance but equals in threat.

They stood at attention, waiting for a command as they closely watched me.

"Lucca." My voice hitched, and their ears twitched.

"This is Wex and Vino," Lucca introduced the two wool balls of monstrosity.

I could feel his eyes on me from the middle of the room. He remained seated in front of a table with a game of chess before him. Only three moves had been made on the board, but I couldn't catch the plays. Not when I was the stranger in the room with two dogs who wouldn't take their sight away from me.

It all made sense. The lack of movement inside the home, the quiet halls. The serenity. *They* were inside. Even with high-maintenance training, Caucasian Shepherds could turn on anyone if they felt their owners were at risk. Always alert, always looking for danger. Never let their guard down, even at home.

As we all stood quietly growing accustomed to one another, I saw their beauty. It was brutal and yet regal against their master.

"Ilias has been keeping an eye on them since you arrived. It was time to bring them home and introduce them to you."

My eyes snapped at his cool tone, and I took the chance to look at him. A clean black dress shirt clung to his body as he sat on the leather cushion, untouched by any trace of death in his eyes or blood from the night before. Casual and detached, Lucca spoke as if my small victory from the night before in the darkness had been forgotten.

It weighed my chest down, but I couldn't concentrate on my feelings or his. The company of who he'd named Vino and Wex outweighed it all.

Lucca stood, and so did they. They followed his footsteps, and I kept my eyes on Lucca. Afraid to look down and make a rash movement.

"Don't be afraid," Lucca murmured as my eyes closed.

"I'm not."

He found humor in my words as he'd exhaled quietly through his nose.

"They are very smart."

His fingers feathered my neck before they wrapped behind its base, pulling my body closer for our bodies to meet. I liked the way he felt against me. Even enjoyed the overpowering sense he brought along.

Lucca wasn't gentle; all his movements were always harsh and direct, but something about them attracted me deeper to his roughness. He handled my body with power, and I could feel how I submitted to his controlling touch.

While in his hands, I found myself at his mercy. It was sickening how easily my body and heart betrayed me. But desire was a feeling I had been deprived of, and now, with him near, it was one I wanted to explore.

It was exhilarating. The touch of a man.

His touch.

How I felt powerless under the weight of his hand and small beneath his tall frame.

I shouldn't let it win, shouldn't allow his strength to excite me. However, as his thumb spread open, lifting my head harshly, I opened my eyes to stare at his cold and dark brown eyes.

I wanted to touch, feel, and enjoy his skin as he did mine, and it infuriated me.

I was supposed to be repulsed by him, *not this*.

I pulled back.

Lucca's hand fell, and his eyes narrowed.

Wex and Vino stood behind both sides of their master, waiting.

Neither of us moved, only our eyes held each other. I should have stayed, played the part. It was what I wanted and planned to do. To be vulnerable enough for him to trust me, but I wouldn't have played *a part*. It would have been real.

"How am I supposed to teach them who you are, and show them who is mine to protect, if you step away from my touch?" While his words were collected, I could also hear their annoyance.

"I've been patient." Lucca's tone darkened. "And I've given you time, Katia. Time to adjust, time to come to terms with this." His hand waved in slow circles and fell. "But right now, I'm losing my tolerance."

My head shook, listening as my pulse quickened. He didn't get it. He was a man. A boss. Lucca had nothing to fear, nothing to feel.

Could he not see the difference?

I wasn't dead inside. *I felt.*

And I could only allow so much because I was already broken with issues I'd never faced. I'd only hidden them. And he was the last person I should allow myself to feel with. Lucca would never care.

"Come," he ordered.

I didn't.

"Now."

My heels took one small step, and Lucca's head arched back. Our eyes fought as he waited, and I took the last step. It wasn't as close as when he held me. My approach wasn't enough for him because his hands gripped my hips forward, and my hands shot to his shoulders, holding on to him to keep my feet grounded by his pull.

Some would call this an embrace as we stood wrapped in each other, but I held on to the distance between our chests.

This couldn't be the only way to convey what he wanted for his dogs. The only way for them to trust me enough to not see me as a threat. And how could we display affection when we didn't do such a thing, and never have tried?

I loosened my hold and stretched my arms, crossing them around his neck. I would give him what he wanted, even if I didn't understand his intentions. Because a part of me was curious where it could lead. But I couldn't see his eyes anymore, and instead of looking into his black shirt, I rested my cheek against it.

A weak moment, but one I enjoyed with his scent so near.

"What are you doing?" I whispered.

His tense body didn't relax. Indifferent to our current position while

I felt the opposite. It was time I made him feel uncomfortable.

"I told you."

"Like you said, Lucca, dogs are smart. You think they don't sense your stiff posture?"

Two could play the game. I just had to keep reminding myself to not lose to the main player.

"I didn't think I was."

Sure.

"Then hold me as I'm holding you," I challenged him.

"I like the way I'm holding you now."

His fingertips dug into my hips, positioning them deeper into his middle. While I felt his excitement through our clothes for the first time, I'd lost any reason because now I wanted to stay rooted right where I was. Feeling the reaction of his body toward mine, the desire I had brought him.

Warmth spread over me in heat waves as the room's air stifled and I'd grown parched and in need of relief from the oppressive ache between my legs. Bearing the need for a deeper breath, I wet my now dried lips. An experience so new that my reactions were delayed between confusion and angst. Giddy even. I wanted to be brave and embrace the delicious torture of my chest rubbing against his as his fingers handled into his mercy.

But as my body rolled in scorching shivers, his body remained as stiff as his dick. As my body heaved in blazing neediness, he stood cool and collected and indifferent. As my eyes glowed with desire, his eyes remained cold.

"I said, hold me as I'm holding you."

All Lucca had to do was entwine his arms around my waist, but instead, his chest bounced.

"You're laughing."

Lucca had turned his face away from view, and I only caught the twitch of his lips before he faced me again. The only humor left was the faint trace in his eyes.

"You believed that I would take an order from you?"

I pushed back.

"I asked."

He jerked me back.

"I prefer if you begged."

*Enough.*

This time, I drew back, twisting away from his grip and far away from reach. Of course it didn't bother him.

Refusing to allow Lucca's touch to cloud my mind and prey over the dangerous desires that intensified each time with temptation, I let go of his eyes. I watched Wex and Vino as they worked through our encounter and focused on them instead.

I extended both of my palms to each one and waited as they carefully watched my move. Slowly, they came closer as I left fear behind. I offered them no threat in such a position, and they sniffed my hands, and their wet nose nudged them for them to turn. I did, and soon I had my fingers entwined in their soft and thick coats.

There, peace and trust. Too bad their master was a harder breed of dog.

"If it means less people inside the house, you should've brought them back sooner." My back straightened, releasing my gaze away from the four-paw weapons that I now considered pups, and I asked, "What time are we leaving?"

Unbothered, he flicked his wrist with a quick glance at his watch and replied, "Now."

# XVI

## LUCCA

RIO WAS BACK FROM THE QUICK BUSINESS TRIP I'D ENTRUSTED HIM with, and he was standing next to Sergio's blacked out SUV. Sergio and Rio weren't capos, but as they both worked so close to Arlo and me, their enforcer title had more weight than most.

I walked down to the stone circular drive while I waited for Katia. I had a few things that needed to be understood before we left for the city. When she excused herself to the restroom, I saw the perfect time without her watchful eyes and perceptive mind near.

My car was parked in front of their vehicle, but I headed straight for them instead.

"Boss," Rio said as Sergio nodded.

"I'm sure Sergio briefed you of what you've missed." I picked a cigarette out of my case and rolled it between my fingers. "That being said, you'll be Katia's shadow."

The severity of my words was evident as I stared into his eyes. This wasn't an easy thing to do. To place such trust in someone other than my brothers. But I needed him to get her to safety if we ever encountered a threat. His life depended on keeping her safe.

Especially after Arlo confirmed we've lost sight of Tino Borelli, the next in line of Los Angeles. The man with the burn-marked hands. His disappearance from California only proved his involvement in the lives taken in Miami. He was here doing his father's dirty work quietly while Borelli Sr. sat comfortably in his throne.

Rio was in his late twenties, always on high alert, and agile in hand-to-hand combat. Sergio brought him in at a young age. Taught him the rules. Preached to him of honor and respect until Rio's mind only saw the mafioso way. By the time he swore his life to Miami, he was no longer the same kid. He was a made-man who towered over his older cousin by a few inches. He had no distractions at home. Rio lived and breathed for the Moretti family now. Even if he ever found someone to wait for his return at night, the Mafia was first, followed by God, then his weaknesses would come.

"I…" Rio seemed surprised, confused even. "As you wish."

"It's not a punishment."

"Never crossed my mind."

"And yet you seem…" I fought for the right word, but nothing came to mind.

"I'm not good with women."

"I'm not asking you to be her friend. Your duty is to keep her safe." I took a step closer and twirled the cigarette into my palm. "Are you capable of that, Rio?"

"Yes, boss."

"Good. Wherever she goes, you go. When you can't, Sergio will step up. However, Arlo and I need him on the streets, and you are the only other one I can see capable of such a task."

"It's my honor."

"I suggest you get comfortable with Vino and Wex quickly. They are back, and you'll be spending more time insid—"

The loud snap of the front door shutting interrupted me. I turned to its sound and watched Katia's long hair swirl in the breeze. Her enchanting green eyes caught mine as she slowly stepped down to meet me. I appreciated the way her legs looked in her heels inside my study, but now they caught the sunray's glow. Her tanned skin urged us to leave. Because I still felt my dick twitch at the thought of how she felt pressed against me. How quickly I was losing my composure around her. How I wanted nothing more than to claim her in my bed.

"Katia." I pocketed the cigarette and stretched my hand outwards. Katia took a quick look at it before she took it, and I brought her closer until her posture mirrored mine by my side. "You've met Sergio and Rio."

She faced them.

I was sure she remembered the day she met them. It was in New York. The day her father dismissed her without a farewell and gave her to a mafia boss he considered an enemy. But she no longer bared the marks left by him on her face. They were now only a foul memory. Yet not one I would forget.

"Not properly. Katia Vitelli."

*Vitelli.* My jaw locked, annoyed by her introduction, and she stretched her hand out for them with a faint smile.

"Sergio." He shook her hand gently and let it go. "Pleasure."

Rio took her hand more carefully, as if she would wound him with just a touch. Perfect.

"Rio." He scratched his throat and dropped his hand. Distant. That was what he wanted to portray. Afraid I would see anything more than respect for what was mine.

"A pleasure meeting you both," Katia said politely and wrapped her arm around my bicep. I looked down at her, careful of her intentions, but there was nothing but curiosity. "Ready?"

This was new, different.

*Hope.*

Something she hadn't allowed herself to believe in.

It was smeared all over her emeralds. She'd resisted it this morning, but she wasn't now. Last night in the midst of my torturous mind and inside death's veil, I had broken a seal inside her.

This was not just new or different, it was good.

I replied with a nod and walked away from my men and to the passenger side of my car with her close in tow. Opening the door, I grasped her hand as she slid inside the black leather seat and walked over to my side. A quick glance at my men behind the wheel of the car behind me, I got inside mine and drove away.

"Where to?"

Her attention stayed on the side mirror as the gates closed behind us.

"*Colour*. It's a shop in one of the main strips of Miami."

I racked my mind through the endless shops on every main strip in Miami but drew a blank. *Colour?*

"What are you getting there?" I needed a hint.

"Pencils."

It was a terrible hint. She could've ordered pencils online or asked for one. I knew there were a few lurking around the house. Then I remembered her lost in the plane with each stroke she made with a pencil that wasn't common, and I understood. Some things were better to pick in person, to touch, to feel its weight until you found what you were looking for.

Even now, I still didn't know what she had been drawing then. I knew so little about her. If I could ask Viktor to look into her past, he would give me everything there was to know, but something kept me from doing so.

Maybe it was curiosity. But really, I wanted to find it on my own and learn everything about her from her own words. It didn't matter either way; I shouldn't care.

I searched *Colour* in Miami on my phone, found the exact location, and placed my phone back inside my suit jacket. It was near a few restaurants, but I preferred eating at the ones I owned.

"Are you hungry now?"

"Do you mind if we eat brunch instead of breakfast?" she asked instead.

"Not at all."

"Then I'll wait for brunch."

Silence returned, and I was thankful for its peace. It was easier to pay attention to my surroundings. Katia may have been oblivious to the threat of taking her outside the home in broad daylight, but I was well aware. While no one would dare make such a bold move in my presence, I wasn't one to let my guard down. I wouldn't pay for such a mistake.

Those born with power often felt untouchable, forgetting the rats that moved in the cracks. I wasn't born with power, I fought my way to it. From the bottom, I'd learned what the streets were capable of and knew firsthand the true criminals who roamed freely in the light.

The game had changed with Katia's presence in Miami. She was the weak link; she was the one to take out. Because the easiest way to get to me would be through her.

For a man like me, I would do anything to assure her safety. Her father and grandfather both couldn't protect their own women, *their queens*, and by doing so, they'd lose respect within their syndicates. Afterall, could you really call yourself a man if you couldn't protect what was yours?

"Are they following us?"

The light had turned red, and I gazed at her. Her delicate jawline tightened as she focused her attention on the side mirror. I didn't have to see the reflection. She spoke of Sergio and Rio.

"Yes."

"You don't travel with a tail."

It wasn't a question.

"How bad is it, Lucca?" Her eyes snapped to mine, but the traffic light changed so I returned mine to the road.

We were near the shop, but Katia couldn't wait for an answer as she pushed.

"How bad?"

"You know the answer."

With her gaze on the mirror, she replied, "I guess I do."

I parked my car but didn't get out. Instead, I watched her. Her hand caressed her thigh. That anxious little tic she frequently fell back on. Katia couldn't resist pulling her eyes away from the mirror, and when they left, it was only to see past me. Surely, following Rio and Sergio's back as they walked deeper into the open area to clear the shop and find all exit routes.

"I won't intervene in any measures you place for safety." Katia's docile tone tipped me off. I could see bits of vulnerability, but I saw right through it. She wanted something.

"But."

"You need to let me train, Lucca."

"There are many places you can, Katia. The grounds are as perfect as they come."

She acted as if I was keeping her from doing laps in the pool. Keeping her from taking a walk, or even a run around the premises. Hell, she could even do core exercises in any room. Why did she want access downstairs so desperately?

"And yet, I know there's a room fully equipped with everything I could possibly need downstairs."

"Along with my men? I don't think so."

"You really believe me a fool to try anything with them, or them to me for that fact?" Her pitch rose, as did my nerves.

This was nonsense.

They weren't ignorant. But was she so blind as to not understand my reasoning?

A dark chuckle escaped.

"What? For once, actually speak to me!"

She was infuriating. Passionate and tempting as her spirit fought me back.

She was distracting.

"It's not just equipment, Katia. Quit acting as if you don't know what all happens there."

"What are you afraid of, huh?" Fire burned her poise with frustration as her cheeks turned a deep rose color while she pointed her finger at me.

"What are you afraid of, huh?"

Long gone was the calculating woman I'd grown accustomed to. Instead, she'd been replaced by someone who spoke out of tone and out of turn, unafraid of who she was speaking to.

"That I'm going to leave? Do you think I will cry myself to sleep because of what I see? Of what I hear? That, *what* exactly?" A thick stream of English spewed from her lips. "I can't leave. I can't cry myself to sleep, and I can't care about what I see or hear. Until you realize we could be stronger for Miami as partners *than* this." Her hands flung between us. "The easier our lives will be."

Katia took a deep breath while mine remained even. Her eyes pooled in nothing more than anger at her outburst, quickly regretting her words. I watched her tuck her hair back with closed eyes, trapping her tears of bitterness.

For once, I was lost. Unsure of what to say or how to react. She'd thrown a curve ball into the game that I wasn't ready for.

I've seen women cry, and while she hadn't shed a tear, this felt different.

Just this time, I allowed myself to speak freely.

"You are right. You can't leave. And while you don't care for what you might see or hear, I do. Because you should care. That's what good people do. That's what people with the same light that shines in your eyes do." Her eyes fluttered open, and any sign of tears was long buried. Instead, her eyes were now soft, frail even as she fought them with her strong stance. "I'm not looking for a partner, Katia. But when I promise to keep you safe, I mean from this world too."

"That's where you are wrong." She shook her head. "This *is* my world, Lucca."

"You're a woman," I said, even when my statement was weak.

"And yet, I know the Mafia just as well as any made-man. You just don't want to see it."

*Perhaps.*

We stared at one another. Neither backed down. Her eyes hardened, and her mask returned quickly, leaving no emotion behind. I wondered how much she had seen. How much had she heard? How much has she suffered in the hands of her own family to be able to hide it all so fast, so easily. A master of minds and feelings.

The answer was *enough*. Katia Vitelli had been trapped long before I came along.

This was the reason I didn't want to learn about her. The real reason I never asked Viktor for a file of her. I didn't want to humanize her. Because the more I did, the more of a threat to me she would be.

"Rio is waiting outside. We should go." Katia placed her sunglasses over her features and faced me.

Our conversation was over, and it felt unsettling to leave it behind. But that was what I did. I couldn't risk saying more. I, too, needed to regain control and step out as if nothing had been said.

I walked out of the car and headed for her door. Katia had already opened it, and I gritted my teeth against saying anything. Instead, I took her hand until her body slid into the open air and Miami's heat by my side.

Our walk was quiet and short with Rio in tow. Sergio was waiting inside as we stepped in but quickly left, leaving only us and a young guy behind the counter.

Long surfer-style hair covered half of his face as he paid no attention. It remained in the sketchbook that sat on the counter. An eraser rested near his drawing with droppings sprinkled around his work area and onto the floor.

"Welcome to *Colour*," he mumbled, with a half-assed wave that showed his lead-stained fingers before he returned back to his sketch.

Soft Indie pop music played in the background. A few plants were scattered around the shop in big pots while rows of materials were neatly placed for sale. Checkered floors spread, mimicking the same white and black colors, throughout the store. It was a quaint little place where the only splashes of color that popped up were the utensils they sold.

Katia had relaxed and walked a few feet away from me, comfortably scanning the shelves. The more I followed her trail, the more out of place I felt.

There was so much material. So much paper, they had stacks and columns of it; supposedly, they were all different. From textures, weights, cuts, and don't get me started on the colored pencils.

I begged to differ that red was red, and black was black. You wanted a lighter black? Pick a gray. Not dark enough?

Just press harder.

Katia stopped ahead of me, and I tried giving her space, but when she kept playing with the same two *pencils, unable* to decide between them, I gave up. While each of her hands held one and her fingers twirled them with ease at their tips, I made my way to her. She had been so concentrated with the unmarked wood sticks of lead that I left some space between her back and me.

"Just get them both," I murmured inside the quiet space.

Her palms closed, trapping the pencils in a tight grip.

"You are just ready to leave."

*I was.*

"It's an easy decision."

"Is it?" Her tone rose, clearly her words meant more.

"You got more to say?"

She exhaled loudly, and I closed the distance, submitting to her sweet cherry scent and faint perfume.

"No," she replied without weakening her grip.

*Give an inch, take away more.* I looked down over her shoulder to the pencils and lowered to her ear. "Why are they different?"

Her head inclined to my voice, as I'd chosen to speak in Italian, and her shoulders fell from their guarded position.

She couldn't see my smile.

"Their lines." Her tongue rolled in Italian.

"How so?"

"One will be thin and easy to erase."

"And the other?"

She took a deep breath. "Hard to ignore."

*Give an inch.*

"Both are important. Take them."

Her head shook as our native tongue triumphed in my favor. When she spun, I saw confusion in her eyes as they blazed.

"Just remember, even if lines can be erased, the mark will remain intact."

"You got more to say, Lucca?" Her defiance was clear as she switched to English.

I've had enough of her mouth, her attitude, and overall the mindfuck.

"I don't have all day. Pick one or both. They are *just* pencils."

"But they are much more!" she spat.

Irritation gripped me and all coolness fled as I stared down at her stained lips. She too felt the change as her body drew back.

"I didn't mean—"

"To what? Snap? Raise your voice to me?"

Her head shook. "No one is around."

I no longer cared. I had given too much, and that had been my fault.

She'd forgotten who I was, who she was to marry, and whose bed she slept in at night.

Fuck giving an inch.

I wouldn't be disrespected by a *Vitelli*.

## KATIA

LUCCA'S BODY WAS TENSE, FIGHTING FOR CONTROL AS HIS EYES STRUGGLED TO regain the violence I'd sparked. I knew I had pushed too far, and I'd flipped a switch I had no power to reverse.

Even in the car, I shared too much, but I had been so blinded with the possibility of getting what I wanted. It had been just us and the small treaty we'd agreed to without words. I'd spoken to him openly, but now my words had been blurred by mixed feelings and the thought of the real lines that were drawn between us.

I had spoken to him out of spite, with disrespect and out of the one place he'd challenged me not to do so, our home.

As I stared at the cruelty his eyes carried, I grew anxious.

I'd played with wrath and menace, and all they'd ever delivered to me was pain. I'd lost my way of composure and the years of practice of hiding my thoughts from my mouth.

All I could now see in his eyes was the same hatred my father cast before physical pain would follow.

I waited and waited because even in public there was nothing these men couldn't hide.

*Breathe!* I demanded myself. *Fight back.*

But as I continued to wait, there was nothing for me to fight back against.

*I'm not broken,* I repeated over and over, and each time that fearful child faded, and determination broke through.

And Lucca never struck. Lucca kept his promise.

Instead, he watched me carefully. His grim demeanor present but controlled. Lucca didn't say a word, and I wished he would say something. React, even if it meant I would fight back because his silence was worse.

His silence was punishing.

Lucca took the pencils from my hands, placed his powerful hand on my lower back, and pushed my body alongside his to the entrance of the store. When the blond shaggy-haired boy came into view, Lucca removed his hand from me, and I yearned for its return. It was sickening to still want his touch, as if it was meant to comfort me, but it was nothing more than to claim his power over me.

The guy behind the counter raised his head as he noticed Lucca's frame before him. Without a word, Lucca threw a bill over his sketch with the same hand that held the pencils. The boy's steel-blue eyes shot wide open when Lucca began walking away.

"Sir, your change!"

He wasn't acknowledged. Lucca only had me in mind as he stepped by my side and pulled me close.

Sergio and Rio waited outside, and while one walked ahead of us in the distance, the other remained close behind us

"Lucca," I managed to utter once we were alone inside his car.

"Katia."

How did he sound so, so unemotional?

I needed to fix this.

"I...I'm sorry."

I felt emotionally drained. Battered, as the memory of my father and rooted feelings had so easily emerged. But mostly, I felt rage. Of how he could get everything I'd worked so hard to master out in the open in a matter of seconds. How the sliver of the treaty had been broken swiftly after weeks of mending. Long weeks of mind games and risks.

All that time lost over pencils and lines!

The car's engine spurted to life, taking away the silence and filling the cabin in its soft purr. His phone chirped, and after a quick glance, he placed it back on the console. I dared a glance, and while his voice sounded controlled, Lucca's rigid muscles and strong jaw showed his temper.

I should have let it go and allowed him to have his moment. I could work my way to mend my disrespect another time. But he felt so distant, and I yearned to regain the close moments we had had since last night. How we'd started the day and spoke as civil humans. As strangers rather than enemies.

But reasoning wasn't my ally, and my spirit had become my foe as his hand reached for the gear. My hand shot out to stop him from shifting. Surprised by my own reaction, I clenched on to his wrist. A terrible move as it now demanded attention with its controlling grip.

My eyes snapped up and his gaze cracked with rage at mine. Finally, a reaction I understood, anger. It was better than his silence, or so I had thought because quickly his hand forcefully removed mine and held my jaw tightly.

I didn't back down. I took his uncontrolled grasp and ire to manipulate the situation. My mind had to catch up fast because his chest now rose with pent-up frustration. It was intimidating to see his eyes darken with such hatred aimed at me, to see his features contouring into the man I hadn't yet met. The boss of Miami.

This was the only chance I had to exploit his reaction.

"Can't you see I'm desperately seeking peace?" My eyes pleaded.

"All I see is how you've forgotten who I am." He seethed, seeing right through my attempt.

My mouth had grown sore from his hold, and I tried once again, but this time I held his forearm, hoping for a break.

"I said I'm sorry."

"Enough said, Katia. You've said and done enough." Lucca's low and dangerous timbre warned.

Fine. I was done with the game. Lucca believed I'd forgotten who he was, and even while it was far from the truth, I couldn't change his mind. It was done. Lucca would punish as he saw fit.

"Then let go of me," I said through my teeth.

His eyes lowered to my lips and down my body. When his gaze returned, he shocked me by doing what I'd asked.

Collected, he placed his hands back to the wheel, shifted gears, and sped out of the parking space. As the streets blurred by, the feeling of defeat weighed heavily inside, and I had no one to blame but myself.

# XVII

## KATIA

TWO DAYS HAD PASSED WITHOUT SEEING LUCCA. HIS ABSENCE WAS another form of punishment. I didn't dwell, nor did I allow myself to feel anything other than indifference.

Because if I played scenarios of how the day could unfold, all the outcomes would be in my favor.

I would expect to slither through Lucca's guarded demeanor. I would expect to grow closer to him. I would expect him to say *yes* to my demands. To get the answers I sought from him. But our expectations were just dreams and often ruined by cruel reality.

Expectations were illusions that delivered disappointment and heartache. Nothing more. All because they were the root of our mind and hopes.

A fabrication.

It was all up to me. I was done trying to put my future in the hands of a man who didn't care. It was time I acted for myself. Lucca had been clear that he didn't want a partner, and since that day, I have stopped believing in the chance to be his.

I was fucking Katia Vitelli.

Not one man in my life fought for my well-being. Not one for my future, so *I* was.

In the past two days, I've grown closer to Vino and Wex. Ran with them along the perimeter of the house. Lounged in the sunroom creating new home designs and spent hours sketching structural lines with them by my side. And both nights, we would sit at the wine cellar with a pint of red and a book in my hand.

Today was the third day that slipped by, but I at least had a knife on my thigh, a workout finished, and a sense of purpose, as the possibility of creating a brand by selling my floor plans to the public was something I could do inside this gilded cage. *I* had achieved what I wanted without needing *him*. And I felt overjoyed, powerful to be reminded of who I was and who I could be.

Lucca might be the head of this syndicate, the boss. I, however, believed that he was the one who had forgotten who I was.

"Ms. Katia." Talia's soft knocks bounced at the entry of the second living room. A place no one ever entered as it was tucked deep into the corner of the house. "Dinner will be served shortly."

"Thank you."

"Will Mr. Moretti be joining you?" she timidly asked.

I stared into her wide eyes and said, "I doubt it."

Talia's lips twisted with a nod, and even after I'd given her an answer, she stood by the door casing, her thoughts keeping her from returning to her duties.

"He's just busy, you know." She tucked her hair back, nervous of overstepping, but her concern about my feelings was stronger than the limits set by the title I carried.

"I know," I replied smoothly. Indifferent.

I didn't want to share further. Her loyalty was to Lucca, her employer, and I've always been one to never speak about private matters.

I ran my fingers through Vino's white coat, and her eyes fell on Vino and Wex as they sat attentively watching her.

"It's nice to see how quickly they warmed up to you." She smiled softly.

"I guess," I murmured while I petted him. "They just crave attention, and I'm providing it."

She laughed. "Nah, Ms. Katia. I've been around those two since they first arrived. They don't get near anyone but Mr. Moretti or Ilias." Her eyes lifted back to mine. "Red or white?" she asked.

"Red."

"Red wine it is." She nodded with a smile and quickly left.

I stood, and my new favorite companions mimicked me. Ready to follow my trail. Wex was the most reserved of the two while Vino usually sought my touch, but they both tagged along wherever I went. They made the loneliness easier.

"Come, I'll walk you outside to use the restroom before dinner."

Vino's white ears twitched as if he agreed. Wex sensed our departure and stood tall before me ready to lead the way.

Before I took my first step, Wex's black fur moved forward, setting the pace with dominance and full awareness of our surroundings. I almost shook my head. He reminded me of his owner as his paws and strut claimed control and authority. Vino didn't mind staying behind; he preferred my side.

Abruptly, Wex stopped, fully alert as we approached the front door. Vino sensed his change, and his wolf-like teeth shone while his body leaned closer to mine.

Lucca had men staged by the gates, and throughout the property, nothing seemed out of the ordinary. When I took a step closer to the door, they didn't stop me or bark. They just stood close in attention. This was new.

With one hand ready to slip under my dress for my knife, I pulled the door open, and a piercing shriek stunned me.

A female with her hand on her chest and terrified features stood inches away from me.

"What are they doing here?" she exclaimed, taking a step back and removing her hand from her body to wave down at the sweet four-legged creatures.

What are *they* doing here? What was *she* doing here, and who was she?

"Excuse me." I peered down at her without letting my hand fall away from the outline of my blade.

"Who are *you*?" Purple-stained lips curled and narrowed blue eyes asked.

*Who am I?*

I almost laughed. Almost.

The dyed blonde-haired woman straightened her posture, but my height combined with the heels I wore wasn't something she could stand up to.

"Katia Vitelli."

Her eyes fluttered and widened. That rang a bell, and today, I enjoyed the weight and burden my name carried.

She tried to hide her hesitation, but she was a fool to the game of confidence and a stranger to class.

"The question is who are *you*, and what are you doing outside my home?"

This allowed her to gain an inch of the lucid power she believed to have. Her hand rested on her hip.

"Anna." No last name was given. Therefore, no one with power. An afterthought. "Lucca is expecting me."

"*Lucca* isn't here."

"I'm aware." She shrugged. "He said I could wait in his study."

Where my knives were? Where I knew made-men spoke openly? The place not many stepped foot inside without him? *I think not.*

"You can wait outside."

Anna's mouth opened, and her chest puffed, choking her boobs against the skimpy and classless green dress she wore.

"I don't think you—"

"No." I stopped her before my blade came out to play. Vino and Wex recognized my warning tone, and both let out a heavy warning of their own as their throats snarled quietly enough to cause panic in her eyes.

"You can wait outside or leave." I gave her no room to defy me, and I shut the door in her face.

She didn't attempt to open it on her own, but I waited a second longer. Trying to piece together what had just happened and who she was before I walked away with Vino and Wex to the back side of the property.

While they ran away to take care of their necessities, I hoped the woman would take the second option, but if Lucca was expecting her, I couldn't intervene in business matters.

It was a business matter, right? He wouldn't be so bold as to bring someone under the same roof I lived in.

A part of me knew he would to prove a point. To prove to me he had no limits, no rules. But I would be damned to allow such a thing under the roof where I slept.

Then, it dawned on me.

The woman from the church.

I looked out into the dark, and as I watched Salvatore's home light some of the night away, my heart sank.

Men in our world were rarely faithful. How could they be, when most marriages happened out of convenience, and they could do as they pleased without repercussions while we were imprisoned by only them?

I knew this.

And since we never spoke of the matter, Lucca was oblivious to where I stood. Yet he was a man. One who was powerful, wealthy, and with looks that easily attracted everything that walked and looked for such things.

How could I not have thought of this? It had been weeks! Had I been so naive to believe all this time that he would refrain from sex? A man like him?

The dogs returned and sat by the door, waiting for me to let them back inside.

*Breathe, Katia, breathe.*

I did, but my palms pricked at the thought of him with another woman, and breathing didn't help the rising anxiety that continued to spread.

With each step back inside, I tried to bottle up the thoughts and images that played in my head.

The things he did behind closed doors.

The things deep down *I* wanted from him.

"Ms. Katia."

I heard my name in the distance, but I was stuck in my head. Frozen by the chilling hatred of this happening to me.

"Are you alright?"

I jerked at the soft touch that pulled me away from my thoughts.

My body repelled any touch, then why didn't it fight *his*?

Mrs. Greco stood with wide dull-blue eyes. Her hands had clamped together on her chest, and I stared at her, observing the resemblance I had missed.

"Who's Anna?"

Her face fell.

It's all I needed. And yet, I waited for her reply. The confirmation I would get, the tells she would offer.

"She's my daughter." Mrs. Greco's head bobbed, trying to conceal the full truth.

"What does she do?" My voice was steady while I felt like breaking.

"She is a designer."

Vague.

"What does she design?"

She hesitated, and I grew tired of the word play.

"Clothes."

*Clothes.*

It wasn't a business meeting.

I bit down on saying anything, gritting my teeth as I stared into her eyes. Then her eyes fell.

I took the blow she delivered but didn't strike back.

She didn't deserve my retaliation. Instead, I walked away from her and the immaculately set dinner table in determined steps.

Vino and Wex trailed behind, and I quickly ordered them to stay. They listened, but Vino whined the further I walked away.

With each step, I ignored the pristine and flawless appearance of the home. An interior that portrayed what many strived to live in. What many believed was happiness. When in reality, it was far from the truth. Facade.

Cheap perfume infiltrated the main room, giving away Lucca's arrival and mockery. I followed the scent, and its path led me to the closed door of his study.

My body shook as memories of the last time I faced a closed door and allowed impulsiveness to lead me to a painful punishment.

But bruises faded, and I was too unhinged to care for repercussions. I will be heard, and I will set his fucking world on fire if he believed I would allow such disrespect.

I wiped my hands over my dress, raised my eyes, and twisted the knob.

Not even a lock had been placed to stop me.

The door flung open, and my face heated as I took in the scene before me.

Blonde hair whirled, blue eyes widened, and immediately calmed with a smirk when they noticed me.

And it was over.

I let my madness win, and in one swift movement, I retrieved my knife. It flung out and twirled in my hand until it lay in a reversed grip.

*Try me.*

Her smirk disappeared, and fear smeared her features.

Frozen, her legs remained spread with her ass on Lucca's desk. Her heels were apart, caging Lucca to the chair. Her dress had ridden up, showcasing herself to the man who wasn't hers to do so, and yet she had smirked knowingly.

My grace and poise had vanished along with any sane thoughts as she stayed in the same position.

I snapped my eyes at him.

Nonchalant in his chair, Lucca sat relaxed with a glass of brown liquor in his hand as he watched me from afar.

While he was composed and unconcerned by my appearance, I spat through my teeth, not removing my gaze from him.

"Get out."

His detached eyes watched the war inside mine. However, the blonde was dense enough to try to talk back instead of listening to the venom that burned through my words.

"You have no—"

My eyes shot toward her, and her mouth shut when she saw the blade spinning in my hand and returning with ease to the grip I had. I kept it below my hips, but the threat was clear. *Get out.*

"I suggest you leave before I teach you how a Vitelli wields a blade."

Her legs closed quickly, moving away from the desk and scrambling down with raised brows. With both hands on her chest, she held her purse without adjusting the bottom of her dress. When she stood next to Lucca in disarray, she had the nerve to speak up *again.*

"You are fucking cra—"

Before she finished the sentence, my left hand rose, and I spun the knife in the air in front of me. I watched the sharp blade spin and waited for the exact moment to catch its smooth edge. A move that earned me many scars until I'd perfected it. When my fingertips pinched the cool metal between them, I brought it back. Ready to be thrown at my target.

With the handle near my shoulder and my fingertips aching to cast deadly pain, I waited.

"*One more word,*" I warned. Longing for her mouth to open.

Her brows pinched together, and her eyes pooled with unshed tears as they jumped from Lucca to me.

I almost wished he would try to stop me so I would have a reason to nick him and finally break his composure.

But Lucca took a sip from his glass, and Anna cried, shaking her head. Her blonde hair whipped in desperation, but all she had to do was leave. It wasn't difficult to understand my words. I had spoken in a language she comprehended.

"Leave."

I took a step away from the door, leaving her a clear path to safety while I held it wide open.

Anna's head bobbed up and down uncontrollably in agreement, but her eyes stared at my weapon.

Impatient for her departure, I lowered my knife but never placed it back in its holster. I only reclaimed my first grip.

Accepting my movement, she beelined toward the door. It was silly, really, because this was the most comfortable grip for me to have. The most dangerous. Yet she considered it harmless as her heels trembled past me, and without another word, she left.

I took a deep breath, hoping to overrule the madness that continued to search for a target.

But the only ones left were Lucca and me.

One step forward, and the creaking door was free. It swung slowly until its loud click pierced through the tension and heat that clung inside the room.

I closed my eyes, but they burned with pressure as I acknowledged the disturbed and deranged feelings. The anger and bile I felt for what I'd walked into.

Twisted with resentment, I lifted my gaze to him.

His tie was intact along with his blazer, and my eyes lowered, catching his belt untouched. That alone eased my hatred, but the damage had been done. If I didn't set boundaries, he would act as if I didn't have any.

I wanted to speak as if I wasn't fazed by his actions. I wanted to speak as if I wasn't rattled to my core by seeing a woman spread out and ready for him. And while we weren't anything but two humans who only caused pain to one another, I was hurt.

It didn't matter how much I tried to ignore his silence or the idea of what this perturbed arrangement meant. *I cared.*

Therefore, I was livid, and my voice was anything but calm.

"Trust me when I say I *will* cause harm to whoever touches you again."

Lucca's mask fell, and surprise filled his eyes.

"All I ask is for respect as your future queen. If you disrespect me, you and Davina will have a matching scar," I seethed.

His brow raised and his lips twinkled with what resembled a grin, but Lucca's eyes held a storm while his head lifted higher. A fucking sitting contradiction.

"Are you threatening me?"

"I'm warning you."

## LUCCA

"I'M WARNING YOU."

This regal woman had just threatened me. In my home, inside my study, as my mind was enraged by her insolence, and my dick grew hard.

Hard to believe her entrance, the power her figure claimed, and how her hand handled a sharp blade effortlessly. Thirsty to taste her crazed body and unstable mind. Her need to punish and claim who she believed was hers. The jealousy that cracked her armor.

I was rock hard to her threat.

As her emerald-green eyes shined with the promise of hurting someone if they touched me, I believed her.

I had gone out of my way to ignore her for days, hoping my silence would make her crave my presence. Hoping it would punish her for how she'd spoken to me in public, but instead, I had fueled her raving spirit.

Anna wasn't planned, but when her text came through, I saw a way to teach Katia another lesson.

I needed a release, a quick fix to ease the demon that lately couldn't be reined in. It didn't ask for blood, and as I had been too busy with the threats Katia had brought along with her to the syndicate, I needed a fuck. Little did I know how far she would go.

But Anna hadn't done it for me. While she was ready for my touch, all I could think of was the tan skin and long legs of a certain vixen I had ready for my taking.

I had been minutes away from telling Anna to leave since my plan to hurt Katia had failed when she hadn't seen me walk Anna to my study.

Therefore, I never anticipated Katia barging inside my study with a knife and threatening Anna.

All I had managed to accomplish while staying away was wanting her more.

And it infuriated me.

To be played by my own game, my own doing, all due to losing sight of who she truly was.

I stood and kept my fists from balling with the wild rage of having her near with a weapon and threats.

"What will you do?" True curiosity sparked in me.

What will Katia do?

She didn't say a word, and I ushered for her to speak with each step closer I took toward her heated eyes.

Again, Katia surprised me by closing the distance between us.

Tall and grand, her lavish might faced me.

Fucking insane.

And yet, it pulled me. Luring me to her striking power.

"Tell me," I gritted.

Her scent triumphed over Anna's, twisting me to her ways.

Silence.

I towered over her body as she silently raised her head high.

My patience for her to speak, for her to feed the demon with details of what she would do, diminished, and I wrapped my hand around her neck. It slid away from her throat until my fingertips felt her velvet chestnut hair. I gripped it tightly, forcing her to keep her eyes on mine.

"As it seems your words have failed you, I'll explain what I would do to those who so much dare to lay a hand on you," I murmured, and my face neared her natural red bowed lips.

"They'll be dead. But not before I will relish in their screams and useless begging." My lips formed a cruel smile. "They will be left unrecognizable." My chest bounced erratically as I continued, "And I will wait until every drop of blood drains out of their body. No fingertips will be left to identify who they were since their hands won't be near their ruined bodies as they touched what is mine." Katia's eyes fluttered. "And if you so much as allowed it." My wrath lashed out at the thought following my threat. "You will hear the cries you say you don't care about, and I will fucking make your life so miserable that you will wish for death to take you as mercy."

I couldn't take back my words as they were the truth. Our arrangement had been toxic, poisonous from the start, and it was time I showed her who she would be married to, who she will submit underneath, and who she will have to be loyal to.

Katia jerked to be freed, forcing me to pull her hair tighter. Too tight.

*Fear.*

So subtle in her irises, and yet I found myself taken aback by the strong feeling of detest I felt knowing it'd been me she'd feared.

Even then, I didn't move.

She wanted to be partners. Fine. I would show her the venom of the demon inside me and rot the idea.

"All I ask for is respect." Her tone stayed sharp. "I don't need your money, presents, jewelry, or even your presence." Katia's words carried a fight she'd never won before me. "Respect." One word, and yet she craved it more than she could express.

She'd been underestimated in our world for being a woman. Taken for granted by being born into the mafia world. Traded and dehumanized.

All she asked for was respect, and I understood her. It was what I'd fought for since I turned fourteen.

"And in return?"

Her eyes closed, and I clenched my hair-laced hand for her to watch me, eager for her answer.

"Everything."

*Everything.* With just one word from her, I could rejoice. Because I knew if I gave her the one thing no one has ever given her, she *would* do anything. Her loyalty and trust would be in me. If only for seeing her for who she was. As the king of the syndicate and with the power I held, to do such a thing would earn it. Making it a sealed vow. All for respect.

It's how I'd earned my brothers, whose bond was unbreakable. I gave them what no one else did. Life, family, respect.

I fought between wanting to break her and making her pay for what her family had taken from me. But my resolve was weak the more I saw the same Vitelli name take away so much from her. And it was her own blood.

Katia had no one.

Before I could trust my words, I said, "Okay."

Another promise I had to keep.

Eyes wide and vivid scanned my face. Surprised and optimistic, Katia's smile broke free.

Fuck her, she made me smile.

She closed her eyes with a head shake and allowed her head to fall against my chest.

Jesus, this woman.

"Don't reel in victory just yet, Katia."

Her laugh was muffled through my blazer, and my grip loosened on her hair, giving her a moment longer with joy.

It was then that I realized how much I liked seeing it on her.

One thing remained, and I was ready to break the developing feelings from furthering into nonsense inside me.

"I won't rush you but know I can't wait forever."

I hadn't meant now, even though all I wanted to do at this moment was bury myself deep inside her. Hard and fast. Punishing her with cruel pounds for getting her way. For making me smile and driving me into undeniable desire.

"I know," she said into my chest.

Katia might see this as a win, but I warned how sex with me would ruin her. She should have heeded my words. Now it was too late.

She would see more than sex. She would want more than sex.

Women always did.

"I won't make love to you," I stated.

"I know."

It was settled.

"Now, put your knife away."

Katia scoffed, pulled away with one eyebrow raised, and did as I asked.

"Afraid of a little knife, Lucca?"

Her words had been similar before when I had ordered her not to keep any in our room. My reply would be the same.

"No, I just don't trust a Vitelli with one." And I had been right.

It earned me a smile I didn't return.

"Speaking of knives," she began.

"You mean the secret you've been keeping?" I asked instead.

"They were never a secret."

Katia shrugged and ran her fingers through her hair, taming the locks I'd twisted.

I liked it better then.

Her eyes found mine with bold sparks as she said, "And you never asked. You just made up your mind that they were for collection."

At first I had. A mistake on my part because once again she had been underestimated for being a woman. That was until the night I saw her wielding them with ease and care as she cleaned each one, but her skill had surpassed my expectations.

How far did her gift expand?

"I meant the secret of carrying one with you."

Katia's eyes never left mine, but I saw the feathering twitch of her right fingers that lay below her hip.

She didn't have to answer. I placed the pieces together.

The frequent touches to her thigh. The soft caresses when she tried to hide her uneasiness and discomfort. Or the times her spirit rose with annoyance and displeasure. Her tell was nothing more than her need to seek comfort.

Then I remembered when I'd asked for all of her knives, and I grew impatient. Because for weeks she had continued with the same tics.

My head fell slightly to the side while I watched her attentively, studying her features. Deliberating whether she'd gone against my order.

If she'd hid and kept a knife in the one room I'd specifically asked not to.

Could she be so mad as to go against me?

Katia didn't falter as I showed her the rage my mind had inspired. It wasn't near the turmoil that conspired against my body. The roaring open fire that heated my core into a smoldering and steady ire inside. Or how my veins popped with livid blood.

"How long, Katia?"

Collected, she closed the distance between us. I didn't move for the simple fact that I couldn't trust myself. And when her hand lifted from her side, I kept a close watch on her.

Her palms stretched out, connecting to my still chest. Her touch nipped my cruel rage, and as they spread onto my sides, dousing my unsettled state with cool fingertips, I allowed her to continue her effect on me.

Katia's fingers slid underneath my suit jacket until they met the shoulder straps of my holster. The kind I didn't wear unless it was necessary, and tonight, it had been.

Then her palms stirred away. One settled on my torso while the other snaked around my side and onto my back and lowered, finding the tucked gun at my waist.

Her eyes claimed she wasn't done, and while I centered my gaze on her turbulent greens, they drifted away along with her body.

At no time did our eyes pull away.

Hers, with a drive to prove.

Mine, of seeing her body lower slowly in front of me.

With her face mere inches away from the evidently hard dick I carried, my blood no longer pumped in lively anger. It reeled in need.

Katia's hands reached blindly forward and roped around my right calf. They dropped in a chain of search, but it had been useless. Not long after, she skipped to the other leg, discovering the knife strapped around my ankle.

She smirked and returned to her feet, vibrating with confidence.

"How long have you carried a weapon, Lucca?"

Katia dropped a lit match, reigniting the wicked fire.

In one swift movement, I held her jaw, pulling her face to mine. Her lips parted, her posture straightened, and her chest pressed against mine.

"You defied me." I lashed over her lips, tightening my grip.

The corner of her lip curled up. "You would've left me defenseless," she confronted me. "Unarmed and easy to kill." Her eyes peered down and back up to mine. "I did what I had to do in order to protect myself."

My hand gave away its force, falling to her neck as I pondered her words. While I would have done the same, Katia did what she always does. Defy, manipulate, *survive*.

I pulled away from Katia. The woman whom I'd agreed to respect, protect, and hate. Hating her ways, her looks, her spirit, even if it was what I desired.

"You know I'm right."

Her hand lifted, pushed, and aimed at my face, but I couldn't allow her soft palm to reach my skin. Not when her tone had lowered, and her eyes softened with the promise of a caress.

A delicate embrace.

I stopped her before the chance was given, and with my hand secured to her wrist, I said, "Dinner should be served."

Her eyes cast away from view as her head turned, keeping the tells of her thoughts.

Katia drew her hand away when I released my hold and bluntly caught my eyes. Indifference and poise was all they gave.

"Will you be joining me?"

"I have work."

My tone was cold, distant.

I would reheat the food myself if necessary, if only to keep her from expecting nonsense out of me. Affection was not something I was willing to give or take. And every touch I gave her was either to pacify my demon or to play our sadistic game. One day, she would learn. Tonight, she could remind herself of it.

She nodded as if my answer wasn't a poor attempt to stay away.

With no further attempt, Katia turned. Before she walked out the door she said, "Move your knight to F3," and left.

Leaving me with an aching dick and the idea of a Vitelli carrying a knife in my home freely, I played the chess move she'd given me. I looked over the open board game by the table and took the offensive move, shifting the game.

A countermove.

I guess it was my turn to send California Katia's wishes.

# XVIII

## KATIA

I HAD FALLEN ASLEEP ALONE, WITH AN EMPTY STOMACH AS MY APPETITE HAD banished due to the contradicting feelings. Twisting me inside and beneath the covers.

From fury, joy, to the downward spiral created by rejection.

All playing a part in my awakening in the late night near a warm body, and during my sleepless night, I had turned toward its heat. Yet not close enough to touch.

Shifting my pillow, I searched through the darkness for him. Past the shadows, I made out his closed eyes and stretched frame. Freed from any restrictions and offered comfort by a blanket.

It seemed wrong to watch his bare and strong figure while he was unaware of my eyes on him. Immoral to the path my gaze slithered as sinful thoughts passed through.

He'd promised respect. Was this not me doing the opposite? Or was it longing for what he'd denied?

"It's late. You should sleep." His voice was hoarse and deeper than ever.

"I didn't mean to wake you." Too tired to master the English language, my exhausted mind spoke Italian.

"Your sleep is restless," Gritty Italian replied.

I smiled.

"I'm aware."

"Close your eyes and go to bed," he chided.

Of course he would, his moody attitude never failed. I rubbed my head onto the pillow one last time until it lay comfortably, and he gave up with a loud exhale.

It stopped as I placed my hand over his strong middle, not caring if he would reject my touch again.

I was too tired and drowsy to think about it, and he never made the effort to remove it even though his body was now stiff underneath. Whether he was too exhausted or just hopeful that I had found the path to succumb to sleep, I closed my eyes.

And in the night, I'd found an ally.

Darkness.


The night was replaced by another bright Miami morning. They all mirrored the next. And after weeks, I'd lost track of time as they all entwined into one cloudy daydream.

## THE NEXT DAY

MY BOND WITH WEX AND VINO HAD STRENGTHENED.

We ran. Endless hours of pushing our bodies until the sunbeams fell high from the sky and our breathing would give. My muscles regained their definition as I ran and pushed my core to its limits. Only I saw, knew, and felt the change.

They now slept at the foot of the bed.

Lucca never mentioned it. Not my body, not their attachment.

And at night, we only allowed our breathing to mix.

## THE DAY AFTER

I COOKED MY FIRST MEAL INSIDE HIS HOME, *TORTELLINI WITH FRESH FOCACCIA*.

I even asked Talia, her father, and Mrs. Greco to join me so it wouldn't go to waste.

I never found out if Lucca had tasted it, never asked. Not even when my body was restless for his warmth beneath the moonlight.

## THE FOLLOWING DAY

THE LIMITED MINUTES OFFERED BY TIME WERE NEVER ENOUGH DURING DAYLIGHT with him. So I focused on myself. It helped to pass time, but the more changes occurred during his absence, the harder it was to ignore the anchor that weighed between us.

A piece of the Vitelli that had left Italy returned with every change. But today, I felt proud because I'd finished the paperwork to launch my brand. Today, I had accomplished everything necessary for it to be sent for licensing.

Yet, Lucca kept me from doing so. Afterall, it involved possible meetings and face to face deals. Safety risks.

As confident as I was for what I'd accomplished, I worried about its outcome.

While I waited for the sun to go down, hoping today could be the day to catch him long enough to talk and discuss my proposal to work, I looked over one last time the envelope I held for dear life.

The evening came and passed.

Lucca remained nowhere to be found.

Funny how time worked. How it could fly with no change and leave you behind if allowed. Or how you could get stuck in its minutes, reliving the past and watching it sweep by into your present. Or suck you into the never-ending routine of déjà vu.

For me, it felt like time had slipped through my fingers mockingly. Waiting for the night as it delivered silence and Lucca's warm body near with my hand over his frame. Because as the sun awakened, so did I, alone.

## TODAY

"Slow down, Wex!"

My order was as weak as my breathing. But it was the one command he disobeyed time after time. Wex had no regard for the cool down period after a run. It was all or nothing for him.

Vino panted by my side, watching his brother trot in the distance.

Eventually, Wex would return, as he always did.

Lucca's property was large enough to run one lap around its perimeter and call it a full workout. In today's excruciating heat that reminded me of the time changing and the season nearing to an end, my legs shook from overworked muscles. I lay down on the manicured grass, promising it would only be for a second to catch my breath. Vino didn't relax. Instead, he sat in the shade I had missed by inches. His pants were erratic, and before my muscles could lock up, I rose back to my feet.

Miami's summer would be cruel.

*Summer.*

I let go of the thought and looked up at the sun. Bright and unforgiving, I squinted my eyes to watch its set position. Its location said it was between the hours of ten and eleven, and we'd been out in the sun longer than usual.

"Let's head back, Vino. We all need water."

As we crossed straight through the backyard, Wex met us eagerly to trade us for comfort and air conditioning.

We passed by the tempting pool until we reached the back door kitchen. I opened the door and waited for the boys to go in before walking inside.

The kitchen was crowded, and when I took my earphones off, I listened to the commotion of pots, pans, and furious whisks jumbling in loud chaos.

"Oh, thank goodness, you are back." Mrs. Greco exhaled, wiping her forehead against the towel over her shoulder.

Confused, I continued on the path to the fridge, picking out a bottle of water and a few ice cubes from the dispenser.

"What's the occasion?" I asked.

Talia kneaded dough by the corner. Strands of hair fell from her loose ponytail as she worked quietly, making herself small and far away from everyone's fast pace. She was lost to the music that surely blared in her ears.

As I waited for Mrs. Greco's reply, I walked over to Wex and Vino and dropped the ice cubes into their bowls.

"Family lunch."

Stunned by the deep and cold tone, I quickly turned to face its owner.

Dressed in the most casual outfit I'd seen him in, dark aegean blue-colored chinos and a white polo, Lucca stood tall in his cloud of malice. I stared, appreciating the ink his arms carried out in the open.

Family lunch?

I didn't have time to think or ask for any details. All hell broke loose in a massive yet crowded kitchen by the amount of bodies inside of it, and before I could say his name to acknowledge his presence, I saw the mere moment it all changed.

Diego, the chef who Talia had described as short, appeared through my left eye, balancing a large pot. Diego's head poked over the side of the pot, missing Wex's backside who scarfed down water from below.

"Katia," Lucca demanded my attention in warning.

I wanted to keep my eyes on him, to have a moment to speak to him as the day had finally allowed it, but I couldn't because his warning desperately begged for me with an arm raised out. However, Diego's yelp caused my eyes to focus on him instead as he tripped over Wex, losing his footing and staggering with the pot.

I pushed back, a futile attempt, as the pot and its contents quickly knocked me down. It had all happened so fast. Only the lukewarm contents and the sharp pain that erupted through my right wrist registered.

Shocked, I looked up at Diego's widened eyes that had filled with fearful apologies. And yet, I feared for him. Wex's body spun, prepared, and shot at him.

I reacted.

In one swift move, I slipped through the floor as I lurched my body toward his. I did not stop until I trapped his collar and pulled him back as hard as I could.

I had no chance against Wex's strength. He jerked my wrist over and over as I continued to hold on, causing deeper pain.

"*Foo!*" *Stop,* I ordered in Russian weakly.

Lucca's command fell at the same time, but his tone held no hesitation as he roared, "*Ostanovit.*"

Wex stopped.

"*Lyezhat,*" Lucca's strong Russian echoed.

Both Wex and Vino listened by placing their heads above their paws and their bodies hitting the floor in unison.

I breathed out in relief as my adrenaline waned. *What had just happened?*

Looking down at Wex's heaving and yet controlled body, I finally let go of his heavy chain. An ache spread over my fingers, up my hand, and onto my wrist.

*Breathe, Katia.*

Lucca's shoes were now in front of me, ruined by the splatters. In an instant, his body lowered into view. He picked my head up with his arched index finger as he searched my eyes, but all I could see was the tomato and basil mess I was bathing in.

"I swear if there were tears in your eyes…"

He didn't have to explain further. The demon in his eyes said it all.

"I'm fine," I reassured him while our eyes locked on one another.

He wanted to believe me, but instead, his gaze scrutinized my face closer, and his fingers spread, cupping my jaw gently.

Too gentle, too unlike him, and too difficult to ignore. I removed my eyes and watched him instead. His freshly trimmed beard, his strong jawline and immaculate Italian tan skin. The hard lines caused by tension and anger as he held me.

"Mr. Moretti, I'm s—"

Lucca's head snapped. The chef didn't utter another word, and when his eyes met mine again, I hated the humiliating state of my appearance. Right in front of everyone so they can see and ponder it in their minds.

It was degrading.

I closed my eyes briefly at the thought of who I was meant to be to them and how I looked now.

"Katia." Lucca's soft tone only heightened the bubbling emotion that creeped into my eyes. The pity I heard.

Fuck, this was bad.

"Everyone, out," he harshly ordered.

"No!" I opened my eyes, and his brows pinched. "Please, stay," I added quickly, and everyone stilled, confused on who to listen to.

Afraid to look at any of them, I kept my eyes on Lucca's inked neck.

"Finish what you have all been working on. I'm really okay."

Puzzled, he remained in the pool of red chunks and orange spice, and eventually gave in.

"Let me help you up."

Lucca said as if he had given me another option. As if his hands hadn't taken possession of my elbows and my legs steadied by his grip. Slowly, I stood with his help, and I was *sore*. Lucca didn't miss it. He just held me tight as he struggled to keep his anger at bay.

"Don't," I whispered.

He shook his head slightly but didn't say another word. We just made our way out of the kitchen in silence, and I was thankful. I didn't know for how long either of us could hold onto our masks.

His, the wrath. Mine, the appearance of control.

"*Fratello.*" Brother.

Lucca stopped, and we both turned to Arlo's voice as he walked through the front door.

Arlo, out of anybody else. It had to be him.

I straightened, lifting my head to the self-absorbed and heartless *in-law* of mine. Then, Lucca let go of his assisting hold and slithered his arm onto the back of my body. My teeth trapped my smile.

Arlo's smirk played with humor as he took in our appearances.

"I won't even ask." Arlo looked down at Lucca's ruined clothes covered in orange and red stains. "What do you need from me?"

Lucca slid his head down, flicking his eyes briefly at me.

*Don't, Lucca.*

"Call Ramos and leave some ice by my door. I also need you to take Wex and Vino out to the mud room."

Arlo looked annoyed at the sound of dealing with Wex and Vino.

"Who's Ramos?" I asked.

Lucca didn't reply, but Arlo did. He wouldn't miss the opportunity to degrade me.

"A doctor. My guess is that your delicate body is in need of one."

In pain or not, my hand twitched in search of my missing knife. Lucca knew it too and took a deep breath, sensing my self-control slipping.

I smiled sweetly. "Or for you. After all, Wex is a bit jumpy. *Hate* for you to get the same treatment Diego could've gotten."

Arlo curled his lips and drew back in confusion. "Lucca?"

Lucca shook his head, and Arlo stood, waiting.

"Just make sure my dogs are taken care of, and the chef cleans the mess."

Arlo nodded and left us behind.

Once his back was nowhere in sight, we turned and walked up the stairs. The silence had grown uncomfortable. So much I wanted to say, to talk to him about, and the timing couldn't be worse.

"I really don't need a doctor, Lucca," I said as he opened the door of his room for us.

"It's just us now, Katia. You can stop pretending." Lucca's hand fell from my lower back to take my right hand instead. He inspected it with light touches and feathering squeezes.

I let him, like a beggar. Taking anything he gave, even if it was just out of concern for my well-being. Was he concerned?

"Family lunch…" I started. "Next time, a heads up would be nice."

"Noted." His fingers ran up and down from my fingers to my forearm, and while it was sore to the touch, *his* touch calmed me. "Now, tell me how bad?"

"It's just a sprain."

"The doctor will make sure of that," he insisted.

"It's not the first I've received. It'll go away in a day or two."

"It's your right hand, Katia. We both know how significant it is."

*You only know because you've seen me wield a knife.*

"Which is the reason I am telling you to cancel the doctor. I know my body. I'll be fine." Our eyes fought. "Plus, can you only shoot with your right hand?"

"I shoot with both."

With a smirk, I replied, "Then, what makes you think I can only use my right?"

Lucca tried to hide his own lips from curling as his head shook.

"I can't believe I'm willing to listen to you," he scoffed. "Fine. Now, how sore are you?"

"As sore as I am every morning after a run."

His head bobbed, but he still hesitated. Lucca struggled to give away his controlling persona. His need to have everything in order. To allow someone else to make a decision.

"I can cancel lunch."

Lucca hadn't noticed, but his hand no longer checked my injury. It just held me. As much as I accepted what he hadn't implied as a caress, I acted as if I too was unaware of it.

I shook my head. "Please don't, I just need a long bath and two Tylenol, and I'll be down to meet everyone."

"Why are you being so headstrong?" he asked. "Are you trying to prove a point?"

"I'm always trying to prove a point."

His eyes lowered to our joined bodies, his forehead creased, then he let go.

Figured.

"I'm going to start a bath. You should change too."

He agreed with a nod, but he followed me into the bathroom. He leaned by the doorway as I twisted the knobs and poured some cherry and eucalyptus-scented bubbles into the tub.

His undivided attention was to me, and the sense of his eyes while my ass bent over the tub to check the temperature of the water was as heated as the steam that filled the air.

"How did you know they responded to Russian commands?"

I sat up, looked at him, and smiled. "They wouldn't listen when I spoke to them in English, and even though they do in Italian, it wasn't as quick as their breed should respond to a command." Lucca crossed his arms. "I thought of Ilias and the fact that you speak Russian as well. It didn't take long to learn them." I watched his tensed muscles and added, "I've had plenty of time alone to do so."

I was learning more and more of his tells.

"Don't get in between one of them again," his tone warned, annoyed.

"Wex would've attacked him!" I couldn't believe it.

"He did what he was trained to do. You'd been threatened."

"It was an accident," I stated.

"He could've snapped at you!" Lucca bit back harshly.

Frustrated, I was ready to fight back and return his icy and sharp tone, but loud knocks filtered from the bedroom door and Lucca left me alone.

All the adrenaline rushed from my body at the turn of events, and my worn body inched closer to the tub. Taking advantage of Lucca's absence, I carefully removed my clothing while minimizing the use of my wrist. A sigh of relief escaped my body as I sank down into the warm water of the large porcelain tub.

I closed my eyes, but they quickly rushed open as his defiant and gloomy temper returned.

"I don't want to fight," I murmured.

His eyes took me in, holding me as tightly as he clenched on an ice bag.

"Then don't." His hands shot outwards, frustrated. "I wish you wouldn't."

He reached over the tub and dropped the bag onto my injured wrist. Nothing showed a sweet or caring gesture, it was just another check on his checklist.

"But you will." His eyes peered down at my soaking body. "It's all you do."

He walked out. *He walked out!* I was so close to throwing the ice bag across the room.

But I didn't because he would've been right.

I missed the darkness, and maybe time had been right. Daylight didn't offer peace. Maybe daylight would always be my foe.

# XIX

## LUCCA

I NEEDED FRESH AIR. IT WAS IMPERATIVE FOR ME TO REGAIN CONTROL AND maintain my focus on the continuous threats that were knocking on every inch of my territory. A task I never failed and refused to. But Katia's presence kept intervening in matters I wouldn't have given much thought to or cared to address before her arrival. Just the mere thought of having her in my home without knowing what she was doing was a distraction.

She was a burden on my mind. One I didn't want but didn't mind at the same time. Because when her greens looked up to me, all I saw was mine, and every day this week I'd killed for those eyes.

Every. Single. Life I took.

I had taken it personally, and my hands were filthy.

This war was meant to be a power shift, a gain for my own empire and foul desires of vengeance. But the more bullets I shot, the more I lost myself in this wicked ache of possession.

I shouldn't have cared if she could throw a knife again. Or how her wrist had swollen slightly from a fall. Or the way her eyes closed briefly in humiliation. But I had. I did, and all I thought in that moment was for no one else to see it—her vulnerability because, if Katia showed it, it should only be for me to see it.

Outside in the humid heat, I picked a cigarette out of my case and rolled my neck in hopes of easing the urge to walk back into that kitchen.

Steps neared, and I was no longer alone with my demon. I didn't have to look to know it was my brother, but he treaded carefully, sensing my dark and consuming demeanor.

"What do you *really* want me to do?" Arlo asked. He'd walked into the kitchen, assessed the situation, and now fully understood where my mind had taken me.

"Something I'm not planning to order." I looked down at the cigarette that twirled between my fingers.

Diego came from a family protected by us. While that had an insignificant say, I couldn't eliminate him as I wished. His family meant something to Salvatore, and certain things couldn't be killed if it meant breaking the duty of honor.

*Honor.* Maybe if I repeated it enough, it would help ease my ire and remind me why I had to let it be.

Then my mind replayed Katia's body slithering through the filthy floor, the way she tried to hide behind the pain as her wrist rolled in Wex's strength, all for a *stronzo* who couldn't do something as simple as walk.

Yeah, I had honor. I lived by it, but I had learned its limit—Katia.

I glanced over at Arlo. Nothing else had to be said. Filthy was who I'd become.

That's how I found myself in front of Salvatore's home with an unlit cigarette in my pocket. The walk over to his house shouldn't have been an issue if I had left my suit jacket behind. Instead, I walked inside ready to leave the humid air behind.

"I thought you would just stay outside and look over the brick some more." Sal's voice cracked, and a heap of coughs followed.

I relaxed when I heard his voice, but I quickly searched for him as his cough intensified and his body gasped for air.

His signature fedora was off his fuzzy white hair, and his back deepened into the single chair that had molded into his body. Sal's fingers shook, holding onto the oxygen tube on his nose. I walked over to the living room, where I'd positioned his chair to view the front door and windows and met him.

He ushered me away, but I didn't listen. I fished inside my suit pocket and retrieved my handkerchief before placing it in his free hand.

I didn't miss the red spot after he wiped his mouth.

Fuck.

Time was a bitch I hated and couldn't defeat.

Sal's tired body gave, relaxing as his breathing returned. He didn't say anything else, and I took it upon myself to sit in the matching chair next to him. A coffee table rested between us, and while he looked away, I watched him.

His pressed dress pants, the perfect lines of his white long-sleeve shirt to his checkered brown and beige sweater vest. All appeared neat and put together compared to his true state, which reminded me of the wedding. How a date wasn't set, how he might not be there by the appearance of his sullen eyes.

Then he glanced at me, and I saw my mother's resilience in his eyes. I looked away.

*Coward.*

"We have a family lunch in a few hours."

"Hmm," he scoffed.

"You should come, get some fresh air and all."

"Will Ms. Katia be there?" His brow raised.

"Yes."

"Are you still treating her like a Vitelli?"

His question had too many answers. I had said yes to respecting her, protecting her. She even walked among my house armed, and yet I still didn't trust her. I still held hatred for her. I still wanted to own her, and I still stayed at arm's length.

"It was a simple answer, Lucca," Sal croaked. "And your silence said enough. My answer is no. I don't want to see the way you treat her."

"Fine," I said sharply.

"Don't *fine* me, boy." His voice deepened, and his eyes lifted. Filled with fire. A sight I smiled at but didn't show because underneath this roof, I wasn't his boss. I was just Lucca. "*Stronzo,*" he mumbled, and this time my eyes cut his way.

"Easy, old man. I'm still the one who makes your late-night coffee."

My comment only fueled his spirit, and he was too quick to complain.

"Which by the way has been too late and brings me to the question, how bad"—he wheezed— "how bad is it?"

Leave it to Sal to measure the danger of the streets by the time he received his daily night coffee. A thing I did, and only Mrs. Greco knew as she was the one who brought it to his home. It started as a deal. When I fought him to move into this home I'd built specifically for him, I never said it out loud. He knew. They all did. Yet, he didn't want it. His reasons could range from feeling like a burden to pure pride. Pride would be the one I would bet on. One night he'd fallen so ill, I didn't give him the choice. I packed his shit and moved it, knowing he couldn't carry it or drive it away.

That night, I saw the end of Salvatore's gun. That night I saw my mother's tired eyes, and that night I turned my back as he filled the chamber with a threat, and as I walked away, he'd said, *"Don't forget my coffee."*

I'd been caught once with a coffee mug in my kitchen late at night. Ilias and Davina had stayed in my home for safety. Davina walked in, too scared to come closer with me inside. All she wanted was bottled water. Before she left that night, she didn't mention the mug, who it was for, or why Mrs. Greco was taking it out of the kitchen. But Davina was attentive, careful, and surely eventually she put the pieces together. To this day, she hadn't said anything, not that I would answer.

I stood, impatient to end my visit with the past. I wanted to walk away from memories I'd kept chained to stay as the cold and vicious bastard only my demon understood. The only way to survive in this hell of a world.

"Why are you really here, Lucca?" Sal asked.

"Diego will be dead by the end of the day."

I was here out of respect.

Sal's lips twisted, unhappy with my words, and his eyes lifted, trying to understand.

"Why?"

"Katia."

He laughed. Full chuckles that dared his lungs. In a roar, he gulped deep breaths, his chest begging for air.

Fucking Sal.

"Happy to know you find his death funny."

"You're a fool, Lucca."

"Don't call me a fool, old man."

"But you are, and I am happy to see it."

His smile broke free, and his teeth shone teasingly. My jaw tensed at the absurdity of Sal's words.

"You are not here to tell me you are getting rid of Diego." He shrugged. "You do as you please with no regard for others." Sal adjusted his oxygen tube and continued, "And you are a fool for thinking I don't know you, kid. You're here because you are losing your edge."

"You don't know anything," I gritted out.

Sal shook his head. His mood quieted, and only a partial smile remained on his lips.

"I think I know more than you right now." His eyes wandered before he announced. "I'll join the next family lunch."

Confused, I wanted to ask why. But I stayed silent.

The truth was, Sal was right. I wasn't really here to tell him about Diego. I wanted to see him. Talk to him, and I hope my mind will be pacified. Instead, I felt more unhinged and unbalanced than when I stepped into the humid air. Just like any other time, I would remain trapped in my thoughts—alone. Because allowing my mind to speak freely will be a weakness.

My phone rang, cutting through our stare, and after taking it out of my pocket and looking at the area code for New York, I had to take it.

"I have to go," I announced, but Sal's hands were already rushing me to leave. "Stay breathing."

His eyes slid, and I smiled, walking away from the ill-tempered asshole I mirrored.

Out in the open and under the beaming sun, I answered as I walked my way back to my house.

"*Pronto,*" I said in Italian.

The voice that replied back in Italian was one I hadn't expected or trusted—Mario Vitelli's.

"Moretti, quite a mess."

"One that I see as necessary." As I stood in the backyard, away from prying ears, I waited for Mario to figure out his next words.

"And yet it has reached a high level in New York," he spat.

"Did you expect it to be any different? After all, it was the Vitelli name who broke a vow."

I knew the troubles and the numbers that kept falling in New York. Los Angeles wasn't only targeting Miami, and while we were their main priority as I had Katia, I hadn't lost soldiers compared to the Vitelli Syndicate.

I was playing smart, tactical, and without any hesitation. Mario was performing like the expected old boss. Behind time and stuck on how it should be. His ego killed his own.

If I didn't believe Enzo would overthrow his father if he switched sides, I would target New York too. I had no trust in Mario Vitelli, or Enzo, but I did trust Enzo's greed.

And Enzo's greed will soon make my empire the largest and strongest in La Cosa Nostra.

Time was always running.

Soon, Mario's time would be over.

"A broken vow?" Mario's voice raised. "How can it be broken when my *principessa* continues to bear my name?"

I held my words from giving away how his insolence for calling Katia *his* princess angered me. How his doubt of her becoming a

Moretti created a wild desire to seek slaughter. How I felt pure malice ignite and destroy any sense of mercy inside, coursing through me like a venomous plague.

I breathed in deeply with a clenched jaw, and my grip tightened, holding on to my blood-thirsty demon.

How fucking dare he question Katia's future?

She was mine.

"Careful, Vitelli. That sounds like a threat."

"Does it?"

"Yes."

"I guess I have a different way of asking about my daughter's wedding date."

No. He meant it, but he couldn't say it out loud. Not while I still had one key witness that could destroy his syndicate, Davina. Katia was the piece that held the promises together. He knew it.

"You'll get the invitation this week. Meanwhile, I suggest you up your defenses."

Mario scoffed and added with arrogance, "I don't need your advice."

"Sounds to me like you do." A smug smile shone as I said, "I need to go. *My* fiancée is waiting for me in my room."

Silence.

I hung up and walked back to the house in search of what had been in question—Katia.

My honors limit.

## KATIA

*FAMILY LUNCH.* WHAT A STRANGE THING TO HAVE. BUT AS THE DINING ROOM echoed with multiple conversations mingling in the air, the only one who thought it was strange was me. The only one unfamiliar to the normalcy of such a get-together.

"Try to keep your knife away from Arlo," Lucca said as he met me at the bottom of the stairs with one hand stretched out for me to take.

His mood had taken a turn for the worse. From annoyance to utter cruelty. Lucca had tried to reign over my presence, but his shoulders were rigid, his jaw was tight, and his breathing was short. He was so far from control he didn't even bother to hide it well.

I took his stiff hand, another sign of the turmoil he was under. Carefully, I said, "Tell your *brother* to behave, not me."

He didn't appreciate my answer, and my smile widened.

"Katia," he warned.

"You are wearing a suit," I stated, moving the conversation along with our steps in hopes of easing his mood.

It didn't.

"I am." He let go of my hand, and a shiver ran down my spine when he hit my lower back instead. The act of possession felt stronger as his fingers held me tighter.

A touch I could get used to by its warmth and claim. The kind I looked forward to as it sparked a neediness in its hold.

"Are you surprised?" he asked.

I stopped and faced him before we walked into the mixed voices in the dining room.

I shook my head, answering his question.

"How's your wrist?" He peered down.

"Fine."

He scoffed, and we fell into silence. He glanced past me, and I glanced at his patterned tie that matched his fitted, dark blue blazer and suit pants.

"Why are you stalling?"

"I didn't think I was," I mumbled.

I was.

"You're nervous."

I felt his eyes and ignored them.

With my shoulders back, I faced the dining room opening.

"Don't be."

"I'm not."

"Then walk in," he pressed.

I did, and the room quieted.

The first set of eyes I found were hazel, distant and harsh—Arlo's. He didn't bother to come our way. Instead, he stayed behind a chair with crossed arms, feet apart, and a blunt sneer pointed at me.

*Happy to see you again too, Arlo.*

Lucca's hand pressed deeper before curling onto my side, pulling me closer in warning. Or was it a plea to behave? A quick glance at his stern eyes answered me. He wasn't one to ask nicely anyway.

"Katia, let me introduce you to Davina and Ilias."

I removed my gaze from him and found the girl who had started it all. He didn't need to introduce me; I'd meet them all.

The doe maroon in her irises retained the same hope and love I'd seen the night of the gala as they looked up kindly at me.

I didn't like it.

Her acceptance of this world was baffling for someone like me. The content they offered in a den of sin. I would never understand her choice to live in this world. To give up freedom and ignorance to the true crime that lived among the righteous.

Davina's hair was now a few inches shorter as it fell in black curtains to her shoulders. Her petite features brightened with a smile I had trouble returning. The optimism and buoyancy it displayed by seeing me. The one whose blood matched the same man who'd scarred her neck, hunted her, and wished nothing else but her death.

Could she be so pure to forgive, to see me as someone more than a Vitelli?

If so, her soul hadn't yet been fully taken by the Mafia, but it was only a matter of time before the corruption, lies, and death would unveil the rotten truth of her future.

The longer I looked down at her thin frame and honest smile, the more I believed she'd in fact made peace with the past. Davina grew aware of my silence, and her posture hesitated while her eyes questioned.

Her reactions gave it all away, leaving nothing for me to hunt or search for. It was an easy feat to read her. Too easy, and with these men, it was a crucial tool to learn how to mask emotions.

I could help her with that.

Putting her at ease, I smiled back, and her spirits lifted.

Davina's flowy black dress swiveled and, her hand lifted and met the chest of the blue-eyed and blond-haired man who'd trapped her in this hell. Ilias.

His stance was nothing more than protective as he held her close to him, but his eyes were the softest I'd seen with her so near.

Love. They could have fooled me.

"Davina, Ilias," I said politely.

"And I'm Viktor."

My gaze slid away from them to the man who closed the distance from the back of the room to us. When his hand stretched out in broad daylight while standing next to Ilias, I saw their uncanny resemblance.

Out of the four brothers, *they* shared blood. They shared blue eyes and blond hair, although Viktor's was a tone darker, but their Russian features mingled in kin.

I took his hand, shook it, and he smiled respectfully before letting go.

"I'm sure you know Arlo." Viktor's hand extended outwards to the asshole by the table.

"Katia," Lucca warned quietly in my hair.

My smile stretched, a fraud.

"Arlo."

"*Vitelli.*"

Everyone stilled.

Lucca's hold stiffened.

Davina's teeth trapped her lips as her chest rose in distress. Ilias's eyes blazed at the sight, and Viktor closed his eyes briefly as if he knew what Arlo had started.

My wrist no longer felt pain, it only wanted to cause it as my fingertips traced my hidden blade.

He'd said it as a reminder to all who stood before me, and as the air turned foul and stiff, I remained controlled by his disrespect and attempt to belittle me.

"Arlo," Lucca threatened.

Arlo raised his palms in fake innocence while I thought of the right words to approach him. I had nothing. He'd just stated a fact.

I smirked instead.

"I'm famished." I gazed up at Lucca and his demeanor calmed seeing how I'd ignored his brother, but something in his eyes still held conflict. "We should take our seats and get ready for lunch."

"Maybe instead of wearing lunch you'll get the chance to eat it this time."

Lucca's hand tugged as I let go of his eyes to chase Arlo's mockery. I slipped through his finger in one determined step to face Arlo.

"Enough," Lucca barked.

Arlo and I stood across the table with hatred-filled eyes.

*What was his deal?*

"It's okay to be intimidated," I uttered.

"Please, you are nothing more than a walking liability," Arlo quickly replied.

Huh, he really believed so.

*"Arlo!"*

Lucca lost his cool briefly and ran his hand over his face as if he was dealing with misbehaving children. He shook his head and pulled the chair out for me.

I sat on the right side of the head of the table. Arlo took the left, directly in front of me. Viktor sat to my left, with Davina taking Arlo's right followed by Ilias.

Davina's watchful eyes bounced between Lucca, Arlo, and I before breaking the silence to relieve the tension.

"Where's Salvatore?" she asked.

Lucca only shook his head. No further explanation was given.

As lunch continued and courses of food came and went, I only paid attention to Lucca's mood slowly easing. How he had relaxed while keeping fragments of his guard high. A thing I was mesmerized by as it was the first time I'd seen it. He had been in such a state of disarray earlier. Even while he didn't smile or join in the conversation between his brothers and Davina, he seemed comfortable.

Envy crawled, knowing I wasn't the one who made him feel such trust to do so and probably would never be able to. Meanwhile, jealousy stirred as I realized I had never felt that way around my own family.

"I checked on Wex and Vino when we came in. Talia mentioned their attachment to you," Ilias said, looking right at me, and everyone quieted waiting for my reply.

I looked down at the dessert I've been playing with for twenty minutes and looked back at him with a slight smile.

"Well, they do sleep inside the room now." I chuckled softly.

Ilias's eyes widened with a smile as did Davina's; then shortly, all their eyes shifted to Lucca, who just watched them back in silence. He hadn't even touched his dessert.

"I'm glad to hear that, really." Ilias kept looking at me, as if he had made up his mind about me.

"Yeah, we all are. They are a true…force," Viktor added as if it was the best word he could describe them with.

Arlo's glare did not disappear, nor did the bullseye I had now permanently etched onto his head.

"How is the wedding planning? Have you picked out a date yet?" Davina asked and quickly added, "Congratulations, by the way."

*Congratulations.*

Was I the only one at this table who remembered the night I was vowed into an arranged marriage? The night I had been traded for power and other people's lives as if mine meant nothing?

Davina bit her lip. I smiled.

"Thank you," slipped through my teeth.

She nodded timidly, and her chest sank in realization of her words.

"Is there a date?" Arlo antagonized.

My eyes slid to his. His smirk only served the purpose to provoke and trigger. I glanced at Lucca, who watched me calmly. He wasn't willing to help; he too wanted an answer.

"Soon."

"Summer is right around the corner." Arlo didn't stop.

"She said soon, Arlo. Plus there's nothing the Moretti name can't get done in time even if it's *right around the corner.*"

Viktor. He challenged Arlo, and I was thankful.

Arlo dismissed us by taking a large bite of his food, and the conversation resumed without me again.

I peered down and to my left where Viktor sat. When my eyes looked up, his deep blue eyes were on mine.

"Thank you," I murmured.

With a slight nod, he smiled. "Don't worry, he can be a pain in the ass at times."

I let a soft chuckle slip through my nose. He wasn't lying on that.

Arlo sneered, and Lucca's eyes hadn't left me all night.

Their focus now piqued my interest. Something was still bothering him, and I couldn't wait for the time it would be just us.

"Are you working after this?" I asked low enough that only he and Viktor could hear.

Lucca's jaw tensed, but he shook his head.

I bit back my smile and returned to playing with my dessert.

Maybe daylight wouldn't fail me today.

# XX

## LUCCA

I DIDN'T KNOW WHAT TO FEEL SEEING KATIA AROUND MY BROTHERS.
Ilias easily accepted her. Viktor had been polite and friendly, and even while his looks were misleading as they hid his brutality, he wasn't one to make a woman uncomfortable unless it was necessary. Working for the DEA, Viktor had become a master of body language and an expert at de-escalating situations. It worked great in my favor as Arlo's mouth was as loose as his temper. Which brought me to Arlo. The one I would have to keep a close eye on due to his short patience and sadistic ways. Although I trusted him fully enough to know that he wouldn't hurt her, if Katia retaliated physically, I did fear his actions and the consequences that would follow.

Katia was off limits. I'd made that clear time after time with each soldier I killed from California. But something had to change quickly because there was no stopping their rivalry and hatred for one another, and as lunch rolled by, their patience thinned.

If they were left alone, it would call for a bloodbath.

While the conversation continued, my mind played over and over Sal's and Mario's words. The date-less wedding and Mario's doubt of what was already mine.

Katia was already in Miami. Her finger was claimed by a diamond meant for my future queen. Her body was still untouched, but it lay in *my* bed at night. In the eyes of the Mafia, Katia would be considered a damaged woman if we didn't marry for the simple fact of her presence in my home. No one would accept a wife who's slept in another bed as openly as I had taken her, unwed, and from her father's home.

*He* would; Pietro Borrelli.

I shook the thought away. No use of thinking such delusions, Katia wasn't going anywhere.

She would be my wife, therefore respected.

My eyes couldn't slip away from *her* as her delicate fingers played with her spoon and the homemade pastry in slow circles on her plate. Captivated by its mess, Katia watched with straight shoulders, her mind far from the banter that spread around the table. She would smile when needed, nod at the right time, and even chuckle softly when necessary. Katia knew how to present the perfect lie, but her poise was striking, as if she belonged in this city and at this table in a tight dark green dress that sculpted her body and showcased her neck and shoulders by its hanging sleeves.

So much skin, so much temptation her radiant skin oozed.

Thirst parched my mouth as the sight of her tongue slipping and wetting her bottom lip unconsciously captivated me before her teeth trapped the corner of her bottom lip. Her makeup was light, a natural look that allowed her features to glow with her undeniable beauty, but her lips kept the deep red stain only I'd seen on her.

Katia released her lip, and I stared at the remaining wetness left over.

*Fuck.*

I was losing my mind in the whirlwind game of desire. Finding a way to control the hunger and the chaos erupting all around was a feature I had to master.

But when she asked if I was working after lunch and I shook my head *no*, controlling hunger would be the toughest task as I saw her reaction of delight in her features.

Now I want them all gone.

I flicked my wrist, checked the time, and Ilias caught my polite way to say, "*Get out*".

"I can't eat anymore," he began. "Please tell your staff everything was perfect as always."

"Will do." I nodded.

Arlo laughed. "If only you knew what it cost some of the sta—"

"Arlo."

My tone stopped him, and he popped his spoon into his mouth with a dark smirk. He pulled it out with eyes that expressed his excitement and happiness to have his hands in an order he would enjoy, Diego.

Katia didn't say anything. Instead, she stared at Arlo with disgust smeared on her lips.

"I need a word with you before I leave." Viktor broke the tension.

"That's our time to head home." Ilias looked down at Davina and stood to help her out of her chair.

We all rose. Viktor, Ilias, and Arlo shook hands and patted one another while they gave Davina a hard time. Katia stayed by my side as I watched them say their goodbyes.

Ilias and Davina made their way to us, and Katia's hand slipped behind me and held onto the corner of my shirt, tugging it slightly.

I had learned Katia wasn't keen on farewells. Uncomfortable receiving hugs, affection, or even kindness. A feeling I too shared, as someone's touch aside from a handshake felt too personal and unwelcome, which was why my posture remained closed and cold to approach.

But she was a woman, expected to receive and give such warmth.

I crossed my arm behind her, hiding her tugging grip and keeping her body near.

"We should have a doggy date sometime. Boris loves Wex and Vino, and we can maybe have a glass of red while they play in the yard," Davina said, eager for female companionship.

She was lonely, it was clear. I had been keeping Ilias away for long hours, and he didn't want to risk her wandering outside with a full war on our streets. It was too risky.

Katia's hand stiffened, but she smiled back.

"I'm sure the boys will love that."

*The boys.* I smiled.

"Brat," *Brother,* Ilias said in Russian with a smile.

My smile fell, and I shook his hand. "Don't do anything stupid."

Ilias laughed, Davina shook her head at him, and he said, "What's the fun in that?"

"Davina."

"Lucca." She smiled with a nod and leaned closer to my brother before they began walking away. Viktor followed them, and Arlo trailed behind as we all made our way to the front door.

Once Ilias and Davina got into their car and drove away, Viktor turned my way.

We were standing by the stone entry, sheltered from the sun's rays by the roof's large overhang, when he said, "You still have a minute?"

I glanced down at Katia and stepped away from her. Her hand fell, and her eyes turned impatient. Ready for the pleasantries to be over and relieved she could walk away.

"I'll let you men be." She smiled with a bright mask, but it turned sincere when she looked over at Viktor. "It was nice seeing you."

"Likewise." His head dipped as he smiled.

Katia left us alone, and Arlo leaned over the gritty material of the exterior wall with his arms crossed. If Viktor had wanted to speak only to me, he would've come or contacted me when Arlo wasn't around, but they always spoke freely around each other. We didn't keep anything from one another, not when it involved the Moretti crime.

"How's Sal?"

"Peachy," I replied, thinking of the ill-tempered grump.

Arlo coughed his laugh.

"Anyway, I'll be taking my vacation days in the department." This caught my attention. "I'll still be able to keep tabs and intel on my computer and such."

"Are you going somewhere?" I asked, appalled.

"No. In my opinion, you need me here more." I shook my head in disagreement. "I'm not asking, Lucca."

"You could be compromised." My voice raised with the absurdity of having Viktor working on the streets.

He smirked. "I won't. Just hear me out." I lowered my gaze. "Lucca."

"Make it quick, Viktor," I ushered through my teeth.

"Shipments will still arrive with no issues. I'll still be working but *from home*. My shit is untraceable, and with the possibility of Tino Borelli in our streets, and threats growing, I am becoming a liability to keep showing up in the department in a suit with the pay of a mafioso."

"Your money is offshore," Arlo stated.

"The fact still remains, I'm not a secret within our syndicate." He shrugged. "But..."

"What?" I asked impatiently.

"I've had a tail for two days." *Fuck!* "It's Borelli's men. I found the recordings today and verified it myself." He took a deep breath and continued, "One day, I *will* be caught in a gunfire, and if I have my government-issued gun on me and shoot back at a known Mafia member that is in war and tied to the mess that is happening in Miami when I shouldn't be involved or targeted, I *will* be compromised."

"A vacation?" Arlo murmured, his head already agreeing to our brother's safety and position.

"You need Sergio and Rio on the streets, and who do you trust most to keep her safe?"

Viktor and I stared at each other.

*Us.* Him.

"Think about it. I'll be here, watching over the target, while I help from the inside. No delays, no waiting until I'm alone, or chasing my ass for a reply. I will have everything live and ready to see their movements without any setbacks."

It was a high risk.

"I risk more by showing up to my office with a tail. I'll end up in jail or dead in a month."

"Being here is a risk too."

Viktor shrugged. "But it's the one I'm willing to take."

I watched him, and as I saw the possibility and the benefit of having Viktor home, I hesitated. He was keeping something. He'd prepositioned this new change with too much thought, almost rehearsed.

"What are you not saying?" I asked, and Arlo snapped his head at him as I continued, "I remember months back your mention of needing to keep a low profile. There were some new people around in your department sniffing. Is that it too?"

His jaw clenched, and my fingers numbed.

"Not in the way you are thinking."

Irritation slithered inside, constricting my muscles, knowing he *was* keeping me in the dark.

"Then explain." I seethed.

My brother hesitated, and I was troubled by it. How was this possible? What could make him hide anything from me? All I'd done was for *them*, for *him*!

His eyes lowered, and my chest caved as my heart raced, and I lost it.

"Fucking speak, Viktor!"

Viktor took a deep breath and looked at me again.

"I mean it when I say my main reason is to keep Katia safe, keep the family safe, and help away from the department."

"But?"

As I held on to the trembles of fury, tension dragged me forcefully.

"But it was more of one person who had given me a hard time and kept a close eye on me, which is why I've kept a low profile and had to distance myself. They have too much suspicion, but…" He rubbed his neck, rolled and dropped his head. "Between getting to know my enemy and their weaknesses, I grew too close to *her*."

I took a moment to think through his admission. He kept this information to keep *her* safe and nothing more. He *cared* about this woman. Jesus, he slept with a fucking DEA agent, caught feelings, and now, she was at risk too.

"What's her name?"

"Don't ask me that."

"Does she know?"

"No."

I picked his answer and body apart for the truth.

"You said she had too much suspicion!"

It was one thing for people to talk, believe, and murmur about our affiliation. Others could swear by it, but we never admitted it. We didn't speak of the Mafia unless they were in our world. It was an enforced rule with no way to mend, specifically the law.

*Cazzo!*

"Suspicion is not knowing." Tiredly, his eyes looked away. "She stopped digging. She won't utter her thoughts out loud."

"How do you know this?"

"She has a daughter."

"My God, Viktor." I stepped away from the door to him. "Not only did you bed a DEA agent, putting her life at risk, but a fucking child!"

"You won't kill a child." He shook his head, reassuring himself.

"But how many have we orphaned?" I yelled. I let go of control and rushed after him. He didn't even fight back. He only straightened as I grabbed his shirt, pushing his body up against the wall harshly. My voice was lowered in hatred. "How many have we left to suffer in the same orphanage as we grew up in? Huh? The one you wouldn't leave your baby brother behind in, even while you took the fucking beatings for him when I wasn't around? The same shit hole that robbed us of a future?"

"I fucking tried! Fuck did I try." His body gave, and his head lowered. Viktor was in pain for what he'd done.

I let go of him and his body staggered, and his head fell onto my shoulder for a split second before he quickly lifted it.

"I love her and her daughter, so I left her."

I took a step away from his words.

"Does she hate you?" Arlo asked, when he really meant, *was she crazy enough to want to ruin your life?*

"No. We both agreed it was for the best. She couldn't risk her position by having an intimate relationship with another agent. Our branch has a *no-fraternizing* policy. Right now is a good time for me to step away."

I ran my hand over my hair, my neck, my beard—I needed a drink.

"I don't want California to find out about them, and the more I help, the quicker the threat to everyone's safety will be over."

"There's nowhere to hide, and no one is ever safe in the Mafia, Viktor. Or have you forgotten?"

"No, I haven't, but war brings a higher chance of casualties."

"Fine," I agreed. "Make sure you lose your tail in the morning." He nodded. "And I want her name. It is not a question."

His eyes flared as his mouth shut tightly.

"Valerie," Viktor uttered, looked at me one last time, and turned, leaving us behind.

I watched his back all the way until he stepped into his sports car. Even when his car left the property, I looked out at where he had once stood. Angry at my brother and the feeling he'd created. Betrayal. It was a similar experience when Ilias brought Davina to me, but this time it was different. Ilias had no idea who she was, who he was protecting, and who he had risked his life for. He wasn't even a made-man then.

Viktor was. He knew what he was doing. Understood the risks and kept it from me.

Viktor did it fully aware of his disloyalty to the *famiglia*, to me, and even then, continued for months.

I turned toward Arlo.

He was just as perplexed as I was.

"It's Viktor," Arlo expressed as if I needed a reminder of who our brother was. It only deepened the wound as a wall solidified, hardening around me and what I had once believed I could trust.

Could I still trust him fully? Trust him to keep her emerald shining with life?

"That's the issue."

Because as much as I wanted to, I couldn't bring myself to cause him any pain. At least not physically. Out of everyone, they understood the things I couldn't overlook. The limits that couldn't be crossed and who I was. The Mafia was first, and they had the power to make me hate myself further than what I believed I already did. This was if I was ever forced to make the one call I dreaded. Their lives.

"He admitted to loving her," Arlo said, but it was weak and failed to deliver its meaning as he too didn't understand such feeling.

I laughed. It was dark and foul.

"Look at what *love* has brought him." I spat the word like a curse.

Love had brought him risk and disloyalty.

"What do you want me to do?" he asked, but for once, he didn't seek my reply.

"Find out who she is and where she lives."

"And then?"

"Nothing. We just need to know where her home is."

Arlo exhaled loudly.

"And do me a favor. Don't fuck someone with a badge. I'm done being tested by my own brothers."

I stepped inside the house without a farewell and headed straight to my office for a full glass of bourbon. I didn't bother with ice. After a gulp, I refilled it and placed it by my desk to discard my jacket. My cufflinks followed, tossing them by the glass and not caring where they landed. I tugged and tugged at my tie, too frustrated to work out the knot.

"Hey."

I stopped, looked up, and saw Katia by the doorway. I needed a minute before I faced her, and yet, I didn't stop her from walking inside. Her hands held a small glass bowl, small red balls rolling as she stepped deeper inside with her lips a shade darker. Her fingers met her lips, and her teeth enclosed a tiny seed in her mouth. Her fingertips pinched it before placing it inside the glass.

"Let me," she offered, and I shook my head.

She didn't listen; she never did. Instead, she placed the bowl in the corner of the desk, and I was able to see inside it.

"Cherries?" I questioned darkly.

"They are my favorite fruit. I pretty much eat them every day." Katia closed the distance, and I kept my eyes on her as her hands lifted, and with her slender fingers, she gently fiddled with the tie.

I couldn't look away from her lips. Their antagonizing color and the taste they would reward if I ran my tongue over them. My tie came undone, and she freed two buttons, allowing my stress to be relieved.

"Is everything okay?" she asked.

But I wanted to test out a theory. Dangerous theory, but control had left long ago, and that was how I found my fingers inside the bowl.

I picked a deep-red cherry and brought it to her lips.

Katia's eyes locked as I ran the cherry over her bottom and upper lip. I pressed it tighter onto her mouth, seeing if she would dare.

She did.

Her lips parted, her mouth opened slightly, and I pushed the cherry slowly until her teeth sunk down its side. She closed her mouth, leaving me with a half-eaten cherry and a hard dick.

My fingers were wet from her mouth and the juice that ran from the fruit. Quietly, she chewed as I kept the fruit over her lips. They were damp, stained, and when a full drop ran from the corner of her lips and my theory had been proven, I took a step closer.

I popped the rest of the cherry into my mouth. I lifted her up with my hand firmly against her jaw so that I could follow the trail left by the drop.

I played with the leftover seed in my mouth while her chest rose and her eyes swirled in need. She looked edible as heat rose to her cheeks, and her hands timidly reached for my cuff. She began rolling them back as a distraction, but I needed her hands where discomfort had become too hard to ignore as my pants trapped my dick painfully, begging for her touch.

The drop was almost at its end of life. I picked the seed from my mouth with my free hand, pocketing it into my pants and pulling her lower half to meet my stiff bulge.

Katia yelped with parted lips. They connected and her hands held my forearms tightly as I pressed her deeper into me. Her head pulled back as a drop hung from her jaw.

I dove for it.

Done with conversations and betrayals for the day, I only wanted to release the pent-up anger that vibrated through my veins.

My tongue licked its sweetness, and I nipped, punishing her skin for such exquisite taste. Because now, I wanted more. My grip tightened around her jaw forcing it back further, and I licked the trail up to her lips, and when I'd found them, I pulled back, taking one last look at their color.

But Katia licked them, and my eyes met her shining greens before I crashed my mouth onto her plump lips, seeking her tongue for the taste of my now favorite fruit.

Katia hummed as our lips collided, the vibration reached my mouth, and I held back a groan as my dick twitched. Her body arched, and I took everything she gave with greed. Our mouths synced with thirst, desperate for more.

She tasted sweet as the forbidden fruit I should've never taken. But as anything forbidden, it only made the craving unsustainable.

Katia's hands clawed my chest, balling my shirt with her fists, begging to continue.

With one hand on her hip and the other tangling her hair between my fingertips, I continued the assault my lips offered as they abused and trapped her mouth fiercely.

Our kiss wasn't gentle.

I had warned her.

My lips punished, my mouth demanded. Now that I had tasted her, I couldn't restrain my cruel hands or brutal desire. Instead, they reigned with need over her body.

I pulled her bottom lips between my teeth before licking its sting away, but as her body arched and her throat gave a raspy low sound, I bit harder.

"Lucca," Katia murmured impatiently, and I was so far gone that I allowed myself to feel and prey without thinking. The only control I had left was the control to demand.

With one hand on Katia's firm ass, I pushed her hips against me again and again, listening to the muffled whimpers she kept from slipping past our lips.

I was ready to take her, to spread her open over the desk and dive my dick inside her heat as her nails dug deeply, bringing blissful pain to my demon.

Her finger touched my cheek, and a memory stole me away.

*"I promise I'll be back, Lucca. I would never leave you behind."*
*My mother's eyes swore, as her petite and soft hand reached my face.*

*It cupped my cheek tenderly beneath the veil of sea dew that sheltered the night. "Happy birthday, piccolo." Her warm touch vanished with her words, and I was alone in front of hell with blood soiled clothes and murderous hands.*

My hand shot out, violently connecting to the one that had caressed my face. Twisting it with force and away until I heard the piercing cry of pain.

As soon as I spotted Katia's stunned expression and pinched brows, I let go. I looked down at her right hand as she pulled it to her chest, taking a step back.

Her wrist reddened, and her mouth opened in disbelief.

"Don't touch my face again." My voice and heart sneered with hatred before I walked away.

I should've never allowed her inside.

Without control, I was capable of anything.

*Anything.*

## KATIA

IT COULD HAVE BEEN A HALLUCINATION MY MIND ORCHESTRATED, BUT THE pressure between my legs and the pain his brutal lips had delivered proved it was in fact real.

Lucca kissed with wicked malice. Its force only offered pleasure, extorting feelings of need and desire. Compelling me to forget and fall deeply in want. And I wanted *him.* Wanted what he offered, influencing my body into surrender. For my mind to tolerate what my heart forbids.

In the heat of hunger, I reacted to what I was given, and my hand reached for his face. It was warm, firm, and his trimmed beard pricked below my fingertips, heightening the mixed feelings of craving.

But it was short-lived as Lucca's eyes held nothing, transforming into black and voided irises as his mind pulled away from me until the pain crashed down.

Incomparable to what my wrist had received earlier in the day, this crushing pain shot through my body as his grip held me without mercy. What used to be tender had burned and was replaced by excruciating agony created by *him*.

I held my tears back as I cried out.

Lucca released me, and instantaneously, I brought my hand to my chest, pulling it as far as I could from his hold. His eyes remained vacant as I searched for him. It was useless.

Lucca had abandoned the present and had been left with cruelty.

"Don't touch my face again."

His threat had been clear, and Lucca had warned me once, but I always pushed all limits. This time, I was met by my own undoing.

He left me behind with pain and trapped the tears that pooled over deception.

Lucca never came home that night, and while my body tossed and my heart ached in his sheets, I curled my body close, knowing he had broken his promise.

Tonight, I bared the bruises he'd inflicted on my body.

# XXI
## KATIA

I WOKE UP THIS MORNING WITH A WEARY SOUL, AN ACHING HEART, AND A shadowed spirit.

I'd been so busy surviving that I'd forgotten to live.

While defeat felt strong, I left the covers and comfort to face my worth.

I followed my daily routine with two Tylenol and pushed through the day with a brave mask. Thoughts of him periodically came and went, and each time, I shoved them aside. If I entertained them, it would leave me with more disappointment.

I liked anger and avoidance best. They empowered my heart into chaos.

Lucca created a monster with every challenge and deny given. One that sought and fought to overrule all else.

As I swam underwater, I made sure to feel the sting of my wrist while it pushed me to the other end of the pool. Each stroke took me into a state of apathy. I came up for air, only to push my feet off the wall and submerge myself beneath the chilling temperature that eased my troubled soul.

With burning lungs, I kicked faster, stretching my hand out and waiting for the pool edge to meet my fingertips. When I made contact with the gritty concrete and smooth tile, I pulled up, gasping for air.

Water dripped from my face and into my eyes as I opened them to the sight of dress shoes. I followed their trail and met Lucca's stare peering down with a plush towel in hand. Seeing as he wore a dress shirt and pants, I knew the towel wasn't meant for him.

I stayed in the water with no intention of leaving. Lucca turned and picked up a black portfolio from the outdoor table that hadn't been there when I arrived. He dragged a chair to the edge of the pool, folded the towel across the back of it, and sat.

Taking deep breaths to control my breathing, I placed my arms on the pool border, crossing them to stay above the water. I let my legs flutter underneath and waited, watching his rugged and powerful features along with the lips that haunted me since I last felt them torturing mine.

I wish I could hurt him for leaving me hot and bothered.

But Lucca's eyes weren't vacant. Instead, they held conflict as his body remained collected. His control was back, and I didn't want to imagine the expense it had taken.

"Pick one, and a date," he demanded as he opened the portfolio.

Three wedding invitations lined the black velvet. All were beautiful and elegant with intricate touches, but one in particular caught my attention. It was black and white with a subtle touch of champagne.

"First," I looked up at his eyes, "I need something in return."

He shut the book, placed it on his thighs, and leaned down.

"What do you want?" he asked, ready to spill money for an answer too soon. Too eager, which meant I had the upper hand.

It was about time I did.

"I have a proposal."

His head rolled, and his eyes closed briefly.

He should've known I didn't need his money.

"A proposal?"

"*Sì.*"

His brow arched. "In a bathing suit?"

I withheld my smile. Damn him for lightening my spirits.

I tried lifting my body off the pool with my arms but failed miserably as my wrist gave in to the pain. Before my body fell back into the water, Lucca stood, and his hands held my arms, lifting me. The portfolio bounced off his legs and into the pool, sinking into the deep.

I didn't think about how his touch sparked my skin. Or how his strength picked up my weight with ease. I also didn't notice how close our bodies stood, and the breath he took through his teeth when his eyes traveled down.

*I didn't feel or see anything.* That was what I convinced my mind to believe, to ignore.

Water rolled down my body, splashing him, but Lucca didn't pull away and his pants dampened. Chlorine mixed in the air as he picked up the towel from the back of the chair. He pulled it apart, stretching it open for me as his eyes preyed on my two-piece light blush-colored bathing suit.

I took the towel from his hands and brought it to my hair, squeezing the excess water that poured down. I didn't cover myself, not yet. I wanted to show what he'd missed, what he could've had but hadn't touched.

The body that wasn't *his.*

Oh so slowly, his hooded and thirsty eyes returned to me.

My lips curled smugly.

"Katia," his deep voice warned as his jaw clenched.

"I have a folder ready. I can grab it quickly," I said casually and twisted my body to retrieve it. Lucca's hand stopped me, his strong hold pulling me back before him.

"I don't need visuals to see the depth of things."

I let my chuckle free and shrugged.

"It paints a clear picture."

"The picture was *crystal,* right from the beginning."

"Are we still talking about my proposal?" I asked cheekily, my attitude shining through.

I struck a nerve. Annoyed, Lucca breathed deeply.

"What is it that you want, Katia?"

I wanted too much. But for now, I settled for a way to escape from the mental-fuck-train I was trapped in.

"It's a business proposal."

His brows pinched. "Go on."

I finished drying my body and tossed the towel onto the chair to face him in nothing more than a thin bathing suit. Lucca's lips twitched upward. He was onto me.

"Should we sit under the shade?" I asked the same moment a cloud rolled over the beaming sun.

*Great.* I tried to buy time to think about my first words, and it backfired.

"Here is fine."

*Fine!*

"I…" My confidence faltered, and I held on to the curiosity his eyes portrayed to carry out my words. "I'm aware most high-profile wives in the Mafia stay home, but I studied too hard and made a successful career for myself to waste it. I poured everything I had in me to get where I left off, and I *need* it back."

Lucca's body turned rigid. He hadn't expected my honesty.

"You want to work?" he asked in disbelief.

I nodded.

"Doing *what* exactly?"

"I'm an architect."

Lucca's lips twitched, impressed.

"Let me get this straight, you graduated, made a successful career, *and* worked in Italy with your family's blessing."

I chuckled. "I wouldn't go as far as calling it a blessing."

His head shook with skepticism. I understood how he felt. Women in our world married younger than my twenty-six years. Therefore, I had the time and guts to maneuver my way and win over my grandfather's conservative and mafioso beliefs. It had been a fight, but I won. When my father found out, he was furious, but it was too late. I'd already started school, and my nonno didn't allow him to pull me out. *"A Vitelli never leaves anything unfinished, Mario,"* my grandfather had said. Funny as his grandson did, and I'd seen her living and breathing strong to tell the lie.

Even to this day, Father has never acknowledged what I've done or accomplished. The only one who waited for me after I'd received my diploma was my grandfather, even if it was only to make sure I did as I'd promised.

"You didn't know," I murmured.

He didn't answer, and I was unconvinced that someone like the control-driven man that he was didn't have a detailed script of my life from my birth to the minute I stepped foot in Miami. I was conflicted and wary as it contradicted who Lucca was, leaving me with, *why didn't he?*

"Your family never mentioned it. And no, I did not look into your past."

"My father made sure no one said a word about it. Like it was a bad dirty secret for his daughter to be educated in a male prominent career," I scoffed. "Wouldn't want a made-man to feel intimidated by a woman whose job should be to warm the sheets and please her man. Not carry a briefcase," I sassed.

The corner of his mouth curled, amused. And yet his features sombered, causing me to panic inside for the thoughts that changed his demeanor.

"I'm not intimidated." His eyes fell to my lips before he continued. "If anything, I'm impressed."

*He was?*

"I actually want to see this folder you've put together."

*Or did he doubt me?*

*If that was the case, bring it on.*

"Okay." With a smirk, I turned.

"Wait."

I stopped, faced him and the towel stretched out for me to take.

With a smile, I continued walking as I said, "I'm all dried now." I made my way inside knowing each step I took his eyes would take the movement of my ass.

Payback was exhilarating, and I wasn't done with it or with him just yet.

## LUCCA

I SHOULD'VE LOOKED INTO HER. DUG DEEP INTO HER PAST TO UNCOVER ALL HER secrets. That was what I did for anyone who entered my life. It gave me leverage, power over them. But I hadn't.

Katia wanted to work, and even if I didn't see anything wrong with the idea of my future wife working, I struggled with the idea of her roaming the streets with a target on her head. I've kept the severity of the threats that stalked Miami, and even New York, from her. It wasn't a topic to be discussed with a woman, but Katia was different and I've stowed away the dangers for far too long.

An architect.

I smiled. Jesus, this woman was beauty *and* brains.

But why?

Most people worked for money. Was that what she needed? All she had to do was ask. I had more than what I knew to do with it. But Katia wasn't one to ask, and I hadn't offered. A mistake on my part since I had a credit card in my desk drawer specifically for her that I hadn't given her. It had slipped my mind, and now I was facing the consequences.

I knew what the answer had to be.

Nothing inside her folder could change the outcome, but I had to come up with a strategy, a smart way for her to understand that the answer revolved around safety and nothing else. That was why I asked for it, to have a minute to think through it without her skin and toned golden body distracting me.

It was cruel for me to give her a sense of hope after losing control yesterday. After I broke my vow to never leave a mark on her body. And I restrained myself from checking her wrist after seeing how her body failed to pull her out of the water, afraid and unsure how I would react or what it would spark.

Katia hadn't mentioned it, and neither had I.

*Was I even able to apologize?*

No, I wasn't, but I had to acknowledge what had happened.

*Was I sorry?*

Yes. No! Fuck, this was new territory, mined and uncharted. But what I did know was that the sound of her cry from pain and the detest and agony piercing through her eyes wasn't something I liked.

Two knocks interrupted my thoughts, pulling me back as the door to my study opened. Katia's fuck-me black heels stepped inside with a *click-clack* cadence that proclaimed power and determination. An attractive sight to see. After a quick glance down her long legs that were exposed in a deep maroon dress that hugged her body, my eyes were captivated by her emerald greens. They were ready to debate and win.

Katia was ready to fight, looking like a businesswoman. The kind that turned heads and demanded attention in any room she walked into. A fucking delicious dream of confidence.

She sat across my desk, keeping her eyes from drifting away from mine. Her spit-fire spirit hardened my dick that hid under the desktop.

"Before you start." I cleared my throat, opened the drawer to my left, and placed the black plastic card in front of her.

Katia looked down at what I'd offered, and her eyes flared.

"I told you I didn't need your money," she said through clenched teeth.

"You think I will use your father's money to pay for the wedding?"

Her lips curled. "I haven't touched his money in years." Katia took a deep breath to calm the fire that swirled in her eyes and the tension in her muscles. "I see where you would misinterpret when I said I didn't need your money." She placed her folder on the credit card and repeated her words. "But I told you I led a very successful business before leaving Italy. Before *you*. When I said I didn't need gifts, jewelry or your money, I meant it."

I didn't like it.

It was my duty to provide for what was mine. How could I be the boss of a *famiglia* when I couldn't provide for its queen?

"You are losing before your proposal is even given, Katia," I warned.

"Why?" she fought. "Because you can't have me paying for my own needs?"

"Yes."

"Lucca, this is absurd."

"Is it?"

"Yes!" Her arms flung while her ass squirmed to the end of the chair.

"If money is your drive to work because your pride won't allow you to take mine, the answer is *no*."

"But it's not!" Her cheeks colored while her hands expressed her desperation. "*You* brought money into this, not me."

"And yet, you are unwilling to accept it. You are not paying for *our* wedding or anything you need."

"Then you won't get your date." She seethed, and this time, I lost my patience.

Katia had no idea of the thin thread of power, change, and questions that threatened her future.

How her own father was ready to toss her to the first bidder as death escalated and money poured out of syndicates.

"Then I'll pick it myself."

My tone was harsh with no room to defy, and yet she still did. She stood quickly. Hatred pouring from her eyes.

"Then so be it. It wouldn't be the first time you lied."

She'd silenced me.

"I wanted to work to stay busy. To have the drive to get up and push through the idea of having to live with you!" she spat as her body vibrated in anger. "To escape from the games and roller coaster of feelings I'm under in this hell." Katia looked into her folder. "But you are just like them all. A liar who is afraid to see a woman as an equal."

My heart beat in an array, wild to her accusations. But I couldn't speak up to defend myself.

Katia's eyes looked down on me as I fought to conceal the wild feeling she'd broken free inside, but she only saw what I'd allowed. A relaxed posture and a careless bastard looking back without remorse. Meanwhile, my chest loathed the constricting pressure that grew with each passing minute. Her eyes lowered, and her head shook disheartened. Katia glanced at the folder one last time before her back faced me.

I'd done it.

I had said no, but it didn't settle well with me. It wasn't the way I had planned; it was messy, and emotions were high without understanding reasoning.

As her hips swayed further away, I caught a glimpse of the fingerprints that marked her wrist. *My fingerprints.*

"I never meant to break my promise."

"Is that an apology?" she said as low as my voice had been, but she never turned. She held onto the doorway with her gaze trained on the wood stain, and when I didn't reply, Katia uttered, "I didn't think so." When she looked back, her hair obscured her features, and I couldn't see her eyes clearly. "June seventh," were her last words before she left.

*June seventh.*

Katia had kept me from breaking my word again, leaving me with gratitude and the feeling of failure. But why did I care? Why did my body sink deeper and my head fall onto my hands? Why did I feel so conflicted?

The yellow folder mocked me, urging me to peek inside and look through what she had put together for me. The chance I hadn't even given her as I'd focused on destroying the conversation before it even had the chance to begin.

I picked it up, opened it, and did what I shouldn't have done. Because as I took note of her previous financials, her intricate designs, drawings, deals, and paperwork to launch her business in the States, I was dumbfounded by the extent of her career and the length she'd gone to prove to me the part of her she desperately needed back.

Stunned by the might it took to get there, the business and financial mind it required.

Fuck, her family had been quick to hide the power she held, and I had done the same. But a part of me knew that even if I didn't want a partner, I would be a fool to ignore it.

And I was no fool.

THE CROWD WAS FUELED WITH ALCOHOL AND SEX DRIVE AS BODIES PILED IN the middle of the club. Lights flickered in various colors as the ground vibrated with the beat of the music. As I waited for Ilias to get here, I pulled away from the glass that overlooked the sweating bodies below and faced Arlo and Viktor.

"Want to tell us why we are meeting in Malvagio's?" Arlo leaned his weight on the wall by the corner and yawned.

Arlo spent most of his time running the streets and businesses we owned. However, I hadn't missed the way he always finished his day here, looking over a certain curly dark-haired aerial dancer until close. He was careful and distanced himself from whispers about his inclination to this club. To many, it looked as if he was in charge of the safety of all our workers that spiraled high in the sky. Our biggest attraction as it added a unique danger and sense of eroticism from any other nightclub. I knew better. Arlo's interest was in only one dancer in particular, and even if I didn't care who he fucked, I feared for the young and sweet girl who'd caught my brother's twisted mind.

If I'd learned something from my brothers, it was how their dicks blinded them into danger.

As I thought of Katia, they weren't the only ones.

Hell, I started a war.

I ignored Arlo's question and turned to Viktor, who was sitting across from us on the black leather couch.

"I need you to look over something for me before I make a decision," I said, with Katia's proposal outstretched for him.

Viktor straightened, taking the folder from my hands. His posture changed the longer his attention looked through its contents.

Music slipped inside the room as the door opened, revealing Ilias's somber appearance. He wore all black and a cap over his head. A look he and Viktor were accustomed to as they worked for the law. But even after Ilias left the force, his cap came out every night. Tonight, it was backward, and before I looked down at his knuckles, I knew I would find them battered.

"You good?" I asked.

The door shut, and Ilias nodded as he stood next to Arlo in the darkness.

I tried not to dwell on the changes and darkness that had changed him in the short months after vowing his life to the *famiglia*. Something I had tried to keep him away from and failed after Davina arrived in Miami. Now, it was too late. The more he followed Arlo's and my steps, the more his morals were corrupted.

The change had already started, and eventually, his heart would become stone and his mind unemotional to the cries. Cold-hearted and unfeeling, like us.

"This is…" Viktor paused, and I met his rounded ice blue gaze. "Impressive."

"I'm aware."

"What do you need from me?" Viktor asked.

"I need all her accounts secured, her paperwork and any credentials passed as Katia *Moretti*, and to start the website with no trace of IP addresses, locations and such. It needs to be impenetrable, all of it." I took a deep breath and asked, "Can it be done?"

Viktor nodded and said, "It's going to take some time—"

"Take however long it needs."

She didn't even know what I was doing. I wanted to keep it that way until the war settled.

"Okay, but first, I need her to talk and—"

"No." I cut him off. "Figure it out. She's not to be aware."

Viktor's brows pinched together, confused. But if I told Katia, she would take it and run wild. I couldn't give her such power, not now.

"Wait," Arlo said, fully awake in disbelief. "Are we talking about business for a woman? For Katia?" I stared at him. "You are serious." He chuckled, unpleased.

"I am."

"What the fuck is happening?" Ilias asked in Russian.

"Lucca is going to allow Katia to work," Arlo replied bitterly in Italian.

I felt all their eyes on me.

"It's *good* business. *Clean* business," I expressed.

Ilias veered his eyes away while Arlo continued shaking his head. Viktor sat quietly with his eyes fixed on the paperwork in his hands.

"It's smart, Arlo," Viktor spoke up. "Katia's business *will* explode, and the Moretti name will have another source of clean money in the eyes of the government. Having her tied into legal contracts and deals will make things easy to hide." Viktor's smile shone wickedly. "It's perfect." He chuckled. "She won't be placed in any legal danger, and money will come and go, and whispers will now mix into the building industry. The revenue stream can be tricky, but large losses often happen."

Finally, someone who sees my vision.

"She will be in prison if caught." Exasperated, Ilias looked around us as if he was the only one who cared.

Viktor closed the folder, stood up, and faced our brothers. "You don't understand. Everything will be legal. It's the Moretti name that will benefit from having such a business drawing out suspicion."

"It's dangerous," Ilias fired.

"It won't be finalized until California is eliminated," I stated.

"She'll be in the public eye, and threats will follow her," Ilias fought.

"She can take care of herself," I added nonchalantly.

It was the truth. Katia could take care of herself in the outside world. The numbers in the folder spoke of it. *I* knew that, and the kind of threats he now spoke of were ridiculous compared to a war.

Arlo scoffed. *"She can take care of herself."*

"You'd be surprised." I shrugged.

Arlo's lip curled with malice, and I watched him carefully as his hatred for her deepened. I could only blame myself, because the moment I'd hid my reason for marrying her from him, I'd lost his trust to see my way.

"We'll see." His smile pushed through, and he left the room.

"He wasn't too kind to Davina at first. He'll come around," Ilias said, following the same path Arlo had just taken out of the room.

Viktor and I stood in silence, and when the music faded, leaving us alone to the vibration of tempo at our feet, I was reminded of Arlo's warning.

Had he meant others or him?

"I have the last of my things in my car. I'm heading to your place. Are you coming or staying?" Viktor asked, breaking through my questions.

The thought of Katia's heat in my bed and her touch over my skin led me to say, "Let's go."

# XXII

## KATIA

THIS MORNING WAS DIFFERENT. WHILE THE COVERS NEXT TO ME WERE COLD and ruffled, it was impossible to not sense his presence.

"Lucca?" I asked, low and deep.

"Morning."

I heard his undeniable timbre reply, and I shot up into a sitting position.

Fully dressed and ready for the day, Lucca sat in the chair calmly looking at me. I glanced at the clock. It was six fifteen, and he looked as if he had been up and ready for quite some time.

"Are you okay?"

"Yes."

"Are you feeling unwell?"

"I'm not sick."

"Is everything okay?" I asked, trying to understand why he was still here. Lucca was always gone before I rose in the morning.

"You ask a lot of questions in the morning."

"You wouldn't know," I fired back.

"I guess I know now."

"Did…did you come home last night?" I hated the vulnerability of my question.

He nodded as he ran his palm over his eyes until they settled back on his thigh.

"I should've mentioned this before, but Viktor will stay here for a few weeks," he announced, a day too late. I'd already caught glimpses of him, but I guess he had finally settled.

"Anything else?" I motioned with my hand.

"Yeah, I'll be out this morning, but I'll be back sometime after lunch. You should have received a few dresses by then. Pick one."

This caught my attention.

"For what?"

"A charity function tomorrow night. You're coming with me."

*Why, thank you for asking. You look so thrilled, Lucca.*

"Charity events are not my thing."

Lucca stood with rigid shoulders and hardened features. Quietly, he made his way to my side of the bed, and I followed every footfall he took closer to me until his shins hit the bed. Anxiety crept into me as his peering body stood above me with his tired and uncaring eyes. When his hand fell along with his body, I froze in place.

Fingertips made the first contact before his fingers clasped, and his hand held my wrist up for him to inspect. It was the first real acknowledgement he'd given for what he'd left imprinted on my skin. When the pad of his finger ran across the bruises he'd caused, oh so gently, my heart ran against my chest.

It wasn't fair. I was already reeling from the fact he'd denied my proposal to work, along with his broken promise. Even then, his touch held so much power over my body's reaction.

All the raging emotions inside me, and his eyes held none. Not upon seeing the pain he'd caused, or remorse for his lie. Lucca didn't care.

I pulled my hand away, and his eyes challenged.

"Pick a dress," he said darkly.

My body fell back onto the bed in a heap when the door shut, leaving me alone with the urge to forget who I was, where I lived, and who was meant to be mine.

A small whine echoed inside the room, reminding me of the two pups who depended on me. I called them both onto the bed, not caring about letting them over the covers. I used their thick coats to soothe the turmoil of hatred and pain. Because eventually, I had to face yet another day.

As Lucca said, the dresses arrived this morning. There were five in total, but after the third dress, there was no need to continue. Its dark forest-green color and low back weren't the only things I'd fallen in love with. However, the high slit over my thigh made it *mine*.

I placed the dress back into its garment bag and dressed for a late workout. Wex, Vino, and I headed down the stairs but abruptly stopped at the sight of Viktor and Arlo talking to each other. Their conversation couldn't have been good, not while Arlo's posture was tense and veins popped throughout his neck in anger.

"Is everything okay?" I asked, taking the last step.

Viktor's lips pulled into a tight line as Arlo curled his mouth in disgust. And where hazel lived in his eyes was replaced by a pristine void of darkness and cruelty.

I should have continued walking, ignore his obviously cruel aura, and forget I'd seen them. But was I really one to forgo a fight? To keep quiet and move on?

No, I wasn't.

"Something bothering you?" I asked Arlo, as sweet as poison.

He glanced over my body with eyes that wished for my death.

"Matter of fact, yeah, there is one in particular."

"Arlo." Viktor closed his eyes.

"Please, don't hold back." I smirked.

"Katia," Viktor's voice warned. "It's not the right time."

I didn't listen. I never did.

Wex and Vino sensed the tension, and both stood on each side of me.

"I've allowed you to speak freely. Why haven't you?"

Arlo's eyes flared with murder because of my tone, and he took one threatening step closer to me.

Wex and Vino snarled, but it didn't stop Arlo.

"I heard a silly rumor." He cocked his head. "How you can take care of yourself?" Mad and deranged, he mocked.

With a smirk, I stepped forward. "Would you like to test such a theory?"

Viktor moved between us with icy eyes staring directly at me, forewarning me of my words.

"Please," he pleaded.

Staring at Viktor's alarm, I debated his warning, but it vanished shortly after Arlo spoke up.

"You think you could hold your ground against me, *Vitelli*?"

My eyes shot to Arlo's, holding on to bitterness, while Viktor whispered.

"He causes pain for a living," he tried to reason. "He may be the underboss, but he was an enforcer for much longer, the finest this syndicate ever had. Still is." Viktor grew desperate as my eyes wouldn't veer away from his brother. "Think of Lucca, how he will react."

*React.* To whom? The woman who's supposed to live in this house safely? Or the grown bastard whose hate was filled by his idea of me?

My eyes slid to him, and I tipped my head toward Arlo before I spat, "He should have thought of that."

Viktor's shoulders tensed, and I dismissed him by shifting my attention to the dark-haired brute.

"I have nothing to prove to you, Arlo, but I've been dying to humble you."

"Would you like to try now or…?" He trailed off, walking backward with his hands stretched out.

I followed his taunting eyes.

"Lucca is going to kill me," I heard Viktor say in the background, and out of the corner of my eye, I caught him pulling out his phone.

It was now or never. As I followed Arlo to the one door I hadn't been inside, I shut it behind me, leaving Wex and Vino behind.

The temperature dropped drastically inside the basement. Fluorescent lights shone over the black concrete room filled with equipment, from weights to a variety of weapons. Two rooms lay in the far corner, and the only exit was the door we'd come down from.

As Arlo stood on a large, cushioned workout mat, rolling his head, I mentally prepared for the pain I would soon endure.

I was no fool. Arlo outweighed me to the point of ridicule. His height was incomparable, and his killer hands matched the bloodthirst in his eyes. My most effective form of attack was speed, the push dagger I had strapped onto my back, and the knife under the stretchy material of my pants by my ankle.

My odds weren't great with two knives, but I was ready to show him how this *liability* could slither and fight.

I wouldn't back down.

I had to be smart and take the defense, watch his dominant side, and study his movements. The tells of each action he took.

Lucca would be furious.

"Are you going to stand there and look at me, or are you going to follow through, big guy?"

"Would you like a *safe word*?" His sarcastic and gentle tone antagonized.

I knew better than to attack first.

With a shrug, my feet crossed, taking a step to my right. Arlo followed my movement, and we danced, slowly creating a ring around us. Eyes scrutinizing, waiting.

"Do *you* need one?" I smirked.

My eyes fell as his left foot slid forward, swiftly his right followed, and his steps rapidly closed the gap between us. Immediately, I ducked and twirled out of reach to face his back. Instead, I found him facing me.

Fuck, even with his size, Arlo *was* quick. Too quick.

Arlo charged, and I sank, dodging his hands. He didn't like that. As Arlo snarled, I steadied my hands to stop his powerful fist from striking me. My side cowered as my arm and elbow received the first block from his fist.

*Ah!* I clenched my mouth shut.

The dread of his blow has vanished now that I'd tasted the pain of his force. It was aching and left a deep burning, but I welcomed it.

Pain and I were close friends, especially from the hands of a man. It wasn't the first time I was overpowered, but it was the first time I could fight back. The first time I wasn't afraid.

I took another blow with a grunt, knowing I couldn't block many more, but this time, I punched back.

Arlo swatted it effortlessly, but he hadn't expected my leg to shoot out to his knee. His leg folded, and I'd found his weakness. Low ground.

His eyes darkened, and we danced with pain as every blow we took, the other blocked, and my kicks no longer connected with his frame. My breathing was shallow, my body ached, and without using my right fist to punch, I'd taken the disadvantage.

Arlo was a skillful fighter, one that didn't blink after a strike. The kind whose body caused pain instead of taking it. However, his endurance didn't compare to mine, and his footwork became slow, drawing his movements to my advantage.

I just had to stay low.

I ducked another hook, legs twirling with momentum, swiping his foot off the mat.

*Thud.*

His large body hit the floor, echoing loudly, and when I glanced down, my eyes widened. Arlo had gripped my ankle. Hand clutching and arm pulling, I fell backward.

*Get up!*

I couldn't. I was trapped between his forceful clutch, but I had a split second before his body could overpower mine from a lock hold.

My left leg curled, my fingers stretched, and my hand clasped around my ankle. My actions were fluid and natural, a compulsion of ease to bear my blade's power.

I fought dirty.

With my knife between my fingers and Arlo's body rushing over mine, I jerked to deflect his raging fist to my face and flung the knife off my fingertips without a clear target.

A grunt confirmed I hadn't missed. After spinning my head, I saw blood decorating his collarbone, and my knife clattered on the floor.

I'd nicked him and awakened the hellhound.

In a roar, Arlo tore away in the distance, and I stood, rushing to dive from his hands. I failed, and his strike launched me back down.

Panic swarmed, my lungs burned, and air vanished as I hit the floor. I gasped, but nothing filled my caving chest. I stared at Arlo's empty eyes with his fist back and ready.

I closed my eyes, ready for the pain to spread.

A gun cocked.

My eyes opened to Arlo's smile. His fingers rubbed his own blood lazily with...*praise?*

"Welcome to the fam, *sis*."

*What?*

"Get away from her," a voice came, low and dangerous.

A shiver ran through me from the malice it held.

The gun cocking was Lucca's.

He was home.

## LUCCA

CRIMSON OBSCURED MY VISION IN RAGE AT KATIA'S GASPING AND ROLLING body lying on the floor.

I cocked my gun, and Arlo's fist fell apart.

"Get away from her." My voice was low, but I couldn't hold the sharp edge that spoke of murder.

Palms out, Arlo smiled at me, but I didn't reciprocate. Blood stained his gray shirt. I quickly searched the room and found her knife on the floor, and I trembled in anger. Raw ire pumped through my body with its sickness. Their feud had driven blood, pain, and me to the brink of losing the balance between my demon and me.

"I was just leaving."

I shook my head while bile rushed within me upon seeing *him*.

"Get out."

I couldn't deal with Arlo now, not when I had a fully loaded gun urging me to unload its weight.

Arlo's brow creased, and his eyes squinted.

*Was he fucking surprised?*

He held my eyes for a moment longer, dipped his chin, and left. I would deal with him later. Right now, I had a vixen to overthrow.

"I told you not to engage with him," I began, walking to her frozen frame.

Katia had risen. Her face was unmarked but the way she carried her weight was uneven, and if I lifted her shirt, it would reveal the reason.

"I told you not to come down here," I roared, waving my weapon to the ground.

I saw her hard swallow, and her hands fell down.

Another step.

"But you ignored my orders."

And another.

"You defy me!"

One more.

"Time after time."

Her back hit the wall, trapped and caged by my last footfall.

Katia's greens held on to the bit of spirit she possessed. It crashed with a shudder when I stood over her body, and I caught its tremble with a grip on her neck.

I tightened my hold, and her eyes held mine defiantly.

"Always a *fucking* fight." I clutched my fingertips, and her mouth parted, taking a small breath.

"Put your weapon down," she rasped.

A dark chuckle flew past my lips. "Do you think I missed your hand slipping behind you? I can only imagine what it carries."

"Take your hands *off* me." Her sneer shook with the loss of air.

Katia's eyes shimmered.

"Or?"

Her hand answered, slithering out in the open with fingers twirling her push dagger into position. Sweat glistened from her skin, and her small gasps held her tensed posture upright, pushing her thin sportswear against me.

The room's low temperature caused the shiver that erupted from her dampened clothes, and the peaks of her chest tightened as her nipples hardened, rubbing against my dress shirt.

Katia's grip was weak, her body was spent, and her eyes pleaded. A request I ignored.

Lowering my face, our breath mingled, and my lips flirted with the soft touch of hers. I needed to walk away. I'd just been under gunfire. A bloody massacre in broad daylight, and my mind still held the adrenaline and souls I'd taken.

Once again, I faced Katia with no control. It was dangerous, the way wrath cracked in twisted desire because of her threat. It was sick, depraved, and yet I craved it. Needed it.

Needed *her*.

My demon raged to take and clip her spirit. But it was her spirit, her useless threats, and her belief in being equals that made my dick hard and drove me to desperation.

I showed her how much her defiance affected me by pushing my painful bulge to her bare midsection. Katia's chin boldly lifted, and her bravado only unraveled my desire.

Releasing her throat to take her nape and jaw firmly, I pressed my scruff against her face, scraping it across her velvet skin to meet her ear. Heavily, she heaved large gulps of air, filling her chest with convulsing pants. The motion vibrated through me, and I groaned at its delicious feeling. I lifted the weight of my right hand, pressing my gun flat over her hair, holding them both in place while her thick locks entwined, leaving the gorgeous and morbid sight engraved into my mind.

Katia exhaled a faint whine.

Fuck, there was no turning back.

"You drive me mad, Katia." My lips murmured against her ear as I took a deep breath of her cherry scent before my lips spread below, and my tongue sought her taste.

I pulled back to stare at her vivid eyes and found her needy features calling for desire.

"I warned you."

Her lips parted, and mine collided onto their lush and rich texture. Like a crazed bastard, I kissed her unkindly and deeply. Our bodies synced as we pushed against each other with strict orders to draw pleasure.

"Now, I'm going to fuck you raw," I vowed.

Katia moaned into my mouth, and her hands desperately clasped my hair. The point of her knife poked my nape, and a tremble coursed down my back. I could have come from its depravity, but instead, I let it fuel me.

My hand rashly fell, tugging the skintight black material of her tights down until they reached her mid thighs. I couldn't wait to free the pants off her body. I spread her legs apart with my knee and cupped her fully with my palm.

She was wet, warm, and sensitive.

My fingers rolled and spread easily over her wet folds, causing her legs to buckle.

I chuckled darkly.

"Fuck you," she gritted out.

I pushed two fingers up her walls, and she cried out.

I hadn't given her time to adjust. I took and smiled at her pinched brows and the agony that brought her pleasure. Curling my fingers, I explored, stretched, and fucked her pain and delight while my thumb pressed brutally into her swollen bud.

Katia's dagger clattered onto the floor as her hands ran furiously over my neck, chest, and arms, pulling and crumpling my suit jacket in tight fists.

*Yeah, fuck me*, the demon snickered.

I watched her, kissed her, and peered down at my hand that disappeared inside her. I repeated the same barbaric steps, needing to see her beautiful need in her features, to taste and trap her pants, and feel her heat sliding between my fingertips as wetness ran down my palm.

"Lucca," Katia sobbed, begging for my torture to ease and her body to release the evil pressure. "Please!"

"First, I need to taste you, *cara mia.*"

I pulled my fingers away. Katia breathed out a whine as her head fell back, exposing her neck. I took the offer and kissed its exquisite grooves eagerly while lifting and holding her close. She rocked against me, and I moaned at the excruciating pressure on my dick.

With my gun in my hand and the other on her ass, I drew away from the wall with her in tow.

I lay her heaving body above the workout bench, removed her clothes, and took in the scattered welts on her flesh. Enraged, I spread her wide for my eyes.

Our eyes met for a brief second before I dove my mouth into her pussy. She jerked, and the thin bench didn't allow her writhing. I placed one leg over my shoulder. I pushed her chest back by taking her nipple between my fingertips and held her hip with a bruising hold.

Katia was bare before me, a sight I couldn't have fathomed in this lifetime by such beauty and irresistible vision. All mine for the taking. To do as I please, as it begged for *me.*

*Mine.*

Mad with hunger and thirst, I unleashed my need by eating her out until my raving brought her to tears. Famished, I lapped, slurped, and dipped. Starved with no end.

"Lucca!"

Her piercing cry howled in despair for a release. As her walls tightened and her back arched, I pinched her bud between my lips.

Katia came in heavy shudders, and before she could ride it over my face, I crawled up her body, rubbing her heat and capturing her hard nipple.

Her ass tried to finish her bliss by pushing her warmth deeper and frantically over my hand, but I wanted to leave her pussy glowing and aching for more.

I slid her body sideways so that only a fraction of her back laid over the low bench cushion. Her eyes shot down at the sound of my buckle and zipper coming undone, and when I freed my dick, she swallowed hard.

*Thrust.*

My groan was short compared to her cry.

Katia's knuckles whitened as she held onto the edge while I drove deep and hard inside her. With each thrust of my hips, I punished her defiance, spirit, and gorgeous body.

I punished her because, now that I've taken her, I wanted no one else.

I couldn't take her graceful and pleasurable-ridden face anymore. I pulled out, stood, and turned her body into a perfect down V. Her ass taunted me while I got rid of my jacket and loosened my tie in a rush.

She had no leverage when I plunged deep into her heat, and her face fell onto the cushion.

"*Mio Dio!*" *My God,* she screamed.

"*No Dio.*" *Not God,* I said between thrusts. "*Il tuo re.*" *Your king.*

"Yes!"

Agreeing, Katia met my violent strokes erratically. Needily.

The slaps of our flesh mixed with our feverish sounds, an erotic melody that ran over my body in ecstasy.

"Come, *mia regina,*" I gritted out.

She met my hips one last time. I took over, gripping her hair back and snaking my hand to her chest, bringing her curving back to my chest.

"Lucca!"

Her walls gripped me inside, taking me even deeper. Katia let go. One more thrust and I followed with my own release, kissing and biting her back, shoulders, and neck.

I then released her and tucked myself back into my pants.

Katia's legs buckled, and her hands caught her body from slamming onto the bench. I smirked as her muscles spasmed to keep her upright.

I fished for my handkerchief. Blood stained one side from pressing my wound earlier. I flipped it, and clean white shined through. I stepped closer to her. Katia's legs shook, but she managed to stand. With her back to me, I slid between her legs, curling my arm to her front and wiping away our release.

"Hmm." Sore and sensitive, she hummed, squeezing her long legs together.

Katia turned, her satisfied and tired eyes meeting mine, but my brows creased at the sight of the wetness that had spilled from her eyes.

I warned her.

I don't do sweet.

I don't do gentle.

And I *was* going to fuck her raw.

But the tears contradicted how her body withered beneath mine.

I wiped them away with my thumb. Even after warning her, I didn't warn myself of the fact of causing her pain.

"They are not what you think." She breathed out shakily and bit her lip, pleased.

Good.

"*Dio*, Lucca!"

Startled by the sudden fright in her eyes, I stepped back.

"You're bleeding!" she explained, bringing her bare skin back to me.

I looked over my arm where my white shirt clung to fresh blood. My movements had revived the blood flow that had stopped earlier, but now it was sweeping through my body in an angry manner.

Katia's fingers ran cautiously over my shoulder and onto my bicep. Her eyes fixed on mine, and her head shook.

Unbuttoning my shirt, I said, "It's just a graze. I took care of *it*."

*Them*. I took care of them.

I slipped off my shirt, and her eyes swept over the furious red mark and veered to the rest of my skin.

"I didn't know."

Her words were labored, and as her hand flew to meet my body with care, I took a step back.

"Don't."

Confused, she pulled her hand to her naked chest.

"I warned you," I expressed coldly. "I fuck without feelings." Like a gun flare, hurt flashed in her irises, a quick flash of abuse I felt nothing for as I'd promised.

It was her fault. She'd done it to herself.

I picked my gun up from the bench, uncocked the loaded gun, slipped the safety back on, and returned it to its holster.

I glanced and left her accusing gaze and ordered as I walked away, "Put your clothes on and go to bed, Katia. I got shit to do."

For the first time, Katia remained silent. Not one word or sound was heard as I left the basement. Maybe I had finally broken her spirit. Maybe I had made her understand who I was. But every step I took further away from where I had left her, fucked and punished, a confusing and unsettling feeling set in.

And I fucking hated her for it.

# XXIII

## KATIA

THAT BASTARD.

*Don't cry, Katia,* I chanted.

Lowering my eyes, I caught sight of the leftover release that had smeared over my thighs and its faint tint of pink. I took a deep breath through my nose as emotion rose, and as time passed, the harder it became to ignore the pain in my body and heart. The beating it had taken from the blows of a former enforcer. The raw and sore muscles of Lucca's thrusts and the burning of my lips didn't compare to the thought of being used.

*You wanted it.*

*You asked for it.*

I had.

Not only did I go against his orders, I voluntarily placed myself in front of Arlo's fists. And I eagerly begged Lucca to take me, own me.

*I* did this.

While I didn't regret it, I didn't think about how I would feel afterward.

Now that I had, and the shade of pink darkened on my thighs with my blood, I knew it wouldn't be the end. I couldn't let it be. I refused to believe I was just another fuck.

I *wouldn't* be. He just didn't know it yet.

I picked up his suit jacket with a smirk and a purpose, left my clothes behind, and walked away wrapped in his jacket with my blades securely at my side.

What had once felt like a broken feeling now made me smile. I'd at least gained the respect of Arlo. And sex with Lucca left me wanting more, even if every step was filled with soreness and pain.

I liked pain.

AFTER I LEFT THE BASEMENT OF TORTURE, WEX AND VINO WERE GONE FROM where I'd left them. A part of me knew they'd followed their master, and with heavy steps, I made it to our bathroom without any peering eyes catching my wake.

Two Tylenol and a burning bubble bath later, I assessed my body in front of a mirror. It wasn't pretty. Not when an iron fist had buried its way into my ribs, the most painful bruise of all. Then, there were faint fingerprints scattered over my hips, bottom, and thighs. A reminder of what sexual intercourse meant with Lucca. Oddly, I was okay with the marks. For once, I did not cower or feel the need to cover them. They didn't make me feel weak.

It proved that I could hold my own against Arlo, someone I'd been asked not to provoke on multiple occasions. And how Lucca's fingerprints were nothing more than his need for me. How he may say he fucked without feelings, but my body suggested otherwise.

Lucca fucked me with passion, feverishly, and while he hadn't been my first, he sure left my body addicted.

With my mind reeling in ways to find him for another dose, I walked out in a thin camisole of satin and lace. In need of making him see I was more than just one of his many fucks. To feel his hands on my body and our bodies dancing with need. Each scenario felt inadequate to crush the dark aura that roamed inside and out of that basement. The same aura that followed him like a prisoner.

I never made it out of the room. Because at times, opportunities fell in front of you, giving you the upper hand. Just like the one I'd received as Lucca crossed the threshold of our door with two heavy legged fur balls close behind.

I bit down on my bottom lip, hiding my eagerness for his touch and the giddiness of our games to begin. After all, they've become compelling.

Lucca left Wex and Vino by the closed door as he walked past me with a pile of rumpled clothes in his hands. He didn't offer me a word or a glance. His attention was aimed straight at the bathroom door. As the door swung open, so did my body. With his back to me, Lucca tossed the clothing into the hamper in the cabinet.

*Yeah, I didn't follow your orders, and you picked up the clothes you so eagerly took off my body from the cold concrete basement floor.*

I suppressed a chuckle. I had felt so hurt and used by him that I'd defied him in spite, but I never thought he would pick it all back up.

That chuckle quickly died as his hand gripped his holstered gun and his pants fell from his hips, leaving me to take in his broad shoulders, back, ass, and bare legs for the first time. I didn't deter my gaze, and he wasn't one for modesty. The one thing I could depend on, and I didn't mind. Not. One. Bit.

Lucca twisted his body, and my gaze trailed over every move his muscles made. From the way they jumped with his powering steps to the way they ran down his arm as he placed the weight of his gun against the chilled marble top. All with controlled force.

I took one step, then another until my hips pressed against the doorframe, captivated by his bare, inked body while he acted as if he was alone. Too soon, the spray of running water filled the room, and Lucca left my vision to drown his demons.

But demons could only be muffled.

I fought between my mind and body.

One said, "*Go to bed.*" The other begged, "*One more taste.*" And yet my soul craved something terrifying, so I followed my body.

I walked deeper into the bathroom, slipped my camisole off my body, and entered the steaming shower.

With his back facing me, I followed the water drops that licked down his body. The way they gently rushed down his strength and flowed to his hips, wishing it would be my fingertips that felt such skin. I knew Lucca wouldn't allow such touch, but I didn't care.

"What are you doing, Katia?" Lucca asked a second too late. My fingers already wrestled the water for his skin.

"Initiating."

His head dipped, and his body moved away from my touch. In that second, it only made me crave it more.

"Well, if that's the case, my dick is hard. You can start there."

I wanted to laugh and smack him at the same time. I shook the violence he pried off me and ignored him and his rejection.

I was smart. There were other ways to touch him.

Picking up Lucca's body wash, I smirked as I lathered my hands with the soap and watched the ink lines of his back teasing me. With palms ready to hold and fingertips eager to explore, I pushed my hands outwards.

"Either you take me for a fool, or you think I can't smell body wash." Lucca faced me, and my hands connected to his abdomen. The shock quickly faded, and I ran my hands up over the defined valley of his torso.

"Neither." I met his eyes.

His hands clasped my wrists.

"Don't." Lucca's voice sharpened.

"You say that a lot."

"And yet, you never listen."

I shrugged. "It's just soap."

His chest rumbled, and he closed his eyes. Lucca was losing his patience.

Good.

My eyes veered to his wound. It no longer bled, but I hated how close to his chest it was. While my bruises didn't bother me, his did.

Submerging my head fully beneath the water drops, I closed the distance until my lips touched and caressed what my hands couldn't. I kissed next to the angry gash and peppered another right below then tiptoed up to kiss just above it. Like his enemy, gently.

"Stop."

I didn't, and it drove him mad.

He firmly pushed me away and into the tiled wall, impatient to remove my lips from his body.

"Go to bed," he ordered, facing me.

Our bodies cooled by the corner as the water hit everywhere but our skin.

I straightened my body, watching him as leftover droplets ran down his hardened features. A walking wet dream.

"I'm here naked before you, and yet, you deny me?" I baited him, but truth mingled with my words, causing his jaw to shut.

"No man can deny a naked woman, Katia." He bared his teeth. "Is that what you were looking for?" he asked, pinching my chin upward. "To fuck?"

I ignored his question, seeking another answer.

"*Any* naked women?"

His fingertips left my chin, taking the crook of my neck fiercely instead. He pulled me closer so I could feel his hard dick that was pressed against my stomach.

Even while my mouth dried and my legs ached for friction, I couldn't lose control. Not now.

I peered into his eyes. He had been watching me all along, hot and interested by my tells, by my cues. Right now, I only wanted an answer, so I waited. Greedy, even if it was in vain.

"*Their* woman," he replied. "You."

*His.* He couldn't deny *his* woman. Me.

The corner of my lips tightened, a small triumphant smile bound to appear. However, Lucca quickly stretched his thumb to its outline, smearing it away and toying with my lips.

"Don't. I'm merely following my promise to respect you." To me, it was enough. "Now." His eyes followed his thumb's movement as it tugged my bottom lip down. "Get on your knees."

Our eyes connected.

My knees fell.

And I licked my lips when all I saw was him. Ready. I was going to drive him wild.

I took him as far as I could and sucked long and hard down and then up his length until the back of my head hit the wall behind me.

*Slowly.*

Oh, so fucking slowly.

My tongue played. My cheeks burned and my lips tugged at him tightly, but my speed never changed.

His breathing changed, charged with deep misery. The same misery his dick endured. All for my gain. The tug of war, the cat and mouse, and the king and queen game we excelled at.

The fight for control we both wanted, but neither of us could beat.

Lucca groaned loudly, and both hands moved to my head as his feet stepped back. I knew what was coming next, but I had other plans.

Even then, I wasn't prepared for his force or the gag that followed. Or the next as he used my mouth for his pleasure. I quite enjoyed his slip of control and the tears that threatened. I was one step ahead, and I restrained the next pull, restoring my old pace.

We fought.

He wanted *hard.*

I gave him gentle.

Slow.

"Keep doing that. It only makes me harder feeling you resist me."

Half the truth.

He liked the fight but hated not being the one in control.

Eventually, I won when a deep, guttural, and rough sound slipped out of his mouth. He pulled out, picked me up, and pushed our bodies against the wall to kiss me.

Lucca kissed me as if he'd been possessed with need. Carnal and hungry, his lips took mine. His hand gripped my face deeply while the other held my ass tightly, bringing me to his bulge.

My body gave into his hold, melted into his kiss, and grasped for more. I'd lost sight of my motives, my plan, and I held on to every dose of his lips.

Our kiss deepened, and I breathed him in, slipping my fingers in his hair and holding on to his neck. On their own, my lips slowed. They turned gentle, and for a brief moment, his did too. They mimicked mine, craving the peace mine offered. For that mere second, he let me in without acknowledgment.

Warfare returned, deadlier than ever. Eyes blazing, strikes loaded.

Lucca's hand found my center, spreading my thighs apart with his leg until he flicked my sensitive bud.

I whimpered from his touch, sensitive from our earlier encounter and responsive to our current game.

Lucca didn't move, my legs already shaking with anticipation. "I have to ask." He shook his head. "No. I need to know," he corrected himself. His lips lingered on mine before our eyes locked. "How long has it been?" He cupped me in warning. "And don't lie to me."

How much could I say? Men in our world expected a wife to be only theirs for their plucking. Virgins and inexperienced for their corruption. Pure and docile for their doctoring.

I wasn't a virgin, even if I was inexperienced.

I wasn't pure or docile. I was already broken before I could be either.

"A while," I breathed.

"How long is a while?"

"Years."

It was the truth. It had been years. My first time was only memorable because *I* had decided on the random and lucky bastard who would take my virginity. Not my family. Not the *famiglia*. Me.

Lucca nodded as if he had already expected my answer.

"How did you…"

"Oh, Katia." He chuckled darkly. "I've fucked many." Lucca pressed his thumb harder between my bud. "But I fucked you hard until bloody." His fingers slid easily down my opening. "No whore does that."

His fingers plunged deep inside, and I screamed in pain.

I was wrong. I couldn't take more of his brutal touch, his cruel fucking for a second round. Not so soon. My own body angrily yelled for the pain to stop. The burning that wouldn't subside as his fingers showed no mercy. The torment caused by his fist connecting to my tender entrance.

I bit back the tears and the following screams, not once backing out of what I'd walked into. Because when my eyes met his demented browns, satisfied by my struggle to not push him away from his brutality, I knew nothing I could do would make him take or give gently.

It was either this or nothing.

I had to take the pain to get his passion. Take his savage demon to get near.

"Lucca!" I cried out, dropping my head to his chest. Ready to give up for once.

I was so fucking close to losing to his vicious touch that defeat hurt deeper than his sadism.

But I felt his smile against me, the stretch of his jaw pulling apart and the slight bounce in his chest.

*My pain made him smile!*

I refused to lose.

My head lifted, and my lips brushed against his skin, tongue running up his neck, licking his inked veins and leftover creeping water. Lucca's head fell further. His neck stretched, welcoming my gentle assault, and his fingers faltered inside me. Sluggish movements that brought back a pang of pleasure after I found the skin below his ear. I took a chance and tiptoed up to him as his body straightened, our flesh flushed against another seeking warmth. My nipples rubbed his chest as my tongue and lips played with his skin. The burn eased, and the pain danced with anticipation.

I moved my hips above his hand and hummed in delirium.

I did it again, and my teeth clamped lightly on his shoulder. "Ahh…"

I wasn't so lucky for a third time.

Lucca removed his hand and gripped my hips tightly, pushing me back and away from his skin. The brittle cold tile shook a splintering wave down my spine.

"I can't." His labored whisper was loud against my ear.

Lucca backed away, but his hands remained firm as his fingertips dug into my flesh.

"So choose wisely, as I'm trying to give you the chance to rest tonight, because tomorrow I will fuck you. You are just deciding how sore you wish to be."

I peered up at his hungry eyes. His chest vibrated with the control it'd taken him to say those words, and when I glanced down at his heavy dick, I imagined the agony of containing his release. The eagerness to set free the build up as I, too, felt the power of the game I'd created.

Lucca's hands fisted on my skin, drawing out my answer.

I smiled.

His eyes were slit with measure. He wanted a direct answer, so I gave it. I held his dick in my palm, and Lucca's eyes, face, and body lost their composure by my touch.

Lucca cut the water off and snatched me up so fast that I wrapped my body tightly to his to prevent being in the way of his wild wake.

With my legs around his middle and my arms holding onto his neck, I turned to view our path out of the bathroom but came up short.

"I know the fucking way." His hand shot out, clasping my jaw and unwinding his mad lips on mine.

Between erratic breaths of need, I kissed him back until I was robbed of his lips and cold air hit my skin by the loss of his. In a quick reaction, my arms spread out aimlessly as my body fled in the air from his toss.

My ass hit the bed first, and I gripped the covers to watch him move like the predator he was.

But I was no prey, and as he crawled over my body and onto the bed, I fought for what I wanted, even if I knew it wasn't possible.

Lucca's frame hovered above me, and when his dick pressed down on my abdomen, the thirst for control swaddled me whole. I pushed my leg down and pushed myself up to turn our bodies. A challenging move to accomplish because of his weight, but surprise was my ally, and momentum was a favor from above. My damp hair draped down my breasts as I looked down at Lucca's vigorous glare. The room had grown quiet from our stillness, but chaos threatened nearby as his gaze took in my position above his.

Caught by his eyes, hesitation stirred, and I didn't dare move.

He smiled, and in a blur, Lucca shackled my neck with his hand. He rolled my body off his until his weight trapped me on the bed. I bucked, but underneath him, I barely stirred. I did it again and again, and each time, I lost to his possessive hold.

My hair twisted in all directions from my jerks, and breathing became a struggle. Panic rose from the constricting feeling of captivity and helplessness.

Lucca never eased with each thrash. Instead, his cruelty lingered, drawing out the fight and enjoying its pull. I waited for the fright to come while his hand gripped my neck and the other held onto my wrists.

But fear didn't show because I was sick. *I had to be.*

I stopped fighting, stopped thrashing, and peered through the strands of hair over my face, searching for his deep bourbon gaze.

"Are you done fighting?"

I shook my head *no.*

A cruel smile formed on his full lips.

"Then why stop?"

*I realized I enjoyed how easily you overpowered me. How I was bare and vulnerable beneath you with no escape and craved it. Because now I know I want to be under your mercy.*

Fucking sick.

"Are *you* done?" I asked instead.

This time, it was he who shook his head *no,* with a hunting smile.

Lucca positioned his legs between mine until they were spread open for him. His eyes calculated me as he slowly removed most of his weight from me. When he felt it was safe, Lucca freed my wrist from his grip. Then his lips crashed onto mine, and my fiery body clung on for more.

His teeth bit, pulled, and stung my lips raw while his hands mirrored his desire for my body. When he pulled away, I pushed back for more, wanting his lips back and his touch claiming my skin.

Lucca only allowed it briefly because he was the one who could claim, not the one to be claimed.

Gripping my leg, he spun our bodies until we rolled. His strength shuffled me with ease, and I gasped, staring down at him in surprise.

Lucca may have been below me, but I had no power as he quickly grabbed my ass, lifting it up and jerking it near his face. He pulled my bottom down, and I lost my balance when my pussy met his eager mouth.

"Lucca!" I gasped, arms out and fingertips clutching onto the headrest.

I was so sensitive, and his tongue had no pity for its assault. Untamed, Lucca devoured me as if he hadn't had enough the first time. There was no room for pain, only pleasure, as he dictated the speed of my hips by his hands and the force of his mouth.

My attempts to keep up with the pace became a punishment that I could not endure. With my eyes closed and my head back, I cried out, shaking from the pressure I couldn't control. I couldn't take it anymore. It was too much, and yet he seemed to have just started.

"Lucca, please," I begged.

My plea was answered with a muffled chuckle.

"Lucca, I can't."

I'd tried again believing my words, attempting to move away. Instead, he managed to gain a stronger grip and long laps with his tongue.

I reached for his head and hair and pulled back. Annoyed eyes shot up at mine. Lucca ran tongue over his wet and parted lips.

"That will cost you."

"I can't." I shook my head between my pants and ran my nails slowly over his scalp.

He closed his eyes briefly, enjoying the feeling. I did it again, but his eyes shot open.

"You will."

Lucca slipped from my hands, and his tongue connected to my bud.

"Ah!" I gripped his hair and pulled his head back again.

Anger rushed through his eyes in warning, and then all of a sudden, the air vanished. I gasped, but my windpipe burned. I clutched onto his gripping hold on my neck as his other hand prevented my hips from moving.

"You are too sore to come with me inside you. But you can and *will* over my face so I can fuck and load you with my cum." Lucca's lip curled. "Do you understand, Katia?"

My god, what has he done to me? I was panting over the loss of air he'd created. I could practically feel my own wetness slithering between my legs as my nipples tightened by just his words. His promise.

I nodded.

"Use your words, Katia."

"Yes," I muttered.

"Good, now *you* sit on my face and let me taste you until there's nothing left," he huskily ordered.

I moved too slow to his demand, and he applied pressure to my neck. My back straightened, and my hips bucked straight into his mouth.

Lucca took over quickly, and pleasure returned instantly. With his strong hand keeping me from breathing freely and the other using my own body against me, it all became too much.

I moaned loudly and panted with each kiss, lick, and slurp until no sound could escape. Only heaving breaths managed to escape my lips as the tighter his choking grip grew.

I was near losing consciousness. High from the loss of air, its pain, and the torturous pleasure his mouth gave, but it all combined into a powerful bliss.

My body shook with heavy spasms, letting go over his face. When his hand loosened, my head fell forward only to be recaptured by it. Lucca entangled his fingers in my hair, holding and pulling it back as he licked me through my quivers until nothing was left as he'd promised.

I was still so high from my release that when my hips were removed from his face, I lowered my hands to his hair and tugged—hard.

"Ahh!" I cried out.

Lucca pushed his dick deeply into my sensitive and sore pussy. The burning and pain wasn't compared to how it felt the first time he'd taken me. And as I tried to pull, push and thrash for a better angle, all my effort had managed was to take him deeper.

With wide eyes, I watched him enjoy my pain through the small smile that mocked along the corner of the lips that had once brought me pleasure.

Lucca didn't give me a minute or two to adjust to his length. He gave me seconds. His hands found my hips, and he used my body for his own purposes, thrusting deep and hard inside me, bouncing my hips up and down with force. Fucking me wildly while hitting the spot that caused my breathing to be erratic, wild, even if it felt like he was splitting me by the raging pain.

"Lucca," I pleaded.

"You. Never. Listen," Lucca's dark voice said between thrusts.

I didn't.

Lucca had given me the choice in the shower, and I'd picked him. He warned me time and again, but I did the opposite. Little did he know, one day I would prove him wrong, and that day would be the day I won. Because in the end, he wouldn't see me as his enemy, but as his lover.

I took what he gave, and as I bounced above him, I felt the pain ease into discomfort with a lace of pleasure. It wasn't easy. Too sore, too drained.

"Katia."

I couldn't look down at him.

"Look at me," he barked.

I didn't.

"Fuck!"

Lucca stopped, and relief immediately returned. While inside me, his hands slid from my hips and up my waist, leaving his mark in their wake as he continued touching my skin until his hands clasped my face.

His thumbs roughly brushed over my jaw, cheeks, and lips.

"Don't look away." His tone was not to disobey.

I kept my eyes on his cruel ones.

With his hands on my face, he pulled down while his hips pushed up.

"Hmph." I closed my eyes from his force.

"Katia!"

I opened my eyes, and he shoved himself deeper.

With our eyes tied, he resumed fucking me, and I loosened my muscles, taking him easier than fighting him. Soon the discomfort eased, and I met his hips.

Fuck, that was all he needed.

He thrust one last time, gripping my face until warmth filled me in soothing spurts inside.

I collapsed on top of him as he let me go. Both our bodies bounced with our breathing. Both spent by our fight. Both satisfied.

We lay in silence, listening to our breathing return to its usual cadence. I breathed in his scent, memorizing the smell of his clean and masculine body wash. The blend of our chaotic time together and the new crossbreed we'd created by our skin mingling.

The aroma was unique, both present and strong, both fighting to overpower. Clashing and yet, balanced. Even our scents fought one another.

Lucca's chest caved, exhaling deeply, and he shifted slightly, ready to slip out of bed. I didn't want him to leave, not yet, not tonight. I took it upon myself to shift off him and into the bed, regretting even trying.

With his heat far from my touch, a chill crawled over my skin, and I battled my foggy mind and exhausted muscles to move.

"I'll get you a warm towel," Lucca announced with indifference and sat up.

"Just stay," I murmured into the pillow and turned my head toward him.

"The bathroom light is still on."

I hadn't even noticed how night had arrived, or how I was able to see him clearly even in the shadows.

"Leave it."

He dropped his head, eyes looking down at my sheet-covered frame, and the laziness that filled my eyes.

"You should soak for a while."

The bed dipped as he leaned back into it.

"Already did."

"You will ache in the morning." Lucca's cold voice carried through the silence, and I questioned why he was so adamant to be alone.

"Are you so miserable lying next to me that you can't stop finding different ideas to be apart?"

"My apologies for trying to help," he quickly bit. "I'll remind myself after fucking you not to offer a fucking rag or ask if you need to soak your body after being someone's punching bag for the day." I lifted my head and chest off the pillow to watch him continue. "Or better yet, give a fuck if you are in pain the next day."

I sat up pulling the sheet along with me to face his wrath and the hypocrisy of his words. How dare he act like he cares? To believe in himself.

"Give a fuck if I'm in pain?" I laughed. "*You?*" His gaze turned to slits. "The man whose fingers penetrated me in the shower with a smile after seeing it caused *me* pain? Or how about the time you smirked after I begged and cried *in pain?*" I clutched the sheet tighter. "Or was that not pain, Lucca?"

My cheeks flushed with heat, angry to explain how those smiles left a trace behind. Upset that I had to give and tell him something I'd preferred to keep inside. Irritated of opening up and showing him how they'd bothered me enough to speak of it.

"Are you done?"

That *stronzo!*

"I wiped the tears off your face after I first had you, not for fun, Katia. I did it because I didn't want to cause you harm or pain while I fucked you." He shifted in search of comfort, detached. "I mean, not unless it's what you want at the time." Lucca's arm creased before he tucked his hand behind his head.

"I smiled in the bathroom after hearing how long it had been since you'd been with another man. I smiled because you confirmed it while I touched you, and your tightness swore it."

I played back our encounters, and while they all aligned, he spoke so unemotionally that I only felt its distant truth.

"And *I did* smile when I saw your pain-ridden face when you sat on my dick. Not because of the pain it caused, but because it allowed me to realize how you can hardly call yourself not a virgin." He smirked. "Let me guess, you've tried almost everything sexual at least once, so no one could decide for you who it would be."

I looked away. My heart hammering against my chest, processing his honesty and how easily he read past my most private secrets.

"Don't worry we don't have to talk about that now."

I met his eyes.

"But Katia, I don't have to cause you physical pain to hurt you." He shrugged. "There are many other ways. Just now, I detest seeing a bruise on your body."

"I…" I was speechless.

"Don't say anything, Katia. This is no pillow talk. Don't look for what isn't there."

While Lucca's insensitivity caused my chest to tighten, and the void inside to collapse all around, I respected his reminder. His warning.

We both remained silent with our eyes fixed on one another, confined to the moment. Limited by words and thoughts. My hands didn't move away from my covered chest, and he lay calmly waiting for my will to settle.

With a nod and ready to feel the pillow's comfort, I told my heart to compose, and my mind to pause. To stop feeling. To stop fixing.

At least for the night.

I pulled the sheet and fully covered my body, but the chill never broke. I pushed my damp hair above my head to remove some of the cause, but after minutes the pesty crawling chills periodically arrived.

I rubbed my feet together non-stop. I shifted around, trying to find a warmer spot. But not once did I attempt to leave the warmth beneath the cover, not to dry my hair, or to bump the thermostat up.

"What's wrong?" Lucca asked in a raspy voice.

"Nothing."

Lucca exhaled loudly but didn't ask again.

I peered over his body, appalled to see him comfortable with merely a part of the thin sheet covering him. Without a thought, I slid closer to him anticipating the warmth his skin promised. Lucca's body tightened by my path, and when my body pressed against his side, his muscles hardened. But when my cold hand landed on his burning chest, he tensed.

Darkness couldn't fail me, not tonight.

It wasn't the first time I'd felt his skin this way, but it was the first time after sex. I knew he didn't want my touch. How he wanted to keep him and I, not an *"us"* in my mind.

It was easier said than done because as I was pressed next to him, my body reacted with comfort and familiarity, something I hadn't experienced before with another human. Stirring something I couldn't fight against my body.

Even so, I had to hide thoughts I hardly understood.

"I'm just cold," I whispered.

Lucca didn't move me away or relax.

"Your fucking hand is freezing."

I laughed and snuggled deeper into his body. My *freezing* hand slid up to find a new and fresh hot spot on his body. It came to a complete halt when I encountered liquid warmth followed by a light jerk from him.

"*Dio.*" I gasped and lifted my head. "You are bleeding again."

"*Leave it.*" He returned my words. "It needs to breathe to heal faster."

I hated how used he was to his bleeding body. How normal he said it as if it didn't matter.

Yet, this was his life, *our* life.

Bullets were served for breakfast.

He never spoke of how it had happened. Always hiding and keeping me in the dark regarding the danger we opposed. That had to change, and seeing his wound, I knew I would forever hate his power by being a target.

"Sleep, Katia," he chided.

I lowered my head to his wound and kissed just below it. His head shook, displeased, and I didn't give him the chance to tell me not to, or to go to bed. I beat him to it with a small smirk.

*"Sleep, Lucca."*

# XXIV

## LUCCA

B oss."

Arlo walked inside my office at Malvagio's without knocking, eyes unhinged in bloodlust waves.

We had a problem.

I raised my hand to stop the Capo who sat across from my desk. This meeting had to be rescheduled.

Arlo's darkness wrapped the room with abuse and his body with impatience. He wore all black, casual. Work attire for a clean-up day, a messy day. It promised a long night.

Arlo had stayed away from my path since finding him on top of Katia with a balled fist. Sadly it hadn't been long enough as my fingers itched for my gun. Craving pain.

He'd defied my orders and still walked alive after his disrespect.

Arlo had been provoked and while he should've walked away, he'd chosen to bruise her body. I'd struggled to pull the trigger on my brother that day, but I was afraid I wouldn't a second time.

"Get out," he ordered.

Emilio's attention bounced between Arlo and me, waiting for my order with alarm and furrowed brows by Arlo's dire demand.

Arlo's temperament and ruthless soul were no secret. And while all my Capo's didn't fear much, they all feared Arlo's devil when provoked and near.

"Now!"

Aware of Arlo's tenacity, I downed my drink.

Emilio stood, and respectfully waited for my nod before leaving the room. Arlo slammed the door behind him so vigorously that he barely missed Emilio's heels.

I took a deep breath. "He's a capo, treat him as such."

"No, he's a little bitch that can't solve his own personal problems."

I ran my hand over my face. There was no point in reasoning in his state. I flicked my wrist and glanced down at my watch. I didn't have time to deal with Arlo. I only had a few minutes to change and leave for tonight's charity auction.

"I need to pick up Katia."

"About that."

Arlo's black boots crashed loudly against the floor. He picked up the remote from my desk and flipped through the channels. I stood and watched him carefully as his eyes trained on the screen. His beard was at least three days old, and his veins pulsed in his neck while his jaw flexed. For once the sound coming from the television didn't get cut off by his channel browsing, and this time, my attention swiftly shifted to the broadcast.

*"You are right, Linda. This could be the hands of a serial killer on the loose. And while the authorities are furiously investigating, panic has swept through Miami and surrounding cities after five females were*

*brutally abused and killed last night."*

*"The similarities are undeniable, Mark."*

*"Indeed, their characteristics, the violence, even how each was left out on strips of heavy traffic to be found by the public."*

*"Really, today is a sad and unforgettable day for all of Florida."*

*"Authorities have not released any information about the victims, or the crimes committed, but advised caution and gave tips for public safety."*

*"We will be right back with..."*

Arlo flipped the channel again and again, covering every newscast running the same story, proving a point.

Quickly, I ended any feeling that arose, cutting off any emotion that I could be capable of. Disconnected and heartless.

This world wasn't ready for it.

"Turn it off."

Silence surrounded us, but my mind reeled with the news reporter's voices over and over. A fucking repeat of the gravity and publicity, out for the law's eyes. The lives robbed of ordinary people, to women who weren't part of a war I'd created.

"This is messy, Lucca. The entire syndicate will now be involved," Arlo rushed. "Rules will be enforced, every fucking move scrutinized by every family. Hell, our own fucking backyard will be questioned."

Arlo couldn't stop firing every thought, deranged with the need to ease his troubled devil without an order to unleash it.

"Have you spoken to Ilias?" I asked, ignoring his worries and working on a plan.

"Yes, and he has been in contact with Davina's father."

"What does the chief know?"

Arlo's face sombered. "Brown long hair, green eyes, slender build."

*Breathe.* I forced myself into emptiness.

"Physically battered until a full clip of lead was emptied into their bodies." His eyes slid to mine. "A coordinated killing spree. Three in

Miami, two just outside the city limits."

I turned.

"You can't go tonight. It's too big a risk, Lucca!" Arlo became desperate.

I ignored him and unzipped my garment bag.

"Your appearance is publicly known!"

Not giving a fuck by his presence, I undressed down to my black boxer briefs and changed into my tuxedo.

"Lucca!"

I laid my untied bow around my neck and straightened.

Arlo had forgotten his place within this family, forgotten who I was, and it was my own doing.

Facing him, I said. "I will never hide. You should know better."

"So you are willing to risk Katia by taking her with you after *seven* women have died just because of her existence? If she dies, their deaths are useless!"

Rage surged in violent waves of ire. The taste of copper filled and lingered in my mouth with the bile of Katia's name and *death* spoken in the same sentence.

But I showed nothing behind my harsh features.

"If she dies, it is not just those deaths, Arlo. Can't you see, *I* will be next? Followed by *you*, Viktor, Ilias, and even Davina," I spat callously. "We will be picked one by one, faster than Salvatore's illness takes him." Placing my guns roughly into their holsters, I sneered. "I fucking know the effect of every move and possibility. That's why I don't barge into rooms." I point to the door he'd entered. "Why, I think before I act. Because I think about all of you fuckers! Even a damn Vitelli."

I stood in front of him, outraged. "So don't question me, Arlo. Instead, do what you do best, and fix the problem. Find a bastard to punish if that's what you need and return to the underboss *I* need."

Arlo's lips curled.

"I count on you to see danger as your playground, so why are you so unraveled now?"

"Because, as your head of safety, you are not listening to my advice!"

"Watch your tone, Arlo." Our eyes fought.

"You will get her killed."

My demon won.

Arlo didn't flinch, but his head reared to the right with the force of my fist. His eyes closed briefly before they cut mine, and I challenged them.

The corner of his brow dripped with blood, and while most believed him to be a devil, he was just a mere human who bled. He, too, needed the reminder.

He touched his split skin with a conflicting smile and brought his fingers together in front of him, watching the violet-red liquid smear messily between his fingertips.

"That was for yesterday. Touch her again, or go against my orders and..." My jaw clenched. I couldn't bring myself to threaten him out loud.

And I detested myself for feeling the division he created inside me. Damn him.


Arlo was the first human I'd spoken to after months of silence. The home for boys didn't question it, and the home didn't bother to take their time with the new kid. In those months and years of mental and physical abuse, I cherished my years of freedom. I didn't miss the childhood I spent running and looking over my shoulder. The years of cold nights and stomach hunger pains. I missed the miserable freedom I knew. Because inside the cruel and low-funded institute of the forgotten, we were treated like pesticides, and out in the world, I at least had my mother.

I'd waited for her return like a wounded animal, staring out every window that faced the spot I'd last seen her walking away from me. But she never came back, and I turned toward the pain given by the warden. At least then, I knew I felt *something*. But Arlo didn't know what existed outside the stone walls. He didn't recognize the leery and longing eyes that were not normal. That pain wasn't the only feeling we were capable of.

*Soft cries greeted me as I stepped into my room. There were six of us. Cramped in spring cots and stained sheets that were only changed when men in suits came in. Shiny shoes, clipboards, and wrinkled noses. No one looked you in the eye.*

*I was the last one who had been granted a shower. The only one who didn't fear stepping into the creeping hallways at night. Us six were around the same age, but the seventh kid who didn't belong in our bunk appeared younger. He was capable of hiding from sight by his small frame in the dark corner.*

*Five pairs of eyes watched my every move, the whites of their eyes shining as bright as the moon, calculating. Waging. We weren't close, and they knew better than to speak to me.*

*I stood above the young boy, and his soft cries hushed.*

*"How old are you?" My voice cracked.*

*Surprised by its tone and hearing my voice again, I sat next to his curled body. The cool stone felt pleasant against my back. This place seemed to always be too hot inside. Even with the windows cracked at night, the breeze reminded me of hell whispers. Fitting.*

*I stretched my long legs over the dusty floor and waited.*

*"Twelve," he whispered, but I noticed how he questioned it.*

*"Why are you crying?"*

*"Because I regret not using the glass to end it instead."*

*What? I peered over at him, questioning his words.*

*The boy stirred lightly and so quietly that it wasn't until I met his red-rimmed eyes that I realized he'd moved to stare at me.*

*He was odd. His speech, his aura, his mind.*

*"We don't have an extra cot."*

*"It doesn't matter."*

*He accepted it easily.*

*Many would fight for it, or prey on the smaller kid. He didn't seem to want to do either.*

*The boy slowly lifted his head and bent his body to mirror my position on the floor. He struggled with each movement. He was in pain.*

*He remained in the shadow, his features hard to decipher, but it was his labored breathing that gave him away. Taking a closer look at him, I saw it. The clinginess of his shirt and the dark stain over his torso.*

*"You're bleeding."*

*"I am. The nurse may clean it in the morning."*

*"Why?" I asked. But I didn't mean the nurse.*

*"I told you."*

I regret not using the glass to end it instead.

*"You did that to yourself?" I asked.*

*"Yes. It made me ugly." His teeth slid over his smile. It wasn't over happiness, it was formed by broken thoughts.*

*I didn't say anything else. I understood. He'd jarred his body to escape his suffering. Little did he know, ugly and evil were lovers.*

*That night, I helped the boy whose name I'd learned was Arlo. Offered my cot and sat at the end, watching him fight his demons in his sleep. And as days passed, an unspoken bond faded into our miserable lives. I gave him most of my food, he needed it more. We didn't speak much those first days.*

*Words weren't needed when two were broken.*

*And as the boys came and went as quickly as they showed, Arlo snatched the cot to my right.*

*It felt normal, to have the wall against me, and him on the other.*

*He never mentioned that night, and often I wondered what he meant by "ending it." Ending what?*

*The creator of his nightmares?*

*The monster that stalked his eyes when closed?*

*Quickly, I learned he'd referred to himself.*

*That night, a boy regretted living, because even after scarring his body, he cried, understanding the damage was deeper than what the glass was capable of slicing through.*

*That night, the boy cried for breathing.*

*That night, the boy did die.*

*It wasn't too soon after that he embraced his darkness, and we found the two brothers we didn't know were missing.*

*We never fought.*

*Never raised a fist.*

*Never allowed anything to come between us. And after long nights in our room learning each other's languages, I watched the lost boys before me, hanging on to every word I spoke. Not a trace of innocence poured from their lost eyes. All of us were different, and yet identical.*

*But as the youngest, Ilias, held on to my tattered pants with bright blue eyes when his brother wasn't around, did I comprehend, I would do anything for them three.*

*Hurting them would be hurting myself.*

*It wasn't until I was leaving, and I had Salvatore tear my siblings' folder from the head of hell's fingers, that I realized why Arlo and I shared similarities.*

*He was a full Italian.*

*He was given to the state of Florida at the age of two after his parents were killed by stray bullets from the same family he would soon work for.*

*I returned for him first, not because I didn't want to tear the other two away from such misery, but because I had no power to do it.*

*Power was what I strived for from that day on. Control.*

*Arlo had filled out, and his height neared my eighteen-year-old body even if he was two years younger. His features were absent from any gentle lines and replaced by a stone-like appearance.*

*He'd walked into the room, missing the Velcro dark gray sack many left with. Apart from the clothes he wore, he left everything behind.*

*He had nothing.*

*And what I could offer wasn't better.*

*Salvatore left us alone inside the musky release room. But not after reminding me with his eyes of how much I could share out loud.*

*"You don't owe me anything. You can walk out of these walls and try living for once. I will always check up on you, and I can help you get started."*

*"Or?"*

*I gazed into his eyes, seeing nothing but emptiness.*

*"Or you can come with me. But I must say, my life isn't mine, and yours won't be either. What I do is not something I'd planned, but what had always been meant to be. It's ugly, painful. Cruel."*

*"Next to you?"*

*I nodded.*

*"And he's part of it." He nudged toward the door.*

*I didn't answer, and his head bobbed, putting the blurry pieces together.*

*"Before you answer, I must tell you, if you choose this path, it means you'll be with those who had a part of what happened to your parents."*

*"I could give two shits."*

*I had been wrong. These two years had done more than physical changes. They'd buried the boy I'd left behind.*

*"You are my family now. And you are wrong. I owe you my life."*

*I stared at him, and after a curt dip of my chin, I walked up to the door.*

*Arlo didn't follow until I said, "Don't worry, we'll return for them."*

I DIDN'T FINISH MY SENTENCE. I COULDN'T, AND I WOULDN'T.

"Understood." Arlo stepped away, and as I walked away, he briefed me quickly. "Security will be increased, and Viktor will have eyes on you both at all times. And you *will* have two tails as you drive. I will be inside the building, and six are infiltrating the catering crew. The others will be around the premises on standby."

*There he was.* With a dark smile, I twisted the knob. "Now don't go making my dick soft."

"Fuck off, Lucca. Don't question me either."

"Never did, *fratello*."

As I drove, all I desired was to find her emeralds, vibrant with life. Instead, I sat inside my car for far too long, moving pieces, strategizing, and following each trail and response. All flawed with blurry outcomes. One thing they all had in common was how clear they became once Enzo would take his father's seat. I didn't trust Mario's support at a council meeting. It was obvious he didn't care what could happen to Katia. However, I needed to find out the extent of their broken ties. I needed to request a council meeting before the wedding. With such a short timeline, and the publicity, I had to move quickly.

# XXV

## KATIA

I'D LOST CONTROL OF MY MIND AND GOALS.

Ruled by greed.

Wanting too much. Wanting what I thought I deserved. As if I knew the things I desperately craved. Respect, appreciation, want.

Who was I kidding? Lucca was immune to them all. Immune to my games and deceit. They had earned me nothing but a fickle heart.

While I stood over my knife casing, waiting for him, dressed as the *principessa* I was, waiting for a man, I knew nothing had changed. The never-ending circle that continuously repeated in my life was only different by yet another timeframe.

Only this time, I was a bride-to-be. A broken but spiteful-hearted woman whose demands have fallen into the hands of a beatless heart.

I knew this because today I'd awoken to an empty bed. Like another fuck. Sore and bruised like a soldier who'd complied with every order.

Even as I knew this, felt this, I still leaned forward and listened closely to the sound of his car tires nearing. I was eager for a night away from this house and with him by my side. But once the car was parked, the sound of his exit or the door closing was non-existent.

Minutes passed with no Lucca in sight, just a running engine.

I gazed out the window, but the tint was too dark to see through.

Something wasn't right.

The feeling had loomed over the house for hours. Viktor would usually wander throughout the house spontaneously, but today his demeanor had changed—alert and glued to his phone. And his easy smile had concealed information. He'd checked on me more than usual, and I misunderstood it as worry from yesterday's turn of events. But at this moment, it made sense, and I should have listened to my instincts.

Once again, I had been left in the dark, and I was sick of it.

The engine turned off, and Lucca stepped out. I couldn't see him clearly, and I hated not confirming my thoughts.

I waited and waited, but he never stepped into his study. Well, I was tired of waiting, so I walked toward the door and paused.

My eyes caught the two moves made since I'd last seen the unfinished chess game. And a crawling chill rolled over my body. I shook my head and left it behind.

I was really growing mad inside this house.

The closer I got to the door, the clearer the steps grew from the other side. I held the doorknob when the footfalls stopped.

One. Two. Three.

Nothing. They just stood quietly on the other side.

I pulled the door open, revealing dark eyes and an even darker aura. It pulled and swirled over me, bathing me in sin's addictive promise.

"Why did you hesitate?" I questioned.

"I don't hesitate." He stared deeply into my eyes.

While I didn't back down from our standoff, his immoral eyes fell over my cherry-stained lips.

"What's wrong?" I asked.

Lucca shook his head, dropping his gaze down on my body. As if his attention on me was needed. His eyes traveled along my neck and over the skin my dark-green dress forgot to cover.

His mood quickly changed to need while his eyes followed my silhouette, tracing each curve and mold on my body and lingering over the long slit of my dress skirt.

A possessive demon lured behind his eyes when they returned to mine.

"You look...good," he said carefully.

Lucca's hand lifted from his side, placing it on my bare back. A deep breath released from between his teeth at the feel of my skin. And with curled fingers and a dominating hold, he pulled me into him.

I felt *all* of him.

His hold never eased, it only tightened, causing discomfort from the bruise near my ribs.

"*Grazie.*" I breathed. "You look..." I thought of the right word, but like him, I didn't dare. I snickered and ran the tip of my tongue over my bottom lip. "Okay."

Lucca looked far from okay in a tuxedo, surrounded by vice and luring arrogance. Immoral, yet seductive. Sinful, but tempting. Brutal power and looks that matched his cold heart.

"How sore are you?"

I struggled with composure, and he did too as his fingers pressed into my flesh. In pain, I parted my mouth and lowered my gaze. The truth was, every step I took ached, every breath I exhaled burned. And assuring my dress concealed my ill marks was difficult to accomplish.

"Don't worry, I'll give you a few more hours."

I smiled at him. He'd meant for sex. Either way, I wasn't explaining.

I lifted my hands to his chest and caught his chest and caught his cautious stare. Raising a brow, I took his untied bow.

"*See,*" my eyes spoke as I slid my fingers across the smooth fabric and tied the bowtie in knots and loops until I created the perfect bow under his white collar and tanned inked neck.

I glanced back at his empty browns. They'd never left. Not once had they stirred away from me. Not away from my face, body, or eyes. Always on me. And while they gave nothing, they told me enough.

The madness inside. The chaos they would soon release.

"Lucca," I urged.

"If you are ready, we should get moving, we are already running late."

Fine. Let's keep playing.

Instead of agreeing with his request, I removed my gaze from him and walked deeper into the room, showcasing the low back dip in my dress.

"I just want to leave a note for Talia to hand over to Viktor." Innocently, I picked up a pen from his desk and looked for a clean notepad. "To remind him to pick up the boys from—"

"Katia, wait."

His warning was too late. I had the drawer open, and I saw a portion of myself captured on paper.

A picture of *me*.

In a coffee shop. Far from here, and in a time where there was no arrangement of us. Unaware, and relaxed in a life I now mourn.

My shoulders sank, and my fingers trapped the image unconsciously, clutching it tightly. I faced him.

Hurt and confusion veiled over me in a rash beat, and just as quickly, accusation followed.

"You lied."

"We don't have time for this," he said indifferently.

"You sa— You said."

"And I didn't lie."

Lucca closed the door behind him.

"Then…"

My heart hammered, shattering the peace I believed I had across the sea. I'd been so ignorant, thinking I had everything under control. How naive of me.

I gazed down at the picture again.

"If not you, who?"

He didn't answer.

My father didn't care enough for a picture, and if he had, all he had to do was speak to Nonno. And if I ruled Lucca out, there was just one man left.

One that would be interested enough to look into my past. One that would have me followed.

"Borrelli," I whispered in hatred. Disgusted. "Why do you have it?" I questioned. "I swear to you, Lucca. I will find out for myself, and you will not appreciate how I will acquire information if you don't speak!"

"Are you threatening to look for trouble, Katia?" he mocked. "You are too smart for a foolish damsel." Lucca leaned against the door, locking his ankles together. "You are past the immature and compulsive feelings that would lead you into real danger." He chuckled. "Don't peg me for a fool. You're a ruthless and deceitful little creature that has mastered the art of survival."

Creasing the picture back into its folded mold, I tossed it onto the desk and faced him. Lucca stood taller the closer I got to him.

"You are right. I'm too fucking smart." I shrugged and continued, "I know I'm the leverage that holds not just my *famiglia*, but now yours too from drowning. The ones you've actually fought to keep alive by trading another life without remorse for it." His gaze narrowed. "So tell me, Lucca. How is keeping me unaware of the bloodbath of our union a benefit for you?" My fingernails scraped his covered torso and swept up his shoulder. "A stray bullet could take away your leverage."

Lucca's hand snapped, capturing my neck and paralyzing me in his strong and desperate grip.

"It won't be a stray bullet, Katia."

*Huh?*

His lips lowered, and the threat kissed my ear. "You *are* the target."

Death hummed with a smile as she set her sights on me.

Knowledge was ice cold, paralyzing my fingers on his arms. Rigid muscles stiff from comprehension. And my heart trembled with confusion.

Women in La Cosa Nostra weren't killed by their own. Tragedies happened due to accidents, stray bullets, and outsiders. Women and children weren't meant to be targets.

I laughed.

I laughed so hard that Lucca pried me away, wary of my reaction.

"Well, I guess since the rules don't apply to me..."

"This is not funny."

My face fell.

"No, it is not. All you had to do was treat me as an equal, so at least I had a chance." A thought came to mind. "Am I in danger tonight?"

"Dire."

"And you weren't intending to tell me, were you?"

"No."

I walked out, numb. His honesty, too much for me to fight. I could've lashed out, asked for more details, but the answer would have been the same. So, I headed straight out the front door, leaving him behind.

A full moon glared and radiated its light in the grim night. But its shine never touched me. It only bounced against the two running and blacked out SUVs behind Lucca's black Maserati. I breathed in deeply, filling my lungs with the peace offered by the salty air, and opened the car door. Inside the car, alone and masked by darkness, I screamed.

I screamed with impotence at the men-ruled world around me.

Screamed because it didn't matter how hard I tried, I was powerless.

Screamed in failure.

Then I stopped, stared ahead, composed myself, and grazed the pads of my fingers across the weapons I had managed to conceal. There were only two, my favorite push dagger on my leg, and a thin stinger-knife hidden in my hair. Custom made to be fixed into my hair roots with a loop at the end. It was my last toy bought in Italy and I hadn't had the chance to play with it. At least tonight, I had it with me.

The passenger door opened and closed. Quickly, his scent infiltrated the cabin, and I faced the window. There was nothing for me to say, so I allowed the quiet to stall, and my eyes wandered to the side mirror. As expected, SUVs followed, and the gates closed behind our tail. As we rolled out on the long road that led out of his private property, streetlights cast through our wake. When we passed one that flickered and another that was busted, he took a long, annoyed deep breath.

*What was it with him and streetlamps?*

Maybe one day, I could bust each one that trailed down his grand fortress. Maybe then I could get a pure reaction from him.

"I don't trust your father. Hence the reason I needed a date for our wedding." Lucca shook the silence. "And I don't trust *you*," he sliced. Lucca's words continued cruelly. "I found the first dead body in the alley of Pecattos. One of my clubs. I didn't think much about it, it's Miami. The second, though, was deliberately tossed by one of my abandoned warehouses. Only a Cosa Nostra member would know I own it."

I didn't dare interrupt him, too scared to stop the truth from flowing.

"I took care of those who carried out the killing. Amateurs, outsiders. That's when I obtained the picture. Borelli was going after what he'd admired from afar for so long. The one person who was promised to him, and the one who was taken from him. You."

I clutched the seat belt, nails scratching the smooth strap closer.

"I've stood my ground and attacked when the right opportunities crossed to the point that not much was left to destroy, and while New York had many casualties, it has turned your father *desperate*. Without Enzo on his seat, I don't see this treaty lasting long even after our marriage." I felt his gaze. "It wasn't meant to last anyway."

What did he mean by that?

"But yesterday, five more bodies were found throughout the night."

"I fail to see how those connect," I murmured.

Lucca's long pause sealed my dread.

"They were all similar versions of you."

My heart broke for those lives, and I felt a change that approached with eerie calm. As if the grain I'd held on to for far too long had been picked. It was so small, yet so valuable to keep for so long. And I accepted the hostile takeover. Hope was for the weak.

"Why are you telling me this now?"

"Like you said, you won't do me any good dead."

Leave it to the rich and arrogant to party for the unfortunate and call it compassion, rolling in cars that could build shelters, and wearing clothes that could warm hundreds and smiles that never faltered by the amount of filler spent on faces instead of filling bellies.

I roamed around them like a hypocrite in my dark-forest-green dress, secretly imagining who they would be without their money.

If they truly wanted to help stop hunger in America, and not just use this charity as a tax writeoff, they could use their money to assure it was spent correctly. But they didn't, because they never truly cared.

"Smile," Lucca whispered into my ear as groups of men and couples nodded his way.

His embrace seemed private to lingering eyes as he played the part of dangerous mogul and doting fiancé. I inched away, laughing as if he'd said something hilarious.

Lucca's eyes narrowed.

I smirked.

As we strutted around, between handshakes, he asked me, "Are you having bridesmaids?"

I hadn't given much thought to our wedding planning, hadn't even cared to ask Mrs. Greco or Talia if they needed help. This marriage wasn't out of love, much less a celebration of two people wishing to spend the rest of their time together. It was arranged. A simple contract that tied promises and power. I was treating it as such. A business deal I had no interest in meddling in between. But now that I understood the severity of what was at stake, I couldn't push it away anymore. I would happily help with the sole purpose of remaining away from my father. At least with this heartless demon, I felt attraction. I knew this devil and understood him. I was more afraid of the unknown. *Call it a win.*

But one thing I was certain of, Mrs. Greco's daughter was not making my dress, and I would walk down the aisle until meeting Lucca's monster at the altar.

But it was only a few weeks away, and I needed a dress.

"I don't really have girlfriends," I said, unconcerned. "I haven't seen my cousins or spoken to them since I left the States, so…" I caught his profile. "Why? Were you planning on—"

"It can be just us two."

I wanted to disagree, to tell him if he wanted his family next to him, I understood. But I didn't. Deep down, I didn't need the reminder of how alone I truly was.

A waiter passed by, tan skin, dark eyes, and a tray filled with champagne flutes. He stopped in front of us, glanced over Lucca, and gave him a curt nod.

"Champagne?"

Surprised by Lucca, I stood stunned when he reached for two crystal glasses.

I didn't take a sip.

"It's fine, Katia." His lips moved against the rim.

"Was that one of—"

His eyes cut me off. "We aren't alone."

I took a sip and savored the bubbly and rich taste on my tongue.

Music played softly, ballads of classic tones that mixed well with conversations without overpowering the lies spoken. But after the fourth couple, I was growing tired of small talk.

Conversations that were forgettable by the next person. The men spoke, leaving the women to chat alone, as if I needed to talk about their recent vacation, or the new clothing line that had been released. And when the men finished, their plus one gushed over meeting me, expressing their happiness and joy for the delightful time they'd spent with me.

I never even spoke. Just a few nods, small smiles, and the occasional, *"Of course."*

We moved from one end of the villa to the other in a historic mansion my eyes couldn't stop appreciating. A structure that took me back to the Mediterranean Sea. Tall Spanish arches and greenery that swept inside in vines. Detailed tiles and stones merged together, reminding me of the countryside of Tuscany my grandfather would take me to visit when younger. It was old, beautiful, and every detail screamed wealth as did the people inside.

"How long do we have to stay?" I asked when their backs were far enough to hear.

"We'll leave after the action."

"When does it start?" I asked. I couldn't keep up this charade for much longer. My body had grown stiff, hiding the pain inside.

Lucca chuckled darkly, and his hand seized my lower back.

He took me away from the chatter. Each step further away we took, the easier I could breathe in. It wasn't until the humid air and breeze hit my skin that I relaxed.

Two females spoke far by the outside courtyard while we remained at a distance and under the low-lit and open porch by the corner.

"Did you take anything?"

"Hm?"

"Your body leans to your left. Your steps while graceful, drag. And your breathing is shallow." He cleared his throat. "Don't worry, no one else can tell. All they can see is power and confidence."

He knew. Of course he did. Lucca didn't miss anything.

"It must have worn off."

His eyes shifted to the door. "Whenever you are ready."

I didn't utter a word, and Lucca bathed in the shadows, leaning against a pillar, watching me.

Somehow his eyes unraveled me by the thought of seeing through me.

Could he see the decay within me? The spoiled feelings? How my survival persona promised to make it out alive even if it meant with blood staining my hands?

"Do you have a favorite flower you would like at our wedding?"

I shook my head.

"A particular champagne? Wine?"

I shook my head again.

"Outside or inside?"

My eyes lowered.

"I don't know if you mean it, or if you are trying to make this difficult."

I thought about it for a second.

"Outside wedding, inside reception. Black and white, not a touch of color. Covered with enough flowers to drown the smell of corruption." *And death.* "Sweet and yet tangy, not too dry. And as for the cake?" I met his eyes. "Cherry flavored."

Lucca smiled.

He *smiled*.

"Done." His smile disappeared. "Are you ready?"

As ready as I could be.

"*Sí*."

The auction went on and on. And the people we were seated with were obnoxious spenders. Deep pocket politicians that would often whisper into Lucca's ear. I leaned closer to Lucca, trying to muffle the endless scents and perfumes my nose couldn't take any more as a headache threatened. I focused on his familiar aroma, wishing it blocked all others. My eyes had trouble adjusting to the blinding shimmers of dresses everywhere I turned, and while the room's light had dimmed, the chandeliers never took a break.

The man on the stage screamed out bids, firing words rapidly without restrain. Overloaded with noise, scents, and light, a metal taste filled my mouth.

"You are flushed and not the kind I like to see," Lucca uttered straight ahead.

"*You* like a kind?" I challenged weakly.

His head dipped, capturing my eyes.

I looked away.

Lucca liked a certain blush, and thinking about the activity that created such a blush almost made me forget the pounding in my head. Almost, because the taste in my mouth lingered as bile warned.

"Katia?" Concern rang in his whisper, and when I didn't meet his gaze, he stood. "Come."

I took his outstretched palm without question. Lucca curled his arm and placed my hand in its crease.

As we walked in unison away from the crowd with my hand gripping his jacket, I couldn't wait to be inside the restroom. Alone.

The longer we strolled through the surrounded gold accents of the hall, my vision played in swirls. Curves and patterns that danced the deeper we walked.

*Breathe.*

I did, and I centered my eyes on one spot to ease the rising nausea. A lady walked out from a door and into the hallway with a smile aimed at her partner, who was waiting for her across the open door.

"Not that one."

Confused, Lucca led me past the happy couple, and the bathroom door opened again. I peered between the two women who'd stepped out. Revolted by the laughter that erupted from the cramped space, I didn't argue.

We took a left and continued.

"There." Lucca pointed to the upcoming door. "It should be quiet."

He opened the door for me, but I stopped him from entering.

"I'll be just a minute." My eyes pleaded.

Taking one look at me, he nodded. But he didn't move. Instead, he scanned the empty room. I, too, turned and faced a closed stall.

There was so much pink and gold that it was nearly impossible not to be perplexed by it. It was too busy and different from the earth and calming tones from the rest of this villa.

I lowered to the ground and glanced under the low opening. The stall was empty. Immediately I regretted doing so when a rush overwhelmed me. My hand shot out to Lucca's chest to stabilize my body.

"Katia?"

God, how I hated the pity in his voice. I used all the strength I had left and pushed my hand deeper into his chest until there was enough space to close the door in his face.

"Katia!" his voice warned.

I locked the door, resting my forehead against it.

"It's empty, Lucca. Please."

The silence that followed wasn't reassuring knowing Lucca would be insufferable if he didn't get his way, but I kept him out.

*Get it together, Katia.*

Taking deep breaths, I made my way to the gold sink. I let the cold water run and placed my hands beneath. A sigh of relief flew past my parted lips, and I raised my head to stare at my reflection.

My eyes had grown dopey with red lines coursing through them when they should've been a clear white. Cheeks filled with red, and swollen lips that couldn't seem to close shut.

Migraines were a bitch.

It'd been years since I had one, but when they came, they completely shook me into a stupor. Usually caused by stress or too much stimulation, it was my mind's way to shut down for peace, since it was the only time I would allow weakness to prevail.

But after a day thinking of the deaths, the threats, my father, Lucca's honesty, and still trying to parade around a room filled with expensive chaos, my reeling mind had said *enough*.

Breathing through the crawling anxiety, I splashed water onto my face, carefully avoiding my eyes, and melted with relief. Over and over, chilled water cooled my skin, and my breathing strengthened. As I bent against the counter, water dripped from my face, and I waited for it to dry on its own. For the droplets to continue their nurture. When the last drop clashed, I turned the faucet off, and looked up.

*Motherfucker.*

This couldn't be happening.

A chuckle bounced out of my chest as I picked a paper towel from the counter and dried my hands without removing my eyes from the mirror. But the more I stared, the more it dawned on me, it was not vision.

I wasn't alone.

"Not now, okay?" I whispered a warning.

The reflection hesitated as it didn't expect my reply, or demeanor. And as he stalled, my eyes wandered over his attire.

Black leather gloves, black tuxedo, black eyes.

He was here for me. My warning wouldn't change that.

But I was so tired, drained, and irritated. He couldn't have picked a better timing.

With a loud groan and a deep breath, I tossed the used paper towel and faced him.

In the corner of my eye the stall door gently swung wide open. A mistake I wouldn't commit again by not clearing the room thoroughly.

Because there would be a next time. I wasn't dying in a pink bathroom.

*I wasn't dying today.*

I rolled my shoulders back with a grin as the sound of his switchblade popped out. A knife fight, I snickered.

I was losing it.

I closed my eyes and counted to three.

One.

Two.

*Three.*

My eyes opened into the void.

Pure blackness.

I heard his first step before I saw it coming, and in one quick movement, my hand fished under my dress slit.

His second stride came, and my fingers twirled my blade into my palm.

Ready, I watched his towering and bulky figure launch my way. Quickly, I ducked and slipped away from his blade. But he twisted rapidly with one foot in the air. Arching my body forward, I eased his kick on my back from striking me at full force. I staggered and glanced over to the locked door.

The man slammed me with an impact that knocked me to the ground.

I groaned when my hands failed to keep my face from hitting the tile floor.

"Katia?" Lucca's muffled voice shook the pain away.

"LUCCA!"

*Thump.*

I gasped in agony at the blazing shock wave that exploded through my face. A full-on collision against the tile by the powerful hands of a man. I tried fighting the compressing weight of his body, but it was useless. My strength compared to his was non-existent in such a position.

*Thump.*

The taste of metal flooded my tongue, and I cried out against the solid floor after the second impact. But he didn't let go. Instead, he harshly shoved the left side of my face deeper into the ground.

I fought through the fatigue, the torture, and his weight, but his violent hands never swayed.

"You bitch!" he said angrily, knowing there was no other way he would leave this room but as a corpse after I'd called out for Lucca. "You will pay for—"

I couldn't care less.

Using his brief speech to my advantage, I curled my finger tightly around my push dagger, and drove it into his thigh.

Curses and groans filled the room, and I repeatedly rammed my blade into his leg, knowing each time I pulled it out, the deeper damage I left behind. His weight shifted from his flesh tearing, and I rolled out of his hold.

The scorching burn from my beaten face fueled me with violent madness. And as I watched him finally see me as the threat I was, I vowed to send him to hell myself so he could feel real fire.

But the coward dropped his knife as he reached behind his waist.

I couldn't allow him to retrieve his gun. If I did, I was as good as dead.

I ran up to him the same moment his gun appeared in my view. My dagger flew, and the gun clattered on the floor along with my blade.

His hand bled and he took a step back. However, the blood from his leg had pooled across the floor, causing him to slip down hard onto the ground.

"You…" He seethed through his bare teeth.

I was on him, straddling his hips, unable to stop.

To see it through.

Death, claiming his eyes.

Hell, opening its gates.

And for eternity to condemn his soul.

Strong hands wrapped around my neck. Clasping tightly and cutting off the flow of air from filtering into my lungs.

I held my breath to keep the panic from rising and raised my knife-wielding hand above me.

One moment, I was losing consciousness, and the next, I had pierced the stinger knife right into his throat. Dragging it out, I focused on his skin. The vein that popped with mock.

With a target in sight, I stabbed the needle blade again and again.

Spurts of blood coated my body, splashing red showers against my face as his grip weakened.

"I told you," I gritted out between jabs "Not. Now."

His hands struggled to reach his wounds as his mouth widened with gargling chokes while I fiercely drained the life out of him. After his arms flopped to his side, and his eyes stared vacantly at me, I stopped.

I pulled out the pick knife from his neck and dragged my body off him. My ass slid against the wet floor until I sat against the wood of the stall, watching blood pour in crying rivers down his flesh.

With long breaths and stretched legs, I studied his black eyes glazing into pits of nothingness.

"And in heels," I croaked, clearing my fiery throat.

The door burst open with splintering wood chips scattering all around.

Lucca's eyes widened when he looked down at me, and he wasn't alone. Arlo stood right next to him, mirroring Lucca's features.

I could only imagine how I looked under their gaze. Sitting in front of a dead body. Filthy with the same blood that decorated the bathroom walls and doors. Calm and at ease after the bloodbath I'd created.

"Katia?"

Lucca's hurried steps neared, and I raised my palm.

He stopped.

I stood, walked away from the dead body to retrieve my blood-soaked best friend from the floor, and straightened.

I offered Lucca a small smile, and both sets of eyes filled with alarm.

"I feel better," I said to Lucca.

But madness still rocked me in its possessive arms.

Lucca continued to respect my wish to stay away. To give me time to compose myself. It was what I had tried to do this whole time, and never got the chance to do.

Both men followed my every step with their gaze, but Lucca roamed every inch of my body. When I faced the mirror, I understood why.

The words bloody and filthy wouldn't be enough to describe what was staring back at me.

The sight of me was morbid. Washed in crimson filth with a busted lip, a split brow that wouldn't stop oozing the flow of a red trickle. I stepped closer and spit the metal taste into the golden sink.

I met the savage of his eyes through the mirror, and when I assured him I was fine, I noticed my wine-colored smeared teeth.

His features clouded, and his head craned, disturbed by my appearance.

"Are you hurt?"

I shook my head. "Can we go now?"

Arlo laughed somewhere in the room, but Lucca didn't find it funny, and I hadn't meant it to be humorous.

Lucca's jaw locked, his neck and face muscles jumping with impotence, and he took a step closer.

Ignoring him, I placed my blades into the sink, and I turned the faucet back on. The water turned a shade of pink as I rinsed my hands and face. I was eager to get the stench of *his* body off me. And I used paper towels to wipe away the dried-up blood from my arms.

It didn't matter how long I spent on each arm, I always found a new spot to clean.

With a dampened towel, I dabbed and cleaned my neck, shoulders, and chest. All I had managed to do was smudge it into angry streaks.

"Stop," he uttered so close I felt the heat of his body behind me.

I did what he asked. And when his hands connected to my hips, twisting me to face him, I didn't fight it. I didn't fight *him*.

His fingers gently glided up my waist, and I closed my eyes when they held my face kindly. Slowly, his thumb ran over my lips, and I hissed.

"I'm sorry," Lucca apologized.

My eyes fluttered open, and as I watched guilt in his eyes, I knew he meant for not getting to me faster.

But *I'd* locked him out. I purposely didn't allow him inside the room to check it thoroughly. It was me who recklessly pushed him out.

I didn't blame him.

I didn't blame him for not coming in and saving me on a white horse.

This was my life.

Just as much as it was his.

And in a life together, there would always be a threat. A new foe who would try to take one of us from each other. Someone who would want his seat.

Lucca pulled me to him, and I accepted his embrace, breathing him in and curling into his chest a moment longer to ease the adrenaline shudders that coursed through me. I held him tight, needing his strength and body to swallow the visions that flooded my soul.

"Yes, she's not harmed."

Arlo must have asked for my well-being.

"Here, put this on. Viktor is bringing the car over to the side exit."

I pulled away, and Lucca shrugged his suit jacket off and placed it over my shoulders. It was useless. My dress was ruined.

Shaking my head, I looked up at him.

"Don't worry, any cameras will be disabled, and our path will be clear all the way to the car."

My head bobbed up and down, then my gaze slid where the body lay.

"Arlo will take care of it."

"Okay," I said, and Lucca pulled me closer to him. "Wait!" I stopped, turned, and retrieved my blades from the sink.

I knew his mind reeled as he watched me tuck my blades back to where they belong, but I didn't have it in me to decipher his thoughts. At least not now. My attention was solely on my weapons.

After I concealed my knives again and stood tall, I said. "Ready?"

Lucca closed his eyes briefly and smiled tightly.

A dangerous smile that couldn't hide the depths of immorality.

I glanced down one last time, finding a familiar pair of boots. I followed their trail up to the leaning and crossed-armed Arlo. A wicked smile rested on his lips, before he gave me a light dip of his chin.

My void replied with the same smile.

"Take me away." This time, I went with Lucca without protest.

As he had described, no one saw us walking away from the bathroom and through the hall. Or slipping out of the villa where his car ran in park.

Ilias's eyes landed on me from across the top of the sleek roofed car. Moonlight shone over his features as he struggled to hide his displeasure.

But it wasn't toward me, because when his gaze landed on Lucca, I saw the trouble he couldn't hide.

"Your brother doesn't look too happy."

"Have you seen your face, Katia?" Lucca replied sharply, but it smoothed when I flinched. "Who could be?"

Bruised face and bruised egos everywhere. The *irony*, I chuckled.

Lucca opened the passenger door and waited for me to slide inside the black leather seat before shutting it. The dashboard illuminated the cabin as gusts of cool air filtered inside, and while I waited alone, I groaned in pain. Adrenaline still pumped, but the darkness calmed the raging emotions revealing my battered body to my consciousness. And while I rested deeper into the cushion, the stronger the waves of discomfort approached. The stronger the pain knocked and fatigue settled.

I wasn't ready for them—wasn't ready to *feel*. But as time coursed, and minutes changed on the dash, it was unitable.

Time only granted the dead.

With power and sinful grace, Lucca entered the car. His composure hung by a weak rope, shaking and losing sight of control. I quieted my aching cries that my quivering lips let out and faced him.

Lucca hadn't moved an inch, with eyes ahead, and one hand crushing the steering wheel of the parked car.

He looked stoic, and yet I was afraid of speaking. Of breaking the hard features that held his composure weakly.

Seeing as he struggled to contain his ire terrified me.

"I…" Lucca began, and his gaze fell on me, conflicted with brutal cruelty and concern. "Are you…"

He was speechless. Tongue-tied by *empathy?*

"Was he…"

Startled by his inability to rein in his cruel thoughts, I spoke. "I'm fine, Lucca." His eyes lingered. "I feel the same as you would after taking a life."

Snapping his eyes back to the windshield, he uttered. "You don't." His voice lowered. "I seek further bloodshed."

I pondered his admission, and as I tried to comprehend the rush, the pain, and death, I didn't see how I felt much different than what he'd described.

I had been picked, attacked, and remained hunted by a man. A man I wished for death, and a city I wanted burned to the ground along with the men who followed him. A syndicate I wanted stripped from power.

I wanted the seat of California empty and forgotten.

Lucca and I weren't so different. I too sought bloodshed, but in numbers only God had the power to take.

In a way, I thanked Borelli for what he'd created—a void that could only be filled by retribution.

Soon, I would show them all the power I carried.

Because I had one thing they didn't—*Lucca.* He would hunt, strip, and burn it all for *me.*

Lucca was my weapon, just as he was becoming my weakness.

"He wasn't my first kill, Lucca. And he won't be my last."

I flinched at the sound of his hand striking the wheel.

Lucca lost it.

"Damn it, Katia. This isn't how you should react," he roared. "How you should feel, or how any of it was meant to happen!"

Our eyes connected.

"He won't be my last because being with you is a death sentence." I raised my voice. "The same sentence I was born with by having a father as a *boss.*" My shoulder rose. "It just changed handlers." Closing my eyes, I set the truth free. "*We* didn't get to choose this life. But it has always been our path, Lucca. Far from normal and unconventional. Why do you think the outcome could be any different?"

Lucca didn't want to see it. He fought against my words as his head shook and his teeth gritted. Even then, he was too smart to not believe in them. He had been trying so hard to keep me far from a world I'd been raised into, apart from the tainted blood that swept in my body. An image he'd already formed and strived to come true. He held on to the vision of how it should be, and how it was meant to be, but had forgotten *I* was a part of it. He'd forgotten the curse that came with a principessa. And he never got to see the young me.

The broken girl.

The beaten girl.

The women I'd fought to become.

"Come here."

I looked over the small space left by his broad and large body on the driver's side and shook my head.

"We both can't fit—"

His hand gripped my hair fiercely, pulling me to sit on his lap. I gasped as his hands manhandled me to how they saw fit. Not once gentle, even if my appearance begged for it. And as my leg dug painfully into the door, the other straddled over the middle console and into the back of his seat.

My neck leaned awkwardly to the side as it hit the ceiling. I ached by its stiffness and position, but Lucca brought my head down to his shoulder and released my hair. Our breaths labored as they both fought in twisted want, for a dose of unhealthy need. To mix desperation, and pain into the sadistic desire our bodies could deliver.

Lucca slipped his coat off my shoulders, revealing my red stained skin and ruined dress. I pulled away from his chest to see his eyes devouring my skin, and his fingers itching for my split lip. He tugged it, and a sharp sting tore my mouth apart. Warm liquid spread over the edge and he pulled my head closer to him. Lucca's tongue slipped and swirled over my bleeding lip, easing the sting by his nipping and tender mouth.

His sounds of satisfaction by tasting me mimicked my own.

Pain and pleasure, a sweet brew.

Unstable and raving for more, our lips deepened.

Shaking and grasping for more, our hands fumbled.

Mine, capturing his belt and working on his pants button. His, raising my ass with gripping fists only to shove me down on his dick once I freed him.

A moan shuddered from my throat as he was buried deep inside me.

"Lucca," I cried, burning with desire.

It was uncomfortable, desperate, and carnal the way we couldn't wait, and I was rendered to pure bliss by need as he rocked my hips.

"Ahh!"

"I know, baby. But I need to get us home so I can take you properly."

"Yes," I whimpered.

"Do you want to come?" His breath skated over my ear.

"Sì!"

"Then move," he growled.

Lucca wasn't going to help, and I didn't know what caused my hips to obey his order, but maybe it was the thought of having free rein to fuck him fast, slow, or deeply. However *I* wanted to. But slow wasn't going to get me off, not now. Not while the cabin heated and sex swirled inside. Not while my crazy still gripped me tightly and death waved from afar.

I wiggled, splitting the dress further up to find the leverage to move in such a confined space. I ignored the burn coming from my muscles, the cuts, and the ache of each breath. I omitted everything if only to feel him close, to have this moment with him.

I rode Lucca while he rode over Miami's streets at high speeds.

Fast, messy…crazily.

# XXVI

## LUCCA

KATIA WASN'T JUST GOOD WITH A KNIFE, KATIA HAD MASTERED THE skill of manipulating a blade. The bastard who died under her hands spoke its truth. Even with an injured wrist and bruised body, she continued as if it was in her nature.

Her eyes were vacant when I'd found her sitting in pools of blood, covered in sweat and gore. The scene had never bothered me if it wasn't for seeing *her* in it. If it wasn't for the paralyzing dread of thinking it was *her* blood.

The sight of her grim appearance had violently rendered me into a spiral madness. A fucking rage I couldn't contain but tried to control. And in those savage minutes, I'd only made it through by keeping my gaze strictly into the life that swirled in her shining emeralds.

The one thing that reminded me that even while they were lost, she was still here with *me*.

And while she'd admitted to killing another man before, I'd placed her in a situation where she had to take another. By doing so, I had taken a piece of her I had never intended. Because while I had wanted to break her, use her, I'd never meant for her and *Death* to be acquaintances.

That was something for me and my demon to bear.

Katia laid her head on my shoulder after coming hard over me. She never moved away, and I didn't push her. Somehow, her weight calmed my heartbeat. And her warmth reassured me of her existence.

I ran my hand across her messy hair as her adrenaline washed away in rapid currents, leaving her exhausted and jaded. My little deceitful creature was losing the fight as her frame molded deeper against mine.

"We are here."

Katia hummed but didn't sway an inch. We stayed in the silence and the darkness for a while longer. But the quiet didn't bring me peace. I thought of what Arlo had found, what Ilias knew, and what Viktor saw. I thought of my next move in grave detail and the city I would soak in crimson.

"Lucca."

Katia tore me away from the slaughter in my mind, and I placed my heavy hand on her back.

"I don't think I can make it upstairs."

Fuck, the sorrow in her voice stung, knowing she felt ashamed by her admission.

I battled between what I wanted to do and what I *should* do. What was okay and how far I was willing to give. *If* I even could.

I took care of those I cared for, and never in such a way. It was always from afar while moving pieces for their future, for their safety.

I didn't know what to say, so I didn't utter a word.

Pulling her bottom higher, I buckled my pants and opened the door. I tried not to embrace what I was doing. How was I going to carry her up as a lover would? Instead I focused on staying steady and maneuvering her body and legs around my sides.

When I took the first step onto the stone entry, her hand wrapped against my neck and her fingernails curled behind my head. Slow and tender, her fingers thanked me, and I clenched my jaw to the shudder that crept.

I wrestled between asking her to stop and giving her what she needed. I didn't want to fight. I didn't want to talk. Not now, so for this moment, I let her win.

The front door opened wide, and my gaze snapped over to my brother, who kept Wex and Vino by his side. Viktor's hair was a mess, and his face was without color. Stony blue eyes held mine in chaos, then fell onto her. He could only see the back of her hair, and his lips curled by not confirming what he'd seen on the screen. While he didn't have eyes inside the bathroom, Viktor had watched every step we took out of the manor.

Viktor's attention bounced back to me, and I raised my hand.

*Soon.*

A quick nod agreed, but his eyes watched her hand placement over me for a moment longer. He then pulled the door further open for me.

I left him behind and headed up the stairs with the mutts in tow.

"*Myjesto,*" I ordered them to stay by the bedroom door in Russian. Wex automatically listened, while Vino hesitated, but finally obeyed with a loud groan.

I set the lights in the room the way she preferred them, a low glimmer, and continued toward the bathroom. With her limbs wrapped around me, I pulled the shower door open and adjusted the water temperature.

A bath would've settled her aching body better, but I didn't want her to soak in his blood. I wanted it off her skin and drained into the pipes and down the sewer along with the rest of the filth of this city.

Katia's legs loosened, and her arms unraveled from around my neck. I held her waist as she steadied her feet, and when my gaze lifted, I tensed.

Her face had deteriorated since the short time I'd last seen it. Her neck had deepened in dark hues of purples and furious red prints. Black outlines took over the edge of her left eye as it swelled, creasing the heavy temples near shut. The corner of her brow was smudged with dried blood from a gash, and her lips stayed parted.

Katia turned her back on me and slipped the thin fabric of her dress off her shoulders. I didn't see a zipper I could help lower, and her ass wouldn't allow the slim textile on her waist to fall by itself.

The only way she could remove it was by lifting it over her head. Katia tugged down, not even attempting to raise her arms to pull.

"Let me." I touched her arm, and she relaxed in consent.

I stepped closer. Feeling her warmth, I caged her body in with my hands low on her hips until I felt the ripped slit of her dress. Fisting my hand tightly with fabric, I pulled it apart, tearing it in quick jerks until she was bare.

Quietly, Katia entered the shower, shutting the glass door and the vision of her bruised body into a rotting memory.

Fuck.

I left the bathroom and kept the door cracked enough to hear, but I couldn't tolerate the wrath, the ire that pricked my fingers, the rage to set loose the demon. I wasn't meant to care, to nurture wounds, or take away pain. I did the opposite.

Wex and Vino didn't follow as I stepped out of the room.

My footfalls mixed with another pair that neared, and when I passed the last picture frame, Viktor came into view. A glass bottle of water in one hand, and a few other objects in the other.

His eyes peered behind me, seeing the bedroom door ajar along with the sound of running water, and when he spoke, he chose Russian.

"она в порядке?" *Is she…okay?* his native tongue fired.

I transitioned to the language and spoke back in Russian knowing our conversation would remain safe that way.

"*Da.*"

"I thought you might need this."

Viktor offered me the contents in his hands. I had bandages and a first aid kit under the sink, but he'd brought the medicated ointment I would need. It was made in Russia, and Viktor had introduced it to us when he was old enough to afford smuggling it into the States. It wasn't regulated by the standards of this country. Too strong and dangerous they'd once labeled it, and yet it had healed many wounds. We mainly used it on others, too stubborn to accelerate the ease of pain. But I couldn't tolerate her pain. Not in this way.

I took the chilled water, ointment, a pill, and the gentle cleaning shit he offered with a silent thank you.

"What did you see?"

"I went through everything. They slipped inside and camped for hours."

"They?"

"Yes. Three men in total. They covered the three bathrooms on the main floor."

I shook my head.

"One of those was filled with women."

"They would've waited for the right time."

Viktor's eyes lowered, and his mouth curled with disgust. When he looked back at me, he said, "When I hacked into their surveillance, they'd already infiltrated the gala. I didn't get access to the previous footage until it was too late."

Viktor was a perfectionist. Nothing he did was easily obtained, and he worked carefully. Something slipping from his fingers was rare, almost impossible. He placed blame on himself for what had happened, but knowing him, it had been out of his power. Viktor had been behind a computer, while I had been feet away from the bastard.

"It won't happen again."

I believed him because Viktor would always strive for perfection.

"I know, *brat.*" *Brother.*

The water stopped running, and I took it as time for my return.

"Oh, Lucca."

I glanced back.

"Arlo caught one of them."

I smiled with the promise of pacifying an inch of my bloodthirst. "Tell him to take him to the warehouse by the canal. I'll meet you there."

I shut the door behind me, placed the water bottle and small pill next to her side table, and turned.

Katia stood tall with a towel wrapped around her. The shower awakened her spirit after adrenaline had extinguished it. It also allowed me to see her features more clearly without the remains of *him*.

The superficial wounds would heal in a few days, but the degenerate need to punish wouldn't until I made those who touched what was *mine* pay.

Her eyes questioned the items in my hands, and her brow furrowed.

I tossed the rest onto the bed and straightened.

Katia's spirit fell.

"You're leaving."

"I am," I agreed. "You should use the ointment before resting."

I turned to leave. One step too short because her hand held me tightly from moving farther away. I lowered my head and spun to glance down at her.

She didn't say a word. Didn't ask for me to stay. She couldn't. Not again. Her hand weakened, releasing her hold but still waiting.

Big green eyes stared at me, holding me still as did the silence between us.

"Take the pill," I ordered.

She didn't hesitate, she simply did what I asked.

"Now put on the ointment."

This time, she held my gaze for a minute too long.

The knowledge of failing to protect and keep her safe weighed deeply inside.

In the dim light and silent request, I shed out of my clothes and her eyes grew. Quickly she snatched the rectangle box off the table and hurried inside the bathroom.

I tossed my soiled clothing on a nearby chaise while walking to my side of the bed. I pulled the covers and the top sheet down and picked up my phone.

**I'll be there in fifteen.**

My latest text read, and I clicked it back off when I felt her presence.

Quietly, her footfalls tumbled one after another and her silhouette neared the bed.

I lay down. She dropped her towel and slipped next to me. She didn't move closer or utter a word. I slid the cover over her body before staring at the globes of faded light above with one hand behind my head.

Waiting.

*Fifteen minutes*, Arlo had promised.

Katia struggled to get comfortable, but if she lay still instead of fighting the pill she'd taken to do its job, sleep would claim her.

She turned in my direction, and I knew what was coming next. Almost anticipating it.

Katia's hand seeking out my body.

I didn't tense, I accepted it in the darkness for the short few minutes I would allow it.

"Lucca?" her sweet Italian accent called me.

"Hm…"

"If I asked you for something, would you see it through?" The Italian rolled off her lips.

Her eyes were closed, her breathing steady, and her cracked lip faced the shadows.

I pondered over her question and removed my gaze from her face, at what *I* had done.

And while Katia could ask for many things, I knew after staring into her vacant irises and blood-covered body that this promise wouldn't be easy to see through.

Even then, I warned in our tongue. "Yes, so be careful what you ask of me next."

She moved closer to me, placing her head against my side.

Groggily, her Italian wrestled slumber as it uttered, "Good. Because I don't just want Borelli dead. I want California to fall."

While Katia slipped into stupor, I lay still in the silence, moving pieces in my head, working my mind in riddles of destruction. Loopholes that could swift through minuscule windows but caused madness—hysteria.

And I was a master of it.

But for now, I had one loose end to handle. And after taking one last look at her sleeping body, I abandoned her warmth and dressed in all black.

Wex and Vino sat attentive. I opened the door and gestured for them to go to her, then closed the door behind them.

I had things to see through.


I took each step eagerly down the trail to the abandoned warehouse, itching to get my hands dirty. Thirsty for red. My demon was loose, and my soul was gone. All I wanted was punishment.

Clouds rolled over the moon and the night hid me in its darkness. Dew spread through the still canal, rolling in a thick blanket of malice, matching the cruel thoughts in my head.

Leaving the eerie silence behind, I stepped inside the wet and rusted metal building.

Old fishing nets and broken boat parts scattered throughout the building on the cracked floor. The smell of motor oil and gasoline lingered even after years of vacancy. The only thing that stood out was the concrete block room at the end we'd built.

Arlo, Viktor, and Ilias quieted down as they heard my heavy footsteps near. They were waiting by the closed door that trapped the future dead.

They all stood, alert.

"You don't need to stay, Ilias."

I offered him the option, but with crossed arms and displeasure marking his features, he shook his head.

"Your choice." I looked away from him and turned to Arlo.

"Where?" I asked.

"I found him in the tree line, waiting for his getaway driver to pick him up," Arlo answered.

"Did it ever show up?"

"No."

I scoffed. Like rats, they scattered in fear, leaving their own behind.

"I recognize him. He was the one who had entered the first bathroom you passed," Viktor added.

With a nod of acknowledgment, I pushed past them and opened the door.

Wet concrete and blood filled my lungs. A smell I found appealing when mixed in cries, and as I leered over the bound sitting body whose face remained low to the ground, I couldn't wait to hear him wail in pain.

I picked a cigarette out of my case and returned it to my pocket. All I needed was one drag to slow my thoughts from killing him by just his sight.

I flicked my lighter open in one swift movement of my wrist and rolled the gear until a spark became a flame.

He looked up.

"What's your name?" I asked, while lighting the cigarette.

He didn't answer, and I took a long pull, watching as the amber ate the tobacco away. Slowly, I blew the smoke out and asked again.

"What is your name?"

Hopeless brown eyes glanced in my direction, while my three men surrounded the shadows of the room. It was pitiful, pathetic. The sight of all the fight gone from his body. He knew what would come of him, and soon. But he took the idea like the coward he was, without an inch of dignity.

These were the worst.

Puppy eyed pussies that faced defeat easily.

"Da-Dario," he stuttered.

*Dario.*

Of Italian descent, roughly thirty to thirty-two years of age, with a nose that had taken too many beatings as it rested crookedly to its right. A left cauliflower ear, and a scar by his jaw.

A fighter.

Well, not tonight.

And by the looks of his appearance it hadn't taken much to take him down.

I took one last drag, flicked the cigarette to the ground, and stepped on it. I made my way to the middle of the poorly lit room. I stood in front of him and leaned back on the metal table. With one foot, I scooted his steel chair back so he could see me clearly.

The chair scraped loudly against the rough ground, disturbing the silence, causing him to flinch.

I was playing with my prey. It was all I had left since I didn't do the hunting. But the fatal teasing toyed with their minds.

"Do you have a wife, Dario?"

The poor bastard cried in sorrow, shattered as if he had a heart and yet his cries intensified.

"A girlfriend?"

His sobs continued.

"A fiancée?"

He quieted.

"Bingo." I smiled when his head shook and fell. "You see, Dario, I too have one. You know that. But do you know the difference between going after a *principessa* of New York, and soon the future queen of Miami to a nobody from your cesspool of waste?"

Dario gripped the chair's metal arms. The rope around his wrist didn't allow his tense posture to loosen, leaving his knuckles white.

"Do you?" Lethal calm swarmed.

He didn't answer.

I pulled my gun and fired the white of his knuckles, shattering the bone and tearing skin. A finger fell off and a piece of skin dangled as it oozed in warm rivers of red, dripping.

"I have eight bullets left, and not one will be for your head."

Tears and snot drowned his screams. His feet jumped struggling against the bounds around his ankles, and as he spluttered in misery, I felt *nothing*.

But I was just getting started.

I fired another shot at his intact hand, then another next to it.

"Ahh!" he howled. "Please, please!"

His ring finger fell next to his middle finger, while his pinky hung from a shred of flesh.

"I asked you a question. I won't ask again."

"No!" he yelled. "No! I don't know."

I chuckled cruelly. "Well, kid, the answer was simple."

Dario's gaze met mine as I straightened.

"She is *mine!*" I roared.

I shot both shoulder blades, and instantly his white shirt drenched in vivid burgundy. The more he bled, the deeper I breathed in, listening to the pain and screams like a favorite tune on repeat. And when they settled into sobs, I moved closer to him and penetrated his wound with my finger. I tore his flesh and ripped it apart.

His head snapped back in a wrenching and silent howl. He couldn't take the pain much longer, not without passing out. As he gritted his teeth, I pulled my fingers away and uttered.

"Where is he?"

Head swaying, eyes fluttering, he was slipping.

I blasted a round into his kneecap.

The scum awakened in loud shrieks.

"I don't know!" he sobbed. "I swear I don't know."

Desperately, he looked into my eyes as if I cared about his state. Puppy-pussy eyes of the man that he was.

"Then *what* do you know?"

"I just stayed with the others, man."

"Where?"

A faint scuffle stirred in the right corner. Arlo's patience thinned, waiting for answers.

"Liberty Square! Sixty-Eighth and Thirteenth!"

"How many?"

He didn't answer, and I discharged a round of lead into his good kneecap. A small drive to keep him talking.

Fuck his mouth did. Piercing echoes of misery rang as loud as the gunshot had.

"*Figlio di puttana!*" he cursed. "*Six*! Six of us should be left."

*Of us.*

"And Tino Borelli?"

"I don't know! I don't know, okay?" he choked. "I just overheard another saying that our Tino was in town."

So it had been him all along.

Bold move to hide in my streets.

I rose, done with what I needed, blood and Tino. I looked over his lead filled body one last time and fished out my black handkerchief from my back pocket. I wiped my face, neck, and turned, leaving him to pay for his sins until I could meet again in hell.

"You will bleed to death—slowly. And with each drop that splatters onto your own pool of blood, know your woman will receive the same mercy I showed you."

And when the door shut with his imploring cry, I finally felt something.

Satisfaction.

I rolled my head and placed the blood-stained cloth back in my pocket. The eerie silence did not allow a whimper to filter through the soundproof walls, not even a whistle. I thought of my next move, my next orders and their domino effect. With the Borelli name in my thoughts they were easy to give.

"Find the fiancée." I faced Viktor. "And when you do, give the orders to our men in California."

Ilias's head snapped, and I cut my eyes to him.

"It's a war, Ilias." He didn't utter a word. "And in *this* war, women are free game." His light blue eyes turned brutal. He understood. Katia was proof. "So go to Davina and keep your phone on you."

With a nod, he left.

I turned to Arlo, who eagerly waited for murder.

"Get Sergio, Rio, Casper, and three more." Arlo's teeth shone savagely. "Make a statement." His smile gleamed excitedly in bloodthirst.

Any other time, I would be the first to unleash hell, but not now.

I couldn't leave Katia for any longer. She was still the target.

The prize.

The *weakness*.

IT WAS LATE. WITH LITTLE SLEEP AND A RELENTLESS MIND, ALL I WANTED WAS TO head straight to my room once I'd arrived home, to the place I knew I'd left her behind, and slide into bed next to her warmth and beating heart. But I wasn't dead, and my promises always came first.

The smell of freshly brewed coffee disturbed my routine, and the surprise wasn't welcome.

"You don't have coffee in your house?"

Sal didn't look up and instead blew on the rim and took a hot sip.

"Eh. I like yours better."

"It's the same, old man." That earned me a sneer.

Sal stood on shaky limbs with a warm robe over his shoulders and an oxygen tank next to him. But his fedora hadn't stayed behind even though he was dressed down in his sleepwear and black cotton pants.

"I'm supposed to send you that." I dipped my head toward the mug he held tightly with thin fingers.

"I heard what had happened. You should have called."

"Probably."

"Is she fine?"

"Yes."

"Did she kill a man tonight, Lucca?" His eyes stared accusingly.

He had the right to accuse me, but I wasn't fond of the way he watched me, needing for me to agree to my failure. But Sal wanted to hear it.

"Yes."

"Her mother had so much fight inside of her too, you know. Well, until he beat it out of her. Did you know he did the same to her, to *Katia?*"

I didn't want to know, but he wasn't finished. Sal came here not for coffee, but to remind me of my duty as a boss and the head of this family. One of those duties was to protect what was ours.

He was here for Katia.

"He beat her so bloody at the age of eight that she was shipped to another country. That child was at death's doorstep and dropped off to her decrepit grandfather who had done the same to his wife."

He placed the mug on the countertop and snapped his gaze at me.

"Every Vitelli woman has died at the hands of their husband, and she is the last in their line. Tell me, Lucca. Will she die at your hands?"

Gripping and constricting, my lungs failed. A suffocating feeling that terrorized even my demon.

"I want to meet her when she wakes up."

I left Sal to return on his own accord. He had made it here, he should make it back. Because what I needed was the sight of her and the feel of life running through her veins with warmth.

*"Will she die at your hands?"*

She couldn't.

# XXVII

## KATIA

H EAVY.

Floating.

That was how I felt the times I woke up.

Whispers came and went. Feather touches marked, and the footfalls never stayed.

And in those short minutes, another pill was swallowed, and darkness followed.

# XXVIII

## KATIA

SUNLIGHT ESCAPED THROUGH A THIN GAP AS THE REST OF THE CURTAINS blocked the day from infiltrating the room. I tried to escape the fog, but the harder my eyes battled the more I felt like giving up.

I wiggled my head and felt a sharp sting from the pillow's touch, waking me. And everything rushed back in a sea of torment.

From death, my grim face, the blows I received, to falling asleep next to a man many feared. The one who I once believed couldn't act like he cared, but that night, his act felt *real*.

But that night left me raw. Opened and vulnerable. Exhaustion and torture took far too much from me. I ran on pure adrenaline. A divine high. Then it had abandoned me, dried and withered into an unappealing reality.

The sound of ears shaking and fury bodies jiggling caught my attention.

I looked around the room and smiled. There they were, standing on the side of the bed watching me. Wex and Vino.

My two constants.

"Good, you're awake."

*Viktor.*

I removed my gaze from the boys and searched the room.

Lounging awkwardly on the floor with one leg bent and the other crossed above it in the air, I met Viktor's icy blues. His head rested on the wall near the bedroom door. He shut the laptop he had lying on his abdomen when all of our eyes were directed at him.

He couldn't have been comfortable.

Shifting to see him better, I tugged the comforter higher, but there was no need. I wore a plain soft-white tee and loose boxers.

Figured.

"Hungry?" Viktor asked, and the promise of food stirred my appetite.

"Why are you here?" I scratched the raspy tone out along with the ghost fingers that lingered.

"Lucca asked." He grinned.

"And *where* is he?"

"He'll be here soon."

"*Where* is he?"

His easy smile hardened. "Not here."

I fell back into the bed, kicking the covers away. My leg muscles were sore and yet, it felt incredible to stretch them out and move around.

I had to get up.

"How long have I been sleeping?" I whispered to the high ceiling.

"A while."

"*Mio Dio*, Viktor!" My arms flung out, and I quickly rushed into a sitting position.

Too quickly.

I ached throughout my body, and while I held my discomfort from showing, a faint tingle stuck around. A blurry prick I couldn't shake. A grogginess. As if my body was fighting against itself. Or *something*.

A thought came to mind. The pills I'd consumed.

"You guys drugged me!"

Viktor chuckled and rose from the ground with his laptop tucked under his arm.

"I would hardly call it *drugged*." I couldn't believe him. "And if I recall, you took them willingly."

"I didn't think it would knock me out."

Viktor's mouth twisted in thought. "Yeah, neither did we. Which is why you are up now. We stopped at the third, or was it the fourth pill?" *Was he joking?* "Anyway, I'll be in the dining room if you need me."

The thought of not being alone for some time made me close my eyes and take a deep breath. I had a sitter.

The clock by my bedside table announced past lunch, and the sight of my phone facing down, charging, got the best of me.

I powered it on, and multiple notifications of missed calls popped up. Most were from Enzo, except a message from Daniva?

I cleared the history and checked the date.

Tuesday.

The gala was on Saturday.

Two days. I *wasted* two days.

I reached for Vino's head that hadn't moved too far from my reach and sank my fingers through his coat as I played the voicemail Enzo had left. It was brief with only two words spoken. *"Call me."* I ignored it, just as he ignored mine after I'd humiliated myself by begging him to take me away from Father's house.

Then there was Davina's text. A simple, *"feel better."* She must've overheard Ilias at one point because these men didn't offer information freely.

Lucca must've given her my number because we'd never exchanged them. *Lucca.*

I found his number, and before I could think of my actions, I pressed call.

It rang once. The long tone cut through the silence with unease, and I wanted to hang up. I wanted to reverse time in one ring. Take it back, along with the insecurity it brought. A childish need. But the uncertainty faded when the second tone was cut short by Italian words and his deep voice.

"Are you okay?" Lucca asked, distracted. Wind tumbled, horns chimed, and loud commotion spread through the receiver. Then it all stopped after a car door slammed shut.

Ignoring his question, I replied. "Hey."

Silence.

"Hi."

More silence. So quiet that if it wasn't for the faint ruffles and static, I would have thought he'd ended the call.

"I'm on my way, okay?"

*Merda*, my stupid heart.

I DIDN'T WANT TO SEE MY FACE. IT DIDN'T MATTER THAT AFTER CLEANING *HIS* blood the damage was minimal. But I did. I stared at my features for at least a full minute. In two days I healed faster than the gash my father had gifted me before arriving in Miami.

And as my face glowed under the fresh coat of ointment, I knew the reason. It may not be magic, but it definitely was as close to it. Or maybe it was a shot of steroids paired with Lucca's favorite brown. Either way, I still looked hideous, but a healing one.

I stretched my arms up as I approached the closet. Arlo's blow to my ribs still greeted me, but at least my breathing returned fluidly. My wrist ached with sudden movements but strengthened. And the kick to my back from the bastard only helped my posture to remain straight.

Overall, I didn't mind the leftover pain that grew as the effect of the pills faded. And while my lips were cracked, I was alive.

I picked a loose and soft cotton dress along with leather sandals and met the boys by the bedroom door. With Wex and Vino by my side, I walked into the hall with my dagger strapped, wearing the most casual outfit I'd worn since living in Miami, aside from my workout clothes.

"You made it," Viktor spoke too loudly, but caught himself quickly. "Sorry," he apologized and took out a white earbud from his ear.

He sat in the same chair Arlo had before—across from mine, with an opened laptop and a bowl of orange soup to his left. Three other placemats had been set, and a few different salad dressings stood between us.

I sat down, and Viktor closed the laptop.

Silence stretched, and while Viktor didn't make me feel uncomfortable or at risk, his effortless smiles were easier to decipher the more time I spent around him. Despite him hiding behind his smiles, to the naked eye, they seemed sincere.

It was what he was doing now, studying me carefully with a half-grin, trying to make me comfortable, open—vulnerable.

"You don't have to treat me like an assignment, you know," I said.

Viktor smirked and leaned back. "Glad you are feeling better."

"About that."

He waited for me to continue.

"I noticed Lucca's ointment was Russian."

"Mhmm…" he agreed.

"And since you are here, and not Ilias, you must be the supplier of whatever it is."

"Correct."

"Then I owe you a thank you."

"No you don't." He chuckled. "It would've expired before any of us used it, so really I owe *you* for not wasting my money in vain."

I replied with a nod, and we settled back to a comfortable silence.

Viktor picked up a grilled cheese sandwich from the large stack of triangle pieces neatly arranged on the platter. The bread was thick and browned in butter. It seemed such a simple dish, but I knew the bread was homemade. It would pair perfectly with the tomato and basil soup that I spotted within his reach.

It wasn't a feast or the usual grand dishes we often ate. It was light, simple—rich. It was clear that it had been made with me in mind. Because after missing a few meals, my stomach wouldn't have tolerated anything heavier.

Viktor took a large bite, and I glanced at the side door that led to the kitchen, debating if I should wait or fix a bowl myself.

"You know—"

My head snapped back to him and while his tone hadn't changed, his blue eyes tinted by a memory.

"You know how sometimes insignificant memories of our childhood beat the ones you wish you could remember?"

His smile did not reach far. I worried about what he would say next, and the point he was trying to make.

"Like the name of the cream your mother used on her own tear-streaked face, but you hardly recall what she looked like?"

I didn't utter a word.

"Well, I guess they proved they weren't so insignificant."

"Why are you telling me this?"

"Honestly, I don't know." He lifted his shoulder, then gentle steps neared. We weren't alone anymore. "Maybe it was the thought of being used for the same reasons."

A bowl of steaming soup and a plate of fresh green salad appeared in front of me. I snapped my gaze away from Viktor and looked up.

Talia's eyes widened as they scanned my face and quickly lowered as her hands shot to her chest.

"My apologies." She ushered, wiping her hands across her flour-splattered apron. Her high ponytail swayed as her head moved from side to side. Her eyes lifted softly, and she offered a mournful grin and quickly left.

"I didn't think they were that bad," I said, lifting the spoon.

"They're not," he assured me. "But while she's aware of who she works for, she's never been exposed to the ugly parts. Seeing it on your face was a surprise." Good, they've sheltered her.

Viktor nodded at my bowl, ushering me to eat.

With a spoon full of tomato and spice I blew out and sipped. It didn't take more than a second before the spoon was back down due to the sting and burn from its heat.

"Here, take mine. I'm not a fan of tomato soup and it should be lukewarm by now." Viktor pushed his bowl in my direction but stopped as his attention shifted to the far corner on my left.

I followed his gaze and met Lucca's dark eyes on me, twisted and far from reach. His inked hands adjusted his tie before they fell back to his side as his strides offered the dominance and violence of his state of mind. Eerie silence echoed inside the walls he'd built.

When his body passed behind my chair, I turned my head, not wanting to miss any further tells of his vicious aura.

My hair flew over my features with momentum, but Lucca hadn't sat down. Rather, he stood next to me, and my head froze in place.

In all black, from his shoes to the pits of his eyes, Lucca dressed for bloodshed.

I focused on the button of his jacket, unsure of how to proceed with the storm he'd conjured.

Any other day, I would have put up a fight. A pull, a jab of defiance. But I was over the games, and a part of me looked forward to his presence. Even if in turmoil.

His fingers twitched before his hand lifted. Lucca's rough palm pressed against my jaw, and his fingers spread, taking my face into his hold.

My eyes closed by his touch and my breathing eased, drawn to his darkness. When they opened, his piercing eyes roamed over my lips, my temple, until they bound to mine.

Then he let go and took a seat at the head of the table. As if it had never happened. And while my eyes were freed, they still felt shackled to where he once stood.

I shook the haze away and glanced down at the bowl Viktor had offered. But I had been so consumed by Lucca's pull that I missed Viktor leaving us alone.

How could I overlook such detail?

*Lucca.*

He was cutting all my senses—my instincts. And slaying every wall in the process.

Lucca was wounding me from the inside out. Slowly taking, leaving me bare with an exposed heart.

And as I realized he had already conquered my mind games, my body tells, I wasn't just looking forward to his presence. *I wanted to be near him.* In *need* of him.

*Damn him.*

"What's the matter?" Lucca asked in Italian.

Nothing if I didn't allow it. But could I? Could I really keep the physical need, the mental greed from filtering deeper?

"Katia?"

"*Niente.*" Nothing.

Mrs. Greco appeared with two bowls of soup, and Talia followed close behind with two salad plates and her eyes on the ground.

Mrs. Greco didn't flinch at my appearance. Instead, she concentrated on the task ahead, cleaning the spot Viktor had once sat and setting the food down. When she offered Lucca's, his hand stopped her from placing the bowl in front of him.

"I'll just take the salad."

Talia moved closer, dropping the plate on his placemat before they both returned to the kitchen, leaving us in silence.

I stared at the empty seat but didn't question who would accompany us. Instead, I sipped the lukewarm soup Viktor had offered. He'd said he wasn't a fan of it, and it couldn't be coincidence Lucca refused his bowl too. Then why tomato and basil soup?

"Why don't you like the soup?" I asked boldly as if I knew he didn't.

"Just not a fan of its taste," he replied and picked a vinaigrette dressing and drizzled it lightly over the greens.

"Hmm. Funny, neither is Viktor."

I sensed his eyes, but ignored them and took another sip of delicious broth.

"You should tell her the truth, Lucca," a croaking voice said, and I twirled to its echo.

*Salvatore Mancini.*

I rose from my seat in his presence with wide eyes, watching the memories of my past unwind. To a time I'd called him godfather, when he was my brothers' instead of mine. A time when our families were at war and not forced into treaties by marriage.

I had been shy and scared. When my mother was around, I would hide near her skirt or in every corner to remain invisible from my father's eyes. And while I was young and confused, I'd always felt safe near the man with the red stone ring.

*"This bush isn't the ideal place to hide, kiddo."*

*I peered up into gentle brown eyes. It was the only feature I found kind. The rest of him was scary, dressed in the same suits my father did. But his gaze was always curious, soft when I was around. Always treating me with care and speaking in a low tone. I had just turned four, and my father constantly reminded me I wasn't a child anymore. That I wasn't meant to be treated like one. Why did he? Why did he speak to me like you would a baby?*

*"I'm four,"* I squeaked, and glanced around to see if any of the gunmen had heard me. If I'd given away my secret hideout.

*"Are you now?"*

*"Yes,"* I whispered.

*Sal sat down on the steps near the entrance, a bit out of reach, but still close enough to hear me. I wish he would leave me. This was a brand-new hideout. One that allowed me to see who came and went, and easy to slip away when my father's car tires rolled down the long drive. The crate I'd learned to remove from the stone wall was an easy escape. I could slither between the small opening and close it before my father could beat me back into the house of screams.*

*"Then you already know these thorns are painful."*

*I did, but I was careful. I moved quietly and creeped small enough for them not to touch me. It didn't take me long to learn my lesson.*

*"My father isn't here,"* I replied instead.

*"I'm aware."* He smiled. *"Can you keep a secret?"*

*I nodded.*

*"I'm here for your mother, although your father believes I'm here for business."*

*My eyes flooded with fright. My father wasn't someone to lie to. He was extremely mean and liked to cause pain whenever I did.*

*"Why?"*

*He didn't answer right away, and I could see his eyes clouded with concern.*

*"Your mother knows the whereabouts of someone I deeply care about, and I'm afraid of what could happen soon."*

*He didn't make sense. My mamma didn't talk to anyone. Hardly even spoke to me.*

*She spent most of her time crying inside her room as I played with her hair.*

*"Could you maybe help me talk to her?"*

*I thought about it, and while I wanted to help, I didn't see my mother leaving her room.*

*"It's very serious."*

*So was my father's fist.*

*Enzo told me I should be brave and stop fear from paralyzing me. That I should pay attention and learn from my instincts. How they are always right.*

*Right now, they told me I should help, but how careful I must be. How I risked wrath, and pain if I didn't plan out my next move.*

*"Okay," I murmured, and rested my hands on the ground. "Stay here."*

*"No, there are too many eyes. Tell her to go to the gold bathroom."*

*"The gold bathroom?" I asked, that was next to my father's study.*

*"I promise no one will know, okay?"*

*I hesitated.*

*"You have my word."*

*With a little nod, I crawled through the dirt and slunk inside the crawl space opening. After placing the wire rack back in place, I scurried inside the house, sprinting toward my mother's room.*

*I knocked once, twice, but my mother never opened the door. I dusted my black dress and walked into the darkened room, but she wasn't in her bed. Quietly, I walked closer to the opened door of her closet. A feeling to run crept in, as if I shouldn't look for her.*

*But I found my mother's face glowing with a bright light as she typed quickly into a small rectangular phone.*

*She didn't have a phone, never seen her with one, and while I watched her tear-stricken face and sunken body holding on to the small rectangle, I knew I shouldn't have.*

*Her eyes snapped, and her hands quickly fumbled to her chest, covering the phone with them.*

*"Katia." She ushered me in. "You scared me, darling. Is everything okay? Is your father here?"*

*I shook my head. "Godfather Salvatu-ure is here." His long name stumbled when I pronounced his full name instead of using the short version he'd requested to call him.*

*My mother wiped her tears and looked up at me with glazed eyes and jumpy movements.*

*"He said to meet him in the gold bathroom."*

*She couldn't stop looking past me, as if a figure would appear. I turned, but we were alone. Her head shook, and her feet paced. One last look at me, and her body turned to hide the device she'd held on to so tightly.*

*It's okay, Mamma. I can keep your secrets.*

*"You didn't see anything. Do you understand?"*

*I nodded.*

*Her nose sniffed loudly and she shuddered when she met me outside the large closet.*

*"Go play, I'll find you soon."*

*I did what she asked for. I left, but I didn't return to my drawings, the endless supply of colored pencils, or the Barbie's that never talked back. Instead, I hid and watched from afar as she walked away from the room she ate and slept in. Her feet were silent as they took each step down to the main floor. I followed her from afar, keeping an eye on father's return and another on her.*

*Mother's frame slithered inside the ajar door of the bathroom, leaving the light off. I took the chance to find a spot where I could keep the door visible without me near. The hall was not an easy place to hide, but the unscrewed air duct vents were friends for someone my size.*

*I squeezed inside and breathed in the dusty space with small shallow puffs. I had to be quiet.*

*"Gianna," I heard my mother's name whispered.*

*I scooted lower. Black shiny shoes against the opened door and a crimson stone revealed whose body it belonged to.*

*"You must hurry, I can't be found here, Salvatore."*

*"I'm aware, but I'm desperate, Gia. Please," he pressured with a gentle plea. "I need to contact Andrea."*

*"I've told you I don't know where she is."*

*"But you do," he fought. "Damn it, I know okay."*

*Silence.*

*"Fine," Salvatore said as his hand balled, and his voice lowered. "Can you at least tell me if they are still okay?"*

*Silence.*

*"Mario won't stop." I heard my mother's soft cry.*

*"And I'm working on that. Please don't run. Not yet."*

*"I can't promise you that."*

*"Damn it, just give me time. Think of the danger you'll bring to them, and that's including your own children."*

*"They are strong."*

*Salvatore cursed too low, and his back leaned against the doorcase. "No they are not. They are children."*

*My mother sniffed.*

*"Stop using, stop plotting, and leave Andrea out of your plan."*

*"It's too late."*

*"No it's not." Salvatore stopped, quickly straightened and turned to the sound from the end of the corridor. "I must go, but please—Do. Not. Run."*

*When people said the walls could hear, the walls could weep, they told the truth.*

*I heard and wept in silence. It was the last time I saw Salvatore, and two days later, my mother was found dead.*

*If I'd once feared father, nothing compared to my next two years of life.*

I was four, and as Viktor had said, insignificant memories beat the ones I wished to remember. However, today, they weren't insignificant at all.

I was four, scared and without a mother's skirt to hide behind.

I was four, and I understood death and pain.

*I was just four.*

If it wasn't for the kind eyes that pierced mine, I wouldn't have recognized the man who stood shakily behind Lucca's chair. But the more I looked at him, the more the memories of Sal mirrored that man.

The strong features, the red stone finger, and the deadly demeanor were all familiar. But his thick black hair wasn't covered by a fedora. Instead the fedora concealed the faint shadow of what his condition had taken. The oxygen tank, and his inconstant coughs were also new.

Salvatore was my father's age, and yet he looked double and on the verge of death's bed.

It was cruel, really, knowing how strong my father breathed as Sal struggled with each puff.

I now knew who Salvatore was. His kind eyes had always been reserved for me when he was around, as if he hid the monster inside, shielding the child he often found in the bushes, under tables, and corners. He could've been like any other black-suited man who walked into my father's study, ignorant and mean to the little girl who hid so terribly.

Instead, he acknowledged my existence, and he was warm while doing so.

Salvatore knew the answers I sought. After all, he was the last person I saw my mother speak to before she died. And during that day and the following, my mother was present, but her mind was too far for me to call her back to me.

"Please sit."

I stared at him struggling with the emotions that threatened the corners of my eyes with memories and the possibility of speaking to him as an adult. Afraid of the answers.

The rough touch against my fingers drew my gaze to it, finding Lucca's calloused hand. He was confused by my reaction, but his demanding spirit didn't ease. It tugged at me to sit, to eat.

I composed my fluttering heart and sat with eyes that were fixed on Salvatore's short footfalls. When he stopped and lowered, our gaze connected across the table.

"You are just as beautiful as your mother was." He coughed.

"Were you in love with her?"

The question flew without barriers. It was the first of many, but by its answer it was possible to determine the correct order.

He smiled but shook his head. "No, not the way you think."

"Then in what way?" I quickly asked.

"I knew her from a young age and cared for her as a sister."

"How?" I fired.

"Lucca, are you intending to explain to her your soup situation?"

I didn't even glance at Lucca, his answer could wait. Salvatore's couldn't.

"How?" I asked again.

Salvatore's eyes narrowed. Gone was the kindness. He didn't like my spirit. Welcome to the Moretti club, Mr. Mancini.

His gaze searched below, and he picked up the spoon. His wool-checkered vest shifted as his other hand removed the tubes from his nose.

"She was my sister's best friend. Practically lived with us when we were young."

Lucca's fork returned to the table forcefully.

"That's enough," he hushed.

But I hardly learned anything!

I faced Lucca and asked uncaringly, "Could I have a moment alone with Salvatore?"

"No," he cut.

"Fine," I spat, and asked Salvatore instead. "Who's Andrea?"

Lucca lost it.

I should've calmed the cruelty he'd walked in with, instead I let it loose.

I flinched as the glass cup shattered into the mantle as loose glass glitters rained down the fireplace. He stood so quickly in wrath that I froze. I'd seen him angry, I'd seen him lose control, but I'd never seen him fucking lost and taken by anger.

This demon, I feared.

His body rushed toward me, and in one swift move, his hand replaced the faint bruises that marked my neck. Gripping tightly, his face lowered with wicked evil.

"Don't ever speak her name in my presence."

His warning filled me with fear.

I fucking *feared* him!

For once, I felt paralyzing dread, the chilling spite of his words, and the promise he didn't elaborate if I went against them. This time, his merciless brown eyes cut through me savagely and inhumanely as he clearly threatened. Seeing the diabolical beast of the man who everyone feared, I understood it.

With his shackling hand wrapped around my throat, and even while I couldn't hide my shaking chest, or the trembles on my fingers, I pulled my push dagger out, and placed it under his jaw.

"Get your hand off me." I seethed.

Lucca's head tilted down to touch the sharp edge that threatened him. Ignoring the blade, his cruel gaze watched me with disgust.

He let go, and I gasped without removing my blade.

"Andrea is whose ring you bear, *piccola.*"

My arms failed, my heart broke, and I froze.

Andrea was his mother.

Lucca gave me his mother's ring.

# XXIX

## LUCCA

S ALVATORE REFUSED TO SPEAK TO ME AND RETURNED TO MRS. GRECO FOR the nightly coffee hour. His disappointment and words followed me everywhere. *"Will she die by your hands?"* While I hadn't believed she would, that day spoke otherwise.

"Leave your bike and come with me," I ordered Arlo as I passed him.

"Where are we going?" He spun and followed me until he jumped into my car.

I shut the door. "Dress shopping."

His head snapped, and I ignored the questions and loathing aimed at me.

"We leave in an hour," he said, confused, as if I had forgotten the plans *I'd* made.

But because of those plans, I was searching for her. I put the car in drive and left my restaurant, Gusto's, in the rearview mirror.

Things between Katia and I had spoiled into hatred. I could see its haze in the short time her eyes locked on to mine. So much sparked around them, but revulsion was its master.

Whether I cared or not wasn't the problem. Because during those days, I used my time to hunt Tino. And while I convinced myself it was for the best, a thin needle pricked with annoyance by seeing her so distant. Lost.

But the knowledge that I had broken the same promise I once vowed to never repeat kept me away from her. I was outraged at breaking my honor. She now made me question my own vow. My word.

I focused on work, the famiglia, and the meeting I would soon face. But, after not speaking one word to each other for days, and her indifference to seeking out my body at night, this wasn't what I wanted to return to.

We were to be wed in less than two weeks, and I had a fucking syndicate to burn. I shouldn't be concerned about her delusional feelings. She had tossed and turned each night, and even though she'd admitted to being fine after killing a man, her sleepless nights had kept me up. When dawn had arrived, I left her by the edge of the mattress as if I hadn't struggled to see her helpless, fighting me even in her sleep.

The door bells chimed at my entrance, and Viktor smiled knowingly with crossed arms at the corner.

"My God, there's so much white in here," Arlo uttered repulsively as he scanned the shop.

There was, as well as lace and tulle.

Mrs. Greco asked if Katia had chosen a dress or if she needed to look for one. I'd told her I would take care of it, and that same afternoon I reserved a private appointment with just the owner for Katia. Then I'd told Ilias to ask Davina to accompany her, giving him the name and time before moving on.

Katia hadn't involved herself with any wedding preparations, but I knew what she wanted, so I'd made it meet her expectations and desires. She might not see it as a celebration or a promise before God, but damn if I ruined the one thing little girls dream of. Did she dream of her wedding day? Had it been for love? Had it been to a killer?

As I glanced around the elegant and silk-filled room, I knew I had found the ideal shop for her. Antique sofas and chaises scattered before a mirrored podium, and I watched Viktor's reflection.

"I wondered if you would come," Viktor cooed.

I didn't find him funny and moved past him.

Davina's head didn't turn as I stood next to where she sat. Her fingers stilled on the catalog she held too tightly on her thighs. She slowly exhaled, and while her eyes didn't lift, her head twitched in acknowledgment.

Without Ilias around, my presence always made her uncomfortable. At unease. I didn't blame her; I was no different from the bastards who butchered her body. I too had men hunting her at one point.

I looked straight ahead, and our eyes met through our reflection.

"Why all the trouble? Why not just tell her you've booked the place and asked me to join?"

"Did you mention that?"

She huffed. "Of course not."

"Good, thank you for coming."

"You say it as if I had a choice."

I chuckled. "True. And not that I owe you an answer, child, but unlike Ilias, I have no desire to make anyone believe I care."

"Don't you, Lucca? Care?"

I watched her head turn toward me in the mirror, felt her questioning gaze, and heard the doubt in her voice.

"No, I don't," I answered coldly, and caught her eyes. "Now, where is she?"

"You can search for her yourself." Davina stood and left.

Fuck, perhaps spending time with Katia wasn't such a good idea.

I followed the path Davina's eyes had suggested and walked deeper into the establishment. A woman, roughly in her early thirties stepped out with silent mumbles of annoyance as she closed the door behind her.

"I should have known." Her fingers circled around her temples, and her strawberry-blonde hair fell against her cheeks.

"Should have known, what exactly?"

The lady, who I could guess was the owner, Maria, froze as her mouth opened wide in a silent gasp.

"Mr. Moretti!" she exclaimed as her eyes scanned my tattooed skin, and her feet carried her a step farther from me.

I raised my brow in question.

"Oh nothing, sir. It's just been a...a day," she stuttered.

"And I hope you are making my future bride hers." I took away the distance she'd created.

"Of course, of course. We are so privileged for the Moretti name to wear our brand."

Of that, I was sure. Money and greed often trumped the moral compass of those you would welcome.

"I'm glad we understand each other. Now if you could leave us alone."

I had hardly spoken the last words before she was nowhere in sight and the white door stared at me. Katia's name was printed in cursive on a delicate plaque.

I opened the door to a frustrated and irritable Italian woman.

"I said, I didn't need—" Katia's gaze bluntly stared behind her through the mirror. "Lucca."

She uttered my name as if she'd found a ghost. However, I had found a fucking ray of heaven that sent me to hell by the filthy thoughts of seeing her body.

As I gazed at Katia's see-through thigh-high tights with lace edges and matching white lace cheeky panties, I was speechless. Her tits were bare and her nipples were hard from the chilly temperature. My dick twitched. She didn't try to cover herself. Instead, her eyes remained on me while mine roamed over her exquisite shape and flawless sun-kissed skin.

I met her eyes and held my attraction, ordering my dick to calm down. But Katia's lips curled, her head craned, and her teeth caught her sangria-colored lips. Their color antagonized me for a taste, and I wanted to prove their natural stain was cherry flavored.

Fuck, my stubborn dick was heavy with a load, and she knew it.

Toying with me, her gaze taunted, and with a flick of her wrist, she pushed the right side of her hair back and her tit was fully visible to me.

*Mio Dio*, I wanted to ruin her body and sink my dick deep inside of her, beating her until her face scrunched in pleasure and her legs wobbled.

I didn't have much time left, but for her, I would find a way to stop it. I would stretch the minutes and seconds and fill her with my cum to remind her who she belonged to. Who owned her body.

"I wasn't aware you were coming."

"I wasn't." I stepped forward.

"Then why are you here?"

I took another.

"I'm leaving for the day."

Her eyes fluttered, losing her bravado the closer I got.

"Where?" she whispered.

"Texas. I'll be back late tonight."

My front met her back, and I lowered my head to her bare shoulder. My lips left their trace while I scattered higher to her neck without our eyes moving away from one another across the mirror.

Her breathing deepened, and she trembled as I took her head into my hand, stretching her skin for my mouth to take more of her neck.

Katia closed her eyes, defeated as she sank deeper.

I smiled.

"I still hate you."

My smile turned into a sneer.

She could hate me all she wanted, but her body—her body craved *me*, molding with my touch like clay. And her words held no power. Not when her skin reacted in need.

*Hate?*

"I hate you too," I whispered, taking her hip with a tight grip and bringing it back to my straining dick.

I hate you so fucking *hard.*

"Can you feel it?"

Katia whimpered, and her eyes shot open as her head shook.

"I can't."

*Was she denying my touch?*

I snaked one hand to her aroused nipple while the other pulled her closer and slipped over the lace fabric between her legs. It was stained and damp with her juices, and I cupped her.

"It seems your body betrays you, Katia."

Her ass backed deeper into my dick, but she quickly turned and stepped back.

"No."

"No?" A dark smile touched my lips.

"Yes, I said no." Her small, yet flawless tits bounced as she stiffened.

*What the fuck was happening?*

"Why are you depriving your body of release, exactly?"

"I don't know, Lucca. Maybe because the last time we spoke you had your fucking hands crushing my windpipe!" Her arms flew in frustration.

Hmm. "But you like it when I use my fingers as a choker, Katia."

I knew exactly what she meant. What she was trying to explain, and yet, I wanted her body more than to waste time talking about it.

"Don't!" she yelled. "Don't stand there and act as if it's the same. As if you didn't break your promise. As if I'm wrong to feel conflicted."

"Fine," I replied through clenched teeth, annoyed by the painful bulge she'd created and the threat of blue balls she implied.

I took a step closer and held her jaw. Her lips had healed, and the bruise by her eye had faded.

"Then explain it to me, and after I listen, you will get on your knees and suck me dry." My fingers squeezed her cheeks. "Got it?"

322

Her eyes narrowed in violent hatred.

"And if I don't."

"Keep playing and find out." I pushed her back onto the mirror. She hissed on contact with its coolness, but her defiant eyes never wavered. And I knew she wouldn't stop playing. "You toyed with me from the moment I walked in. You proudly wanted me to see every inch of you in this delicate fucking dream of fabric, and you teased the wrong motherfucker." I pressed my covered dick against her. "And you *will* fix it."

"Or I might bite it off."

I grinned. "I like pain, sweetie."

"You..." Her hand pushed against my chest. "You—"

I kissed her sangria-colored lips, but instead of wine, grapes, or citrus flavors, cherry was all I could taste.

Cherry lips, fighting, crashing, delicious.

When they synced and gave as much as they took, I stopped.

"Me, what?"

Her cloudy gaze struggled against mine, and her head fell onto my chest as her hand gripped my suit jacket.

I froze. It no longer felt like her mind was trying to craft or con. This was real.

"Speak freely. You don't have to look at me."

"You made me fear you."

The broken whisper struck brutally, plowing down over the fraud of my beatless heart with a strangling hold.

It was what I had wanted from the moment I agreed to this sham of marriage. However, hearing it from her fragile lips, and yet the strong spirit she was, constricted my breathing. It twisted and gripped me from the inside as if I was on the receiving end of agony.

Maybe I was because the torment in her voice spread through me like bane.

"You make me question my instincts. You *blind* me, Lucca." My hand ran beneath her hair, listening to her accusations and the truth she'd set free. "I don't recognize who I am anymore."

*Smart, beautiful, dangerous.* She hadn't changed, if anything she had become a bigger threat than ever.

"Are you done?" I asked, composed, and damn if I didn't stare at hell when her eyes flared quickly as she glared at me.

*I listened, Katia.* You too made me question my actions. You too blinded me. And I too didn't recognize the man whose thoughts wandered to a fucking woman in the middle of creating a blood painting.

But I couldn't worry about theories I was incapable of feeling, or ideas I didn't want to be a part of. I liked my life just the way it was. Vacant. Nothing more than her body to sink into and a fucking empire to rule.

My fingers spread over her mouth, and I dug my thumb deep and low into her bow lips.

"You were loud and clear. Now, you do what I asked."

*Make me show you what will happen if you don't. Come on Katia, another round.*

"I wish it would've never been you," she spat, aiming to hurt.

"That's alright. It would be a sixty-year-old dick you sucked instead."

Her hand quickly fell to her thigh, and her fingers ran across it, finding it empty and stripped of any weapon. I smiled. She sneered, and her fist flung.

*I don't think so.*

I gripped her jaw and shoved her into the mirror, taking her balled fist. Ambers of ire kindled. This wasn't what I'd come here for. This whole scene wasn't how I'd envisioned it. How I'd hope to start or finish. Instead, it was fueling and tumbling, deepening into pits of endless hostility.

"Your dagger is one thing, Katia, and one I acknowledge I deserve. But don't *ever* raise your fucking hand at me, much less your fist unless you want to be treated as a fucking man." My words touched her flushed face. "And while I don't fear you, I can lose the small thread of respect

I hold for you."

Katia's brows furrowed.

"Were you not just fighting my touch because I caused you pain? Because my hands inflicted *fear?*"

Her eyes lowered.

"Yes, I listened." Our faces were mere inches apart. "You want to hurt me?" I asked, and her vivid greens fogged. "Do it while you fuck me violently." I pulled her body closer. "Cut me, bite me, draw blood if that's what you need, but do it while your mouth chokes on my dick, or while you ride me in pleasure. But never outside of sex. That's not a marriage I will honor."

I could see tears of anger pooling in the brims of her eyes. Her face was dotted with splotches of red, and the veins in her forehead were filled with wrath.

Her hand swatted mine off her face, and she gave me what I wanted. *Another round. The fight.*

At least this time, we both agreed and understood our limits.

Katia gripped my blazer, pulled it to her, and turned so my back pressed against the mirror.

Damn. I had a feeling sweet pain would soon arrive in rapids of ecstasy.

I grinned triumphantly. Katia didn't. She was driven by pure anger and need. Her hands fumbled with my buckle, and as much as I liked watching her temper loose, I wanted another taste of her lips.

I tugged at her face and my lips sought out for her soft and warm mouth that lingered in dipped cherry.

I drew back and our eyes connected. "Have I mentioned how divine your body is in only high tights and lace?" I pried another kiss. "Or how the color white against your golden skin makes me hard?" I hauled her back for one last taste and groaned when my lip stung painfully by her teeth.

"Shut up," she spat as her hands freed my dick.

I pushed her head down with force and shoved her mouth deep as I moved forward with her lips wrapped around my shaft.

"Look who shut up instead."

Her eyes fluttered as she gagged with threatening tears.

Her teeth came out to play, and fuck if she didn't shut *me* up quickly. *Dio*, this goddess.

She sucked, she fought, and I couldn't hold on longer with her eagerness to cause pain and pleasure, submitting my request and agreeing to my terms.

"Just like that, *cara mia*." I hummed, reeling my fingers around her hair, roaming and gripping their thick and smooth texture as her mouth messily kept up with my sharp thrusts.

Her teeth disappeared and her cheeks hollowed, sucking me deeply in and out. I gave in to her tempo and groaned like a little bitch. I wasn't even bothered by the power she held over my dick, or the desire she drew out just for her.

Her deep tugs pulled my eyes away, forcing me to tilt my head back as my balls tightened. *Cazzo,* I couldn't hold my release longer, and Katia knew it as she shifted with hands firmly, gripping my thighs.

"Katia." A deep moan clung in my throat, and I emptied my dick into her mouth.

She took each drop, and did as told, milked me dry.

I picked her up by her waist, and her legs immediately clasped around my hips. I kissed her hungrily, and while her cherry taste lingered with a bitter taste, I lavished her mouth and pressed her against the mirror.

Her hands clawed and fumbled with my shirt buttons. Our bodies couldn't wait, and hers thrashed up and down with her dampened lace creating the friction she begged for.

"I'll take care of you," I murmured into her ear, and nipped it as her palms ran over my now bare chest as my shirt tumbled to the ground.

I took a nipple into my mouth, sucking, biting and swirling my tongue around its stiff pebble. Katia scratched my shoulder, and I bit harder.

"Ahh!" she shouted in pain.

She did it again, and this time her fingernails didn't just scratch but stung as they pierced my chest. In a loud pop, I let go of her nipple as I moaned a groan of the sweet torture she was putting me through. I dropped my head onto her neck.

When I lifted my head again, I found her wicked smile and vicious sense of victory. I craned my head slowly, watching her in dark humor.

I hadn't even begun.

"I'm going to make you beg."

Her green eyes widened at my promise as her pants escaped rapidly.

She stared. I stared, and we both stood still as a classical lullaby played in loops inside the room. It didn't match our fire, our threats, nevertheless the need that pulsed between us. It had been a second too long away from her body. A second for my promise to scurry and join the notes of peace with the war mine vowed.

Then I unchained my demon.

I was on her like a ravenous predator, flipping her body and pushing her head onto the mirror. Her mouth parted and her breathing dampened the surface by her little suffocating pants, and I dragged her ass to my front.

She whimpered with large eyes. When I spread her legs with my feet, I traced her sight.

I found the reflection of *us*. The hand that gripped her hair, forcing her head to the cold mirror. The bow of her back as her nipples teased the glass with spread legs and a perched ass. Sheer stockings, white lace, and a pure fuck-me expression reflected back. All while my heavy hand seized her hip and placed her against my freed shaft. My tattooed covered body was clear under broad light while my rumpled shirt lay on the floor. And while my black pants hung over my ass, the zipper toyed with my erected dick that sought another release.

Fuck, this vision would hunt me.

I pressed my body to her back and whispered as our eyes connected through the reflection.

"Are you going to deny me now?"

With my eyes trained to her emeralds, I hooked the thin panty lace against my fingers and tugged. A loud and short rip blended with her moan as I pulled the shredded fabric off her sensitive pussy.

"Are you?" I asked deeply as I balled the lace into my fist.

She didn't reply, trying to omit my answer. But I wanted to hear it. I wanted her to cry it out, and for her heart to hear it through its vibrations.

Done with the reflection, I wanted to see her body before me.

I shifted, teasing her entrance while my hold on her hip slithered to between her legs.

Katia suppressed a moan, closing her eyes, and I slid my fingers through her wet folds. So fucking wet, so responsive, and yet so fucking stubborn.

"Answer me, Katia."

Silence.

I applied pressure for an answer, and when she still fought, I used the scratchy-soft lace against her bud.

"Uhh!"

"Still not an answer, *cara mia.*"

I rubbed in tight circles, causing her legs to buckle and her ass to squirm. When her thighs ached to close, I drove my foot further, leaving her spread for my torture.

"*Lucca,*" she implored.

But that wasn't the begging I'd promised. I dropped the lace to the floor and dipped a finger deep into her walls.

"Ahh!"

I pumped, toyed, and smeared herself over her opening repeatedly.

"Are you still denying what's mine?" I growled, frustrated by her impertinence of even trying, and the resistance to retract her insolence.

Katia shook her head, and I pressed deeper. Her lips parted wide, dampening the mirror. Her hair was tousled, and her features clustered in heaps of bliss as I showed her sensitivity any mercy.

"Come on, just admit it."

"Hmm." She thrashed.

"Fine," I snarled. "You are going to listen carefully," I threatened, and she nodded. "You are not going to fucking move from this position. Do you understand, Katia?"

Pants and tunes echoed.

"*Do you understand?*" I pinched her bud.

"YES!" she shouted.

I smiled, demented, and watched as her legs shuddered, and her palms tensed on the wall.

With my hands on her sides, I slid them down her ribcage, her waist, and stopped at the curve of her hips the same time my body lowered.

I bit the bottom crease of her ass cheek, and her leg jumped.

Dark chuckles rumbled from my chest, and I twisted in a squat to find the source that could pacify my violent hunger.

I watched as my fingers spread her apart and ate. I'd made a mess I needed to clean, and fuck if my tongue didn't. My pace matched her soft cries.

My fingers plunged, my other hand kept her on the spot, and my tongue raved over her bud and circled in mad want.

"Lucca, please!"

She withered above.

Still not what I wanted to hear, so I continued my assault.

"Lucca!"

Katia tensed, and I pulled away.

"Argh!" she screamed when I took away the release she'd tried to steal.

I smiled and looked up. Her head fell between her arms, and she found me beneath, mad eyed and glistening lips that shone sinful teeth. Her needy eyes begged, frustrated.

Her eyes followed my head, and hers shook furiously.

I did it all over again, and again, and my flight would be delayed until she *begged*, and gave me what *I* wanted to hear.

"*Per favore,*" cried my demon in satisfaction. "No, I'm not denying you." Finally, she answered, followed by promises I will hold on to. "Please, I won't deny you again."

I pinched her sensitive and swollen bud, extracting as many vows that could escape.

"I will never deny your touch."

I released her, and her droopy eyes watched in relief. I stood and took her face with both of my hands. I turned her fatigued and pent-up body back to the mirror and leaned against her.

"Now tell me what you want."

"*You.*" She breathed.

I kissed her and chills crawled down my spine as her nails scraped before they dug into my scalp. I lifted her leg off the floor, hooking it against my elbow and clutched her hip, securing her high from the floor. Spread out and ready for my dick to be buried.

She rubbed herself against me, and I closed my eyes to the euphoric feeling of friction my shaft painfully demanded.

"I'm going to beat you to exhaustion," I hissed in her ear, and her hands clasped my hair tighter while her other leg snaked over my hip, ready for me to follow through with my carnal oath.

"*Si.*" She fucking purred and clawed, and I plunged my dick in one deep thrust all the way to its base. "Ah!"

Katia bit my shoulder, and I pounded brutally. Her movements were created in pure ecstasy; the kisses, the bites, the tongue that ran over my skin, to the hands that gripped, scratched, to the nails that broke skin. And each one of those crazed touches provoked the demon to continue his needy abuse of her body, drawing all of her needs and bathing in its pain and pleasure.

"*Mio Dio, cara mia.* You take my dick so good." I hummed and drove harder. "And you feel like fucking glory." My fingers dug while our lips toyed one another. "You drive me mad, Katia."

"Lucca," she begged.

"Soon, I promise." I nipped her jaw.

"I can't." Her face fell while her bottom quivered. *So* sensitive.

"Please!"

I glance at the reflection. The beating my dick was giving, and the flustered body that took it. Crimson swirls decorated her wailing hands as they scattered over my tensed muscles. The clinking sound of my belt matched each pound, and the parted mouth that stretched out above from the gorgeous princess of mine.

"Look at me," I ordered.

Her eyes opened, but they weren't on me, instead they drifted to our reflection.

"Hmm."

"You can now see how you come and soak my dick."

Her wall tightened, and I was ready to bust inside of her.

"Now you can see how I empty myself inside you."

"Ah!"

She cried out as her body tensed and her pussy quivered into release. I snapped my eyes to her face, watching it unfold as she drifted in pure pleasure. And with one head to her nape, I kissed her parted lips and pumped once, twice until I too gave in to her.

I stayed buried inside for a moment longer, catching my breathing and controlling the demon, locking it in for another time. And while my head tucked on the crease of her neck, she slowly trailed her trembling fingertips across my back, shoulder blades, and up to my head.

Her touch was too intimate. Too raw. I peeled away from her skin.

"Don't stray away from the guards or Viktor." I tasted her lips one last time. "You got it?"

Exhausted and satisfied, Katia offered a small nod.

I pulled out and released her. Her legs buckled, and I watched as she struggled to stand straight with a grin.

I tucked my dick inside my pants, picked up the ruined shred of lacey underwear, and my shirt. After I put the soaked fabric into my pocket, I slipped into my shirt and worked on my buttons, all while her eyes watched me carefully.

"I hadn't paid for those," she managed to utter.

I scoffed.

"Add it to the account."

Engraving her vision of her shuddering and fucked body next to the smeared mirror, I said, "And whatever dress you choose, make sure it's for a queen." I turned, but her voice stopped me from pulling the door open.

"Lucca?"

My head tipped toward her, but she didn't say anything. She just stood there naked and vulnerable, unable to speak her mind.

"I'll call you when I'm on the plane heading back, alright?"

Her chestnut hair swayed, and her doe greens glowed.

"Be careful."

Two words, but they meant so much more coming from the Vitelli I took freedom from.

Two words pierced me deeper than I could possibly fathom.

And in two words, she'd said too much.

I walked away, eager to leave the cloak of need and her unspoken thoughts. I couldn't bear them. Didn't want to. So instead, I left, ready to submerge and face the future I was crafting. The plans I had mapped, and the play of deceit for my gain. Our gain.

Miami's gain.

# XXX
## KATIA

I WALKED OUT OF THE DRESSING ROOM IN A DAZE WITH MANY FEELINGS AND thoughts crashing against one another. And while my body tiptoed in blissful satisfaction with curled lips, I couldn't help damning my heart.

I could feel it forming. I could feel it beating.

It was the minutes that were offered. The moments I stole in the short encounters that made me feel alive.

But in this life of greed, blood, and death, they were more than power. They were riches that the underworld didn't provide for those trapped in its sin.

I'd been born in blood and bound to the Mafia.

*I was part of the sin.*

For once, in those fleeing seconds, I felt more than just duty.

I felt the fear of losing someone. The fear of never having that *one* more second. The terror of being all alone—again.

If I'd found a splinter of glee in this cruel, and callous reality, I couldn't abandon it. I had to pick it, even if it meant it was from one of the heartless men that ruled it.

"Any luck?" Davina's marron eyes glanced behind me before they bounced back to my eyes. A small smile played over her features when she realized the owner had left me on my own.

She wasn't a fan of strangers, and that made two of us. But her timid smile hid too many questions.

"I think so." I offered her a smile.

I found the dress moments after Lucca had left me high in release, surrounded by various dresses that hung around it. Somehow, before I gave up the search, my eyes had narrowed to it. It'd fit my exact physique, and it didn't matter if I had to fight the skirt to search for my blade. I knew nothing would come close to its elegant bodice.

It was the dress I would be marrying Lucca in. It was the dress he would tear me free of on our wedding night. So instead of walking out in it, I left it behind only to be seen again on that one day.

"I can't wait to see you in it. I have no doubt it's beautiful," she added.

"Thank you," I said, and scanned the empty room. "Where is Viktor?"

Her face lit up, and her body bounced, turning and motioning for me to follow.

"Ilias arrived just as Lucca was leaving." Her smile returned with a snicker. I watched her closely, and while only half of her face was visible, I could see she knew something I didn't.

"What is it?" I asked, and slowed my pace.

Her black shoulder length hair swayed as she shook her head as if it wasn't anything important but answered. "Ilias likes to tease and push Lucca a bit too much for pure enjoyment."

She stopped before we could walk out to the main floor and continued, "Even Arlo does when they are not all…" She searched for the right word.

Brutal? Cold hearted? Assholes?

Hell, take a pick.

"Scary."

I laughed.

"Sure, *scary*." I chuckled, and her smile widened. "And what was he teased for again?"

Her face tinted a faint rose, and the color traveled down to her neck.

"Well, Arlo had said, and I quote, *I can only think of one reason we are late to our own flight.*"

"And Ilias?" I questioned.

Her eyes lowered. "That by his rumpled shirt, and messy hair he could name *it*."

What an odd interaction. They joked with him.

"What was Lucca's response?"

Davina's head tilted in my direction and shrugged. "The only way he does. With threats, sneers, and a few choice of words."

Now *that* I could see, I smiled.

We both stepped into the open entry and two sets of striking blue eyes shot in our direction.

"Thank fuck, I'm starving," Ilias announced, and his gaze fell onto Davina. She walked away from me to meet his outstretched arm, and once she was tucked inside, his eyes lifted. "Good to see you again, I'll be joining you guys for the rest of the evening."

I gave him a nod and turned to Viktor's scrutinizing gaze.

He smiled.

I smiled back.

He chuckled.

I held mine.

"Are you hungry?" he asked.

"Yes, but first, I would like to stop at one last place."

"Where to?" His brows scrunched, and he glanced down to his wristwatch.

"I need to get Lucca's wedding band."

Viktor's smile reached his eyes, and when he twisted his head toward Ilias, they shared a look.

"I know the place."

Turns out the place was one that had an affiliation to their syndicate. The Mafia had their own little shops, towns, and streets that were tied to them one way or another. It could bring safety, but it also meant danger when it was places you often frequented.

This jewelry store in particular had over-the-top security, and I didn't think it was due solely to its large equity figure. *Lo Splendore* wasn't a small business run by an Italian in the corner of a city. It was a store that viewed the crystal-blue beach. It dripped with brilliant elegance in dim lighting and shining chandeliers.

Viktor and I waited to be let in as two of Lucca's men stood outside. Ilias and Davina decided to stay behind, and I was thankful. As much as I enjoyed their banter, I wanted a moment alone. Even if that meant with Viktor close by.

Viktor looked at his watch again.

He'd done it once in the wedding boutique. Three times in the car, and it seemed he wasn't done.

"Is there something I should be aware of, Viktor?" I asked, staring straight ahead at the man who was nearing in an all-black suit.

"No."

"Do you have to be somewhere else?"

"No."

"Then why are you continuously looking at the time?"

He shook his head. "You sound like him, you know." My eyes slid to him, and he finally answered in a loud exhale. "I have alerts set for when we are out in the open. I keep looking at my watch because I want to make sure nothing has changed."

Huh.

The man offered his hand and said kindly, "Mrs. Moretti."

I shook it and returned my hand to my small clutch.

"*Vitelli*," I corrected him. "Soon to be Moretti."

"Of course!" His chin dipped. "Congratulations on such a joyful time for you."

My smile tightened, but to him it only showed cheer.

"Right this way, I have the room set up for you." He motioned for us to follow him and added, "Mr. Moretti prefers privacy."

Viktor stepped closer to my side as I followed the man at a distance, and he murmured, "Why do you do that?"

"Do what, exactly?"

We walked past the empty sales floor. By the looks of it, Viktor's call wasn't just to expect us, but to cater solely to us.

"Correct him."

"Because *I am a Vitelli*, and I don't bear his name...yet."

It was simple. I was unwed, and that title came only after we both said *I do*. Until then, I was just another sick Vitelli.

Viktor's hand gently touched my upper back, and he uttered, "I walk in first."

His tone changed at the sight of the newly opened door, and his easy smile and demeanor shifted to cold and stone-like.

Viktor's craft wasn't just reading people, it was transforming into another persona in seconds. A smart and ruthless skill when played by him. He was the chameleon of the family.

I waited a few seconds by the seamless door casing. I was alert with one hand near the edge of my skirt while paying attention to Viktor and my surroundings.

"Aren't you coming?" he quipped.

My eyes narrowed, and he shrugged.

I suppressed my chuckle and walked into the room. The man who had provided his name as Joseph explained the sections of rings he'd placed on a large glass casing. And while he spoke with no end, I stopped listening after he'd said they were all Lucca's ring size. I studied the tall ceiling and their structural beams that could sustain its shape and heavy mounted stones. I trailed the lines and angles, playing them in my head until I ran out of walls and molds to look at.

"And on this—"

"Thank you, Joseph, for your time," I cut him off. "I'll take it from here."

He smiled and left with a curt nod.

"What took you so long?" Viktor chimed as the door closed.

I walked closer to the large collection of wedding bands. "Are you telling me you are not interested in the grade, materials, and metal of each one of these?"

"You got jokes, huh?" He glanced over at the casing.

I guess I did.

The selection was too broad, and as I stared at the case filled with diamonds, I avoided choosing one of them. Lucca's taste was too refined and strict to wear something flashy against his skin.

"The guy mentioned how Lucca preferred privacy, as if he spent many hours here. He must come often." I leaned my hip over the glass and faced Viktor.

He smiled knowingly.

"If you must know, Katia. No, he doesn't. I know my brother. If he wanted something, it would be specific, and only a few items would be displayed similar to his request. My bet is, he comes in, takes a look, and walks out."

"Hmm."

"But if you are trying to find out what kind of *things* he buys here." His brow lifted, and I waited. "It would be a new watch." He paused and smiled crookedly. "Cufflinks." His palms waved. "Or custom-made brass knuckles. Nothing delicate, nothing *feminine*."

*Good.*

With a smile on my lips, I returned to the rings.

My eyes roamed row by row, absorbing all the colors, from gold, silver, black, to gray. The forms and edges of each were unique.

This would be more challenging than finding a dress.

"There are so many options, it's—"

"Diamonds?"

"No."

"Good choice," he replied and fired questions. "Black or gray?"

"No."

"Silver?"

I thought about it for a second, but while our marriage was far from traditional, I wanted his band to match the ring he'd given me.

His mother's.

"Gold."

"Okay, that narrows it down some." Viktor quickly rearranged the bands until only one casing remained. "Now, the first four that you are drawn to." His hands ushered me forward.

I did.

"Now eliminate two."

I took each band and returned two to its padding.

"Pick one."

I traced each edge and detail, feeling its grooves and twists. Both bands were similar, and yet unique.

I loved them both, and as I stared at them, I couldn't decide which would bear his finger.

"Do you think he will wear it?" I wondered, lost in gold.

"Yes."

"Have *you* ever thought of marriage?"

"Yes." My head turned to face him, but his eyes were down on the various rings. "But it's not something I see happening. Not with what I do."

Viktor shared, and a part of me thanked him for doing so because he didn't have too. As his thoughts pried him away into memories, I could see the sorrow of his admission.

Viktor had someone special.

"Not *with what you do*?" I echoed his words. "Lucca is getting married."

"As a boss, he has to, Katia. And you've always been in harm's way by being born into this life."

Even though I knew this, his words stung. Because if it hadn't been me, another woman would be walking down the aisle for the same reason I was supposed to, duty. I was just offered before he sought out his future queen. In fact, we were never meant to meet. Never meant to coexist.

I repeated his words in my head, and uttered, "She's not affiliated."

He didn't have to reply, his tensed body answered.

"I wish it was *that* simple."

Two knocks erupted throughout the room, and I was left with burning questions. Joseph stepped inside and waited near the opened door.

"Have you found anything that interests you?"

"I have," I replied, and drew my shoulders back as he walked closer. "Which one of these is one of a kind?"

He moved closer, looking at them, and he quickly replied, "The one on your left."

"Great." I smiled at the gold band. "This is it. I'll wait for the payment information so I can clear the wire transaction, and please add the sole right to its design."

Joseph blinked, taken aback by my request but quickly regained his composure. "There's no need, Miss. Vitelli. We already have an account on file."

I stared at the man, finally looking directly at him and his shiny slicked-back hair.

"And per my request, you can disregard that account for this purchase. I will take care of it, and please don't forget to hand me the paperwork while you retrieve the information I asked for."

His Adam's apple bobbed, and without another word he did as told.

"*Fuck*, I bet you drive *him* mad," Viktor whispered nearby with glee.

Yes, I did.

**TEXAS**

# XXXI

## LUCCA

NEUTRAL TERRITORY. THAT WAS WHAT I REQUESTED WHEN I HAD called out a council meeting and how I found myself on a private flight to Houston. But this city was far from corrupt. Texas was one of the main streams that traveled all across the States and into our cities. A gateway that we all benefited from, with resources and people we all used throughout.

*This is as neutral as it gets.*

Our rules were simple. Every boss must travel with only one man by their side.

Council meetings were secretive for the safety of each syndicate. The exact location and time was only known to the bosses to rule out any leaks or threats. They were rare and requested when an issue needed to be discussed in person. An issue that could potentially harm La Cosa Nostra.

Due to the rules already being broken, I didn't trust Borelli.

I didn't trust this meeting.

But this was one way I could get him out of California to see the bastard. Even if it was surrounded by family members.

"Why not take him out now?"

"I'm going to act as if you didn't speak, Arlo." I glanced at my watch, fifteen minutes until landing.

"But I did."

I faced him.

Arlo sat on the opposite side of the cabin, but his seat faced the back of the jet. He repeatedly tugged the knot in his tie, uncomfortable to wear a full suit. While his clothing had changed since becoming my underboss, he still preferred his dark jeans and black tee on messy days. The others, he spent it in dress pants and a black tee. Never a tie.

"You know the answer."

"And yet, I'm asking you." His light-brown eyes challenged.

I took a deep breath. "If he dies, or any of us don't return to our cities, the famiglia will crumble by mistrust." My eyes fell to my last drink for the day. "If he dies," I repeated, "they'll know it was me. Unless he steps in Miami, in the eyes of the council, he is not a direct threat to me. I need to assure you that our rules are still in place."

"Tino is in Miami," he spat.

"Do you have proof, Arlo? A fucking picture, or someone alive that can confirm?"

We knew it, which meant the whispers would have eventually made it to the other bosses. But that was all they were. Whispers, rumors.

"Then why are we even here?"

For my next move. To look Borelli in the eyes, knowing he was oblivious to what I had planned.

To cause chaos.


KATIA. KATIA. KATIA.

Every thought and every step I made across the street was with her in my mind. The promise of keeping her safe was my top priority. I wouldn't have believed it if it wasn't for the weight that dragged inside of my chest, the constricting pressure to eliminate all threats to what was mine.

Miami.

Katia.

KATIA.

"Rana sent me a text," Arlo whispered as we neared the side entrance of Calabria's. "Looks like they finally made it. Were you aware of Katia needing to run an errand?"

I stopped under the shade of the overhang of the roof and turned.

No, I wasn't aware, but what bothered me was Viktor and Ilias not mentioning it.

"Where?"

Arlo faced the wooded line behind the establishment, eyes scanning the few acres of the secluded land in which the winery stood. A few couples walked the manicured and shaded grounds, enjoying the gentle breeze against the Texas heat.

*Calabria's* wasn't just a winery, it was a quiet place for tourists to enjoy a stroll while taking sips of the most refined wines of Italy. Private enough for a meeting, yet open to the public to avoid scandals.

A place where to some, we were just another suit walking through for exported goods. We were hiding in plain sight along with the rich.

"*Lo Splendore.*" Arlo smirked, turned, and opened the door.

Huh, the jewelry store.

I walked into the smell of aged wood and grapes, leaving his smirk along with any further thoughts of Katia's errand behind. There was no room for nonsense when soon I would meet every boss in person. It was time for business, not for distractions. I knew this.

*Then why was I still thinking of her?*

I adjusted my eyes to the dim lighting and welcomed the cool air inside. Glass walls showed case rows of wine bottles while tall wood tables scattered around the open space. A mix of elegance and old Italy mingled together as expensive touches were added in the establishment. The main room was absent of any seating aside from the few leather and tapestry chairs in the corner where a young couple shared smiles and gleaming eyes with each other.

Three men were accompanied by a female, all dressed in executive clothing. They all gathered around one of the tall tables with an opened folder in the middle, and as a waiter neared to refill their empty wineglasses, the female denied them all their next pour.

By the way her curly dirty blonde hair shook, and how her posture remained strong even as she stood in high heels, I knew she held all the cards in their exchange.

The waiter returned behind the grand half-oval bar, set the bottle of wine down, and whispered to the waitress next to him. The young girl looked up, noticing us by the corner. Her eyes widened, noticing she'd missed our entrance. Quickly she wiped her hands on a rag as her steps rushed to us.

I took one last glance around as I felt unwanted attention.

The couple was still enamored with each other, paying no one around them a thought. But when my eyes returned to the one full table, I met her eyes.

The men talked around her, unaware of how her attention had shifted away from their dealings. Instead, hazel eyes took me in with questions beneath their hard gaze, uncaring of how they studied me so bluntly.

Only the eyes of the powerful were capable of holding notice as she did.

But I wasn't here for her, or to answer to the leering eyes, I was here for Katia.

I broke our contact and peered down at the pixie haired waitress whose smile covered half of her face.

"I have a private meeting," I muttered.

"Of course, it's right through this hall," she said, waving her hand toward the direction. "It's the last door at the end." She began walking as she continued, "It's probably my favorite room, with all the barrels of wine around," she gushed, and I read her name tag. *Mindy.*

"Thank you, Mindy. We can take it from here."

"Of course, some of your party has already arrived." She finished with a nod and left us alone in the corridor.

Arlo stepped beside me, ready for the unexpected.

"Not a word," I uttered, and pulled the door open.

The waitress had been right, the large room was filled with barrels and boxes of wine bottles lining the walls. In the middle of a large wooden table, I met the eyes of killers who I mirrored, standing before brown leather chairs with one man behind each.

Only one boss was missing, Borelli.

The first to move was no other than my future father-in-law. I tasted copper bile at the thought of being kin to him, tied even if it was by marriage.

*All in due time,* I chanted to my demon. *All in due time.*

Mario Vitelli stretched his arms out, a welcoming gesture even I didn't believe. A gesture I didn't trust.

In the next hour, every move, every word had a reason. An underlying agenda I had to pick apart and decipher, and Mario Vitelli was putting a front of union in front of the others.

I stretched my hand out without a smile, and we shook hands.

"Moretti." His smile tightened.

It'd been months since I last saw him, and under the distress New York was under, Vitelli hid well the toll it was taking on him. I watched him carefully for a second longer, and against his hard features, and the fine wrinkles around his eyes, I failed to find a trace of Katia's strength on him.

"Vitelli," I replied and moved past him to meet the boss of Las Vegas.

It was the best way to remove myself from the image Vitelli wanted to portray without disrespect. After all, we weren't alone.

Alonzo Costa offered me a grin as we both closed the distance. It'd been three years since he'd taken over his father and held the gates of Vegas. Before I took the title of the youngest boss in La Cosa Nostra it had been Alonzo who mingled with the old ways until I'd come along. Our alliance was simple, we both saw the flaws of not moving with time.

"You should've called," he whispered through his teeth, blue eyes striking in question.

I offered my hand, and as he took it, I leaned closer to reply, "It wasn't safe."

Alonzo's eyes narrowed but didn't show any other gesture. Instead, we pulled apart with tight smiles as the reminder of where we were and who surrounded us didn't allow an open conversation. He ran his hand through his jet-black hair and gave Arlo a curt nod.

"Guess I'm not the only one who traveled with their underboss." His head tilted slightly to his right.

A tell he did too often for me not to pick up after the several encounters we had. I watched him closer and lowered my voice.

"I guess not."

A wolf-like smirk took over as he straightened, nothing more. Nothing that confirmed my suspicion. But there was something that told me I had learned my ally's weakness. His right-side hearing was impaired.

"Lucca," he warned without a threat. "Don't forget Chicago."

"I have a pretty good memory but thank you."

Alonzo let out a dark chuckle. "I'll be calling you soon."

"Talk to you then." We shook hands once last time, and I stood next to the empty seat between him and Stefano Russo, the oldest boss and most cynical bastard of all. His closest tie was Mario Vitelli. It seemed fitting.

He offered his weak hand out to me. Another hand to shake, another close lip smile to give. A distrust shared.

With an open jacket and a large belly in between, he said, "It's been a while."

"It has. Hope all is well."

Stefano Russo shrugged, and his loopy cheeks shook. "It is when I don't travel."

I grinned, surprised he even announced his annoyance out loud to meet in person. But by the looks of his freckled bald head, and the weakness to hold his own weight in trembling limbs, I was more surprised if Chicago didn't have his coffin ready.

My eyes caught the man behind him. His son, Mateo Russo. I returned his curt nod with Alonzo's words playing in my head. *Guess I'm not the only one who traveled with their underboss.*

Seeing Mateo for the first time, age ready for his father's seat, I questioned his title as capo even more..

"Business couldn't wait," I replied to Stefano.

"We should take a seat," he said loudly for everyone to hear. "I'm sure Borelli will be in shortly."

I dismissed Stefano's arrogance. I wasn't here to make Chicago an enemy even if his ruler had no manners to address me.

We all followed Stefano and sat in silence. The wedge and ties between families was clear.

Mario Vitelli and Stefano Russo; New York and Chicago.

Alonzo Costa and I; Las Vegas and Miami.

As I sat between them, I could finally see it in person. The reason I had agreed to marry into the Vitelli family aside from my own immoral desires.

The shift of votes now played in my favor. My word now carried power between families. I couldn't lose, and it was an addictive feeling.

In the middle of the table, a large spread of cheeses, roasted crackers, dried meats, and endless grapes laid for picking. Only Stefano dug in as if it was a meal. A glass of water rested next to an empty wineglass, and a knock broke through Stefano's chewing.

Vitelli's man walked to the door and allowed the pixie haired waitress to step inside with him close in tow. Mindy pushed a small cart of wine bottles inside a metal bucket of ice with eyes that couldn't meet anyone in particular.

*Could she sense the killers of which she neared? The sin and danger that sat before her?*

The young brunette cleared her throat. "I will be leaving the bottles for you all to enjoy without any further interruptions." She cast a look behind her before she continued, "But before I do, I will go over the five top selections I've brought with me." Mindy cleared her throat again with another leering glance behind.

Poor kid. She'd stepped into a world even her imagination couldn't comprehend.

"The first is a thirty-year aged—"

"Just pour them," Stefano Russo mumbled.

She cowered, and Stefano's eyes glimmered happily at its sight. *Mio Dio*, this was hard to watch. The fear in her eyes, the twisting of her fingers, the hesitation to move forward, all while causing excitement to others.

The waitress nodded and made her way to Stefano. Vitelli's goon let her go as Mateo neared, escorting her to his father. A bit overkill. I was sure Arlo felt the same because once she went over the wines and finished pouring Stefano's choice of wine, Arlo only followed her small steps to us with his eyes.

I hadn't planned on another drink until my return to Miami, but after hearing a certain bottle, my interest won.

"Thank you," I said after smooth red filled my glass.

She smiled timidly and walked a few steps to Alonzo.

I took a gentle breath in as my lips touched the brim and took a sip.

It was a blend made from the fields in Tuscany. Aged with fermented grapes with a bold and yet subtle hint of ripe *cherries*. The wine played with my tongue as I pulled the glass away. Silky, tart, alluring. Not dry enough for my taste but its sweet savory elegance reminded me of someone who would. Someone who I could enjoy such glass with if only in their presence.

*Fuck.*

I placed the glass down.

Vitelli's leery eyes followed the girl all the way to the door, and when she left the silence returned.

My watch read ten minutes after. If Pietro Borelli didn't walk through the door in five minutes, the meeting would come to an end. No words would be exchanged, and I would have to move through my plan without a clear wage of repercussions. But before my mind had the chance to begin its course of countermoves, the bastard walked in.

Tall, in an all-black suit that matched his eyes and contrasted against his full white hair, Pietro Borelli made his entrance. His son, Tino, was nowhere in sight.

An alarm blared in my head with the knowledge of Tino in my city without me. They knew it, and while I had known the possibility of Tino not showing up next to his father, I took the risk. I left Katia alone.

The severity of the chance I'd taken grew against me. All I had was the trust of my brothers and my men to keep her safe.

In the end, this was the outcome I'd wanted. I just hadn't known the suffocating grip it would cause. It couldn't be fear. I feared no one. *But did I fear for her?*

I dragged my thoughts and shoveled them with murder. I sipped on red as my demon thirsted for blood and watched as my sadistic heart imagined his last name obliterated by my hands.

*Soon,* I promised. One by one.

"No need to stand." His palms opened.

I hadn't moved.

Borelli slid his chair out as his eyes roamed around the table with small nods to each boss. But when he met mine, our war spoke in freedom.

The lives he'd taken.

The lives of his men I'd taken.

All for the prize he wanted, the prize I had.

I had to pick my words carefully. A strength of mine, but with him present in the same room, I had to be cautious about making any accusations.

"Where's your son?" My question was a simple thought, but my tone was the first punch I delivered, causing interest around Tino's absence.

The first seed of many I would plant without allegations.

Borrelli's arrogant smirk and answer, his own ruin.

He never traveled without him.

"He had important business to attend to." His capo brought a wine bottle to him. He declined it. "But he sends you his regards."

"Just me?"

He chuckled and glanced around. "Of course not. What have I missed?" he asked and faced Stefano Russo.

Stefano dusted his lips with shaky fingers and raised his glass to wash down his gluttony.

"We were waiting for you. You sure you don't want some wine?"

"I don't have the taste for wine."

"What about some cheese? How about some salami? It's seasoned to near perfection."

My eyes slid to Stefano, perplexed by how a man of his age could eat and gush over food as he did. Even startled by his fixation over a fucking charcuterie board instead of business.

A quick glance to his son, Mateo, whose eyes were ahead and away from the conversation with a tight jaw, and the more I questioned Chicago's order.

"No disrespect, my friend, but I'm only here on duty." Borelli squared his shoulders.

*Friend.*

We had no friends.

Stefano leaned back, finally taking his first break from working his mouth muscles, and all eyes were on me.

I'd played over scenarios, picked and placed the right amount of information to give in front of the eyes of sin. To me, this was a simple chess game. This table was an open board. And while I was here to defend, I would be taking the first move.

"There's a threat that concerns us all as it's causing too much attention toward our organization."

Now, I had their undivided attention by taking offense. I kept my words strong, while my tone took charge.

"A target on a Vitelli, soon to be Moretti," I quickly added, and fished inside my jacket pocket. I threw the picture that was dated a year ago, with Katia's face out in the open for all to see. "I took that picture from someone who took orders by an affiliated man."

Stefano shifted closer to the picture while Borelli stayed composed.

I felt Alonzo's eyes, but mine watched Vitelli, uncomfortable by his daughter's face as it silenced the rumors into truth. Although, he was more concerned of how the revealed secrets would perceive him than the safety of his only daughter. He didn't fool me.

I turned my attention back to Borelli.

"If by an affiliated man, you mean one of us, that's against code." Stefano's puffed lips curled.

"And punished by death," Alonzo's words sliced in bloodthirst.

"This is a grave accusation, Moretti," Stefano warned.

"And yet, I haven't spoken a name," I replied.

Borelli didn't twitch. Calm, collected, and in control, he kept his posture, but the more they spoke, the more a vein popped across his forehead.

"I heard about the five deaths in your city. It made the news nationwide. Some named it a serial-killer on the loose while others called it a killing-spree," Alonzo said next to me, stating the facts and setting the whispers to rest. "The characteristics of the victims are uncanny to your *fiancée*."

Borelli broke character, I didn't.

I liked the sound of *your fiancée*.

"Mario," Stefano spluttered. "You must have something to say."

Cornered, Katia's father spoke. "Like Moretti has said, we are at war."

Of course Vitelli's words wouldn't help me. No war was known to La Cosa Nostra, it had been private. Taken and forged without rules, until now.

"Who is it, Mario?" Stefano cut clean.

Mario Vitelli didn't answer, so I did.

"I can't prove it, yet. Which is why I've requested this meeting."

"If you can't prove it was an affiliated man, there was no base to call this meeting!" Stefano's tone raised and a bead of sweat rolled off his temple.

"It will be when our organization hits the news if the next victim is the daughter of a suspected mafioso, Russo." My patience was running thin. "They will connect the prior deaths and tie them to hers."

"My question is, why is a woman, a Vitelli, targeted by one of our own?" Alonzo abruptly asked, tired of the broken stories and hunting for the truth.

My eyes met his bright blues. They were wicked and demanding answers. While rumors often began with one person, the wind carried the whispers and split them. When they arrived, they were nothing but shattered shards of information. Most far from the truth.

But I knew the tales Alonzo had heard were untouched. I made sure of it.

Then it dawned on him.

His jaw tensed and his eyes turned to slits. Alonzo's rigid shoulders fell back onto the chair, and he faced ahead.

"Borelli, you haven't said a word!" Stefano's face matched the color of his wine.

"I'm just as surprised," Borelli spat.

"Was there ever a deal made between New York and Los Angeles?" Alonzo fueled the match I'd lit, and chaos ruptured through.

I held my smile and watched how the order crumbled. The curtain pulled from the sham as egos and lies collided. The fatal and unspoken slaughter that hung above, and the trigger-finger tics that begged to deliver bloodshed.

Curse words flew around the stiff pressure in the air, and our men grew tense as the sway of deadly outcome creeped.

Stefano's hands shook out over the table to cease the madness, but his weak muscles gave up to their weight, and he shouted, "*Basta!*" Enough.

Vitelli sat back. Indignation and anger clouded his eyes as his mouth opened in disbelief by the brutal truth out in council.

Borelli stood rapidly, and his chair scraped loudly against the floor. A well-acted performance as his face flared in rage, offended.

"I will not sit here and be accused of any of this nonsense." His palm hit the table.

"I hadn't done such a thing. I asked a mere question between bosses," Alonzo said, unbothered.

"But it brings allegations!" Borelli flung back. "This is not the way of council, and disrespect comes with a price!"

Stefano sat quietly, his eyes swinging from one head to another, watching, listening, taking it all in. His closest ally, Vitelli, had broken a vow. But the boss on his right had broken an oath. The one thing we lived and killed by, sealed by blood. It was sacred and treated as such.

Borelli could deny it, and I had no proof to say otherwise.

He wouldn't be walking out of here alive if I did.

Dead on the spot in the back room of a winery while we sipped on its riches.

Vitelli finally spoke up. After all, he was also sitting next to the boss who'd caused so many casualties to his city. He would do anything to stop it.

"No one accused you of targeting my daughter, Borelli. No disrespect has been made. Now, sit so we can finish this meeting."

Borelli's eyes slid to mine. Their black bottomless pits spoke of his promises and ruthless plans he sought to fulfill. Rabid in massacre.

I held them and smirked.

"I will do no such thing!" He stood straight.

"Before you leave," I stated. "I requested this meeting only for one reason, and that was to inform all that Miami's borders are closed. Therefore any visit into my city would be treated as a threat and eliminated as such."

My words carried power, action. A clear warning of execution if bridged.

"Until this threat is resolved, we are all at risk," I added as if I cared for their lives.

"You have my vote. Close it down," Alonzo spoke up.

Borelli's nose twitched in ire.

*Check.*

"Vitelli?" I asked.

"The safety of my daughter is a priority, *sì*." A lie I ignored after hearing his vote.

Borelli's breathing deepened.

*Check.*

"Russo?" I asked.

Stefano stared at his empty wineglass before he looked at me. Full lips quivered as sweat poured from trouble.

He nodded.

I glanced at Borelli.

*Checkmate.*

"You don't need my vote." With a sneer, Borelli turned and left the quiet room.

That was my cue to leave. Because while I wished to stay until the surge of victory could subside inside, I had corralled Borelli into action, and I was still states away from home.

From Katia.

"Gentlemen."

I walked away without any further words to give. No nods, handshakes, or closed smiles to offer. I got what I wanted. Miami was now a no-man's-land. I was free to kill anyone without question, no matter of title or affiliation.

I had work to do.

Arlo kept up with my pace as we moved through the corridor. Chatter grew the closer we got to the main room, and as I turned to take the side exit we'd entered, I stopped.

"Lucca?" Arlo asked.

I circled around until I found Mindy's surprised face behind the bar.

"I want a bottle to go." I pulled a billing card from my jacket. "And a box delivered to this address." I tapped it. "Charge it to that information."

I slid the card across the bar and her pixie cut swayed in agreement. Mindy quickly left to retrieve my order.

"Seriously?" Arlo scoffed.

"Sir." The male waiter stepped next to me. "A female from earlier left me her business card for you."

I looked down at the paper between us and took it as Mindy returned with the bottle I'd asked. The card read *Natalie Arrington.*

"Let's go." I grabbed the bottle and made my way out of the building and into the hot Texas air.

I took a few steps before fishing for my phone and making the first call.

"*Da.*" Yeah. Viktor answered in Russian.

"Do not leave the house. Eyes open and above," I replied, hung up, and moved to the second call.

"*Zdarova.*" What's up? Ilias mumbled in Russian.

"There may be trouble. Stay in my house if needed."

"Wait!" Ilias's voice cut off, and I moved on to my last call.

"*Pronto,*" Sergio answered, Italian heavy in his tongue as loud female moans filtered through the receiver. "Boss?"

"Tell Rana, Fer, and Mimmo that they are needed in Rio's perimeter. Get Beppe to fucking do something too."

"Casper and Emilio's men are already covering—"

"Do as I ask."

"Yes, sir."

I ended the call and hopped inside the car. Arlo turned the ignition, the engine purred to life, and I closed my eyes for a brief minute. I needed a drink, and I didn't mean wine.

"Did it not go as you planned?" Arlo asked.

It did. It was the best outcome and scenario I could've fabricated. I now just needed to see a set of vivid greens full of life to finally escape from the adrenaline and burning blood that had taken over.

I gripped the bottle and smiled. Damn cherries.

# XXXII

## KATIA

THE CLOCK READ PAST ELEVEN, AND LUCCA HADN'T RETURNED HOME OR called. While I hadn't asked about his last-minute trip to Texas, I noticed after arriving home that Arlo was gone too. They'd left together. That alone spoke of how crucial it was for them both to leave the city without its boss and underboss. It also showed the limited number of people aware of their absence.

Since I'd gathered and roped around the missing pieces, and understood how private this meeting was, I was growing impatient by his silence. I worried about his safety as time passed.

Slowly dread swept inside, creeping through the cracks of my dimmed thoughts. The loneliness only grew with the darkness inside the room. The one friend I'd counted on now hunted me with visions I'd only dreamed of. All conspiring, to my dismay.

I'd tried to occupy my mind by sketching on my tablet. However, as I held the cool and thin touch-screen pencil, the feel of my stringer-knife and its thin needle blade took its place.

My grip loosened with small trembles, and I closed my eyes. It slipped as I broke into a cold sweat, dampening my hands. But instead of cold chills traveling over my body, I felt warm sap over my hands. I snapped my eyes only to see red.

I scurried away from its feel, shaking it off and wiping my palms over the white bedsheet, and while they were clean, the ghost's blood lingered.

*No, no, no.*

The dreams were brushing into reality. Stirring memories of bloodbath and recreating scenes I couldn't flee.

I tossed the tablet and pencil to the side, and searched for my phone. I looked at it one last time in case I'd missed his call.

Needy to escape in his voice and calm demeanor, I tucked my pillow tight to my chest and lay over the mattress, watching as my phone mocked without his name written on its screen.

"Vino, Wex," I called out to my two beasts and patted the bed for them to get on it, unable to wait alone with my mind tricks.

Quickly they both jumped, and the bed dipped under their weight. They tossed and circled around its edge trying to find space for them both. Wex flopped, and pinned my hips down as he laid his head over them. Vino snarled and shoved his nose to Wex's neck in an attempt to move him.

"Stop fighting," I cooed.

Vino growled and grumpily laid next to him, pushing me down onto the bed to place his head on my torso.

I huffed under their weight, and their bodies heated. Maybe Lucca was right. They were too big for our bed, too heavy to be treated as lap dogs. But at this moment, their warmth and long coat calmed the roars in my chest, gently easing death's shadow.

I laid still, pinned beneath their frame, wide eyed and fingertips stroking their fur to replace the sin—even if it was temporary.

For nights, I'd relived that night, and maybe I wasn't as strong as I thought I was.

I had killed a total of three men in my life.

The *first* wasn't intended. I hadn't been the one who'd bled him to death. Leo did, but I was the only reason for his death. Not once did I ponder over his life.

The *second* was a poor bastard who'd stolen from me. My grandfather ordered his hunt.

*"No one steals from a Vitelli, dolcezza."*

I was sent to condemn him to death by identifying him. Without batting an eye, I watched as they beat him to a pulp, but as his screams grew, I took the gun my grandfather had offered and ended his misery. My grandfather didn't shy me away from the ugly. Instead, he taught me to embrace it. He wasn't a kind man, but to me, Nonno's treatment almost showed care. Care to acknowledge the blood that ran through my veins and the weight my last name carried. Nonno's attention was the closest thing to affection I'd experienced. At twenty-two, I believed death brought us closer. As if I'd gained his respect as a woman by taking the life of a man who'd threatened our reputation.

The man's death was fast, simple, and not a night passed without me losing sleep over it. After all, I was broken, or so I'd thought.

Maybe it was the intimate way I'd taken the life of the *third* that night at the gala. Or the way I watched his eyes void of life while I sitting in ire calm, in a puddle of his blood. Immersing myself in his essence.

Or maybe what really haunted me was *myself*.

The way I'd disconnected and slipped into the thirsty fog of inhumanity. Either way, evil consumed my spirit.

My phone ranged and I answered, closing my eyes.

"Talk to me," I whispered.

Lucca took a deep breath and exhaled into the receiver.

"Why are you awake?" his deep and raspy voice asked.

"I can't sleep," I admitted.

"I will talk as long as possible before the call drops. But first, answer me." He paused. "How bad is it?"

Of course he knew. Lucca slept lightly, any small stirs or sounds quickly awakened him. My tossing and turning hadn't gone unnoticed. But as I'd struggled with new feelings, and their revelations followed by the fear he'd inflicted, I'd stayed away. I was furious with him and ignored his presence, acting as if the life I'd taken didn't bother me. I believed he wouldn't notice it or sense it in those days. However, Lucca had always seen through my farce, lies, and deceit since the first day we met.

Once again, darkness failed me. Instead of concealing my troubled mind, it revealed it in its shade.

"It's just me, Katia. I won't fault you or speak of it again." While his voice was firm and cold, they spoke in truth.

"It's the silence."

"What happens in the silence?"

"Dreams break my peace. No, not dreams. Vivid memories." My hand slithered away from Vino's soft coat, and I covered my closed eyes, pushing my palm against them as if it could erase the images.

"I don't think I have it in me to be a coldhearted killer," I uttered.

"Want to know what I think?"

"Yes."

"You don't have to *have it in you* to thirst for death. *I* think you are strong. I am convinced that your mind slips away as you take a life but returns shortly after for *you* to acknowledge it. And I think after you do, it will never bother you again."

"What if you are wrong?"

"I'm never wrong," he stated.

"Talk to me," I repeated, hoping this time my admission could die along with the memories.

Lucca stayed quiet for a short while and eventually gave in.

"Are you sure? Anything I say won't ease your mind."

"Yes," I answered, and Lucca spoke without aim, freeing words and tales of his past.

"I don't like tomato soup because it was what I mainly ate at the orphanage. Talia's father, Carlo, used to pass basil around to the boys, and I used to stash them for my brother's soup to have some decent taste."

"He didn't have to, but his kindness was probably the only thing any of those boys, including myself, felt in those years. And while my time there was short compared to the ones who were left before they could speak, I loathed it the most. Because unlike them, I knew what awaited me on the outside. Freedom."

"Inside those walls we just—existed, and Carlo's small act made me face reality. It's what made me stop wondering about the length of my stay. It's what made me see the truth. So when I bought my first home, I asked him to work for me, taking him away from his reality."

When Talia mentioned her father worked in a home Lucca used to live in, I never thought of that *home*. It never occurred to me that he would be the gardener and nurturer of the same grounds in which Lucca had been abandoned.

"Did you ever think of running away?" I dared.

"No." He paused. "I waited."

*On what? Or who?*

*Salvatore?*

"Then it was too late. I had three younger brothers to keep an eye on."

My mind spun with questions. How did he end up there? Where did he live before? But most importantly, where was his mother? Did she die when he was young like mine did, or did she abandon him?

Lucca was right. His words didn't ease my mind. Instead, they broke for the lost teen who'd once hoped for freedom.

"I must go. I can hear the static growing the longer we are in the air," he explained, and as much as I didn't want him to stop talking, I heard the cracking reception buzzing in my ear.

"Okay."

"Oh, and Katia."

The ongoing call scratched in weak beats.

"Yes."

"I will make sure you never have to feel this way *again*."

Lucca said in a riddle, and after the line disconnected, I clutched my phone tighter and curled deeper into the two large beasts. But his voice remained fresh in my mind. His tone and timbre lingered as his riddle played over and over.

In the break of dawn, I woke up wrapped in the warmth of his arms, entwined with his body as our limbs were woven together. I allowed sleep to claim me again, and as I sank deeper against his body, I solved the riddle.

*I'll kill for you.*

# XXXIII

## LUCCA

THEY ALL SPOKE TO ONE ANOTHER. A CONVERSATION I'D PULLED AWAY from with a glass of brown swirling around and around, mirroring the way my mind worked relentlessly as I waited for Salvatore to arrive. I was tired.

Sleep had become a luxury. All I did was think, play, and scheme. At this point, everything I'd done and planned to do stopped revolving around the syndicate, the *famiglia*, and it had everything to do with *her*.

Everything had shifted. The power, the threats, *my thoughts*. It was dangerous, really. To lose control of my emotions and actions. All driven by sleep deprivation and cruelty.

Vengeance; the sweet and consuming rage that crumbled empires.

It was all I felt because after leaving Texas, the acts of violence had escalated into bloodbaths. As if the weight I carried wasn't enough, I now had more innocent lives caught in the crossfires. I had taken my private jet back to Miami, drained by the meeting and knowing my streets could be streaming in red. And while I made my point without any misunderstanding, I left with each boss' blessing, and the underlying warning couldn't have been clearer.

A no-man's-land.

A war zone.

But I had to stop the death tolls.

I had to stop Tino Borelli at once, and I was ready to share the plan with Salvatore.

"Lucca, are you listening?" Arlo asked from the right corner of my study. The place he always found himself in when we were all together, standing and with arms crossed.

I didn't remove my gaze from my glass. Instead, I brought it to my lips and took a long sip.

"You haven't said anything." Arlo should know, I always listened. No matter if I was a prisoner of my mind, *I always listened.* I always watched carefully, and never ignored the thoughts they shared, the tone they spoke, or the aura that mixed in the room.

It all mattered.

"Salvatore isn't here *yet.* I am not repeating myself twice."

My eyes lifted, locking onto his. He wore his usual attire, all black, but today instead of jeans, dress pants hung from his hips. Arlo remained quiet, but his displeasure and annoyance were clearly etched on his features.

Viktor pulled his phone out of his gray pants. He, too, stood by the corner next to Arlo, but he leaned against the bookcase with furrowed brows and paid attention to his screen. His fingers sped across the device, and he eventually returned it to his pocket. I met his steel-blue eyes that popped against his short sleeve white button-up, but he didn't utter a word. Viktor just sank deeper into the books.

I didn't ask if there was a problem. I trusted him to address it when it was necessary.

"They are all hers?" Ilias asked close to my left.

I dropped my glass onto my desk and watched his back as his hands left imprints over the glass casing that housed Katia's knives.

"Yes."

"This is quite a collection. All with different purposes, grips, blades." Ilias slid one of the compartments open. "There's even throw blades and brass knuckles in here." He inched closer. "Are those diamonds set on—"

"I would close that if I were you," Arlo warned before I had the chance. After all, Arlo had seen what Katia was capable of with the same blades in question.

Ilias shut the drawer and took one last look at the glass before running his hand through his blonde strands, turning to us. He shrugged with a mischievous grin.

I guess some things would never change.

The door burst open, and while everyone turned to the abrupt entrance, I took a deep breath and drowned the remainder of my drink.

"Guess you finally remembered you had a consigliere," Salvatore wheezed as he walked in with pressed black trousers, white long-sleeved shirt, and a formal sleeveless sweater vest. His black fedora rested low on his head, and while his shoulders were straight, his posture was curved from age and sickness.

His ill-temper remained intact while he slowly died, and his power was strong with every weak breath he took. But his mind was as sharp as the first time I met him.

I couldn't stand seeing him slowly deteriorate and hated the deep wrinkles and the struggle it took him to just get here. I hated knowing that soon the last of my blood would be six feet under.

By his missing oxygen tank, this was supposed to be a good day for him, but his weak limbs couldn't deceive.

"I never forgot." Seeing him only worsened my mood.

"Hm." He scoffed and stood over the unfinished chess game. "I don't have all day." Salvatore pulled his gaze away from the board and sat across from my desk. "How did the meeting go, and why are you just now calling me?"

I guess thirty-six hours later was not acceptable for Sal.

No one spoke, and Sal's eyes gripped me tightly. His displeasure was still tight on his lips from the last time we'd been together, upset at how I treated Katia.

I decided it wasn't the time or place to talk about that day and how he'd overshared the past, or how I'd lost control by the sound of my mother's name. Instead, I focused on the task at hand. Blood streaking streets.

"It went as expected," I replied. "In Miami's favor and blessings."

"But I wouldn't be here if it went so *smoothly*." He drew out the last word and coughed. "So what is really the problem?"

"Borelli's son acts on his behalf, *for now*."

"That's not a surprise." His hands waved in front of him, as if that didn't matter.

It didn't. The man with burned, scarred hands would be dead soon.

Salvatore's fedora tipped up, and his gaze cut through my thoughts.

"You are going to order his death." Appalled, he saw my plan. "No one gave you *that* blessing, Lucca."

"Not with those words, but the votes were in my favor. Any visit to my city will be treated as a threat."

Sal's head shook, and his chuckle erupted into heaps of gasps.

"You closed off Miami to the *famiglia*?" Sal's voice raised with disbelief marking his eyes.

"Until Katia is no longer a target? Yes, I did."

He glanced around the room, watching each one of my brothers.

"You all think this is a good idea?" He pointed around.

Trying to settle his anger and calm his breathing, I explained to him.

"The moment Borelli targeted Katia, he knew he'd gone against La Cosa Nostra amendments. He'd sealed his deal, and I made sure they saw it my way. The news and the possible threats to the other bosses made it much easier for my argument to be valued." My thumb slid over the engraved cuts of my empty glass cup. "Borelli wasn't smart enough to bring Tino into the meeting. He left him here, and while I had no proof, I raised the suspicion and all the pieces moved in the right direction." Sal settled as he listened carefully. "Even Alonzo Costa asked if there was a deal made between the Vitelli name and the

Borelli."

An act I wouldn't forget and will repay when needed.

"How did Mario handle the accusation?"

It wasn't an accusation, it was the truth. Thankfully, Mario never made it public. It was a private arrangement, just like the one I'd made with his son. And while every boss knew it by the whispers of their own informants, it had never been from the lips of New York.

Hell, even I understood Borelli's outrage because of a broken vow. I, too, wouldn't have given up or backed away from what was promised to me. It was the way we lived and coexisted. But Borelli's mistake was not taking it to the council. His mistake had been chasing after Katia instead of the man whose words now meant nothing. Borelli's flaws worked in my favor, and after taking Katia from New York, *I* made it public who she belonged to.

"With indignation, he didn't deny his vow. But he also didn't recognize it. Which only leaves me knowing his word is as good as a dead man. Useless."

It took a minute for Sal to think through the play in which I had been a pawn, and I showed him how the board was full of threats.

"We knew this," Sal muttered mostly to himself as he thought of Mario.

"While the Borellis breathe, we will always be watching our backs. And until the marriage is fulfilled, Ilias and Davina will remain in danger."

"Or until Enzo takes his seat," he chimed with a nod. "Have you found Tino?"

"We have a strong lead," Arlo answered. "Even if he hid better than the rats underground for so long."

"Which is how I'm planning on flushing Borelli out of Los Angeles and into our streets," I added.

"His son's death." Realization shimmered in his eyes. "The closing of Miami's border."

I nodded.

"This is too risky, Lucca."

"It must be done before the wedding. Our streets are starting to suffer with Borelli too far to reach. I've run Los Angeles into shambles with time, but they still have manpower and loose cannons thirsty for Miami. If I take them both out, the city will be too weak to rebuild with no one to guide it."

"You are taking out a whole syndicate, Lucca!" His Mafia blood thickened.

I was. Not only for her, but because I won't risk Miami falling.

Sal's gaze snapped at Ilias, the one who in his eyes had started a domino effect. "You best be keeping your promises, boy."

"I'm still made, and Davina is safe," Ilias shot back.

Salvatore's lips curled, and he acknowledged me next. "Where will you be after you kill the son of a boss, huh?"

I didn't reply, and out of the corner of my eye, I saw Viktor's smile.

"I said he should take Katia away for a few days." Viktor's head lifted. "A honeymoon before the wedding, per se."

"I'm not hiding." I cut Viktor a look.

"But you are not," Arlo argued. It was the same conversation they tried to make me listen to earlier, but this time, there were four against one. "And unless you would like to explain to the bride-to-be that you are killing a boss's son to draw out Borelli just days away from her wedding, and leaving her here, like a fucking sitting duck…" He trailed off.

"Or you can just send *her* away." Viktor lifted his shoulder, offering an option we all knew would never happen. Its sole purpose was to win their argument.

"She's not going anywhere without me."

The room heated by my claim and silence stretched, seizing any debate. I dared anyone to say it again. To argue how her safety would be in better hands than mine.

It didn't fucking matter if she was taking the next flight to a remote third world country, Katia wasn't leaving my sight.

"Then it's settled." Salvatore stood with a grunt and dipped his fedora. He was done with this meeting even before offering any council.

"I'm not leaving," I stated.

He turned and walked back to the chessboard. His slender fingers slid the knight by the queen, making a move, and as always Salvatore's words struck deep.

*"You always protect the queen."*

When he left, his words hung on and bounced inside the room like a recording.

"Get out," I ordered.

Viktor and Ilias walked out quietly, but Arlo stood by the door. Waiting until we were alone to speak his mind.

"You can't be here after Tino's death, not for a few days at least. If she dies, so will Ilias and Davina."

I was fucking aware.

"It's not hiding, Lucca. On the contrary, it would be placing Miami first."

I didn't want to talk, I wanted silence. I wanted peace to brew from the chaos I envisioned. Instead, I thought of her and her safety.

My eyes slid from his and to the open door that filtered high heels walking straight toward our direction. The menace of my thoughts and Miami had arrived.

Arlo's demeanor lifted with a wicked smile by seeing her.

"Well, it seems you have healed. Ready for another round?"

He jabbed, insinuating another match between them as her footsteps approached. Once they stopped, her voice was clear and strong as she bit back.

"How's the shoulder?"

Any other time I would've smiled at her quick reply.

"Oh, the graze?" Arlo scoffed. "That bitch was hardly a scratch."

"Arlo," I warned.

Katia walked past him with a smirk, and I stared at the elegance and wit she carried with her. "Really? I could've sworn your shirt was drenched by that *scratch*."

*Mio dio,* these two. When will they stop?

"You need something?" I asked, breaking the dangerous tension and banter, and motioning Arlo to leave us.

Katia watched as the door shut before facing me. Her long legs were bare as her dress was a few inches shorter than most, hugging her body in sophisticated seduction. Her fingers slipped away from the tablet she carried to tuck her hair behind her ear. She then looked down and unlocked the screen.

"No, I don't need anything." She bit her lip, and my dick reacted.

"Then what is it?" I couldn't hide the short and curt tone of my words.

She leaned over my desk placing the device on it, but my eyes zeroed in on her tits peeking through its heart-shaped bodice.

So much skin, glowing and in plain sight for my taking.

"Are you busy?" she asked in an innocent tone.

Games, she was playing them now, while all I wanted to do was let my shaft play inside of her. I knew Katia felt the dark pull of the meeting I'd just finished. Yet, she decided to enter and toy with my mind. Why she had to make things so difficult was beyond me. But the small smile in the corner of her mouth, and the light in her eyes, wasn't foul. She was…*happy?*

My palm caught the curve of her leaning neck, bringing her closer to me.

She'd gotten into the cherries already, and her stunning eyes darkened into forest green at my touch.

"Why are you really here?"

Rose pink spread across her chest and rose up to her cheeks. The striking color heightened her golden skin and my eyes roamed around its flush.

Katia slithered away from my touch as she stood straight. My eyes followed her teasing hips as they swayed around the desk.

Lost in her curves and drawn to her wicked game, I sat waiting for her move.

Next to my sitting position, I rolled my head back to see her towering body next to mine. The mischief on her lips hadn't disappeared. If anything, it'd turned giddy.

"I've been working on something, and I thought you might want to look at it."

Fine, I'll play along.

"Okay."

Her ass perched, and her back curved as she reached over the desk to retrieve the tablet she'd laid out. My Adam's apple bobbed as she took longer than necessary in that position, grabbing something that could've been taken easily with an outstretched hand.

I pressed my lips together, hiding my smile from the needy mood she was placing me to. My dick hardened and my bulge stung against the constriction of my pants.

Katia slowly tortured me, turning her ass in my direction before facing me.

Her smirk was clear as her eyes hunted her prey.

But I was no prey.

I devoured.

## KATIA

MY MOOD WAS AT ITS HIGHEST. HIGH ON SEX, HIGH ON FEELINGS, *HIGH ON HIM.*

He sank into his chair with the same cold, unbothered attitude as usual. His scent lingered strongly between us, a mixture of clean with a rough touch of leather and whiskey. The empty glass spoke of his first drink. It wasn't even noon yet, but the stress in his muscles expressed the morning he had. Even then, his scent danced in attraction, luring me deeper into the trap. His dress shirt stretched over his shoulders, and his tie hung perfectly in place.

I wanted to mess it up and pull it free. To feel his inked skin beneath my fingertips and ruffle his silky hair. But first, I needed a buffer.

The icebreaker that could help my forwardness.

With my back to him and my ass high in the air, his eyes burned into my body. He too wanted this.

His pent-up body wanted to sink his dick and release his mind. And I ... *God* ... I wanted it to happen.

As slowly as I could, I picked up my tablet from his desk and watched him in hunger.

"I drew and fixed a flaw within your home. You might want to look at it." I baited.

Lucca's brow quipped, and a husky chuckle erupted, followed by his running hand scratching the short and trimmed beard I enjoyed when it did the same but between my legs.

"Did you, now?"

"Mm-hmm."

Our eyes locked.

"I must warn you, I'm a bit unstable at the moment, Katia."

I felt it, saw it in his hooded eyes that stared back at mine. But there was no stopping my greed, and blindly, I saw his warning as a promise.

I'd tried to slow his sinful rhythm of need. Through gentle touches, I tried to make him see me as more than just another fuck. Meanwhile, I'd learned I too enjoyed fucking him violently. Because as I thrashed below him, it didn't matter if his fingers marked my skin, or if his thrusts punished. It only proved that desire and want could be delivered in many forms.

I scooted between his legs, and his hands automatically clasped my thighs. Lucca didn't acknowledge the tablet in front of him. His dark eyes and even darker aura kept my eyes tranced by their veil of brutal hunger.

It was all in his eyes. The way they spoke without words to reveal his sadistic thoughts. The way his gaze made my body react, and the room to quiet with the heavy and suffocating fog of danger I'd twistedly craved.

"It'll take just a second," I murmured, but we both heard the lie.

"If you wanted to fuck, that's all you needed to say."

I tucked my bottom lip in an attempt to hide my smile and hovered over him.

With one hand grasping the arm of his chair and the other holding tightly onto the screen, I uttered onto his lips.

"I want to fuck." I evaded him quickly and continued my ruse. "But first." I nudged the device against him. "I don't like it when my time is wasted."

His eyes closed, taking a deep breath, and I smiled as his patience thinned.

The joys of driving him mad was seeing it firsthand.

"You have three minutes before I bury my dick deep into you."

My eyes widened by his threatening tone, and when he opened his eyes, he'd meant every word.

I omitted my argument and quickly opened the file I'd saved of my sketch. His eyes lowered to the screen.

"Two minutes," he said coldly.

To avoid missing a beat, I spoke in rapid Italian. "The structure downstairs, your *work* area, is a death trap. The only exit, or entrance, is the door that can only be accessed through the staircase. It's a disadvantage in case of an ambush. But to avoid someone coming in through a full-sized door in the corner, the grounds outside are suitable for a half-sized side exit that can be stretched out into the property and can be hidden even from the outside. The frame and beams can hold the change."

My fingers swiped to the next slide and traced the outside corridor that could be overseen by a small man-made mountain of bushes and greenery until reaching the outskirts to safety. I dared a quick look at him. He was listening and following every word that I fired.

"While I highly think it's taking the words *extreme caution* to another level, as if someone could be as suicidal to attempt a hit on your own property. But your title and our way of living doesn't allow any measures or risks to be ignored.

"You've built this manor, this fortress to fit *you* and your men. However, you and I know what the future and your position will require. What's my duty, and what I should bear in our world."

An heir.

Lucca stood as fast as my heart beat once. With his body pressed against mine and the outline of his hard dick straining against my abdomen, his fingertips trailed until they curled with a large fist of my hair. He tipped my head back to fix his eyes on mine.

His eyes darkened with gleaming fire, and I stood surprised by his abrupt change.

"Do it." His free hand took my tablet, tossing it to his desk. A rattle crashed as objects fell onto the ground by the force of the device, and his hands caged me as they held on to me. "Now your time is up."

His leg spread mine apart, raising my dark blue dress until it stretched to its limit. I clutched onto the arms that held me, but soon they both fell as he freed his shaft.

It was all so quick, sudden and erratic as if I'd sparked a violent might to take me. Right here and now. No kiss, no touch, just an aggressive want to sink deep into me.

Lucca lifted my dress higher to spread me even further. His hand bruised my ass, lifting it from the ground, and setting me over his desk to align with his hips.

His finger curled around the thin strap of my lace underwear, and a short rip echoed sharply with our breathing.

*Thrust.*

Raw and brutal, I took him in.

"Ah!" I gasped and clawed at his covered shoulders. "Lucca," I begged for a second, but Lucca didn't give me time to adjust, instead he pounded again, deeper, and roughly.

Sweet pain and ecstasy rolled in rabid waves as he lowered my back to his desk. His palms hooked under my knees, opening me wide to his vicious strokes.

"How many will you gift me, *cara mia?*"

He asked as I bucked.

"How many, *mia regina?*" His hand slipped until his fingers grasped my throat tightly, demanding an answer, but my eyes held his, watching as they raged out of control.

I shook my head, not understanding and missing what ran through his mind without an answer to give.

"Answer me!" he roared, and his punishment continued in savage beats.

"Hmm!" I whimpered as his dick hit over and over aggressively into the blissful spot only he'd discovered.

"How many versions of you will mix with my blood?"

My mouth parted with realization. I tipped Lucca over his consuming need with the slight hint of our future, *kids*. My gasps grew weak with the stray air I mustered inside my lungs, and I flung my hands over his face. And while his hips pounded repeatedly, my hands were the opposite. They were gentle against his jaw, as my fingertips caressed his lips and scratched over the prickles of his short beard.

"As many as it will take to fill the halls with chaos!" I shouted through a moan.

Lucca leaned down until I tasted whiskey. His hand released my throat as he kissed me, but his hold lingered on my neck. Wild lips matched my own and nips stung as my chest soared, and as our bodies synced, my heart cracked with any remaining barrier left.

He didn't respond, it wasn't needed.

He too wanted it. He too sought out the same future.

His phone rang, but he didn't stop causing the pleasurable sounds that escaped me. The ringing stopped only to begin again.

"Fuck!" he said between my lips, and his hand lowered on my sides, tracing my skin while I met his hips for release.

I was so close, my breathing erratic, my body on fire, and as my throat dried thirsty in gasps, air, and him, I rubbed my pussy against his shaft.

"Hmm." A short sound from his chest vibrated onto mine. I enjoyed the feel as I slid and rubbed myself over him. "Now, you must be real quiet." He smiled wickedly.

"Huh?" I whined.

*"I doubt you are too busy to answer my call, Moretti."*

I clamped my mouth shut with my hand as my father's voice was loud by my ear. I watched the evil smile that Lucca revealed as it yearned for my whimpers, the gasps, or his name called out in pleasure.

"Extremely," Lucca answered evenly and composedly, while I couldn't contain the small whimpers that filtered past my lips and hand.

I closed my eyes, but he pinched down on my nipple causing exquisite pain. My body curved as I attempted to stay quiet, but instead I took him in deeper.

My gaze returned to his, pleading. Lucca's smile reached his eyes. He wasn't willing to make it easier on me, if anything he wanted my father to hear me.

It was sick and depraved the way he wanted to show his claim, and yet, it heightened and fueled my greed. As if it made me want it even more. As if I too wanted him to hear how I enjoyed my time in Miami. How he'd lost the fight to ruin my life.

"I'm done with games, Lucca. I want a meeting with you before the wedding."

Lucca's hands moved to my hips, arranging them only to fill me again in a different and harder angle.

*Mio Dio!*

My feet tried to land on any surface for leverage, but my heels made it difficult to rest on anything.

I was at his mercy, with no leverage, and my father's voice by my ear as our bodies met louder and louder by his thrusts.

The phone grew silent, and even as I tried to breathe out through my nose, I was loud, raspy, and infuriated by holding on to my sounds. The pleasure.

"I'll set it up."

Lucca's mouth found my nipple, and he bit it the same moment his fingers found the swollen sensitivity between my legs, pinching it, until I came with a loud and muffled moan. Tears escaped as I couldn't let out the intensity of my release any other way.

The phone fell into another long silence as Lucca rode my release. "I must go, Vitelli. I have pressing matters to attend to." The mockery was cruel in his low voice, and yet Lucca still chased his own release.

*"Vaffanculo!"* Fuck you!

"I'm working on it," he gritted out, and ended the call.

I shook my head at his triumphant and pleased dark grin. When his lips lowered to catch mine, all I could do was take them in a whimper.

"Three," his husky voice rasped. "I want at least three." Then Lucca came in harsh spurts filling me with his cum until his spent and satisfied body hovered over mine.

"Three or more," I promised.

He gave me one last kiss, and our eyes met. And as I watched the whiskey brown return, he simply said, "Pack a bag, we are leaving tomorrow for a few days."

Then he was off me and just like that, the lover vanished, and the boss returned as he moved away from my body to compose his appearance.

"Don't wait for me, I will be late."

I watched him in a daze as he left me with his cum running down my legs and onto his desk. But he briefly stopped at the unfinished chess game.

"You want to know the irony of chess?"

*What?* He had just fucked me while my father heard every slipping sound. He'd admitted to the idea of our future—children, and how many. He had just ordered me to pack a bag as I stood on shaky limbs with no further information of where we were traveling, and he wanted to talk about *chess?*

His eyes briefly swept over me, and he said, "The queen holds more power than the king."

# XXXIV

## LUCCA

RUNNING A SYNDICATE ON A COASTLINE HAD ITS BENEFITS AND ITS disadvantages. It was easier to keep track of the streets, the homes, the roads, and transactions made on soil. But the Atlantic Ocean was my neighbor, and Miami was filled with ports, channels, and many canals to cover and maintain under surveillance. It was tough to know all the cash transactions made on water. Or keep up with the waves of tourism that flooded the piers and harbors with boats. But I did, and I knew every shipment and exchange that took place.

However, I hadn't been hunting a simple man but a made-man with endless resources and hiding skills. A careful and sharp-minded individual.

I'd fucking found Tino. It hadn't been easy. Yet, this was my city, and eventually the current would drag my victims right into my hands. After connecting Katia to the first few dead bodies, Ilias spent most of his time investigating and following through all transactions made on shore and deep waters.

"The owner of the yacht died seven months ago." Arlo placed his earpiece in. It matched the same Viktor had given Ilias and me before we left my home. "His children are fighting the wife for it. They've been in court all this time with no settlement made." Ilias huffed from the driver's seat. "She saw the cash offer for a rental as an easy yes. No paper trail to lead or harm her in court."

"How many men stay with him?" I asked.

"Six to seven, including Tino." He checked his watch. "We are twelve in total, and everyone is already waiting near the marina."

"This will be loud." Attention was the last thing I needed.

Water carried a sound like an echo. Too many ears, too much room for error.

"I gave Davina's father a heads up. He'll hold the response time for five minutes." Ilias caught my glance from the rearview mirror.

It may seem like a short time, but MPD was one of the largest municipal police departments, always ready for a night of high crime and quick to cease chaos. Nevertheless, Chief Price would deliver without questioning.

"I'll be notified when the first call comes through. The clock to make our exit will start then."

*Five minutes.*

We creeped to a stop and waited inside the vehicle for Viktor's instruction to exit through our earpieces. As we waited for his *all clear* of any surveillance recording, and an open view of our surroundings from above, Arlo shared in detail our next moves.

"Sergio and Mimmo have been monitoring the boat for a few days. It hadn't moved since we returned from Texas."

If the information Arlo received earlier in the day was true, it meant they had planned an attack tonight. There wasn't another reason to stay docked in a marina aside from trying to avoid detection by reducing traffic.

"His soldiers move around the boat wearing casual beachwear to avoid suspicion. Casper is going to assure our path is clear to access the boat. He should be quiet."

Casper hadn't received his name solely for his bald head. The soldier was as quiet as a ghost.

"Rana will be close behind Casper to give us the signal for us to follow along with Sergio and Mimmo."

Seven of us in one boat. Too many footfalls, too much noise. Once inside, nothing could be predicted. Not within the short time we had to execute the attack before authorities were notified.

We had to be clean, quiet.

*At least until the end,* my demon whispered.

"You mentioned twelve. Who are the other five?" I asked, my eyes taking in the calm port.

"Emilio and four of his men will be on standby." Arlo didn't feel the capo was needed.

"Good work," I mumbled and fished my phone for any notifications.

"Fuck off." He scoffed out a chuckle.

My eyes slid to his and while mine warned, Arlo's gleamed for slaughter, excited and eager to inflict pain.

"Lucca?" Viktor's voice chimed in my right ear.

I glanced out the window and replied in Russian. "*Da.*" Yes.

We all waited for his voice to come through our earpieces.

"I've disabled all video and internet access. The perimeter is for half a mile, but I have no clear view from above." I didn't miss the irritation in his tone. "I can't go low enough past the mist without detection. You'll be going in blind."

So be it.

"*Andiamo,*" *Let's go*, I ushered in Italian, and opened the door to the sound of seagulls and the smell of the seashore.

A boat's horn blared from far, and a mixture of music blended from the few boats that lit the marina. Ilias and Arlo walked before me, and I tapped my knuckles on Ilias's back.

I met the hard touch of his thin bulletproof vest that hid beneath his clothing.

Good.

Ilias didn't react. He knew what I was doing. I did the same to Arlo, but instead my knuckle connected to his flesh. Hard and unprotected.

His face swiveled halfway, revealing his broad smile and thirsty eyes.

I couldn't fault his perturbed ways, the high risk, and the game of death we played. I was addicted to its drug too and treated every hit as if it could be my last, knowing one day the trip would end with a bad blow. But today, I couldn't take that risk.

I held the safety of *them* and the syndicate.

I held Katia's safety.

Streetlights shone over the main boardwalk that connected the darkened aisles of docked boats. My gaze was aimed at one row in particular in the west corner. I didn't need light to see how the yacht swayed at the end.

Our walk to meet my men was short. They all hid beneath the night and underneath the shelter of overgrown woods behind the large storage building.

Emilio stepped forward and offered his hand. I shook it and faced everyone.

"In and out. Be quiet and don't be seen. Got it?"

"Yes, boss," they all replied.

"Everyone knows their positions?" I stared at each man. "Good, now let's go make a statement. Arlo?" I quipped, giving him the go-ahead.

"Casper, you're up." Arlo lifted his chin to the scattered boats.

Casper nudged Rana, and they both trailed ahead and disappeared into a blind spot. A few short minutes later, only Casper resurfaced into the dimmed and yellow boardwalk lights. The farther he walked, the more the dew and darkness cloaked him into a ghost of a man.

Rana then followed Casper's trail, and it was our turn to set course into the blind spot.

Emilio and his men dispersed across the border of the property, leaving Sergio and Mimmo behind.

Arlo walked silently in front while Ilias stayed behind me. We moved united and attune to one another as we stayed under the edge of the overhanging roof. The metal building creaked loudly against the gusts of wind, offering a barrier of sound.

I kept my gun tucked into my waist, though I wanted its weight in my hand. If it wasn't for the location of this hit, things would be different. I wouldn't be able to torture and toy the bastard who'd hunted what was mine.

Keeping my breathing steady, I waited and waited.

Rana's signal was nonexistent.

Ilias shifted behind.

Arlo's attention remained straight ahead.

And I stood still while my heart began beating out of rhythm. A match between bloodthirst and restrain. A drum of uncertainty for the future of one human in particular.

"Lucca," Viktor spoke clearly into my ear.

"Hmm," I hummed in acknowledgment.

"I've secured a second vessel if needed. East side, boardwalk number four—"

"Is there something I'm unaware of?" I uttered, annoyed at the extra precaution. Sure, we always had escape plans and different points of hideouts, but Arlo already had one boat ready for a quick getaway if needed. Securing a second vessel seemed too extreme.

"Docked on slot five," Viktor continued as if I hadn't interrupted him. "And no. I just can't take the chance."

The chance of me dying, along with the treaty that promised his baby brother, Ilias, another breath.

*Croak. Croak.*

"Is that...?" Ilias asked.

Yes, Rana. Croaking.

"Believe it. Now, let's go," Arlo ushered.

In a loose formation, we set off under the boardwalk lights. Small waves crashed beneath the pier, and the wind picked up in a whistle. A blue heron watched us as he stood on top of a wooden post, fishing, scouting, hunting for his next meal. He screeched on our approach until our presence wasn't welcomed, and he flew away before we reached him.

Our pace didn't falter, and with each boat we passed, the closer to Tino I got, and the more unstable my mind spun with visions of crimson.

I spotted Rana by the edge of the boardwalk with a ladder rope hanging next to him and a man slumped by a post, sleeping without the possibility of another day.

*One down.*

With no time to waste or another thought for the dead, I went up first.

Once my feet rocked in the late eighties model yacht, my adrenaline kicked in, and I struggled to keep up with the plan. With the idea of clean, quick, and quiet deaths.

Casper leaned against the side of the cabin. Only a fraction of him was uncovered by the shade of the tower above. He motioned for me to continue as a bundle of cooling flesh lay to his left.

*Two down.*

The deck was low-lit by running lights sprinkled through the main floor, betraying every step I made with a shadow. It didn't matter if the dew buried the moon. We couldn't all remain unseen for much longer.

I steadied my breathing. In, out, and in again as a rolling chill spread. Not for fear. For excitement. For the high of steel in my hand as I picked and screwed my silencer to its place. For the knowledge that the risk had grown and the job would be messy, bloody.

Arlo and Ilias were quick, meeting me to the rooted spot I'd stayed.

I motioned toward the floor lights that would alert our positions. A change no one was expecting by the age of the boat.

We all stared down, waiting for my command.

I turned to our surroundings, to the scattered boats with no lights and the ones that blared music. We were out in the open, exposed, and suspended in time. But there was no time.

Damned if we stayed, damned if we moved.

Rana caught up, and soon Sergio and Mimmo would too if we didn't *move*.

I nodded to my right, and Ilias and Casper took position.

I nodded to my left, and Arlo and Rana took position.

Guns drawn, waiting.

I nodded forward.

All four went, and I followed Ilias.

Our steps weren't quiet. There were too many at once, and when we made it halfway onto the boat, two quick pops were fired.

*Three. Four down* and an organized chaos followed.

Shouts from inside the boat rang, and the motor kicked in gear.

My body swayed with the momentum, and I steadied my footing while two of my own ran to the bodies on the floor. The rest of us sped inside to stop the vessel from taking off, straight into the sounds of commotion.

*Clank.*

The yacht powered down and everything went pitch black.

I ducked down, waiting for the fire to start and the screams to echo. I couldn't see past my hands and my eyes fluttered to adapt to the dark.

"Lucca?" the earpiece sounded with Arlo's voice.

"Hmm."

"One is coming to your right."

I closed my eyes and listened carefully. With my arm stretched and my finger on the trigger, I heard him clearly. His next footfall, his last.

I shot, hitting my target and bathing in blood splatter. He'd been too close.

*Five down.*

"Clear." A flashlight flickered inside the cabin, and Ilias stood by the entrance door. "Anyone else should be down that door."

With the new lighting, I peered down at the body on the wooden floor. I nudged it with my foot for any movement, but as blood pooled out from his chest, there was no coming back.

I shot him once more and wiped my face.

"You good?" Arlo uttered with careful eyes.

No. I was losing my edge. Losing my control to my demon.

"Shit," Ilias cursed, and all eyes zeroed on him. "We got five minutes."

My demon chuckled.

Without a single word, I walked away from the body on the ground and headed to the door.

"Start your task." I pointed at Rana as I passed him. "Cut the fucking light off, Ilias, and help Rana." Darkness surrounded us once again. "Arlo," I whispered.

"Right behind you."

Perfect. Just us two quietly lowering into the ground level of the yacht.

"Time?" I whispered.

"Four minutes," Viktor's voice replied.

Two hundred and forty seconds remained to find my target. Inside a layout I wasn't familiar with. Yet, I knew boats. Yachts and their designs all resemble each other. It was why I had the inside of mine custom-made. This was a simple luxury model that hadn't been touched since bought.

Arlo and I made it to the end of the steps. I placed my back flushed to the wall and closed my eyes, listening.

Upstairs, feet scattered, and small splashes hit above. But I wasn't interested in the deck or the captain's cabin. I was interested in what was on this level. Then a muffled whisper and distinct ruffle was made by the east end.

A loud gear knocked with an echo, and the lights flashed until they flickered on.

"Two minutes," Viktor announced.

There was nowhere for Tino to hide. He was cornered and trapped like a caged rat.

After a quick glance, we were clear of any threats.

I walked with a purpose, uncaring if he heard my steps and position clearly. I wanted him to. I wanted him to know I was coming for him. That I was just a few steps away to deliver his death.

Behind me, Arlo lowered and dropped a red before the retracting door. Then he pushed against the door, and it coiled open.

Tino Borelli stood in front of a king-size bed, greeting me with the blues, greens, and a mixture of eighties pink decoration. Arms spread wide, *unarmed*. But a flash caught the corner of my eye. The oval and golden trim mirror showcased another body inside.

In the reflection and in between the old Miami colors, I saw the barrel of a gun pointing at my head. It was so close. Only a thin wall separated us.

I didn't react, although my demon twitched.

"MPD is en route," Viktor whispered in warning.

*Redecorate. The demon smiled.*

I took a step and flicked my wrist.

*Pop-pop.*

Six down.

Before the sixth body hit the ground, Tino snatched a 9mm. *That was more like it.* Unarmed wasn't something we mafiosos did, unless planned.

I lowered my gun and pulled a knife while Arlo targeted Tino in point blank range with his weapon.

"I would've said you were lucky due to time management. But you should know, Tino, I can always come with new ways to torture."

Tino raised his head. "And sign your own death sentence?"

I chuckled.

"Has your father not shared the news with you?" I wiped the blade, toying with him. Tino waited for me to continue, but with his gun drawn at me, I didn't like the odds. "Arlo?"

Arlo fired his gun, and Tino screamed. His body bent forward, his gun fell, and Tino wailed in pain, bringing his injured hand up to his chest. Blood decorated the palm-printed bedspread with red. His brown eyes sneered, and his brows crinkled together, surprised I ordered his harm.

Angered by the bullet hole in his hand, he shook his head as dread filled his gaze. "What is he doing?"

Arlo circled the room with the red can he'd picked up from the corner, and Tino's question was answered by the strong smell of gasoline. The stinging scent I'd grown familiar with, and I knew it was a smell he knew too well.

"What I'd promised the council. Taking care of the threat in my city at any cost."

Tino shuddered as his eyes begged. "Not this way, Moretti."

Seeing the power stripped away from him was as fulfilling as the high I sought from risk.

To watch how a grown man regretted facing me. How his eyes apologized for ever coming into my city to hunt what was mine. Seeing the moment he understood I didn't care about his title or ties. Tino tried to hold it all in. But the more gasoline Arlo splashed, the quicker his untouchable and strong ego crumbled.

In record time, I broke a skilled mafioso. A son of a Cosa Nostra boss. An heir to a syndicate.

In record time, I ruined him without pulling a trigger. All I did was find his weakness by learning every detail of his life.

All I did was add gasoline.

I looked down at the bloody mess he held close to him. The current of crimson that trailed down, dripping onto the floor. And past the gore, I saw his scarred-burned hands.

"You know, some said after your wife died, you grew strong. You were feared."

Tino straightened. His slicked black hair glistened while his jaw clenched, holding onto a string of fickle force.

"But in reality, you grew weak and fearful of one thing. Fire."

Repulsed, he kept his eyes on me.

"Too bad you couldn't save her. At least your hands reminded you each day after your failure."

"My father will come for you," he spat.

"That's what I'm hoping for." I smiled. "Oh, and while you're in burning pain, think of how your father could've saved you from the same death your late wife suffered."

"Lucca, you need to get out now!" Viktor said in a rush through my ear.

*Soon.*

I slipped my knife back into my pocket and reached for my lighter instead. With my free hand, I pulled the picture he'd used to target Katia. I lit it and watched as the end burned between my fingertips.

"Moretti," Tino gritted out.

"Katia gives you her regards." I took a step back, Tino took one forward.

With Arlo by the door and Tino rushing closer, I lowered the glowing image.

Tino froze.

*Burn*, my demon wished.

I dropped it.

*Whoosh.*

Tino's eyes spread as he retreated to the end of the room, but the trail of petrol trapped him in the middle. The flames grew, and the old, dried bedroom quickly engulfed in heat and smoke.

I turned as his screams began.

"Moretti!" he hauled.

I kept walking, leaving the burning man in misery and imprisoned by nonfunctional windows and gusts of angry fire. The heat touched my back as it spread at rapid speeds.

Arlo's strides quickened as smoke clogged our exit, and when he emerged onto the main ground, Tino's screams turned into torched wails and kindled whimpers.

"MPD is on scene. Hurry!" Viktor announced.

Arlo and I were the last ones out of the yacht and on solid ground. We both walked calmly around the marina until we evaded the blue wave of Miami without detection. Law enforcement stalled, watching the fire, stunned before they sprang into action, screaming for medics and the fire department. They ran toward the fire to notify those around of the now flaming yacht.

"Ilias?" I asked, knowing he could hear me.

"By the tree line," he replied through the earpiece.

Arlo set out toward the direction, crossing a running car with the lights off, waiting for us.

I hopped inside the front passenger seat, finding Ilias behind the wheel. Arlo climbed in next to Rana and Casper.

Before I got the chance to ask, Ilias said, "Sergio and Mimmo left with Emilio and his men."

He passed me a rag and sped away.

I ran the fabric over my face and caught the tall fire reaching high in the sky through the side mirror.

It was a beautiful sight. The kind I didn't let go of until it was gone from view.

*Seven down.*

Finally, Tino Borelli was dead, and I only had one Borelli left before extinguishing a bloodline. But first, I needed to get Katia out of the city.

# XXXV

## KATIA

THE MOUNTAINS. LUCCA BROUGHT ME TO THE MOUNTAINS. IF I WASN'T confused by our silent plane ride, I was now.

Had I missed something? Had I said something that caused him to give me the cold shoulder? And my God, if he looked at his phone one last time, I was going to lose it.

I stared out the jet's window as we descended onto a private landing surrounded by heavy greenery and endless valleys.

"Where are we?" My question was distant and after the long ride, I was just glad to see land.

"Montana."

*Montana?*

Once again, expectations were my enemy.

While Montana seemed beautiful, there was so much green, and it welcomed us with little light. I tried to stay positive. To not dwell on the uncomfortable silence I'd endured for hours. Lucca wanted to take me away before our wedding, and after the blissful few moments I'd stolen the past couple of days, I wanted to remain optimistic about our time together.

Maybe he wanted a different scenery, it was just…not what I had expected or packed for. My suitcase was filled with bathing suits, summer dresses, heels, and sandals. This trip required long pants and closed-toe shoes.

While I loved long runs outdoors and sunbathing, *this* was the real outdoors. I was out of my element.

"How long will we stay?" I wondered.

"A few days."

My eyes flashed away from the gorgeous view to him.

Feeling my gaze, he removed his attention from his device and stared back.

"You should wear your seat belt when the plane is landing."

That's it? He wasn't going to offer anything else?

The jet's tires squealed, and gentle jerks shook inside the cabin.

"Looks like we already have." I smiled, but it was forced as I struggled to keep my thoughts and questions to myself. There wasn't a point, and I didn't want to start this getaway, or early honeymoon, with a fight.

I knew honeymoons in our ways of marriage weren't traditional as most didn't marry out of love, only duty.

Was I romanticizing a simple trip into something more?

Either way, it was just him and me. With this opportunity, I was going to seek out more of those minutes that made me feel alive.

I powered off my tablet after saving the blueprints I'd started for the downstairs renovation he'd agreed to yesterday. When the plane came to a halt, I stood and retrieved the few belongings I'd scattered, tossing them inside my tote. The golden zipper closed shut, and I hooked the bag on my shoulder and waited as he watched my every move.

Lucca took the glass of brown and drowned its contents before he rose before me. His gaze roamed over my frame and stopped at my bag. With an outstretched hand, he offered to take it.

It was such a simple gesture. Yet, after feeling unseen by him for hours, my tensed shoulders relaxed as my heart eased, and the tightness in my chest evaporated.

I gave him my bag and took a step closer. I raised my hand, but before it connected to his cheek, I settled for his chest instead.

His eyes calculated every blink and breath I took, and my hand slithered up to his neck as I dived for a kiss.

We had never kissed outside of sex, and his lips didn't move for a second. It had been the longest second I'd faced, and it brought a mixture of feelings of rejection and anxiety together. The kind that weighed your chest in silent torture. Then his lips gave, and I took as he closed the small distance by dragging me to him.

His kiss wasn't gentle. It was slow but never gentle.

And as I experienced this intimate moment wrapped in his arms, and the taste of liquor in his devilish lips, maybe Montana was indeed the right place after all.


I HAD LIED. MONTANA WAS NOT THE RIGHT PLACE. IF I THOUGHT MOSQUITOES were a menace in Miami, Montana's were the devil's spawns.

Before arriving here, I believed I could live and thrive in any environment. But I'd been humbled, and I was a city woman.

I felt guilty for feeling so unhappy, knowing *this* was the destination of my getaway instead of the blue crystal waters of the Bahamas or Bali, knowing his yacht remained docked while I was *here*. I even sounded like the spoiled *principessa* many believed me to be. But as I itched my legs furiously, frustrated by the countless buzzing that flew by my ears, and the continuous weird animal sounds, and the frog that wouldn't stop croaking since we arrived at the cabin, I was enraged.

"You'll bleed if you don't stop scratching, Katia."

I hurled my gaze in his direction. Humor danced clearly in his eyes even from afar as he grabbed our bags out of the trunk of the car that had waited for us at the terminal.

I didn't know how much longer I could hold on before I snapped at him. After all, he was the reason for my discomfort.

I closed my eyes briefly and mumbled silently, *"Deep breaths, it's just us."*

Did I hear a soft chuckle? No, I couldn't have.

"I'm glad you find it amusing!"

He smiled. A real one. That alone relieved my annoyance.

"Come, you'll enjoy the inside."

He wasn't kidding. It was beautiful and breathtaking how the outside could hide the structure and intricate interior. The whole backside of the home was covered with floor-to-ceiling windows inviting the view of the calm lake inside. The light pendants, cans, and chandeliers were unnecessary during the day as natural light illuminated every corner of the house. Tall ceilings with accent oak beams hung from above, and the pillars around held the architectural weight allowing an open and inviting feel of peace.

Montana was prettier by the minute, and if I spent each day wrapped in bedsheets and in his scent, it would become the wildest state to be in.

"It's stunning."

"Thank you. I knew when I bought it, it would be difficult to visit often, but I got it anyway. Probably paid more than I needed to, but the view was worth it."

"It is."

His phone rang, cutting through the harmony in the house, and he quickly silenced it.

It all changed. The calm had rolled into chaos as Lucca returned to the distant and untouchable man that was so hard to pull apart. And while his darkness always lured me, today it was disheartening.

"It was a long flight. You should rest." He loosened his blue tie without meeting my eyes.

I *was* tired, and the hunt for a glass of red wine would be my first task, but he hadn't meant for *us* to rest.

"What if I'm not tired?" I tipped my head back.

Lucca's jaw tightened, but he never glanced at me. Instead, he turned and said, "I have work."

*Don't*, I told my heart.

*Don't*, I said to my breathing.

*Don't*, I warned my tears.

*Why are we here?*


I FELL ASLEEP ALONE, WOKE UP ALONE. LUCCA'S SIDE OF THE BED HADN'T even been touched and the morning light filtered through the window. It blinded me as deeply as the acknowledgment of his absence.

In a quick heap, I left the light-colored room that was meant to bring tranquility but instead delivered irritation. While the cabin was grand, it didn't compare to Lucca's home, and as I searched through the halls for him, I pulled my robe tightly around me. My hair was in disarray, my face puffy from sleep, and only my teeth had been brushed all by the need of finding him.

The need to give him an ear full and set my boundaries.

I passed the white and brown oak kitchen, dismissing all details as I focused on finding an Italian man. Not just any Italian, but mine.

Door opened, elbows on the desk, and inked hands over his face, Lucca sat in front of a book wall. The clean white desk seemed out of place by its color. Lucca wasn't light and never searched for its tones. He was the contrast I could only see as the bright window shined daylight over his bowed shoulders.

He seemed exhausted in the same suit he'd worn yesterday, and for the first time, I'd met an unkept Lucca. While irritation still clawed, his features and distraught appearance took over with worry.

"Lucca?" I called out his name, wondering if he had fallen asleep.

Red-rimmed and heavy lids slipped away from his hands. He looked drained.

"Have you slept at all?"

He shook his head, and a messy strand of his dark brown hair toyed with his brow. I wanted to pull it back as if it didn't belong to him, as if his appearance troubled me. And it did.

"Come," I muttered for him to follow me.

I wanted to take him to bed and force his mind to rest. However, Lucca shook his head, and I didn't have the patience to treat him with calm.

"I'm not asking, Lucca. I didn't sleep well and I'm tired."

Lucca's eyes closed briefly.

"Please," I uttered. "I don't want to be alone in bed."

He stood, grabbed his phone, and met me by the door casing.

"Just for a few hours, alright?" His words stumbled.

I nodded and turned as he trailed behind. Lucca took a quick shower and changed into a pair of black sweatpants, and this time I was the one who trailed after him. The bed sank under his weight, and without hesitation, I sought out his warmth.

Lucca didn't tense and his body didn't pause beneath my touch. Only his eyes shut, and his hand repositioned on my back. His body didn't even fight me, it embraced me for the first time. It could have been the lack of sleep or the stress that radiated off him, but I failed to think and just felt his desire to feel me close to him instead.

But as the unforgiving light infiltrated through my lids, I tried to find the remote to close the blinds that hung high. I didn't even get the chance to twist before Lucca's palm pressed over my back with fingers spread.

"The blinds," I explained.

His throat trapped a low sound.

"Blinds." His voice rose firmly, and a beep echoed. "Close."

Magic.

The blinds shut by command, and I rested my head on his shoulder.

My fingers roamed over the valleys of his abs, and the lines of his chest, exploring and soothing his mind to succumb to unconsciousness.

"Why did you really search for me?" Lucca asked heavily.

I didn't dodge the answer. I wanted him to know and understand my limits. With him against me and beneath the covers, I spoke the truth.

"I won't stay here if I'm meant to be alone. I can do that in Miami. At least in Miami, I have the boys."

"And I cannot stop when I have work, Katia."

Discouraged, I answered. "I know."

The Mafia would always be first.

# XXXVI

## LUCCA

KATIA?" I CALLED OUT AFTER WAKING UP WITHOUT HER HEAT PRESSING against me.

Silence answered me, and I shifted my weight to glance around the empty room. I'd always been the first one out of bed. The one who always left a spot empty, our close proximity a memory. I lived on a routine. Wake up, work out, shower, get ready, work, and catch a few hours of sleep before starting the same pattern all over again.

By the time Katia woke up early enough to see the next sunrise, I would already be gone and deep in sin.

It was how I functioned, routine.

Today, everything was off.

I was the one alone, and as a creature of habit, the change didn't sit well with me. I felt as if I'd slept for days, groggy and aching. I needed to move.

Nothing good ever came when I stopped.

After a quick glance at the time and the endless missed calls on my phone, the pit in my chest grew with tension. It had been five hours. Five too many in broad daylight. I was lucky to get close to that during the night, and even then, every morning my mind rushed to get going. Today that rush had become erratic, and I left the bed with my phone already in my ear as I went to the bathroom.

Arlo didn't answer, and while I played every voice mail, listening to his tone and urgency to call him back, I dwelled on the reasons that could've kept him pressing for my call.

I hopped into the shower to rinse off sleep and scrub off the sense of lost time. It had been useless. I dried and dressed myself with the same urgency I'd left the bed with.

*Something was off.*

It was the same feeling I hadn't shaken since leaving Miami. The same pressure that bubbled all day yesterday. But today the magnitude only increased in a force I couldn't shake or carry. Even the quietness inside of the home didn't align as Katia hadn't made a sound. There were no footfalls or creaks. No signs of movement.

*It was too quiet.*

I walked out of the room dressed in dark jeans and a plain tee. I didn't even bother to put my shoes on, I just needed the quiet to stop. To find her.

My phone rang as I walked down the stairs, and I answered before the second ring.

"*Pronto,*" I answered in Italian.

"We have a problem," Arlo replied, and my steps slowed.

While our phones were secured thanks to Viktor's built walls, we were always careful. There was always a risk, a threat to be recorded. Right now was no different, and I detested how I couldn't discuss or hear the details of such problems.

"The rooster is not following the trail, and some of his chickens are causing scuffles in the pen by drawing too much attention."

What the fuck? That was the best Arlo could come up with. An idiotic analogy to explain how Pietro Borelli hadn't left California, and some of his soldiers were now in Miami, causing havoc in the city.

"I'm sure you've seen the news."

I didn't reply.

"You haven't."

"No."

"Two more have been found."

My body stilled. Borelli must've given the orders after finding out about his son's death.

"The conditions of the bodies were bad and bold."

Two more lives had been taken. Meanwhile, I slept in a state too far from home to solve anything, counting on others to follow my orders, and *nothing* was going according to plan.

Things *always* went as I planned.

Things always went *my* way.

"And the rooster?" I asked, calling Pietro Borelli what Arlo had as I checked the last door of the house for Katia.

"Some said it caught the bird flu as it mourns, but he hasn't been seen leaving his coup yet."

The last room was empty.

"Stop with the fucking nonsense, Arlo!"

He chuckled, missing the annoyance and my tone of urgency. I knew Arlo's bile humor enjoyed the chaos, sought it, but as I glanced out the front window, then hurried to the back of the house with no sight of Katia, I couldn't entertain it. Something was brewing. I could feel the cracks expanding and filtering away from my control.

"I'll figure it out." I stepped outside through the back door. "I'll call you back with new orders soon. We are running out of time."

Ending the call, my eyes adjusted to the cloudy midday light, and I quickly scanned the grounds for her dark brown waves.

"Katia?" I called out.

Nothing.

*No one knows you are both here.*

"Katia!"

*No one could have known.*

"KATIA!"

*She is far from danger.*

But after time had passed without any sign of her, I rushed down through the brushes. I took each paved stone through the heavy greenery and to the outstretched dock.

By the rocky beach of the lake, I found her clothing and turned to every side with no luck.

"Katia!"

"Yeah?"

I heard from far away, and my chest caved as I exhaled.

With my eyes out to where her voice had traveled from, soft swooshes of water followed. After a few short seconds, her head peeked out from the tall trees that covered the right side of the open lake.

Katia smiled upon seeing me by the shore, but I was too unraveled to return the gesture. I almost felt mad. No, I was furious by my reaction. By her!

"Get out," I sharply ordered.

She smirked, and instead of listening, she pulled her hair back and into the water. Her arms swayed in rhythm to keep her above the surface as she floated on her back.

"I don't think so. The water is nice and chilly," Katia said to the sky.

It was too much. The loss of routine, the sense of lost time, the knowledge that my plan wasn't coming through. The fear I'd felt, along with my control slipping, was too much. And yet, this woman decided to toy with me.

I didn't think twice. My shirt hit the muddy shore, and my pants slid off my legs. In just a pair of boxer briefs, I submerged my body into the cool water, following her laughter. I swam underwater as the water stung my heated body. The moment she saw how close I'd quickly closed the distance by emerging to the surface, Katia's laughter faded as her green gems shined wide. Sensing my dark demeanor, she attempted to distance herself, but it was too late. I'd already gone beneath the depths of the lake, capturing her ankle and pulling her back.

Her legs kicked as I shook the water off my face, watching her arms push against the water, fighting my strength.

Useless.

Now that she'd provoked me, I wouldn't let her get away.

She tried rolling and kicking her free leg against me, but I caught it too, causing her to use only her arms to stay afloat. With both ankles shackled by my hands, I pulled hard, and her face went underwater by the force. I used the momentum of her body and water and held the back of her knees until my hands reached out and grasped her bare ass.

If her struggle hadn't already made me hard, her naked and wet silky skin did it.

Katia's head resurfaced in loud gasps as she coughed out of the chokehold the water had put her in. Her hands quickly shot out to tightly grasp my neck while she caught her breath. When her eyes peered open, catching mine, she stared deeply into me with caution as mine held no humor.

"You are awake," she spluttered innocently.

A fucking fraud. Nothing innocent was engraved in Katia, and I was more awake than she could possibly imagine.

My hands slipped from her ass to her back and firmly gripped her neck as I swam us closer. My feet touched the muddy ground while remaining underneath the water. With her legs now wrapped around my waist and her tits pressed against my torso, I held her naked skin tighter against me, feeling her, touching her, watching her until I believed she *was* before me. To ensure my mind wasn't playing tricks and I'd found her.

Naked, swimming, unharmed.

Her doubtful gaze locked with mine.

"I—"

I stopped her words with my lips, pouring things I didn't understand, like the touch of fear I hadn't felt since I was a teen. Or the frustration of knowing I couldn't lock her and chain her to a cellar. The bitterness and failure to acknowledge I couldn't seek my revenge for what the Vitellis had taken from me or her.

I had been a fool.

*She* made me a fool.

Because now, I would deliver wrath to whoever took *her* from me. A Vitelli.

And I hated it.

I hated the weakness she'd brought with every strong step she took with poise and elegance.

I hated her for it.

I felt no love for Katia. It was a dark obsession of what belonged to me. And while I'd seen with time how her eyes had grown soft and her need to be near me had increased, I had warned her not to.

She did what she did best. Didn't listen.

Now she wanted my attention, closeness, and intimate moments. Things I didn't do because I was incapable and uncaring for them. I had a wide variety of things to take care of. Cities to protect, cities to burn. Men to rule, men to kill.

Cruel bastards fucked, whether it was their women or empires, but never fucked with feelings, and yet she made me *fear*.

Fuck her.

"Don't fucking disappear from me like that. Do you understand, Katia?" I threatened onto her lips.

With her forehead touching mine, mouth apart and eyes closed, she breathed, "I just left for a swim."

*Mio Dio*, she couldn't give up.

I tightened my grip on her head.

"I won't," she quickly answered.

"Now, why are you naked?" I nipped her bottom lip and slithered my palm down and up her side, brushing my thumb over the edge of her tit.

"It's called skinny-dipping."

"Yeah, well, it screams *'fuck me'*."

"I'm surprised you caught that after all the time you've spent ignoring me." Her fingers weaved into my hair before she had full fists and my head pushed back.

There it was, the spirit I knew she couldn't contain. The spirit she'd tried to simmer yesterday as I didn't meet her demands and expectations of a doting partner.

With my head pulled back and the delicious tug she gave, a dark chuckle erupted from my throat.

"We'll see how much you like getting fucked in the water."

I snapped my head away from her fingers to catch the confusion in her bunched brows. My hand slithered from the back of her neck to her throat.

"I hope you take a *deep* breath," I said in one second, and the next, I submerged our bodies.

Sick, was what I was.

Her lower body strained to pull up. The movement rocked her pussy up and down against me. I came up for air and smiled as the clear water allowed the explicit scene underneath.

When I pulled her body up, water splashed as she thrashed for air. I pressed her closer to me, slid my boxer briefs down and buried my dick inside her.

Katia gasped as her eyes furiously fluttered against the running droplets.

"Lucca!" she yelled, dubious to believe what my wicked mind had done.

Her tits bounced as she caught her breath, and when my lips curled, her stunning emerald eyes widened, excited. She crushed her lips to mine while she tried fighting our bodies underwater, but with every struggle, the more my body shook in carnal need to feed my demon. With one buck of her hips, I held her waist and sank my dick deeply.

Our mouths battled for control, but my strength couldn't compare to hers while I drove inside her. Katia heaves mixed with whimpers as I continued fucking her in the open lake.

Water chilled our heated skin and her struggles never eased. Her thrashing hips never stopped, and my pounding never took mercy.

And as I rammed into her, drowning her in desire, it made me *wild* with savage demands for the creature I couldn't have enough of. The one that gave my demon what it needed.

I was so close while lost in the sight of her and in the fight. Lost on how she took me, scratching my arm and curving her spine for me to deliver each thrust to her needy and tightening core.

My skin crawled as I continued to fuck such a divine woman into release. She begged above the surface and took me underneath.

I watched each tell, fascinated by her. My hand moved from her throat and over her wet face until reaching and grabbing her hair. Katia's body slowly lost the battle, spent and spiraling into release. I pulled her closer. Her hands hooked around my neck, and her breath brushed against my mouth as water fell over her face. Her breathing was erratic, and her whimpers were untamed.

Such a breathtaking sight.

"Lucca." My name fell from her swollen lips, and my eyes shut at her plea.

I held her hips and sank inside her warmth over and over as I walked closer to the bank. I couldn't hold on much longer, and neither could she.

Her fingernails sunk into my flesh, breaking skin, and my head rolled in pleasure.

"Please!"

She whimpered when she felt her bottom leave the water, asking and begging for her release. I stole a kiss and laid her against the rocky beach. I pinched her nipple, and her lips parted as I grabbed and bent her leg to my side.

My knees scraped the sharp stones, and her back bowed with every thrust as the pebbles rubbed her skin raw. The pain only intensified her chase for release, and I used her body as a rake to draw out the pleasure pain brought her.

"Ahh!" Her throat cut out her moans, and her head flew back.

I unleashed my mouth and tongue over her throat and down her hardened nipples.

"Lucca!" Katia cried out.

I pulled away, watched her pleasure-ridden face, and pinched her bud, making her buckle wildly beneath me.

I felt her release, the warmth and bliss she rode, and sank again to chase my own.

Holding her face, I took her lips and kissed her until I left all of me inside of her.

Every thought, hate, and fear she'd caused in such a short time. And while my arms shook from holding myself up, I could've mistaken it for something much deeper.

Eventually, my worn-out body won, and I crushed her underneath me as we both fought to even out our breathing.

Katia's fingertips danced over my back and up my hair. I didn't move. I didn't want to, not yet. Instead, I waited a few more minutes until I was sure a rocky imprint would be left on her skin, and I slid back into the water. She raised herself up onto her elbows to watch me as I rinsed the gravel off.

I walked back to the shore, and Katia's head turned, following my every move as she lay in an exhausted and satisfied cloud while the water played with her toes. I picked up my pants, slid them on, and collected our clothes from the shore.

I made sure not to look in her direction again. I had the vision I wanted to replay for the rest of the day.

"Don't disappear again," I ordered and walked past her.

"Lucca!" she warned.

"I have things to do and people to *ignore*," I threw back. Little did she know, I wasn't ignoring her. I was trying to keep us both alive, along with the Moretti name.

"You are taking my clothes!"

My back already faced her and the calm water.

"It's called skinny-dipping in the open air. Careful with the bugs."

I didn't have to turn to know her hand had slid to her thigh, searching her bare leg for the knife that had become a part of her.

"Lucca!" she yelled, and I didn't miss a step, putting more distance between us.

# XXXVII

## KATIA

LUCCA DIDN'T LIE WHEN HE SAID HE HAD PEOPLE TO IGNORE…ME. HE'D spent the rest of that day in the bright-colored office with the door shut. All while I still had the memory and marks of our time together. I'd eaten alone and drew in the spacious and quiet living room, too proud to even attempt to go to him. I'd found a bottle of red he'd brought with us, a cherry tempting label I couldn't resist. Before I knew it, I'd drained every drop. I just wanted to drown the silence, not myself, with pity.

Maybe I'd been wrong. This was never a getaway. It wasn't a time for us to spend together or give me a glimpse of his thoughts, the events in his life and factors that made him who he was.

A cold-hearted bastard.

I knew of Lucca just as much as I had that first night I met him. Nothing.

Yet, I knew I wanted and craved his presence. It was maddening to not be able to slip through his barriers while he'd crumbled mine.

When I woke this morning, the only clue of him making it to bed was the rumpled sheets on his side of the bed.

I hadn't heard him come in, I hadn't felt him near. But after the way he'd taken me in the lake and the empty bottle I'd picked up this morning, I'd slept deeply by the toll my body had taken and the alcohol I had consumed.

But I wanted to say, *the hell to pride* and go to him. It had been easier in my mind because when I stood in front of the door he hid behind, I hesitated. Yet I pushed the door wide open, looked at him in the eyes, and followed through with my terrible plan.

Terrible, because I told him I was going on a trail and the closest thing I had to shoes were a pair of designer flats. His lips curled, entertained. Lucca agreed to join me if only to see me struggle and fight off nameless insects.

But we never made it too far because Lucca took me against a tree, then he bent me against a rock and fucked me as wildly as a fucking animal.

Then the high of his skin and our lips was short lived after we returned to the cabin, and the feeling of being just a fuck settled.

He left me by the front door without a word, and I had no fight left.

Later, I drifted to sleep before the sun could set, just to let the pain go away.

My phone rang. My phone. I'd forgotten I brought it. As I hunted its shrill sound, I could only think of one person who had contacted me via phone since coming back, Lorenzo.

After tossing a few things around my suitcase, I found it. But it wasn't Enzo, it was our brother, Leo.

The shock of seeing his name on the screen did not even cross my mind, I only knew it couldn't be good. We barely spoke.

"Leonardo?"

"I swear, Katia, you better be far from that damned forsaken city," he roared and spoke so fast, it was hard to follow his voice.

Out of the three of us, Leo was seen as the most reckless and unstable.

Unstable by how his emotions bested his actions, and reckless as his knives shot at any living creature for the fun of it without a thought of repercussions. Leo was the definition of bloodthirsty without a mind. People feared his presence.

He was selfish without an ounce of remorse, and Enzo always cleaned up his mess. But this time, Enzo couldn't fix the problem. *I* had to.

"Answer me!" he screamed.

This was bad. Leo was engulfed deeply into his deranged thoughts, swimming in its bottomless pool of sin.

"I am." I wouldn't give my location over the phone, and he didn't ask knowingly.

"A fucking fire!" He laughed without humor, enraged. "He just couldn't wait, could he?"

He made no sense, and having *him* on the phone, unhinged, and screaming in ire, chilled my body. My sight fogged out as the scene of calm lake water and Montana's landscape from my window shifted into chaos.

"Is...is Enzo—" I breathed.

"What? *No*, he is fine." Air filled my lungs, relieved and confused as ever. "He couldn't get a hold of you, saying you hadn't returned any calls or texts for fucking *weeks!*" he accused.

Okay, then who couldn't wait? Who was he speaking of, and what fire?

"Are you guarded?" he asked.

*Were we?*

"I'm with Lucca."

He chuckled darkly. "That bastard. Good."

It seemed Leo preferred my answer, and I could hear how he pulled away from the conversation after finding out what he needed. But I hadn't, and I needed to keep him talking.

"Now tell me what's happening?"

"Chaos. A divine one to watch but…" He stopped himself.

"Damn it, Leo. I will fucking cut you up if you don't tell me!"

"Borelli's son is dead," he snapped. "Let me guess. You think you are on a cute little getaway. Hell, maybe even on a honeymoon." Leo laughed cruelly. "Think again. Stop daydreaming and think like the damn Vitelli you are." The line disconnected.

I had been a fool and taken as one.

How fucking dare *he* leave me in the dark after everything, after killing a man who'd threatened my life?

How dare he treat me as if my hands were pure?

How dare he make me feel belittled!

I threw the phone in a haste onto the floor and paced.

"Ahhh!!" my scream rattled out of my chest, echoing and bouncing off each wall in anger and pain. Pain for being ridiculed and allowing my guard down.

How naive of me to believe the thought of *him* wanting to be with *me*. For believing he had planned time for *us*.

It all made sense. His foul mood, the endless calls, his detachment. While Lucca was here, his mind was far away, moving and scheming. Deceiving *me* when all he had to do was speak to me about the threats as a partner. We would've been stronger together during this time. Fuck, I would've supported and cheered his wrath on.

*I believed in a lie.*

And Lucca and I would never be more than a good fuck.

Shocking currents of grief stroked my heart, and its lightning burned through my veins.

I couldn't cry, I *wouldn't* cry.

I'd brought it upon myself.

I was blinded by so-called riches, and they were nothing more than fakes.

"Katia?" I heard his voice, distant and careful. "Are you hurt?"

My head flung to his standing frame, tall and unbothered by the open door. And all I could remember were the words I'd once said when he'd placed the ring that decorated my finger.

"Don't act as if you care."

With a small tilt of his head, his eyes narrowed. Guarded. It was an instinct, ready for lashes that would rip open his cruelty.

"Fine, I won't." His dark eyes slid down the shattered screen of my phone that lay on the wood floor, and he asked with a clenched jaw. "Enzo?"

"No, *Leo*," I spat back.

His posture straightened. *Yes, Lucca. Leo told me more than he should have.*

"I will be packing my bag and heading back."

"No you are not."

I quickly closed the distance and looked up at his spiteful eyes with balled fists.

"Try me," my whisper warned.

Lucca smiled and scoffed. "What could possibly make you this…" His head shook with his unfinished sentence.

Upset? Enraged? Fucking furious?

"I don't know, Lucca, it could be you and *your lies!*"

His lips curled, and his chin dipped down. "Lies are for those who fear death. I do neither."

I held my ground even if his gaze radiated retribution.

"But you have!" My hands flung at my sides.

"What? What have I done?" His temper erupted as his voice raised in outrage. Like a punch, my chest drew back, and my eyes fell away from the bile.

I broke.

"You made me believe you were taking me away to be with *me*. As if there wasn't a false motive behind it."

I couldn't look at him, not after my voice shook at the end.

"When did I utter such nonsense, Katia?"

My eyes fluttered shut, trapping the promise to not shed a tear even if my breathing took the blow of his merciless words.

"It seems to me the only one who lied to you was yourself."

Sometimes words needed to be freed.

Spoken, written, loose.

Sometimes they were never meant to create a sentence.

And sometimes, I wish they held no power.

# XXXVIII

## LUCCA

S O MUCH TO DO AND NOT ENOUGH TIME TO SEE IT THROUGH.

Katia wanted to return? Fine, I assured our departure that same morning. I too needed to be back. My phone never stopped ringing, and this trip was a waste of time while I could be out on the streets and showing my face to our men.

The threats had heightened after killing Tino. I knew this would happen, but Borelli still remained in Los Angeles. But with my streets weeping in blood, some things were inevitable. My presence in *my* city was one of them.

I'd spent the entire trip back working from my phone and tablet. Not once did I acknowledge her piercing eyes that punctured my body with pain. There was nothing I could say that would take that away.

I knew my faults, and not sharing the dark side of business was one of them. Ilias had once told me not knowing the threats was more dangerous. That was before he'd sworn the oath to la famiglia. I never understood him then, and even now, I still didn't.

But Katia knew the war our marriage would cause. She understood the danger, and not once had she run toward it. Katia had been bred into this world and molded for survival. It was an instinct only those born in danger comprehended. Even with our ten-year gap, Katia was more mature and aware than any other twenty-six-year-old woman.

The Mafia stole innocence and peace, hers being one of them.

Katia wasn't a submissive woman, she was just fucking smart. She was loud and vocal with her demands but never fought when it interfered with someone's safety, including hers.

She was careful, cunning to those who only saw the beautiful exterior, and watchful. But she was also fragile, hopeful, a contradiction for only me.

I would deal with Leo when the time came, as it seemed some didn't respect the boundaries placed in our...relationship? No. Our arrangement.

I had never lied to Katia. However, I omitted the real reason for our time in Montana. My reasoning had and would always be to keep her away from the filthy reality of our world. I couldn't see myself changing, or believing it was the wrong thing to do.

A black-out Escalade waited for us at the private landing strip. Arlo, Viktor, and Ilias waited outside the running vehicle. I'd expected Arlo, not the whole welcoming party.

I stood from the leather seat, emptied my drink, and picked up her bag from the floor.

"I can get that." Katia's accent was heavy on her tongue. It always was when something bothered her.

Her gaze focused on my hand.

"I'm aware," I replied, and turned to the open door.

Miami's cool and humid breeze swirled in the late evening. A few streaks of sunlight fought the darkness as I went down the plane's stairs.

My brothers met me as I waited for Katia's descent. She didn't take the hand I'd offered on the last step, and I struggled to ignore the raging need to show her some fucking manners in front of my family.

Viktor shot me a look before following her trail back to the SUV.

I watched every sway of her hips, every step she took to the flow of her long brown hair in the breeze.

"I'll get the rest of the bags," Ilias mumbled, leaving Arlo and me alone.

"I'm guessing it didn't go as smoothly as you had hoped," Arlo murmured as Viktor opened the back passenger door for Katia.

It wasn't until she was safely inside that I turned my attention to Arlo.

Black combat books, black-blue jeans, black tee.

"Tell me you've found a hideout."

Arlo grinned.

"Viktor found where some of Borelli's soldiers are hiding," he said excitedly. "There has to be more somewhere, but for now..." Arlo trailed off.

For now, we would take care of the ones we had eyes on.

I glanced at the running SUV. We needed to drop Katia and Viktor off at home. We only had four days before the wedding, and if I wanted Borelli eliminated, I needed to focus on getting him in the city. Therefore, I removed any distractions from my mind.

One in particular.

Katia.

Because after his son's death, the word out on the streets for the head of Los Angeles had shifted. It was now smeared with wild madness. Unpredictable, and I needed him to fall into the trap I'd set.

A part of me knew he was coming, and soon. But I needed to keep pushing and hurting him until every breath he took was with me on his mind. I had cornered and broken him by killing his son. Weakened him in the eyes of his syndicate. Although, I needed him shattered to leave the safety his throne provided and to enter the hell my city would greet him with.

Katia didn't stir when we all huddled inside the vehicle. Even with her sitting in the middle and me on her right, she never allowed her body to touch mine. She didn't utter a sound or a glance in my direction. Ilias tried making conversation. It was one way. Everyone felt the tension in the cabin. The annoyance and wrath she radiated.

I ignored it.

Inside our bedroom, Katia beelined to the bathroom while I changed into another dress shirt. I debated on leaving without a word, but my feet carried me to the sound of running water. The valves squeaked shut, and I stared at the wooden door for a second longer before I knocked. She didn't respond, so I let myself in.

Katia leaned back on a plush towel as her body soaked in cherry scent. The lights were dimmed, and a few candles flickered in peaceful waves. Bath bubbles covered her silhouette, and I traced her necklines.

In silence, I watched her.

The strands of hair that had fallen from her updo. The way they tickled her collarbone and teased the water. Her parted lips and gentle breaths. Flushed cheeks and sun-kissed nose.

Striking.

Breathtaking.

Infuriating.

Then, her eyes opened, and her vivid greens watched *me*. They roamed from my face and down to my feet until they landed on my chest for another second.

I had changed into all black. She was aware I was leaving.

Our eyes met again.

Our eyes fought.

And neither one of us said a word.

I turned and left her alone with the silence. No goodbye, no regard for her feelings.

THAT NIGHT, I KILLED THREE MEN AND TORTURED ANOTHER.

That night a total of eleven Borelli soldiers met hell.

I was drenched in death and taken by depravity. And when I got home, I was greeted by an empty bed.

It was the last thing I expected, and in my immoral state, it was dangerous. The ideas and visions my mind lured me to execute. The evil punishments my demon shook with.

The things I wished to do to her.

She wasn't safe from me. Not right now.

I headed back to work even if the distraction was all I could think about from that point on.

## KATIA

I HADN'T SPOKEN A WORD TO LUCCA SINCE WE LANDED IN MIAMI. NOT ON THE plane ride, in the car, or inside his home.

After his eyes glared down as if it was an inconvenience in his life while I had sought a peaceful bath, I didn't want to be near him. Near his essence or scent. For the past two days, I'd slept in a separate room. I doubted he even noticed because even a glimpse of him was nonexistent.

In those days since our return, security had increased, and countless men were gathered around the house. I felt unease by the amount of precaution and urgency everyone carried. I wasn't the only one. Wex and Vino were also highly alert and unfriendly to the bodies roaming around the premises and within the halls. It was safer to keep them away, as I too didn't feel friendly or calm enough to prevent slitting someone's artery if they glanced at me the wrong way.

The boys and I had something in common. Raging impotence.

While I didn't want to worry or care, with every hour and minute that passed, I wondered about Lucca's wellbeing, and with every second that passed, I detested myself for it.

This morning, Mrs. Greco knocked on my door. Her old ways didn't seem pleased to find me in a guest room. Even as she hid it terribly, she announced the last thing she needed to mark off for the wedding.

The marriage class and meeting with the priest at the church.

I chuckled at the marriage class. The one every *famiglia* member had to attend in order to be married in the eyes of God.

My heart didn't feel pure or ready to face the church I had been introduced to, so I didn't get ready. I didn't leave the house when the time came, nor did I move away from the bed.

I was too hurt to care.

Too sensitive to face reality.

Lucca's words still ricocheted in my mind, and since nothing I could do or say made him feel the same way he'd hurt me, this was my way of pushing back.

"Katia." Two knocks bounced urgently at the door.

"Go away, Viktor."

"I'm coming in," he quickly added, and the door opened.

Viktor stood by the entry in a full light-gray suit that complemented his striking blues. He had an umbrella in his hand as the upcoming storm the news had warned us of had arrived in haste on the Miami coast.

"We were supposed to leave ten minutes ago to meet Lucca at the church. Why aren't you ready?"

I sat up and ran my fingers over Vino's white coat.

"The weather."

"Damn it, Katia! I know I said to give him hell when you arrived home, but *this* is not the time." His head shook, and his lips thinned in frustration. "Fuck!" Russian flew from his lips as I watched him pace.

When he stopped to face me, his shoulders straightened.

"*This* wasn't it." His fingers waved around. "If anything, this was the worst thing you could have done."

I stood up. "*Good.*"

Viktor's eyes lowered, and his nod was reluctant. "I will tell him you are unwell." Viktor didn't utter another word. He walked away, closing the door behind him, and I suddenly felt unconfident about my actions.

In the time I'd spent with Viktor, the short conversations, the looks, the warnings, and even the quiet moments where words weren't needed, he'd slowly crawled into my trust. The kind I didn't even have with Enzo or Leo. Somehow, the disappointment in his eyes was the one I would've thought an older brother would feel.

It was uncomfortable to experience it. The compulsion that crept in to find him and ask for him to talk to me. To tell me what he truly thought, to confide in him.

To have someone in this fucking hell who cared.

Instead, I stayed in the room as thunder rumbled from above and waited for the storm to barge inside.

The door burst open, and Wex and Vino quickly stood alert. Their growls were loud, and their bodies were ready for the threat.

Lucca.

"Are you dying?"

I moved away from the desk and stepped farther away from his ire.

Two days. We hadn't seen each other for two days and this was his greeting. Of course he wouldn't come in trying to work through our issue before we said I do. No. It was Lucca. He wasn't done hurting. Punishing.

"No."

"Are you running a fever?" His chest bounced while he stood in outrage.

"No," I whispered.

His jaw clenched, his palms turned to fists, and a deep rasp bubbled from his throat as his teeth shone briefly. When he stepped closer, so did the four-legged beasts.

Lucca's eyes snapped down at Wex and Vino, their reaction

infuriating him further.

This was a disaster.

He opened the door wide and ordered them in Russian to leave. They listened to their master with apprehension. Their slow steps and snarls weren't timid. They wanted to be heard, wanted to remove the cause of tension.

Lucca slammed the door, and his gaze fell on me.

"You made me look like a fool." His voice was slow, even, dangerous.

The calm in his tone sent a shrill up my body, and my fingertips ran cold as I faced his eerie hate.

I'd seen Lucca lose control when memories of his mother resurfaced. I'd experienced his vicious words and the evil that emerged after staining his hands red, and I'd face his demon when freed. But there was something different about this calm, silent loathe.

It didn't matter how many sides of Lucca's anger I confronted, this one was by far the one I hated.

I didn't fear him. I feared the damage and gravity of what I had consciously done.

I only wanted to push and fight back one last time before it was all over. Before I took the name of the man who didn't care for me as I did for him.

Meanwhile, I added to the weight that was dragging us apart.

"Do you know how it feels to be sitting in front of a priest, watching as minutes pass by without the woman you are meant to marry next to you?"

I breathed in through my mouth as he spoke deliberately.

"Why now, Katia?" He trapped my name between his teeth. "Why, when I waited for *you* in *my* church?" Lost was the calm. His voice mingled with the thunder's roar.

"*Your* church!" I finally fought back, pointing my finger.

"Look around. You are not in Italy anymore." His dark-navy suit opened as his hands waved furiously all around. "My church is now yours, and I'll be damned if I allow you to come in between."

"That was never my intention, Lucca. I—"

"*You* have fifteen minutes to meet me downstairs." He took one last step closer, and even with our distance, his low threat was clear. "Don't fight me on this, or so help me God." He looked around the room, and as he turned his back on me, he gave his last order. "And don't let me catch you sleeping anywhere else than in my bed again."

Tears rolled down my face, finally setting them free.

Free to escape the pain and the shackles I couldn't break free of.

Broken.

I no longer lived on my own. I wasn't an architect or had the business I'd worked so hard on. I was just a shell, property condemned to do as told. Even my fighting was in vain to win a sliver of freedom, and even my name would soon be gone.

I was suffocating and painfully dying as my mind harmed and my heart ached.

I was drowning for my future.

In the unhappiness and pain I couldn't shake away.

*Was this what my mother felt?*

Was this what drove her into madness?

# XXXIX

## LUCCA

I T WAS THE SECOND TIME I'D STEPPED INSIDE THE CHURCH'S FRONT DOORS today. It should have only been once, but earlier I'd sat inside the priest's office next to an empty chair while watching the minutes go by alone. As soon as Viktor's text had flashed across my screen, I excused myself and left straight for my place, where I knew I could find and drag Katia's healthy body back with me.

While I was a mortal sinner, I had an understanding of my faith. After years of following the scriptures, it was the only thing I held as close to law. The church was the one thing I knew where I stood. I'd made peace with it from a young age even after seeing the cruelty in the world. Because if I believed, my heart could accept how my mother rested in peace for eternity in a better place far from fear and pain.

I hadn't fully understood my devotion until Katia threatened my beliefs by disrespecting the church and our vow we would take under God in two days.

If it hadn't been for the peace the church offered me, I wouldn't have been able to walk alongside her. Or even taken a closer look at her red-rimmed eyes. How her sage green veiled in sadness, resignation.

I could work with hurt and hatred, but not with *that*.

The priest, too, saw the change in Katia. His gaze often shifted to her, waiting for her to speak her mind, her troubles. Katia didn't. She only smiled and shook her head at his questions as if she had nothing more to offer.

Her light and spirit had dimmed.

"Miss Katia." Father pulled her attention back to him. "Lucca."

"Father," we both said, and she softly smiled.

"Let's talk openly. If not in the house of God, where else?"

With her eyes low on the ground, her head inclined my way.

Was she questioning how open she could be? How much could she say?

I couldn't read her.

"Marriage in our church is more than a pretty ceremony and fleeting feelings," he began, and Katia turned to him. "It's a sacramental marriage. A lifelong commitment to each other. One that is only dissolved by death. A marriage between you both and God."

The priest's eyes bounced between us.

"Are you willing to continue with this knowledge?" he asked Katia.

I couldn't face her. I couldn't see the doubt in her face, the dread. But mostly, I couldn't face her after knowing the sin I'd committed by taking her free will. By taking on an agreement that meant a commitment until death.

Even then, there was no turning back. She was mine. My queen, my future wife.

"Yes, Father."

My body relaxed.

"You are entering and accepting this marriage, this vow without force or pressure?"

Bile rose as my skin crawled, and the longer Katia took to reply, the deeper I fell with worry. This was the place she held the most power.

Then I felt her touch. Her fingertips slid over my forearms, gently trailing down until her hand curled with mine. I stared at our joined hands. My mother's ring on her delicate finger, the place it belonged.

I cast a look at her.

Katia's smile reached her gleaming eyes. Small tight lines formed at the ends of her brows as her teeth shone brightly. And with a glowing radiance, she said, "It's what I want, Father."

She didn't answer the question.

Want, what a dangerous word with endless meaning.

We could always want, even if it hurt. Even if we wished for a different outcome.

The priest carefully watched her. It didn't help that I sat quietly without a smile to match hers. I only looked ahead at the brick wall with a hammering heart.

"Lucca?" he asked.

"Without force or pressure," I replied.

The priest nodded and quickly moved back to Katia. Her hand twitched underneath mine as she couldn't flee from his attention.

I placed my free hand over hers, caging her between both of mine.

"And you both are willing to conceive children?"

We couldn't marry in the Catholic Church if we said no. Thankfully, I remember vividly our conversation about children. *Three or more!* Had been her words. Loud and ridden in pleasure.

"Yes," we echoed, and this time, our eyes met.

"Lucca, I would like to speak to Katia, alone."

I freed my hands and stood. Her eyes widened, but her false smile never faltered. I walked out of his office and closed my eyes against the stone wall, waiting for this to be over.

Today was a mind game.

From the moment she stood me up to the careful words she used.

I was spent.

Borelli still ruled my mind, Katia reigned over my control, and the vow I would soon give to the church governed inside. The thoughts of her family arriving tomorrow also lingered, and while I hadn't offered them to stay under my roof. The threats were still here and scattered around the city.

There were so many moves, so many pieces, and I couldn't see the end.

The unknown was driving me mad. Insane with scenarios and countermoves, and yet Katia weakened my mind with her defiance and spirit.

She became the weakness I had tried so hard to divert.

The heavy door opened, and the priest smiled.

Hesitantly, I faced him. "Everything alright, Father?"

I waited for his words of advice and disappointment, but I received the opposite.

"Indeed, Katia is ready to wed. She even mentioned how she got to know you in the mountains." His brown eyes glowed with joy.

He'd fallen into her deceit.

I walked inside with a void in my chest, appalled by the father's content and Katia's docile aura.

I signed the marriage license he'd placed before us and didn't miss the way her hand trembled when the ink smeared her signature.

Our marriage would be sealed on Saturday after he would perform the ceremony.

The priest ended our meeting with a prayer, and as we walked from the back of the church to the front double doors, Katia stopped to take one last look at the ceiling before wrapping her hand around my arm. The deception of being strong and united in public.

The sky mirrored my troubled mind, and I opened the umbrella I'd left at the edge of the church. Katia's timid smile thanked me before she sneaked under the shelter I offered. I kept a close eye on the hoax she portrayed out in the open as her hands held the plastic envelope close and free from the rain. When I opened the back passenger door to the SUV, I stretched my palm for her to take.

After shutting the door, I glanced over at the second black-out Escalade and gave Beppe a nod as I crossed to the other side. I hopped inside the large SUV and ran my fingers over my dampened hair. I caught Rio's eyes in the rearview mirror, and he immediately removed them to speed away from the church.

Katia looked out the window while her fingertips played against her thigh. The light cream-colored dress she wore contrasted her golden and smooth skin. Her makeup had been minimal, but she'd taken her time to conceal the puffy and dark areas under her eyelids.

She hadn't slept. That made two of us.

"You didn't have to lie," I said, glancing down at the envelope between our seats.

Katia didn't face me as she whispered, "I walk inside the house of God just like the sinner you are, but I don't lie on sacred ground. I spoke the truth."

*"She got to really get to know you in the mountains."* The priest just failed to realize how far off her statement was from good.

We remained silent for the rest of the ride, and while I trusted Rio, I didn't want my personal life whispered on the streets. The more they believed the bastard I was even behind closed doors, the best it was for us.

Nightfall arrived as we pulled into my private street, and after weeks it seemed someone had finally heeded my threat and fixed the busted streetlights.

Somehow the simple sight of them running without a flicker eased my breathing.

"Wait."

My hand shot out when we arrived home and her body tensed under my touch. Stunned by her reaction, I pulled back.

*Katia had cowered.*

Dumbfounded, I stared at her delicate frame and lowered my gaze with no thought of how to proceed.

Rio exited the car, and while it ran with the air at full blast, heat spread under my skin. My hand then had a mind of its own, and wrapped by the nape of her hair, until I made her face me.

"You are afraid of me now?"

Her eyes watched me carefully, and I caught her hand movement, creeping and slithering closer to her skirt slit.

Fuck.

I let her go, and her hand stopped.

My God, she was fucking with my head. I couldn't even tell if this was real, or a craft of her game. It was how far she'd swept my senses to the point that if this, us, right now was real, one of us might not make it out alive.

*Me*, I wouldn't make it out alive because I had vowed to protect her. Katia would slowly rot every cell in my brain until I couldn't think straight for our protection, and I would be the one filled with gunpowder.

I had to pull away and think straight. I was so close to ending this war, I couldn't let it crumble before my eyes.

"The rehearsal dinner has been canceled." I cleared my throat. "Instead, we will have a small dinner with our families tomorrow night." Disbelief shone in her irises. "Your family will stay here tomorrow and leave after the wedding."

Her cherry-stained lips parted, and her shoulders slumped with the news I had kept from her. I'd waited until the last moment to deliver them, knowing the impact of having her father sleeping under the same roof could mean to her. Hell, I didn't want that man in my home either, or one of her siblings. If anything, a private dinner with both our families called for chaos.

"How long have you known?" She cleared her raspy tone.

"A month."

"How long has Mrs. Greco known?" Her voice died at the end.

"A month."

Katia's eyes widened as her brows creased, and she rubbed her chest as if I'd delivered a punch but didn't utter a word, a tone, or a whisper. Only her eyes offered her hatred.

She pulled the car door open quickly and stumbled out into the rain, and when the door bounced shut, I was alone with the silence and the havoc of my mind.

I SHOULD BE GOING OVER THE WEDDING SECURITY WITH ARLO, CHECKING ALL the boxes and guaranteeing no misunderstandings. I should be going over the arrival of Katia's family tomorrow, warning everyone to expect everything and nothing at all. Instead, I heard Arlo talk circles while all my mind went over was Katia's simmering anger.

It was unsettling. She'd held on to a farce for so long, but now that anger cracked through, it wasn't long until her spirit would shatter and for her emotions to weep.

She was a high-heel ticking time bomb.

"Whatever you've done, fix it!" Viktor roared as he slung the door open in my study.

Shocked by whatever caused the abrupt entrance and the anger aimed at me, I sat perplexed by his vicious rage. He didn't care who was inside or who he'd interrupted. Hell, he didn't even mind that it was *me*, who he raised his voice to.

Sal's eyes shot out and his upper lip curled while Arlo smiled with crossed arms, patiently waiting for disaster.

"Careful, *fratello*." I seethed.

"I don't think so. I am done, *brother*." Long steps rushed toward me, but they stopped as I stood.

"You are *done*?" I questioned.

His jaw tightened. He knew he wasn't done until death.

"I am done watching how you slowly break her. If that's what you wanted, congrats, you've achieved it."

Sal's features shifted from disbelief to interest. He too wanted to know what Viktor was referring to if it revolved around Katia.

"I have done no such thing."

"Then you are blind, or you've chosen to ignore it." His eyes narrowed. "This is what you wanted all along, wasn't it?"

I said, "*Careful*." I moved away from my chair and stepped away from my desk.

"What could you possibly gain, Lucca?" Viktor grinned coldly. "I'll answer that for you. Nothing but misery."

Rage burned in coils of fury at his disrespect for intervening and believing he could influence how I handled Katia.

"Did you know she had hardly touched her food for days? That tonight she moved the casserole from one end of her plate to the other? How she was so taken by rage that she couldn't take a bite? Have you noticed the circles under her eyes? What about the fake smiles, Lucca?" He dug deeper.

"That's *enough*."

Low and cautious, I spoke, meeting him in the middle of the room. Our eyes fought, but Viktor was too far gone. Too enraged and lost by emotions.

"Did you know she's the reason your little streetlamps shine with new bulbs?"

*Huh?*

"Yeah, she made sure it was scheduled the day before you took her to Montana." Viktor's cloudy blues locked on me as he shook his head.

"Fix. It."

The fucker turned his back on me, and I couldn't fault him. I was the one who'd placed him to take care of her, guard her. I just didn't think it would be from me.

"Where is she now?"

Viktor didn't halt his steps as he mumbled, "Downstairs, beating one of your men to a pulp."

Arlo whistled, and I raised my hand to cut him short. "Don't."

"Viktor!" I yelled, and he stopped by the doorway. "You allowed her to walk downstairs and fight one of our men?"

"No, *you* did by showing me how much you fucking gave a shit."

My body launched in his direction, but I was quickly stopped by Arlo's strength. He caged one of my arms, but I fumed in rage and lost sight of who Viktor was to me. All I could see was his disrespect.

Ravid in anger at Viktor's retreating back, I slammed Arlo into the bookshelves, and I punched his side with my free hand to chase after the imbecile who thought talking to me in such a way was acceptable.

His hand snaked to the back of my neck, and as I fought, our foreheads connected.

"You are losing control, brother," Arlo spoke in Italian with labored breaths. "He did what you asked. He did what he told you he would do." His grip didn't lighten as I continued to fight. "We don't hurt each other in hatred. Never have."

I looked into his hazel eyes. The same eyes I had calmed since I was fourteen, and yet for the first time, they were trying to do so for me.

"You can't lose control, *fratello*. Not now."

*Not now.*

I controlled my breathing, eased the demon, and closed my eyes briefly before Arlo let me go. I rolled my shoulders and pushed him off me before I walked back to my desk where I'd left my unfinished drink. The contents of the drink were drowned in one sip, and I quickly rolled my sleeves. I now had one intention: find Katia.

All she'd done today was defy me in every way. It was erratic, and I knew I wasn't the only one lost in the madness of our lives.

"Fucking children is how you are all behaving," Sal chided between a cough as I walked past him. "Fucking fix it, Lucca!"

I ignored the old bastard and walked out of the room with Arlo following close behind. With my hand on my back, I drew my handgun out and opened the basement door.

The temperature dropped drastically to the low cool setting of the room. Every step I took down the stairs, cheers, laughter, and conversations grew louder. Even from above, I couldn't see her frame or hair through the large crowd of made-men that clustered in the corner.

After the last step, my tense muscles ached for release. With the echo of the door closing, a few of my men turned. They quickly moved away from the rowdy circle, and the closer I approached, the more others followed in the same direction with wide eyes.

My demon was loose. It was evident in my walk, aura, and gaze. No one would dare come in between.

Grunts and puffs grew louder under the fluorescent lights, and I couldn't get close fast enough. But each soldier that moved from their spot, the other turned to see the cause, me.

It wasn't until I was in the front row that everything fell silent.

I hid my shaking body and the hatred that gripped my hand from unloading my gun at everyone I faced. I buried the heat crawling behind my neck and the pounding that beat in anger, causing my breathing to race.

I wanted to watch and stare at the eyes of each man that had decided to stay as if this was a fucking show. As if there was a match between soldiers and a bet to be won.

But it was *my* woman who they watched. Who they deemed okay to receive filthy fists connecting to her golden skin.

And yet, I only saw her.

Drenched in sweat with black matching shorts and sports bra, Katia stood in the middle above a man. Hair strands escaped her ponytail and while some flew around her face, others stuck to her skin. Her chest bounced as she peered down, thirsty for sips of pain.

Katia was so lost in delivering and taking physical pain to ignore her internal distress that she didn't notice the silence that flooded the room into stillness. The eyes that watched us, and the demon that filtered around.

I was now part of the show, but this show wouldn't end well for anyone. Not until my hands checked her body for any hint of purple.

Blood was smeared over the mat, and as I scrutinized every inch of her body, I couldn't find the source aside from the man on the floor who moaned. With the small amount of fabric that covered her body, there was no sign of bruising. At the vision of her adrenaline-crazed body so at peace with the chaos, I stood dumbfounded.

Katia *was* used to fighting men. She was used to letting her wild rage free to punish even while others watched. This wasn't the first time she'd fought against men in the Mafia. It couldn't be, not while she seemed so accustomed to her surroundings. Attuned and ready for more.

The grip on my gun tightened, understanding the environment she'd been allowed and introduced to. It angered me that she sought physical pain to numb the one inside.

Katia's head fell back taking a large breath, and as she straightened, her eyes opened to reality. Slowly, her face turned left, and our eyes met.

A fucking deadly dream.

A dangerous obsession.

Katia was my wild weakness.

She didn't cower. Her eyes never wavered, and her stance never relaxed.

While I held her shining sage green eyes captive, my tone spoke with menace. "I will murder each and every one of you along with your whole family line if anyone so much as touches her fucking hair." Katia's gold brass knuckles tightened as her fists balled. "It's not a threat." My eyes released her and roamed around the sea of mafiosos. "It's a vow."

"You are to protect and respect her. Not to harm or treat her like the motherfucker next to you!" My voice rose. "Disrespect me in my house or my word again and I will educate you all on the meaning of torture until I burn your last minutes of life in fire."

An ominous silence spread through the stream of nodding faces.

"Did I make myself clear?" Apologetic and casting eyes agreed. "Now, get out."

Slowly they all made their way up the stairs, and I found Sergio at the end of the line with crossed arms, waiting to be the last one out. His eyes fell to the floor before me, and when I took a closer look, I saw the young boy's busted face.

Domenico, his younger cousin. He turned eighteen three months ago and was initiated shortly after. Eager, quick to follow orders, and ready to please, Sergio's cousin was now tossing on the ground in pain.

"Get Mimmo out of here and clean him up," I ordered. Sergio's rigid posture eased as he walked closer to the boy. Arlo met him, and they both picked up the groaning kid. "And Sergio," I added. "Make sure he understands what reckless decisions lead to in our world. If not, this may be his only lesson."

"Yes, boss." Sergio's head dipped, and with Arlo's help, all three disappeared up the stairs.

As I turned back to Katia, there was still one body comfortably sitting a few feet behind her. I shouldn't have missed the blond hair in the crowd. However, as he sat back and relaxed in the iron chair, he hadn't been seen in the sea of dark hair.

Viktor had only left Katia long enough to speak his mind before returning to her.

"Nice speech."

Katia turned to the voice, surprised to see Viktor.

Our eyes connected, and I could see Viktor ready to continue but my attention shifted when Katia said, "Don't harm the kid. He was the only one who stepped up after I pressured."

*"You can't lose control, fratello. Not now."*

*Not now.*

I placed my gun behind my waist and took a deep breath as I stared at her wild eyes.

*Not. Now.*

"Don't harm the kid?" I scoffed. "I think you did just fine, Katia. And he's not a kid. He's a made-man who made his own decision."

"He wouldn't even punch back!" Katia's temper returned, and my demon twitched.

I was tired of seeing her in this room and the idea of her fighting with my men, I took a step forward and roared back. "As he shouldn't have! And yet, it didn't seem like that made you stop."

Katia shook her head.

"Tell me, how many brawls with mafiosos have you encountered?" She stepped back.

"Tell me, why did you act against my orders to stay out of this room?"

Her lips curled as her breathing grew unsteady with every inch of distance I removed from us.

"Tell me, Katia. Whose face did you see instead of the man you fought, huh?"

My fingertips snapped to her jaw, and I pushed her head high to watch her answer. The loud scratch of iron against concrete caused her eyes to fall, and I didn't turn to the sound of the chair or the eyes that watched from afar.

I didn't care, I had my answer.

*Me.* She wanted to cause me pain.

"Leave," I warned Viktor, and he finally listened as I heard him step farther away from us. I tipped her head again. "I asked you a question."

"You asked many."

"Then answer me!"

"Too many brawls, Lucca. It's how I learned to fight. My grandfather was right. It was vital for my life." Katia snatched her face from my hold. "I'm thankful he did. If not, I would've been dead by now." I tasted blood as she continued, "And I acted against your wishes because you'd gone against mine by keeping the arrival of my family and their stay from me. My god, you've had weeks to mentally prepare for the chaos. You only gave *me* a night!"

Katia's palms extended over my chest, and she pushed her weight against me. Her force was weak as she tried shoving my body away. Resentful and enraged, she tried again, and this time, her palms formed into small fists.

"You gave me nothing!"

Struggling to see her breaking madness, I held one of her wrists between our bodies. Her arm fought to be freed, angering her further by the feeling of helplessness.

Tugging her close, I asked between my teeth, "Whose face did you envision, Katia?"

Katia pushed, and I pulled. She writhed, I held her tighter, and when she wouldn't face me, I *made* her look.

And I saw them. The unshed tears that threatened her hatred rim-filled emeralds. The teeth that captured her bottom lip as it shook, and the slight twitch of her button nose. Katia was losing her fight to the battle of hurt she'd held inside.

In a broken whisper, she replied, "My father."

Stunned by her answer, my hold loosened, but her will had already vanished and her hands slipped to her sides with no fight left. My gaze followed the lone tear that fell, and my chest clenched at its sight.

This wasn't my little cunning creature with forest fire eyes I'd vowed to protect for the rest of my life. This was the broken girl she'd imprisoned for years with deep wounds of hurt as agony poured from the past.

I couldn't take away the pain or comfort her without tearing her further. Without giving her the sense of care. And while I detested her cloudy gaze, the red in her eyes, and the tears that flowed, I stood watching her saddened features, unknowing how I could stop them.

My hands spread to her jaw and neck as I lowered my lips to her cheek. My mouth trapped her tears and the salty taste of their pain. Slowly, I brought her body flush to mine while my face slithered close to her ear.

"Don't cry, Katia. It weakens me."

Small trembles turned into involuntary body tremors as her tears molded into cries.

They did exactly what I'd expressed, weakened me.

I struggled between walking away and staying. Neither was something I wanted to do. If I walked away, I wouldn't know when they stopped, but if I stayed, I wouldn't know how to take them away.

I was at a loss, so when her head dropped to my chest, and her delicate fingers curled around my arms with fists full of fabric, I stayed.

Standing still while tears dampened my dress shirt, I kept my hands and fingers intertwined with her silk chestnut hair.

I stood there for long minutes without my chest relieving the misery that crept inside, and a part of me wanted to understand her pain.

# XL

## KATIA

THE DARK SKY CONTINUED TO CLAIM THE EARLY HOURS OF THE NEW DAY as soft thunder rocked the silence. I was lying next to Lucca, and while his breathing was even, I knew he was awake.

We didn't touch through the night, and even now, my body remained far from his warmth. He'd seen me weak as I had lost all composure yesterday, and while my mind played with the tricks of want, need, and hope, I'd grown numbed by the time sleep claimed me.

Today was the last day before I said *I do* to a killer whose hands I craved.

I was worn, confused, and outright dreading seeing my family. Because now, I felt too much.

I'd wished the next time I would face my father, I would smile brightly and show him how he'd lost. How even in misery, I prevailed, and he couldn't touch me again. I wanted to look Enzo in the eye to show him what he hadn't been able to do without me, and I'd dreamed of facing Leo's compulsive demeanor to teach him how a woman could handle their emotions better.

Instead, my eyes were puffy, my heart scorched, and my will splintered.

Lucca hadn't uttered another word after his chest soaked up my tears. Last night, he'd just waited until my rough breathing settled, and my eyes ran dry before he placed his hand low on my back and guided me out of the room and into ours.

His silence had been enough, because at least then promises couldn't be broken, and words would've been tainted by deception.

"Broken streetlamps remind me of the first life I took and the last night I saw my mother."

My heart raced in my chest as Lucca broke the silence inside the room. I didn't move. I lay paralyzed as I listened to him share a part of him.

"It was the night before my fourteenth birthday. We'd been running for so long that I began believing my mother's fear was all a creation of her mind. I don't remember a time before just us, and in the early hours of the morning, she dropped me off on the curb next to a large stone building.

"She held my face one last time and vanished into the darkness. I never saw her again." Lucca shifted. "And while I bathe in the dark, I can't stand seeing a broken streetlamp."

I breathed quietly through my parted lips in ache as my soul grasped a fragment of his past. The troubles he'd buried without allowing others to see them.

"I've made peace with who I am, Katia, and what I can't offer. But I owe you a thank you. While I am a proud man, you deserve the reasoning behind my gratitude for something that may seem minor, but to me..."

Lucca trailed off, and as he opened the door of his past in the dim hours of the morning, I wanted to venture closer to what made him, *him*. He was right. To me, the broken light didn't concern me. I had scheduled and assured the repairs with Viktor before we left Montana. At a time,

I was still riding high on the riches and ideas for our future. Little did I know, it was a rooted wound tied with foul vines of memories.

I risked a glance and found his eyes open, watching the ceiling as if he was searching for something more than the roof lines. His relaxed breathing contradicted his rigid muscles, and when he felt my eyes on him, they lowered as his head leaned to meet my gaze.

"While I tell you this, I also have a motive."

Of course he did, Lucca didn't do anything without a gain even if it was to say thank you.

I tugged the bedsheet closer to my chest and gently nodded against the plush pillow.

"What do you want from me, Lucca?"

"Peace."

"I don't understand."

He exhaled deeply and flicked his eyes away before they returned to me.

"I never asked about your past, but I have a clear picture of the man your father was to you, and I know the position your brothers had placed you in."

"Yeah..." I quipped.

"I also haven't shared my issues with your family and as they will arrive today, I need peace between us for at least a day." His hand ran over his jaw. "I can't have the war, your family, the threats, and you clouding my judgment. I can't control the other or you, but I am asking for peace for just one day."

I flipped over onto my stomach with a taunting smile I couldn't hold. I balled the pillow under my chest as I lifted my head to watch him carefully.

My, my, was Lucca trying to negotiate a treaty between us? A truce?

The corner of Lucca's lips twitched, and he gave me a look.

"Are you asking to be partners today, Lucca?" I smiled.

"I'm offering you support with your family today."

"So you want to partner?" I rested my chin against my palm.

"Katia."

"Lucca."

"Stop smiling."

I couldn't. It was plastered all over my features. The victory for him to agree that together we would be stronger even if it was for a day. The victory for something I'd asked for, even if love wasn't involved.

The trust.

"Just because *you* asked so nicely."

"All I asked was for one day of peace with you." He tried to make it clear, and it was.

Lucca needed us to see eye to eye and ride the troubles of his mind knowing I would be okay, and that he could count on me.

"Now, stop smiling."

My chest bubbled, and a laugh erupted by his testy tone. Lucca grumbled with dark eyes, and in one swift movement, his strong hands grabbed my hips and dragged me on top of him.

With our centers connected while the sheets writhed along with our bodies, I felt the outline of his dick pressed against me. I watched his brown eyes untamed as his breath feathered my lips.

I dampened my lips with my tongue and clutched onto his neck while my leg snaked around his hips. While we stared carefully at one another and our scents mingled, I failed to care about tomorrow or the following day. Because today we would be partners.

"I'm not good with peace," I murmured against his mouth.

"That's alright. You have tomorrow to wreck me."

Lucca collapsed his brutal mouth free, and his lips controlled mine. I kicked the covers and sheets off for our skin to mend to one. His hands ran furiously and gripped my sides, ass, and thighs, and I rocked my body to their assault.

I was flushed as heat coursed over my flesh, and I wanted him inside me. I wanted him now, hard and fast, to seal the vow of today. My hand slithered down his strong back with nails that stung its path. This caused his skin to crawl in a shiver and his mouth to falter by its sensation.

"Deal," My burning lips agreed, and my hand slipped between us, and I gripped his hard dick. "Now, fuck me." I tugged at his shaft, and he groaned.

Lucca did. He fucked his frustration and the stress he had been holding onto inside me brutally. Bruising and cruel thrusts. Stinging kisses, and painful touches, and each pound and sexual torture he gave, *I wanted more*. His troubles and torment to stain and use me for pleasure.

I came hard, coating his dick with my release until he emptied himself inside me. Our passion mixed together as he collapsed on top of me. Our scents fused as we both gave in to our desires, and I lay over the ruined white sheets, sore and satisfied.

Reluctantly, Lucca pulled away and stood. His eyes slowly roamed over my body, and he surprised me when he leaned back to steal a kiss before heading inside the bathroom. It took all my will to leave the bed behind and cover my body with his discarded button-up. However, knowing Lucca was behind the door, I chased him.

Lucca stood over the sink in boxer briefs. I admired his taut muscles and inked skin from afar while water ran, filling the sink halfway. He shut both valves off, and I met his eyes in the mirror.

A razor knife lay over a small black towel next to a clear jar of white mousse. His hair was tousled from my fingers and vibrant red smudges joined the black of his tattoos from my touches of our time together. While relaxed, his eyes calculated my every move as I walked closer. I leaned my ass on the counter until I slid onto the cool surface. He spread my legs open to cage himself between them.

I heard the loud crashes from above as the storm continued outside of this home, and as the skies rumbled and the earth shook from thunder, bolts coursed inside the quiet bathroom with electric awareness.

My hands found the shaving mousse, and I picked the brush inside. I peered up into his eyes, and they didn't stop me as I touched his skin with the soft bristles to coat under his jaw and neck. I placed the jar back in its spot and tipped his head from side to side, examining the line to clean against his trimmed beard. I did it all under his sharp gaze, and when my fingertips touched the familiar cool metal of a blade, I grasped its natural feel against my palm and faced him.

Our eyes locked, and a nervous flutter pricked my fingers.

The chime of rain harshly hitting the windows was loud and my breathing mimicked its blast as I raised the blade to his neck.

Lucca's jaw tightened, and with a slight tug, he inched away.

*"I just don't trust a Vitelli with one,"* he had said more than once, and yet here I was, with a blade inches away from his neck. Inches away from the vein that popped as blood ran through his body.

My hand slipped to the back of his head until my finger clutched his short hair, bringing him closer and pulling his head back. Lucca fought with how far he would allow his neck to be exposed, but his eyes blared in fire as they looked down on me, and when I brought the blade closer, he craned his head further and closed his eyes as the knife connected to his skin.

The blade slid effortlessly against the pressure of my fingertips, and it swiped clean without a drop of blood or a mark left behind.

Maybe now he could trust *one* Vitelli with a blade. Because I have mastered the art and precision of wielding one, and he wouldn't be harmed by my hands.

Lucca was afraid of me drawing conclusions, fabricating feelings and ideas that would never be there. But did he not see what he'd just done? What his actions solidified while his mind said otherwise?

Lucca *trusted* me. He just couldn't see it.

I kept my heart at bay along with the smile I struggled to hide, and I rinsed the blade in the sink only to return to him and continue to shave his taunting flesh.

"My father will push you," I murmured while concentrating on my task.

"I know."

"And Leo will provoke."

"Mh-hm," he replied as I slid the blade again.

"Don't react, okay?"

Lucca chuckled. "Katia, I hardly speak when I have to, let alone react to games."

This was true, but…I stopped cleaning the blade and glimpsed up.

Both of his hands grabbed my hips, pulling me closer and his head lowered.

"The only one who tests and causes a reaction out of me is you."

"I mean it," I pressed.

"So do I." His thumb ran against the crease of my bikini line and slid underneath the edge of his shirt to feel my bare skin. "Now, finish. I must leave soon."

With a nod and satisfied with his answer, I drew the knife back to finish what I'd started.

Lucca was right. He was a man of a few words, and I pushed and continued to push until I could get him to react. To know and see some emotion in him, even though it often pained me.

I let my worry free from my chest and savored the last minutes of calm before chaos erupted, giving the tropical storm a match of its own. Because I knew our family feud wasn't over, and our bad blood was too thick to ease years of hate.

THE HOUSE MOVED AT HIGH SPEED WITH THE NUMBER OF PEOPLE ROAMING around. From a few extra helping hands in the kitchen to men walking around from one end of the property to the other. There were too many bodies and yet, after Ilias picked up Vino and Wex to stay over with him and Davina while we had visitors, the house felt too vacant without their large paws and growls following my wake.

I watched the news for an updated weather report. It was the second day that rain poured and thunder roared, and while the news promised a short time of clear skies tomorrow, an outside wedding was a risk.

"Oh, Ms. Katia!"

I muted the screen inside the one room that housed the large television and turned to Mrs. Greco. A pile of folded sheets rested on her arms, and her breathing was labored as she stopped by the entry arch of the second living room.

Seeing her stress-ridden eyes, I asked, "Do you need help?"

She shook her head. "Oh, no. I have it, darling, but there are a few centerpieces that arrived if you would like to look at them."

"I would love that, thank you," I replied politely, making a mental note to do so.

"I actually wanted to touch base with you." Mrs. Greco stopped talking as she glanced to her right. I too moved my attention, and Lucca appeared with his eyes drawn to his phone before they snapped to face her as he entered the room.

"Afternoon." Lucca tipped his head toward her then his gaze found mine.

It was impossible to overlook how I followed his footfalls or the pull of the dark, condemning aura he brought along. How I stood eager to see him walking toward me in this part of the home he rarely explored just to find me. How this morning I withered in pleasure in his bed, only to get fucked all over against the countertop after holding a knife to his neck.

I wanted to pull his black tie free from his charcoal wool vest and free the first button on his white shirt to stare and trace the ink lines of his skin with my fingertips. Because today we'd agreed on peace and tomorrow, I could worry again about my heart.

For a moment, his eyes held mine captive as heat flooded his browns. Then his eyes fell to the curves of my body that was wrapped in a silk champagne-colored dress.

"I apologize for interrupting," he expressed, and his mouth parted to continue, but he abruptly stopped.

I followed the cause as his eyes veered to the silent news screen.

*The search for justice continues for the deaths…*

The red banner across the bottom of the screen read, and I noticed the tension in his shoulders. I switched the TV off, and he snapped out of his mind. Lucca turned back toward me, taking a deep breath.

"You are not, sir. Will you join Ms. Katia for lunch?" Mrs. Greco was oblivious to the news coverage and the change in Lucca's demeanor.

"I can't, I was just stopping by briefly." Lucca took the last two steps until his hand pressed against my lower back.

"I'll leave you both alone." She politely smiled. "I can speak to Ms. Katia about the possibility of moving the wedding inside due to the weather another time."

Lucca's fingers twitched, and he glanced down.

"You want an outside wedding, correct?" he asked, and I nodded. "The wedding will be outside, Mrs. Greco, and we can push it until the sky is clear if needed. If not, I'll assure the church is ready."

"Of course." She grinned sheepishly and left.

"Stop smiling," Lucca said with a knowing look, and the hint of humor adorned his lips.

"I must say, I'm growing inclined to this so-called peace day." I chuckled at his ruffled features, and added with sincerity, "Thank you."

I turned to him, and his hand moved along the base of my back. I picked an imaginary piece of lint off his tie, and his eyes fell.

"I didn't want to call, and I needed to pick up some documents I left behind this morning so…"

"Yeah."

I pulled back from his clean and peculiar smell of sand, wool, and whiskey breeze to stare at him. His eyes appeared at ease, but the longer I kept them from leaving mine, I saw their violence and bloodthirst.

"Lucca?" I pushed, and my palm touched his chest as my fingers spread around his warmth.

Lucca's eyes fell to my hand, and he looked away.

"Your family will arrive shortly after four, and dinner will be served at five thirty," he explained in monotone. "I should be back before anyone arrives."

"Is that all?" I pressed again, and a twitch of his lips gave a small, grim smile away.

"What else would there be?" He dropped his hand from my back and tucked a loose strand of my hair to the side. "I must go. Stay inside, alright? The weather is rough."

The weather…right.

"If that's the case, stay in."

His eyes narrowed, and his throat rasped a chuckle.

"I'm not afraid of the rain, Katia."

A pressure weighed deeply in my chest, and I needed the assurance of his words to carry some away before he walked out of the door.

"We are still talking about the weather, right?"

A devilish grin answered *we were not.*

"Don't change. That color is striking on you." Lucca was already pulling away.

"Wait." I trapped his wrist. "Be safe."

Lucca didn't look back, he didn't nod or acknowledge my words. As if he couldn't face them or the care behind his wellbeing.

Regardless, the words flew free, and the sentiment for his safety was evident.

# XLI

## LUCCA

TIME HAD RUN OUT, AND EVERY MINUTE PASSING BY WAS BORROWED. California was in chaos after Borelli's son's death, and we'd lost sight of *him*. There was the chance that he could be walking through my city seeking vengeance.

It was what I had wanted, but I couldn't confirm if he had fallen into my trap.

I had anticipated California's uproar, and after all the scheming, the toughest task was dealing with Borelli's men. It was expected. His soldiers were scattered all around, unruly and lost with the new changes. Some in Los Angeles without sight of their boss. Others in New York fighting a battle with no end. Not to mention the ones here, in Miami, following his orders, while watching their syndicate crumble.

Now, the entire famiglia had their fingers deep in the havoc. The longer it took to tame the loose ends, the more reckless the madness grew.

All four bosses couldn't agree on the possibility of naming a new head for California with Borelli still alive. Their thoughts were all based on greed and self-gain, believing they could have one of their own running another city when in reality, Los Angeles had its own ranks. But the situation was difficult with a target on a boss who no longer had a next in line.

In the middle of La Cosa Nostra's disagreement, I found out there was one bastard in particular who wasn't helping to restore order. No one other than my fucking future father-in-law.

Katia's father wanted to co-rule California between the four families. It would never work, I knew it, and the others did too, which was why the votes were divided. It should be Los Angeles third in command who should take the seat. Someone that would reclaim peace between all the syndicates. A man others trusted as their own and respected.

Instead, Mario slithered and whispered in ears about his plan and my involvement.

He spoke as if I backed him in this plan, creating the two versus two. This shouldn't even be up for a vote. It was mad.

I sped through my streets, too lost in ire to give a shit about the slick roads. I just wanted to get home and keep an eye on Katia after hanging up with Alonzo Costa. But before the call ended, I made it clear to Las Vegas how I didn't share Mario Vitelli's idea of progress.

*Progress.* The old man wanted progress. It was laughable.

There had to be something I was missing.

Something I'd overlooked.

It was unsettling, and my demon warned.

Because all Mario Vitelli was provoking was for this war to continue against my city after I would kill Borelli. And it drove me mad not seeing or understanding his end game aside from pride.

Now I would have to face him in my own home, knowing the troubles he continued to cause. Because men kept pouring, and we were starting to get hit from all angles.

Then, there was the shift I felt. The sway of power like a sound of crumbling dust falling off a pick as it slowly chipped my empire.

I pulled my car onto the deep and gravel road that led to Salvatore's home. I had to calm down. I needed Sal's advice and thoughts before I could lose control with the Vitelli that slept in my bed. I couldn't share this with her.

"Sal?" I roared as I opened the front door.

All the lights inside were off. Nothing had been disturbed and an uncanny silence traveled through the house, causing a rousing alarm to settle. The dread engulfed my body as I glanced at the chair he spent most of his time in, empty and without a mug resting on its side table under the darkness.

Darkness. It shouldn't be dark. The house should be covered with lit lamps. The low static sound of the radio he kept on through the day should be humming through the walls. Instead, it was too quiet, haunting.

"Sal?"

I picked my phone out of my pocket and shot Viktor a quick text as I walked through the silent halls.

**Where's Katia?**

Viktor texted back immediately.

**She was last drawing on her iPad. Feet over your desk.**

*She was last.*

**Not last. Now.**

I peered into the kitchen. It was empty.

"Sal!" I yelled.

My phone vibrated against my palm.

**No change.**

A slither of constraint diminished in my chest, but I couldn't shake off the worry feeling.

**Don't lose sight of her.** I texted back and pocketed my phone back.

I didn't attempt the upper floor. It always remained vacant, forgotten. Instead, my feet pushed through the hall straight to his bedroom door. I pushed the door open to the smell of disinfecting alcohol and woods, and my body froze.

"Sal?"

Immediately, I rushed to his body as he sat slumped against the side of the bed. A low whistle of air escaped from the tube far within his reach, and the oxygen tank lay sideways by the corner.

He still wore his sleepwear. Salvatore never made it out of his room this morning.

*No, no, no.*

My hands shot to his face, cupping his soft wrinkled skin. It was cool but...I slipped my fingers to his neck and pressed down.

One.

Two.

I counted through the trembles that coursed through my fingertips, and as I stared at his closed eyes, calm features, and slouched shoulders without the feel of his heartbeat, mine drummed loudly, raging inside its cage.

"Come on, you bastard!" I cupped his face and shook him.

*Breathe.*

I took a deep breath, balled my fingers, and tried again.

One.

Two.

Three.

I laughed.

It was faint, subtle, and yet, it meant life. I pressed my fingers deeper to count each beat and pulled his head onto my chest. I reached for the air tube on the floor and maneuvered the tangled cord to place it under his nose and around his head.

My fingers fell, knowing his heart rate was low and weak, and I sat with him for a minute longer, trying to calm the dread that wouldn't dull even through relief. I needed to carry him to his bed, but the urine smell filled my lungs. Sal soiled himself. Angered by the thought of how long he had been alone weighed me down. I helped him back against the bed to find a fresh pair of silk sleep pants.

I moved swiftly, changing him, and once I pooled his old clothes on the floor, I picked him up and carried him over to the bed. My phone rang as I stared at him as he slept, and I answered while covering him with a blanket.

"Yes." I scratched my throat.

"The plane will land shortly," Arlo's voice broke through the receiver.

"I'm aware." Sal shifted his head. "Bring Mrs. Greco to Sal's and call Marissa."

"Lucca."

"Do it." I hung up.

I watched the rise and fall of Sal's chest. It grew stronger as the minutes drifted by and all I did was stare at the man who once took me from hell while I couldn't take him away from his.

Tires cruised loudly outside, and I stood over him. I placed my hand on his forehead, feeling the warmth returning, and slid my palm over the peach fuzz on his head back.

"I never feared you, but I feared for you."

I looked at him one last time and stood. Every step I took away from him felt wrong. However, I couldn't stay, his pride wouldn't allow anything more, and the Mafia in his blood wouldn't appreciate me if I stepped away from my duties.

It was our way of life.

Arlo and Mrs. Greco exited the car and rushed under the rain to meet me on the covered front porch. Her face was stricken in worry as her hands clenched together to her chest. Arlo held her elbow as she walked up the stairs.

"Marissa will be here shortly," Arlo said without emotion, and I tipped my chin with gratitude knowing the nurse would be staying with him along with Mrs. Greco.

"Is he alright?" Mrs. Greco rushed. "I stopped by early this morning, but he was still sleeping, and with tonight's dinner, and the wedding tomorrow, and all the preparations, and—"

"He's stubborn, Mrs. Greco," I cut off her panicked rambling. "Sal is now in bed. Please make sure he eats something."

"Of course." The dull blue hue of her eyes stewed over his well-being.

"One last thing," I added. "*You* changed his clothing, understood?"

"*Mio, Dio,*" she uttered before agreeing with a tilt. "Yes, sir."

Mrs. Greco quickly slipped inside, and I watched her back as she scurried deeper into the house.

"Is he *alright*?" Arlo said behind me.

"For now."

"Should we call the doctor?"

There was nothing they could do, no medicine to help, and no further treatments as cancer had eaten him away rapidly.

"No."

"Want to talk about it?"

I faced him.

"No."

I walked away into the heavy rain and got into my car while the daunting feeling of turmoil broke through in rage.

"Lucca?" Katia's sweet Italian accent called out for me.

I turned toward the opened walk-in closet door as I secured the last cufflink and met her vivid emeralds. She ranted about flower arrangements and the dinner menu as she walked closer. Her tongue rolled thick as it always did when she was flustered. Her hands waved all over, expressing the stress she wouldn't admit to as her family would be shortly arriving.

She hadn't changed as I had asked, and my eyes roamed over the silk champagne dress that slipped over her curves and the thin straps that held the fabric loosely, dipping low into the swells of her breasts. Her long bourbon hair teased her glowing skin as it lay in messy and taunting soft waves.

Katia was a wicked sight of spirit and sin, both a desire of mine.

My dick twitched, growing hard at the mere sight of her walking before me, the diamond on her slender finger, and the long black nails I wanted to feel puncture my back. And as I looked at her how lips, stained in red without the need for lipstick, I wanted to taste the cherry flavor they promised.

"Everyone is here on our side," she continued.

*Our* side.

My dick was now stiff and heavy inside my pressed pants.

"But Salvatore hasn't made it yet. Should I search for Mrs—"

When she stood in front of me, I grabbed her by the back of her neck. Her eyes widened, and her tits swelled against my chest.

"He's unwell and apologizes for not making it tonight."

Katia's mouth parted, and her hands flew to my arms, nails gripping, and blood rushing her cheeks.

I had her twice this morning, but it wasn't enough. I needed another taste, another touch to lose myself deep inside her while everything else felt unsteady.

*I wanted her.*

"Is everything al—"

I shut her mouth with mine, running my hands furiously over the dark curtains of her hair and brought her face, her body, her fucking soul closer.

Katia didn't hesitate. No, she, too, craved the high our bodies would reach and the unleashing of our troubles onto one another. Her fingers fumbled with the button of my pants as I ravaged her lips and neck with my mouth. I pulled her hair, stretching her neck as she freed and tugged my dick with her delicate fingers.

Our hands were wild, rough as they touched, and our kiss was carnal, hungry.

I couldn't hold on longer with her hand pumping and her sultry sounds of need. I flipped and bent her over onto the glass top of the island cabinet, pushing my weight against her back. She gasped loudly at the forceful shift of our bodies. I brushed her hair to the side of her face as I pressed her cheek against the cool glass. While I had her pinned beneath me, my free hand slipped her dress up and over her round ass.

Katia was bare, only a lace knife holster wrapped around her right thigh. My chest rumbled deep in appreciation for the depraved sight of the glistening blade and her naked flesh she had covered in just a thin silk dress. Katia spread her legs apart, and the motion caused her ass to wiggle and rub my dick, and I groaned.

"*Per favore,*" she begged in Italian.

I gripped my dick from its jerking need and placed it near her entrance.

*Thrust.*

I gave her what she wanted. I took what I wanted, and I beat my dick deep inside her over and over, losing all control inside her damning body.

"Lucca!"

Katia cried, and I closed my eyes, listening to the slaps of our flesh and the sounds she couldn't hold.

I clutched her side as I rammed inside her and lowered my mouth to her ear.

"That's right, *cara mia*, you will take it all."

I bit the sensitive spot behind her ear, and she whined.

"Ahh."

"Every sore step you take, you'll think of me," I whispered. "And every word your swollen lips utter when you speak to your brothers, you will remember who bruised them."

"Yes!"

"And while you sit in front of your father, my cum will run down your leg, and you will remember you are *mine.*"

"Sì!"

My hand reached her front, and I rubbed my palm into her sensitive bud, pressing and extracting out her screams that only took me deeper.

"Say it, *cara mia.*" My voice lowered with warning. "Say it out loud. Say who you belong to."

"You!" she cried. "*I belong to you.*"

My balls tightened as a shrill ran in my spine hearing her affirmation, and I emptied myself inside as I heard her scream in union to our deal.

I rode our release until my dick was pleased with her broken and satisfied moans of ecstasy. I slipped off her and cupped my hand over her pussy, catching our cum and smearing it against her folds.

Katia purred, and as I tried to defy gravity with my hand, I murmured into her hair.

"*Mine.*" I pushed off her body, watching her shaking legs and perched ass. "I'll meet you downstairs."

I wiped my hand over the discarded towel I had used and picked up my suit jacket from the hanger. I walked, slipping my jacket over my shoulder and tucking my shirt back into my pants with the memory of Katia's words.

Loud chatter echoed downstairs as I headed down to meet my brothers. My study door was left open, carrying out the sounds of a few laughs and foul words. I adjusted my tie one last time and walked inside into silence.

The first pair of eyes I caught were doe-like as they watched me carefully. I guess some things would never change, and Davina's fear would be one of them. I didn't blame her. At one point, I wanted her dead and far away from this family as she'd caused such a headache. Now, even if it had been the starting point that tipped the scales into war, it was the reason I had a wild, high-spirited, and lethal creature that I could fuck my control out on.

It was enough to not wish or find her as a cold and lifeless body.

"Davina," I greeted.

She was dressed in a long black dress that matched her mid-length raven hair and dark eyes, and while she now lived in Florida's sunshine state, her skin was fair and unscathed from the sun.

"Lucca," she replied politely with a faint smile, and her hand twitched to the arm she clutched on to.

I didn't return her smile, and instead, I nodded at Ilias and walked past them. I needed a drink because while Katia's scent lingered, my thoughts sank back into the crucial time that neared.

After I poured and drowned my first glass of brown, I refilled it and added three cubes of ice to sip through dinner and turned to the four bodies inside my study.

Arlo stood by his unclaimed corner and Viktor the chair he was accustomed to while Ilias and Davina stood near the entrance. They all wore suits, and they all looked at me, waiting.

My eyes landed on Davina.

"Leonardo and Lorenzo will both be here, as you are aware," I stated, and I could see her struggle to not show any emotion. Sadly, it was etched across her face. "And while it's not the first time you'd seen them," I paused as I watched Ilias's jaw clench and raised my brow to him before returning my attention to her, "it's a fact Leo will push and provoke *any* reaction from you. It's imperative you don't." Davina's brows curled, and her chest drew back. "You understand how it will make trigger fingers happy, so keep your guard up and continue doing what you do best. Which is keeping an eye out, learning shit you shouldn't."

Arlo chuckled at the end, and I cut my eyes out to him.

"Don't. Not now."

Arlo raised his palms with a cunning smile.

"And don't fucking add to the tension, do you understand?"

He smirked.

I glanced down at Viktor, whose stress was clear, and bounced my eyes around every gaze inside the room.

"It's the dinner before the wedding. It should be enough for you all to understand I do not want an issue to arouse or for Katia to worry, am I clear?"

I didn't wait for their reply. My tone alone threatened pain to whoever went against my orders. There was no one who detested the Vitelli name more than me. If I had to entertain my temper, so could they. I stepped out of the room to Katia's heels clicking above.

My fucking regal queen took each step down with power and grace. Her shoulders were back, and a fresh coat of lipstick adorned the lips I'd tasted just minutes ago.

No one could see the nerves through her strength. But I did because, somehow, between the dark looks, the hate I'd cultivated, the fights, and the quiet moments, I saw my enemy as a possibility.

She took her last step and placed her hand over my extended one. Her chest and cheeks still held the touch of fresh fucked pink, while her face glowed as bright as her eyes did.

Katia glanced behind me at the knocks that traveled from the front door. I caught the small tremble of her hand and trapped it between mine.

I failed to understand the power her family had over her. The captivity of dread shackled inside and the influence that trapped her mind into a sick play.

How far and deep did the damage go?

How cruel had the abuse gone?

By the small comments Katia expressed and the short tales Sal shared, I knew Katia's younger days weren't colorful. They were black and gray like mine. But, as I watched her breathing change and her muscles tighten with the inability to remove her sight away from what hid behind the door, I grasped the true beating she had taken for such vulnerability.

It was trauma.

Knocks bounced through the door again, but this time, I took her gaze away from them. I pinched her cheeks between my fingers and pulled her face until her eyes met mine. Long gone were the playful swirls of her irises, and I despised it.

Without a thought, I closed our distance and spread my fingers over her jaw. I slid my rough hand and thumb across her chin and onto her neck, pinning her head with my touch and bringing it to me. Our foreheads connected, and her lashes fanned while her eyes surrendered to my gaze, and I breathed in her alluring, sensual smell of cherries and sin.

"No one deserves such power," I uttered. "Don't let them have it."

Katia didn't say anything. She only stared at me, reining in any weaknesses and bathing her wicked spirit in will. Then the deviousness returned as her eyes ignited, soul burning. My cunning creature stood before me.

"Smile."

Her lips curled with an immoral smirk.

*That's right, baby, you don't cower.*

Ignoring the gazes behind me, I pulled away and touched the base of her back and gently pushed her forward for her to walk before me. Our feet matched each step toward the entry. When we faced the iron and wooden door, I took a breath and pulled it open.

All three Vitellis stood tall in black suits with three more men behind them.

My eyes landed on the first man in the diamond shape form they'd created.

Mario Vitelli.

The man I least wanted to see after finding out he'd worked against me during this time of war. The man who'd caused Katia harm continued to wound deeper.

My face was void of emotion, and when his teeth gleamed with a treacherous smile, he spoke.

"Moretti." He leered. "Or should I call you *son?*"

A cold stream of malice settled into my bones.

Son.

One word, but he delivered it with blunt guilt for the lives he'd taken.

This night would be nothing but a ruthless game, and I would kill him.

Just as he'd killed my father and mother.

A bullet to the chest, another to the heart, and the last to his head.

# XLII

## KATIA

LUCCA TURNED TO STONE AFTER MY FATHER CALLED HIM SON. IT COULDN'T be a coincidence. The feud between our families lasted for years, and I had no idea how deep my father's involvement ran. What could he possibly have done to earn Lucca's despise for the Vitelli name? To hold such hatred and hostility toward him?

The more I watched them both look at one another, I feared for the bad blood and venom they both shared.

This was bad, and Mario hadn't even stepped foot inside.

"You can call me by my last name," Lucca's dark voice advised, and I heard its danger.

My father's smile stretched wide, and his brown eyes were filled with bitter laughter. He looked as he had months ago, strong, and healthy to continue to torture for years to come.

"Father," I greeted to cut the tension. The moment he heard me speak, his eyes sliced me, and his features flashed with disgust.

I didn't drop my gaze. I wanted him to see the same spite my mother's eyes held for him. "You don't speak unless spoken to," he spat.

Somehow his blow never reached my heart. Somehow, I knew standing next to Lucca, in a city that wasn't my father's, and the expectation of his poison aiming to strike was the reason it never did. It slithered.

I smiled.

"This isn't New York, and you're on my front steps." Through Lucca's steel fingertips behind me, I kept my breathing steady. "I speak openly in my home, which you've been invited to, so I expect your respect while speaking to me."

In the corner of my eye, on my father's right, Enzo's lip twitched.

All too quickly, a charge swayed as Mario Vitelli's hand rose with a red stricken face. Out of habit, I waited with my face held high for his punishment.

But the punishment never came.

Lucca caught my father's swinging hand by his wrist and took a dominant step forward. The ire and power that radiated with threatening force towered over my father.

Enzo, too, had placed his gripping hand over father's forearm. The same hand that etched the letters NYS in black ink. He remained behind our father, but his defiance was clear even after he let go, but Lucca wouldn't move away. I watched Enzo, too dumbfounded to believe he'd stepped between father.

Lucca's jaw clenched tightly. He was losing to the wrath that drowned his body.

Arlo, Viktor, and Ilias stayed feet away behind Lucca while Davina was pushed farther from the commotion. And each brother stood ready for *any* order.

I brought my eyes back to Lucca and to my brothers, who waited alert while the men behind shifted dangerously on their toes.

"You lost any right to her from the moment she became *mine*." Low and dark, Lucca sneered. "I won't allow you or anyone to harm her in any way without consequences," he threatened. "Don't raise your hand at her again, Vitelli."

My father shook in anger, a vein popping across his forehead. When he tried to snatch his arm away, Lucca let go but he never cleared my father's path to me.

Leo stayed still, quietly with his head angled toward Enzo. He wasn't too concerned about the scene that played out in front of him. He didn't add anything. Not his usual smart comment, wicked smile of enjoyment, or even a gesture of regard.

It was unlike him.

It was frightening.

Nothing was right, and my skin shook with crawling shivers.

My father breathed heavily, and his gaze slid over to me. He rolled his shoulders back, and without a word, he turned. Enzo and Leo both stepped out of the way as he walked toward the SUV they'd traveled in. The three men who came with my family followed my father. He spoke a few words to them and entered the car.

That was it.

This reunion lasted *minutes*.

Two of the men joined my father inside the SUV while the other walked back to Enzo. Enzo gave him a quick nod, and the man I didn't recognize went to the back trunk. Two large duffel bags were dropped at the bottom of the stairs before he jumped inside the passenger side.

Red lights rolled across the paved entrance, and my father was gone as quickly as he'd arrived.

"My father never intended to stay overnight. My apologies for his… sudden departure." Enzo's careful tone expressed. "Meanwhile, we—" His hand waved from Leo then back to him. "Don't want to decline the offer out of respect for the agreement we made. That's if your home is still open."

*What was happening?*

My eyes shot to Lucca who watched Enzo too closely. He saw the same thing I did. There was a wedge between the Vitelli men. Broken ties and clashing views.

"Katia?" Lucca asked.

Lucca was asking *me* to decide. His face was blank, and I couldn't read his expression.

"Could I have a minute alone with them?"

His eyes hardened as his jaw twitched. He glanced at my brothers for a moment, then turned his attention behind them to his scattered men who walked through the premises.

Lucca didn't want to leave me alone with my brothers, but I wasn't afraid or worried about Enzo or Leo. They'd never caused me physical pain. Because in an odd way that I hardly comprehended, they cared for me in their own twisted way.

"Please," I added.

Lucca took a deep breath and tilted his head.

"I'll be in the dining room." His fingers woefully slipped away from me, and he cast a glance over at the men he was leaving me behind to. "Enzo, Leo."

They both nodded, and Lucca stepped away from me and into the home.

I closed the distance between my brothers and me, allowing the door to shut. A loud click echoed behind us, and I faced Leo first.

"What's the matter with you?" My mask was long gone as I regarded him without a filter.

"Good to see you too."

"Cut the bullshit," I sneered.

Leonardo took a deep breath and smirked.

*There he was.*

"Done. What exactly do you want to know?"

"Leo," Enzo warned.

"You didn't interfere, snap, or say anything to make matters worse. Why?"

"Did you want me to?" Leo skidded my question.

"Why?" I asked again.

Leo shrugged. "Tomorrow is a day to celebrate."

*My wedding?*

I laughed. Leo gave two shits for it, even though it was meant to bring peace between both families and resolve his fuck up. It was a bad joke, but his features didn't change. They were calm and casual.

"You are serious," I murmured.

His head rose, and under the pendant light, the long scar that traveled through his brow was clear for me to see.

"Like the dead."

And I believed him.

My head jerked to Enzo, who shared Leo's seriousness.

"Fine, all I ask is for you both to keep this dinner and your stay civil."

"That's the plan," Enzo chimed, but Leo's lips swayed to the corner.

"Leo?" I asked.

"*Mia sorella.*" *My sister.* "I wouldn't do anything to ruin tomorrow. Of *that* you can trust."

What I didn't trust was his smile.

## LUCCA

THE DOOR SHUT BEHIND ME AS MY MUSCLES TWITCHED IN RAGE. I SHOOK MY shoulders, finding my brothers near and itching for news, but all I could think of was the woman I'd left behind with the wolves.

"Is—" Arlo began, but I raised my hand to cut him off.

I picked up the glass I'd left by the entry table and pointed at Viktor, then to the corner of the door.

The silent order was given. *Stay behind and be alert for her.*

It had taken a lot to walk deeper into the home instead of staying where I'd placed Viktor. But Katia needed me to respect her wishes in front of them. I trusted her judgment and her need for time alone with the two men she shared blood with.

The smell of basil and freshly baked bread thickened the further I walked. With each footfall, I struggled to quiet the stress and anger Mario had built inside.

He showed up on my doorstep to lay out our differences. But they were never blurred, not for a minute.

The truth was, I would kill her father.

I knew this the day I turned sixteen after Salvatore spoke to me like a man. While I didn't blow out a candle, I'd promised to see it through.

Mario and my father started a war after a bad deal was made and promises were broken. A few years later, my father turned up missing, and so did my mother and me. But we weren't dead, no. We ran as my mother feared my fate would be the same as my father's.

She'd never explained to me who I was and why she'd always looked over her shoulder. She never explained why her suitcase hid a gun and spare bullets. Or why she needed to teach me how to shoot a gun and fight, when the other boys my age played outside ball or punched their fingers into rectangular video game systems.

I never questioned her. I listened and learned.

A Catholic doting son.

It was never proven who had killed my father. However, when my mother was found with the same wounds as he had, the *accidental* car wreck couldn't be overlooked, and the message was clear.

For years, I worked my way up in the syndicate with Sal by my side.

For years, I waited, planning and slowly working to become the head boss Miami needed.

Because when you were at the top, the one who made the orders, and the one who people feared, nothing was out of reach. Not even the head of another syndicate within the Mafia.

Any rule could be broken.

It only took patience and smart thinking to avoid leaving a trail.

Katia delayed my plans. It worked even better as this union could dismiss our bad blood to others and create an alliance for those left alive in that syndicate instead of searching for vengeance.

While at times, I had a consuming hatred for my own reeling mind, it kept me one step ahead and focused on my endgame.

Today was no different. That was after his suggestive admission of my father's death. Then when I'd seen his hand rise, ready to strike Katia, I lost all reasoning with the need to shoot him on the spot.

My God, I was so close.

So close to losing *everything*, and *she* had been the one who had created such a turbulent will in me.

It was Enzo's response to hold his father back, as well as Leo's quiet attitude, that brought me back.

Something wasn't right, and I knew I had to see tomorrow through.

As I sat at the head of the formal set table, I sipped and watched the brown liquor swirl inside the cup. I paid my brothers no attention and focused on the melting ice and the sweating drops that ran through the wedges of the clear-cut glass, trying to comprehend what had been happening in New York and had occurred outside of my doors. Hell, what continued to brew on the front stone steps.

"Do you think Mario will show up tomorrow?" Arlo asked.

I cleared my throat. "He can't afford not to."

Mario had to. He wouldn't disrespect me so boldly. He didn't possess the balls it would take to show his true colors to the Mafia.

"Any word on Sal?" I asked, needing assurance to relieve some of the dragging anxiety that clutched my chest.

"He's awake and eating."

*Good.*

Salvatore had to be there tomorrow. Not by duty, but for me.

"Should we be staying?"

I heard Davina's voice quiver and drew my eyes away from my glass and aimed them at her.

"Are you afraid?" My question was detached.

Davina sat between Arlo and Ilias on my right, and as she glanced at both sides, she shook her head.

"No," she replied, meeting my gaze.

"Would you like to leave?"

"I stay where Ilias stays." Her answer was expected.

"Ilias?" I asked next.

His icy blues didn't like where I was heading, but it was necessary. He wanted Davina, and while she'd grown and hardened since I first met the skittish girl, she was still too inexperienced to this life. She still struggled to hide her emotions and fears. She didn't understand our way of life, which was why we rarely married someone too...*normal*.

Davina was strong, but her own doubts enabled her to accept the underworld.

"Where else would I be?" indifferent, Ilias replied.

My eyes dropped to Davina.

"When you agreed to him, you agreed to this family. Don't question where you should be, *child*."

Her eyes narrowed at the word I'd called her the first night I met her. The night I threatened her with another target on her head.

My point wasn't to belittle her, it was to awaken her, and I had. Because now her brown eyes darkened to the point of becoming pure black.

Anger, memories.

That was what I sought to bring out of her. Now, Davina was ready to face Katia's family.

To face Leo, the man who'd drained her blood and left her to die on the snow.

The swinging sound of the heavy front door followed by an echoing shut alerted Katia's return. I drowned the contents of the fiery liquid of my cup and waited for her sage green eyes to emerge into the room.

I saw Viktor first. He stepped out of the way, and Katia entered the quiet room. She looked fucking gorgeous. Confidence was high on her shoulders and eyes that searched mine to show it. Strength, power, malice. They all revolved around her like storm clouds of might.

We weren't as different as she believed.

We weren't as different as I believed.

Both stained by death and childhood nightmares of punishment.

Both scared and welted into adults of pain.

Meanwhile, I tried to shield the screams and absurd cruelty of the underworld from her. It was the *one* moral thing I could do. It was the proper way to protect and keep at arm's length the woman I would spend my life with.

Through all this time, I was a fool.

A blind man.

Too stubborn to see, *she was just like me.*

A mold of clay that kept spinning on a potter's wheel while time carved the solitude, smoothing the scars and joining the damages until casting a fickle heart.

All created by the blood-drenched hands of those in our lives.

Too driven by tenacious cruelty.

Two descendants of Mafia royalty whose pasts kept colliding until our present caught up in rolling hatred of those who came before us but bleeding into each other.

I stood and stepped to the chair on my left and pulled out, open and offering where she belonged. Our gazes wouldn't break apart, and my mind whispered the words she'd once uttered into deaf ears.

*"I can't leave. I can't cry myself to sleep, and I can't care for what I see or hear."* Followed by, *"This is my world."*

This *was* her world.

And I was a stubborn man for ignoring it.

Questions popped inside her gleaming gems, but I was learning those answers, petrified of what they meant and where they led. Therefore, I had no reply in my eyes as our distance vanished by the clicking sound of her heels.

"Lucca." Her voice was laced with sweet poison, luring the one thing I'd established.

I had vowed respect and protection to the woman whose Vitelli blood coursed through her veins and branded her with a part of the killer who'd destroyed mine.

I had agreed to an arranged marriage without knowing we were both the outcome of one man.

Some said hate was the beginning stage of a rotting heart. How could they forget greed?

Greed for power.

Greed for money.

Greed for yourself.

Greed caused hatred, and greed was the ink of a rotting heart.

Mario Vitelli was splattered black by it, therefore decaying his own line. His legacy.

I would break that cycle, creating a legacy he would never be able to lay his eyes on.

I offered Katia a stir of a smile, knowing I would end it with us. The future Moretti line wouldn't suffer at the hands of such wasted air and space of earth. There would be a time when our children would only be descendants of Mafia royalty, and their only lessons would be the cruelty of our underworld and nothing more.

We would be alive to guide and teach the ways of our life.

Because this life of ours was nothing more than a game of chess.

Calculating. Ruthless.

Some pieces fell and some were taken out. But, in the end, it was all a corrupted game. A game where the king and the peasants were ruled by one queen.

DINNER STRETCHED INTO LONG AND UNCOMFORTABLE MINUTES, BURSTING TASTE buds that filled our mouths with rich foods, and surface conversations that no one carried further. Minutes passed by of Leo's gaze fixed on his one failure—Davina.

She hadn't cast one look. Not one care. I hid my smile, watching as the little raven-haired girl crumbled with time but remained aloof on the exterior.

But I could see it, and so could Ilias. His right hand hadn't appeared above the table at all. Surely, a heated weight he had placed on her thigh. While Davina wouldn't so much dare a gaze before her, Ilias had.

Leo and Ilias were playing a secret war, surprising not only me but Katia too as Leonardo sat peacefully in his chair.

Katia's attention bounced from one head to the other, calm and yet careful to the rising tension as we chewed through our loss of appetite and silence because if we continued to take small bites, the less we had to speak.

I had nothing to say, and instead of playing with my food anymore, I sipped the glass Talia had refilled. I swirled my tongue into the bitter flavor of my favorite aged bourbon.

The last course had been served, and all plates were smeared with uneaten cherry-chocolate cake. I cut my cake once with my spoon, but it never entered my mouth.

I had never been a fan of sweets.

*Until her.*

The lone cherry tempted my gaze, and I plucked it from the swirling syrup it lay on. I popped it into my mouth, and with the leftover liquor taste, a faint taste of Katia lingered in my mouth. But I was missing something.

Her skin.

Her mouth.

*Her lips.*

So it couldn't compare to the suffocating pleasure she brought along with that addictive taste.

Katia's eyes fled to mine after she found the cherry she wanted to steal from my plate missing. Her eyes narrowed to my mouth as I played with the seed with my tongue.

Her throat jumped with realization. Her lips curled on the corner, and her fingers danced closer to the hand that nurtured my bourbon.

I followed the dance of her fingertips around the rim. I watched them pick the glass from my grasp and her lips connected to the brim mine once were. Now both of our lips left an imprint on the glass as she brought the drink back to the table, in front of her and away from my reach.

*That little menace.*

Our tug of war was interrupted as Enzo broke the silence.

"Still planning the wedding outside?"

At that same moment, thunder crashed, shaking the house and clattering the windows and flower bases into a prance.

Katia turned to her brother, who sat on her left with a shrug.

"If the rain stops long enough for the ceremony."

"I'm sure you have a backup plan. I can't imagine you wing-ing such a special day."

Katia pushed her hair off her shoulders, quietly contemplating her next words.

If only he knew how little Katia had done for our union. How little she cared about the details. How much she tried to hide the looming day.

If it hadn't been for my questions, it would've all been a vision from Mrs. Greco and Talia.

Katia's fingertips twitched on her shoulder as her elbow rested on the table. She had no idea what to say or what the plan would be, and she grew insecure under the eyes that latched on to her.

Enzo's eyes sparked, and so did his brother's. A smile spread across both of their faces as they watched her tongue-tied.

"It's okay, Katia. It isn't a secret for them." I saved her from scrutiny. "If the sky doesn't clear, we will move to the church, then leave for the reception." And I added for her, "I met the priest after we spoke today, so it shouldn't be a problem. You don't have to stress over the rain."

Katia's hair swung with tinkling wide eyes. Her teeth trapped her bottom lip, but she couldn't hide her smile. *"Thank you,"* it said.

"An outside wedding in humid air and Miami's heat. Sounds like torture under a full suit," Leo said in the back.

"I couldn't help but assure you of your discomfort, *Fratello*. Really, all I thought of was you on my day." Sarcasm was thick on her tongue.

"Don't mind him." Enzo cut his brother a look that Arlo and I caught, and we shared a look of our own. "We are happy to help tomorrow with any preparations if needed."

"Thank you," Katia and I echoed together.

At some point, the animosity changed from bitter to a sharp tang of mutual agreement. The conversations passed on from the weather to even fucking cheese and wines that paired best with them. The dinner was a mockery of two families trying. Trying so desperately to behave and balance our inner monsters as we stooped down to twit discussions. All for the name of peace.

We would never like each other, of that we all agreed.

By the time we were all done with the ridicule of unsaid emotions and true thoughts, I craved nicotine.

Ilias and Davina were both eager to leave. As I stood to excuse myself outside, they slipped away from the boiling chaos. They said their goodbyes without too much fuss, and I walked outside the back door with Enzo on one side and Arlo trailing us close behind.

The rain poured and cascaded off the hanging shelter of the roof we stood under. The smell of wet grass mixed with muck and the thunder hid any words we uttered into the storm.

From where I stood, I could see the bulb that lit over the deep corner of my property. Sal's house was far and yet close to my reach. The lone light that hung next to the front porch reminded me that inside that house, life still flickered. And on the opposite side, I could see

Katia through the window talking to Leo while Viktor stood nearby. He would nod here and there to her as if she was asking for his point and needing his speech to mingle with hers.

"It seems I've misplaced my light," Enzo muttered with a hanging cigarette between his lips, tapping his hand over his pants pocket and reaching back to his suit coat.

I fished for my metal lighter and ran my thumb over the engraved Moretti crest before offering it to him.

The gears worked under his thumb, and fire bloomed. He handed it back, and I lit my own rolled tobacco, watching how the first long inhale ate away the tip. I closed my eyes briefly, and as I exhaled.

"Will your father cause trouble tomorrow?"

Dark eyes and a dark heart replied, "No."

"You sound too sure when it is not your own actions that I am questioning."

His index finger and thumb pinched the end of the bud, and he blew out to the side before turning to face me. As he replied, I noticed the small scar hidden beneath his short beard by the corner of his jaw.

"You are right. But I know he can't. That should count for something."

*Something.* I huffed.

"Now tell me, Lorenzo, I know where I stand with your father. Will that be the same with you as a boss?"

Arlo kept quiet behind me. His hips swayed at a snail's pace with crossed arms as he listened to every word and promise two families would share.

I hadn't taken another hit. The amber burned brightly while I waited for Enzo to speak. Because his next words would change the course and shift the future.

"Katia is allowed to feel the way she does about me. She can craft and believe me to be someone who didn't care for her and continues not to. The truth is, I never had much power to change her fate. Her duty."

He looked inside, watching her as he continued, "Don't get me wrong, you are no better man than Borelli or me. But I knew she at least had a chance of not suffering the old ways of a mafioso."

"What do you mean?"

"You were the greater evil in my eyes. Closer to her age than any boss. A cold-hearted bastard that would at least control his iron hand even if her mouth often sought one." He chuckled. "By me looking out for her future, I saw the possibility and power we could both have by this arrangement. What two syndicates could be if united. Funny, all I had to do was think about her."

"You mean, while you were cleaning up after your brother." I didn't let him off easily. To stand as if he didn't offer his sister to save both of their titles.

Enzo shrugged. "Yes, and no. I saw it a bit differently."

I waited for him to continue.

"New York would've come after your brother. *An eye for an eye.* Then kill what was meant to stay dead, his woman. *No loose ends.* And we would've gone to war, Moretti. While my sister faced Los Angeles, by duty." Enzo took a long drag. "And in the end, I would've gained nothing by losing her. Sure, cleaning after Leo gave me an alternative, but at least I chose it with more than myself in mind."

Enzo was more thoughtful than I'd perceived. And while his reasoning made sense, it didn't take away the immorality of his actions. But who was I to judge?

He could paint in different colors and distort it how he wished. Either way, I had Katia now. The how no longer mattered to me.

"What makes you think I control my iron hands?"

"Because while we are both cruel, Lucca, our dicks don't twitch at the sight of pain on a woman." He paused. "Well, at least not ours."

Arlo's sharp intake of air and soft chuckle blew near my ear, and Enzo snapped his eyes to mine.

"And by the looks of it, I was right."

While Enzo was right, I didn't agree. It was unnecessary.

"How long before your time comes?" My question was bold, disrespectful even. But Mario wasn't here, and something told me Enzo wouldn't share our conversation.

"Soon."


THAT NIGHT, KATIA WAS FLUSTERED ABOUT US SHARING A BED. THE TRADITION of bringing bad luck into our marriage by sleeping with me the night before weighed heavily on her.

Hadn't she seen *we* were the bad luck?

That our way of life had deemed us doomed from birth?

It was comical to see her so riled over such nonsense while we lived day by day with death's laughter on our front step.

I told her to shut her mouth and lay down. It'd earned me her slicing eyes and wild cursing lips. Eventually, she ran out of threats and temper. She crawled into bed, fire forest eyes still burning through the coils and ashes of her thoughts. Nevertheless, I fucked them into bliss.

I took her rage and stinging nails for my own pleasure and devoured her fighting tongue until satisfaction.

It wasn't until she lay over me that I asked her about her childhood.

It wasn't until our bodies cooled and our breathing settled that I asked her about Italy.

It wasn't until she closed her eyes that she asked me for another day of peace.

It wasn't until her breathing evened in sleep, that I replied.

"One more day."

# XLIII

## KATIA

CHURCH BELLS RANG IN LOUD HARMONY. EACH CHIME COLLIDED WITH the uneven beat of my heart. A numbing sensation scattered between my fingertips and swept over my nerves, casting chills beneath my skin. The thundering bolts of merciless clouds above had settled into a lullaby of soft sprinkles. A dull mist carried along with the shadowed sky that passed through the church as a glimmer of sunshine infiltrated the horizon.

I kept my eyes high above the second-story window of the church, watching as a few seagulls flew quickly while they had the time to escape the threatening return of rain. Their beaks opened in the air as they let out a *ha-ha-ha*, and *huoh-huoh*. It was a natural call they made, but I smiled as I imagined their laughter for defying nature.

They disappeared into the open air, and I lowered my eyes to the countless bodies that walked with closed umbrellas into the church. Oblivious of my gaze on them, or the short time we had to perform the outside wedding I wanted.

After all, you could only defy nature and fate for so long.

Nature, the rain.

Fate, marriage.

My thoughts quickly shifted to the man I would meet shortly next to a priest. In front of witnesses and under God's eyes.

Today, I would marry Lucca.

Today, I would bear his name.

Today, and so forth, I would be called Katia Moretti.

*Mrs. Moretti.*

I played with my smile with a cherry pinched between my fingers, thinking, and...*hopeful?*

I had given up hope, and yet, here it was, knocking the air out of my lungs and punching my chest with worry for heartache. I shook my head.

I had asked for one more day of peace. I wouldn't waste it in fear. Not today. Instead, I pulled the memories I'd spent underneath his body this morning, dragged the unsaid words, and bathed in the lips that stole my breath. I listened to the echo of his promise as he left me in the room I now stood in alone.

*"You will meet me shortly, and even God will know you are mine."*

A shiver scurried in sweet possession. The idea to belong to one man and him to me.

The idea of our spirits uniting and our souls meeting.

Even if he only felt the hold and the idea of me being his.

It was more than I had anticipated. More than most arranged marriages had.

So I would agree to his seizure of my being. I would agree to the terms of who I was to him and who he was to me.

It was more than I had imagined.

More than what a cruel mafioso should be capable of, and yet, given to me.

It was not settling, It was twisting and mending.

One inch, one wall, meant more could be broken.

And today, time wasn't my foe but my friend.

Soft knocks bounced against the old wooden door. My eyes snapped as it opened slowly, and a glimpse of blonde hair fell to the side before deep ocean eyes peaked in.

"Can I come in?" Viktor asked as he walked in, and I chuckled.

"Why ask?"

"So you can't say I didn't." Playful white teeth shined with a smirk.

Viktor and all of the brothers dressed identically. Black tuxedos, black bow ties, black buttons on a white shirt tucked beneath a black vest. A white rose with touches of cream, gold, and champagne encircled the tiny flowers and was pinned over the right side of his jacket with a needle. On the opposite side, the color of steamed milk pressed and popped in the fabric sticking out of its pocket.

Watching Viktor, I imagined Lucca matching him, but his bowtie wouldn't be black. It would match my gentle white dress.

My gaze was drawn to his hands. They were wrapped in a small black box.

"What are you doing here?" I asked, raising my eyes.

"Well." He looked around the empty room, proving a point. "Keep you company. What else?"

I chuckled.

"What do you have?"

"Oh, this?" Viktor waved the box as if it was meaningless. "Oh, just…you know? Lucca's little and inexpensive wedding gift."

A gift?

I'd said I didn't need or would ever ask him for anything. Yet, my lips parted. Smiling. *He wanted to.*

"I can take it back or throw it away if you want. You know, no fuss."

I felt my brows raise as he took a step backward, keeping a close eye on me.

"Take another step, and you'll learn how I can reach my knife even through a weighted dress."

Viktor burst out laughing, and the gleam of pure ease and cheer that erupted from his chest was contagious. The smile that agreed, and the eyes that shone.

Viktor seemed light and happy. Hopefully we could spread that feeling out to the growing crowd outside. But who was I kidding? It was filled by made-man.

"Since you've asked so nicely, I'll leave it with you."

I reached out until I cupped the leather box and looked up.

"It also comes with this." His hand disappeared inside his tuxedo and revealed a small envelope.

I snatched it out of his fingers before he could keep it out of my reach and turned to the table. I placed the letter and box on the marble top and pulled out a diamond flap envelope.

"Will you give this to him?" I placed the envelope in his palm.

Viktor flicked his wrist, eyes catching the hands of his watch.

"Fine, I'll be quick. We don't have much time before the sky pours over us."

His body twirled, and I faced his back.

"Wait." I hurried.

Viktor's eyes rushed.

"His ring." I took the loose ring off my thumb and stretched it out between us.

His face warmed, and he took the ring.

"You look beautiful, by the way," Viktor said, leaving me behind with the gift Lucca sent and the words trapped inside a closed envelope.

I turned, picked it up, and tore it open.

In neat writing and messy ink, his words marked the paper and stamped my heart.

*Something blue.*

*Something new.*

*Forget something old.*

*Forget the war around us.*

*We are past the rules and the war of us. Now, tell me. How does infinite peace sound?*

*With me.*

*L*

My heart soared. It yelled as my heart opened and clung to his written words. The promise, the question.

Tears pricked my eyes. Threatening to ruin the makeup that took the artist an hour to create, threatening my soul to pour with the feeling of belonging. Of finding a brutish bastard who cared for *me*. Who wanted me by his side without saying the words out loud for the wind to carry them away. But instead, engraved them in ink to be re-read. To be touched.

Lucca might believe he was incapable of love, but this, this was the beginning. And I'd never been more eager for my future. Giddy and optimistic.

I clutched my chest between my hands as a smile broke. As time slowed. As the weight freed by emotion and fervor.

In just a few short minutes, I would say I do. But now, it would be true, real. Bonding.

I carefully dropped his letter into my tote bag, afraid of losing such a gift if placed anywhere else but in my belongings. The black leather square box stared at me, and I couldn't wait anymore. I cracked the lid open.

A tear fell on the beautiful and rare light blue diamonds that adorned a comb hair piece. But it wasn't a normal comb. They were thin and dangerous needles. They would easily penetrate skin and slice while deep in flesh, only to continue its torture when ripped out. And as tears fell, I laughed, smiled, and wiped my nose.

It was gorgeous.

It was me.

It was mine. *From him*, and it made it that much more meaningful.

Without hesitation, I turned to the full mirror on my left and placed the intricate silver hair piece. I dabbed my eyes from any remaining tears and pushed back. Staring at the woman who looked back in a wedding dress fit for a queen, his queen. A woman who stared into my eyes with a hairpiece that took the place of a crown, and as she mimicked my curling lips, I felt complete.

Ready.

I was walking out of this room as Vitelli and walking out of the church as Moretti.

May the living be ready for another Moretti.

# XLIV

## LUCCA

KATIA WANTED A BLACK AND WHITE WEDDING.

Not a touch of color.

There was nothing colorful but the deep dark colored dresses of women scattered across the large lawn. Some guests were seated on the adorned chairs while the wedding planner and staff worked diligently to dry and cover the remaining seats. Time was of essence as clouds rolled, mocking the shimmering sun and hiding it over again with heavy pools of smoky pearls high in the sky.

The chatter thickened in the large crowd, and familiar faces stopped to congratulate me. I heard endless wishes for our union and saw flashing smiles for days.

Some seemed sincere, others felt forced, and a few were out of respect.

Blurs of wedding workers passed through my vision. Scurrying with flowers at high speed.

*So many flowers.*

She'd said *enough flowers to drown the smell of corruption.*

*Say no more, Katia.*

Quickly and in record time the lawn transformed into a bed of flowers. They bled from above and swept through every inch, dripping with fantasy and poise.

Their perfume lingered in a condensed dome around the premises. The smell of corruption was extinguished by nature, the leftover odor of petrichor, and white blooms.

I thanked the couple in front of me, and politely stepped toward the wheelchair pushed by Mrs. Greco.

"Is everything running smoothly? Would you like me to check—"

Sliding my gaze up, I shook my head, cutting her stressed tone.

"Everything is perfect. Thank you for all your work."

Her timid smile formed wrinkles around the corner of her warm eyes.

"A wheelchair, Sal?" I jabbed and concealed my smile.

"She won't let me walk!" he spluttered in Italian.

"Oh please, you won't make it through a Catholic wedding on two feet." Mrs. Greco snapped back into an old Italian accent.

Her eyes widened, catching my glance.

"My apologies," she mumbled quickly.

My chest bounced in a scoff.

"Please don't. Feel free to knock his ego anytime."

Sal's features contoured into displeasure, and his lips shook into angry incoherent mumbles.

"I'll give you both some privacy," she added and dashed a few steps behind to meet Talia and Carlo.

"Can't believe a boss invited the *help* to his wedding."

It held no conviction. I almost cracked a smile at his bad-tempered snap.

"Says the man who enjoys the company of some of the *help*."

He coughed loudly and reached behind him to grab his air tube before mumbling. "If this cancer doesn't kill me, fucking allergies will." Sal pulled his fedora lower and breathed in clean oxygen, and continued tickling his throat, ignoring every word I had spoken.

"Come on, old man, I have a spot for you."

I moved behind him, catching the tank attached to the back of the chair, and pushed us to the side.

"Yeah, wheel my ass up close. I don't want to squint too."

"Could you lighten up?"

"Says the man who hasn't smiled," he mocked.

Sal's body relaxed back into the black leather, and he swung his head high and around our path.

"I never imagined so many flowers and white at your wedding."

"There's black too."

"I expected that."

"What did you envision?"

I asked and made contact with three pairs of eyes.

My brothers stood at alert by the altar canopy facing the crowd and watched as I rolled Sal closer to the front row.

"I don't know. Not this. It's beautiful, almost dreamlike."

"Well, you aren't sleeping, and this isn't a dream. It's just what Katia wanted." I scratched my throat and pushed him forward to the front row. The spot closest to me.

"Lucca." Sal wheezed, and his fingers waved for me to get closer.

I stepped up before him and lowered.

Shock flooded my senses as his warm and wrinkled hand pressed against the same cheek my mother had once held. But as I stared at his brown eyes, I found my mother staring back at me.

The touch didn't last but mere seconds, but it was long enough to knock me into a daze.

"I'm proud of you, *figlio*. She would've been too."

"Don't go soft on me now," I croaked through my tightening throat.

"Never." Sal smirked.

I cleared my throat and straightened. It was just another wedding. I had attended many, and somehow this one felt different. Vulnerable.

"Lucca." My attention was drawn to the sound of Viktor calling out my name.

We met in the middle, and he pulled out an envelope. There was no need for explanation. With a quick nod, I took the envelope and placed it inside my suit jacket.

It was hers.

"I must return to Katia and bring her down to her father. The ceremony is starting in minutes."

"Go," I ordered with a dip of my chin.

Viktor's blond hair disappeared among the crowd, and I took a deep breath, scanning over all faces and corners. Slowly my steps carried me between two bodies.

"Everything is secure," Ilias whispered with a brisk glance.

Good.

"I don't think I can place my back behind so many people," Arlo muttered, tugging at his cuffs. His discomfort was apparent, and while I too felt vulnerable with so many people out in the open, evil roamed, outweighing the pure.

"If you don't wish to sit in the front row, don't *fratello*. A seating arrangement doesn't reflect your importance in our world or mine."

Arlo's chest slightly caved, accepting his disturbed feeling and the weight I'd lifted. Then as if he hadn't fidgeted with irritation or spoken with doubt, his wicked smile flashed.

"Break a leg." His mayhem eyes twirled until they moved away from mine to survey every inch before he headed to the edge, turning and walking farther to the back.

People began taking their seats, dimming the chit-chat into quiet whispers. Katia's reserved front row for her family remained empty, while mine slowly filled, starting with Sal. Two empty seats were unfilled next to him, Viktor's and Ilias, as Davina's brown eyes rested solely on the man by my side. On her right, Mrs. Greco sat next to Talia and Carlo. Her daughter, Anna, hadn't been invited.

My eyes flew to the threats that loomed above. The long Catholic wedding would have to be kept shorter than custom as the rain would soon catch up.

"I'll stay until Viktor returns and everyone is seated," Ilias uttered, eyes peeled in the direction Viktor had been last seen.

The envelope inside my chest pocket burned, and my fingers itched for the thin paper inside. But just as the envelope burned, the eyes of many flickered over my skin, watching my every move. Watching for a weak moment, they could replay among others.

It was the wedding of the year. A known union all wanted to witness. A play of a tale for the future of Miami.

It was finally here.

Two tall bodies emerged from the left corner. Both walked with purpose with their heads bowed to one another while words were exchanged. Arlo followed their backs with his gaze while mine trailed Enzo's and Leo's steps closer. Once they were out in the open and walking up the aisle, I removed my eyes from them and waited for Viktor.

I didn't wait for long before he appeared.

Both he and Ilias took their seats, and I took my place inside the outdoor altar.

"Lucca," the priest said as he walked closer to me before hiding under the hanging flower canopy.

"Father," I greeted, the same moment I heard the classical violinist strike a loud note. Everyone stood. Everyone turned in one direction.

My head snapped to where Katia should appear, and with each second that music played with time, the tighter my chest grew.

I had never been a man of emotion. A man of nerves.

Yet, it took all of me to keep my own legs from failing. For my knees not to give and for my breathing to steady.

*It took all of me to hide behind the mask of the heartless.*

Then I saw her, and I ran numb.

Only my heartbeat drummed and pumped inside, hammering in powerful wallops that shook me.

She was beautiful in all white.

A dress that shimmered with lace and touched her skin and body with a gentle caress.

A veil over her face that couldn't keep our eyes apart.

A sight of golden skin, green eyes, and white.

A vision I never wanted to forget.

And her smile.

Her smile brightened the depths of my heart. The pitch-black void that hadn't been touched. I hardly blinked, and when I did, it was quick, too afraid to miss a single step. Too afraid to miss a second.

Katia glimpsed around. Wonder and joy shined past the veil, touching every flower with her gaze. The second it returned to me, they glimmered in awe.

Happy, eager.

*Or was it love?*

I was so captivated by her, I didn't care for the man who walked alongside her.

I was too mesmerized by her gripping regal beauty to stain such vision with thoughts I didn't welcome at the moment.

At that moment, I only had eyes for *her*.

My little creature of wickedness.

But I blinked, and death danced with disaster.

# XLV

## LUCCA

**M**Y MOTHER WARNED ME ABOUT HESITATION. HOW IT HAD THE POWER to root your feet. The power to paralyze a being. Or would the fear of losing someone triumph over such a power? Or would it leave you too fear-struck to move?

Could they shake hands and form an alliance into despair? The feeling of all hopelessness.

While she'd spoken in hushed whispers next to me in my bed, her tales were always lessons told into the ears of a five-year-old. Nighttime stories of confusion and uncertainty. Words to understand and feelings to conquer.

But there was one word she'd never covered.

Desperation.

*And desperation can overtake you with madness.*

I blinked, and I saw it too late.

The glimmer of a scope.

The shine reflected into the corner of my eye.

Time flew by with the wind in swirling gusts. Fast, furious, and yet too slow.

Too slow for the speed of a bullet.

Too fast for erupting chaos.

First, the lone loud *pop*.

Second, the exploding flesh.

Then, the havoc.

I didn't hesitate, and while fear clawed, ripping my chest by her parting mouth and wide eyes, desperation took control when I saw her back, turning to face her father as another *pop* ricocheted into my eardrum.

Echoing in a deafening death.

Blood splattered all around her, and she fell to the ground by her father's weight.

Screams pierced all around, bodies ran in all directions.

I rushed to her.

I rushed to retrieve my gun out in the open, eyes wild and looking in all directions for threats as I *ran to her.*

Adrenaline pumped, and bullets fell all around.

Katia struggled on the floor, her hands pushing the weight of the dead. But her howling cries and shaking body weakened her as his head pressed against her chest.

"I'm here, baby," I yelled past her cries, but she wouldn't open her eyes.

She cried with fists punching and pushing against Mario.

I slid onto the floor, wrapped my hands beneath her arms, and pulled her toward me. I shoved my foot down the body with my soles. Katia tried to fight me, trying to break free from my grasp, but we had no time.

I kicked us backward on the wet floor.

She kicked the body off.

Shaking red fingers gripped on white, her hands tugged on the heavy skirt, bunching the long trail away, and I turned our bodies to face the ground.

I kept pulling, dragging, and towing her beneath me. Shielding her quivering body.

Between the deserted rows of empty chairs, I placed her on the floor and flipped her over.

With a gun in one hand, I cupped her cheek fiercely with the other.

Crimson splashed her face in heavy specks, and gore sprinkled with remains that were once a part of her father. They created all sizes of freckles on her skin, dusting her features, neck, and chest. Dark red particles of torn flesh.

Her veil had disappeared. The lace over her arms was shredded, and her dress was ruined in deep red.

Dark hair stuck together in livid curtains of red wine.

Katia was showered in blood by the second bullet that struck the back of Mario's head. And if she was a few inches taller, that high-caliber bullet would've struck her too.

My gaze raced over her body, trying to find out if the first bullet had touched her. But I found no open holes.

I pulled her convulsing body to me and concealed her face between the crook of my neck. Holding her and pushing my hand on the back of her head as I took in her quivers. I lifted my head to the chaos surrounding us.

Men poured from all directions while others scurried inside the church for shelter.

Death spotted the floor with men.

Some enemies.

Some mine.

And gunfire dipped the white pure flowers in blood, corruption, and evil.

I found Arlo, Rio, Sergio, and many more walking upward toward the danger in a formation. Guns bouncing with each shot, eyes devoid of feeling. Arlo's gaze met mine, and I saw their diabolical need for torture. His left hand stretched, and he lifted his thumb, index, and middle finger out to me.

*Hold.* It warned.

Hold.

I crushed Katia to me and turned in the direction he aimed.

In the corner by a small brick column, Ilias fired with no protection as he placed Davina behind his back. He also had a heaving Sal who stood on weak legs, Mrs. Greco, and the priest. All between the stone wall shelter and him.

*Where is Viktor?*

I couldn't see his blond hair or his deep blue bottomless eyes searching for me. His presence was nowhere near his little brother.

Shots flew near Ilias.

Davina screamed with her hands covering her ears, eyes shut, and far from reality. She was taken by trauma and memories, lost in the bullets as the brick crumbled to dust as it fell.

Ilias turned, head low, back out into the open like a shield.

He was trapped.

I pulled my second gun from my shoulder holster and waited for him.

"*Novak!*" I roared, pulling him from the slight cover as his head swiveled back to my voice.

An ice storm rippled in his chilling eyes, and I stretched out my hand to him.

Realization dawned, and Ilias's lips fluttered rapidly with violent orders. His eyes, while desperate, centered on my fist that signaled him to hold. His hands moved fluidly as he reloaded another magazine into his empty gun.

I looked out to bastards that had cornered my family into execution.

Gun cocked, left hand itching, and index finger burning, I flicked my fist down.

Once.

Twice.

I stretched my palm out and began raining hell. Katia clutched on to me, and I brought my hand back to her hair as the ear-splitting hammer of my gun released the massacre.

Ilias pushed bodies into the church, shielding them until his back retreated inside.

In the midst of assuring their safety, I had placed us both in grave danger.

I squeezed Katia closer to me, making us smaller to the whistles that soared past us. I acted out of pure instinct and rage.

*Protect, protect, protect.*

I pulled my gaze away from the curled body of white and red in search of Arlo.

*Hold!* His hand implored with tension and snapping veins.

Hold?

We were sitting prey!

*Cazzo!*

I'd lost control. I'd been bested in my own city. My own wedding. At the doors of the church!

I'd been handed on a platter with an apple in my mouth.

I had been outplayed.

Katia was consumed in shock, deep in its grip.

Thunder tore through the darkening skies. Soil vibrated beneath us, rumbling our bones with bitter chills. My head reared back, and I felt the first drop.

The cry from above.

The icy bite of my sins.

The demon I would set free.

I dropped my head and cupped her face as rain fell over us.

My thumb ran over her cupid bow lips. My hands smeared the raindrops away as it streaked her bloody face. Her lashes trapped the water in flutters, and her eyes drowned in mine. They *screamed* for help.

Her eyes gasped for air, suffocating me in her own dread.

Fear stricken.

Paralyzing despair.

"Not now, Katia. *I need you.*" My lips raced against hers. "I need you back, baby. I need the strong woman. The cunning. The outsmarting. The spirit. Come back to me. Come on." I shook her. *"Damn it, Katia.*

*I need you!"*

Katia's eyes slammed shut, and she wept. Sorrow sobs shattered, her chest heaving. Despite the wrecking pain, she furiously nodded.

"That's right, Katia. Come back to me," filtered through my teeth. "Bring the raging wildfire in your eyes. Let me see the deep-green-forest blaze."

Her chest expanded and fell. Deep breaths filled her with strength, and her exhales pushed out the weak.

Eyes shot open in jaded fury.

I kissed her.

Urgent, wild, passionate.

"Take this, shoot on your way, and stay close," I rushed.

Katia nodded, clutching the gun with her delicate fingers, and then snapping into action. Her hands were filled with lace, silk, and tulle. She bunched the dress into a bundle, revealing her long legs. Her fingers slipped to her thigh, and she pulled out her blade, twisted it, she held it in a reverse grip. With one hand heavy with lead and another with sharp promise, both hands were filled with danger.

Katia tried to turn in preparation for our escape, but her legs caught the long train of her dress. Her body tossed, and she fell to the muck with a groan.

"*Puttana!*" The harsh curse fueled her ire, and she slipped her knife to the end of her feet. It sliced the fabric, and she tugged and tugged with no give of its strong train.

My eyes flew back to Arlo, pushing her hands away. The loud rip muffled between the firing bullets, the howling thunder, and the heavy raindrops.

The dress was still long but wouldn't drag her behind. I wanted to cut it off and leave it by the forming puddles. But we had no time. We needed to move.

I needed to take her to safety and kill all those who had threatened her. Butcher and carve them with lead.

"No fear, Katia."

"None."

Arlo signaled us to get ready.

We moved closer to the end.

"To the stone pillar," I instructed.

She nodded.

Arlo opened his mouth to shout, "Now!"

"*Go, go, go!*" I yelled, and bullets sputtered in unison.

I shot.

Katia shot.

Hisses flew by my ear, whooshes disrupting near.

All aimed in our direction.

Rapid fire of automatic rifles against handguns.

Fire spread through my side, branding my flesh with burning metal and stunning speed. My body reared from the blow.

With my teeth gritting, I growled in pain and rage as I pulled the trigger. I hit my target right below his left eye. His body slumped to the ground, and I pulled the trigger again to shoot the man beside him, but only the clicking sound of the slide locking was in my ears.

I was out.

Empty.

I tackled Katia's body, taking her with me as I ran the last few steps toward cover.

I pushed her against the wall and searched every inch of her body.

She was unharmed.

"*Dio.*" Her hands waved. They rolled over the tear in my suit jacket without touching it.

There was no time to fret. I discarded my jacket and vest. Red swept spreading over the white shirt, and I ignored the pain to reload my gun.

I looked back at her, but her eyes were trained behind me.

Fuck.

I followed her gaze while raising my gun.

He stepped out of the shadows.

Leo's long, scared face stepped forward, hands up.

"It's just me." Sweat, blood, and in labored breathing, he stood.

He tossed the automatic rifle to me, and I caught it with my free hand. Then he reached behind, bringing another from his back and tossing it again to me. I placed my handgun on my waistline and strapped one of the rifles onto my back, ready.

He had three more latched on to his back, and he picked one up for himself, then retrieved a knife. He twirled it into his palm, holding it tightly in the same position Katia held hers.

Enzo and Leo hadn't carried heavy gunfire. They came with handguns just like us.

It seemed Leo had collected prizes during his killing spree, and showered me with his medals. I couldn't turn them down. I needed ammo and gun power.

"Where's Enzo?"

He stepped back into the shadows. "Looking for Borelli."

His weasel name alone caused my vision to blur deep in brutality.

"Father is dead," Katia whispered to him.

Leo had no sympathy for his father's death. But his eyes scanned her body, and his brows deepened after seeing the carnage and disarray of his sister's appearance.

"I know." His hand stretched out. "Come, I'll take you to safety."

I kept her from moving.

Leo's eyes narrowed in surprise. His mouth parted to speak, but it quickly shut.

"*She's my sister.*" He sneered. Enraged by my distrust of her safety.

Had he looked around? It was hell on earth in pure daylight, out and in the open for everyone around to hear, and *we were* in the middle of it all.

And he thought I trusted him blindly for her safety?

"I kill in the shadows," he said calmly. "I move through the darkness and shield behind their clouds. I can get her to safety faster than you can. Don't confuse my cruelty for those I don't care for the *two* that I do."

Gunfire continued, and his eyes shifted to the open space for any upcoming threats.

"I could have killed you, Moretti. Your back faced me, and you

failed to see *me*. But that would only harm her, and I wouldn't hurt her."
He stretched his hand. "We are on the same team, *hers*. Let her go, so I
can make sure my sister lives."

Fuck.

How could I hand her to *him?*

Place such trust on whom months ago threatened my brother.

"The shadows are only big enough for one body," I explained.

Our attention shifted to my left. Arlo was losing ground.

"Then I'll make sure it's hers."

I nodded.

"We don't have much time to slip away, Moretti," Leo said,
distracted by the large open courtyard.

I turned to Katia, her eyes already dreading my next words.

"*No.*"

"I'll meet you shortly, alright?"

Her head swayed from side to side.

I stole a rushed kiss, unable to let her go without one last taste.

"No fear, Katia."

"I fear not for myself. I fear something happening to you. You are
already bleeding, Lucca!"

"*Moretti,*" Leo warned.

"That's foolish. It's just another day. Now go." I pulled her head to
my chest and placed her in Leo's hand.

"There's a secret passage that will lead you to a bunker. It's inside
the priest's chamber. Katia knows the way. Look for the small door
behind a large mirror. I'll find you both after."

"Who all knows?" he questioned its safety.

"Just us and my brothers," then I added. "Ilias could've taken a few
already. He'll open the door for her."

"Got it."

"Go!" I ushered Leo.

His eyes thanked me as he tucked Katia into his side, and he
disappeared along with her emeralds and white stained dress.

A part of me knew I should've never let her go.

Another knew we had no chance of coming out alive if we stayed together.

*Then, why did I feel as if my demon wept?*

# XLVI

## LUCCA

I CROUCHED LOW ON THE FLOOR AND TOOK COVER.

One by one, I extinguished life.

One by one, they dropped to the ground.

My knees scraped against the grain floor while I moved from one corner to the other. Kneeling, then squatting.

Each time I shot two rounds into bodies.

Each time, we gained ground and pushed forward.

There were so many.

They. Just. Kept. Coming.

I had the manpower to take down syndicates. Miami, New York, and Chicago were the biggest in numbers. But my men were scattered and placed on the path we would have taken after the ceremony. Streets were crowded with soldiers as civilians walked aimlessly with hidden guns. Cars parked, waiting, and rows of soldiers waited minutes away from where the reception would have been.

The reception would've been flooded with made-men.

*I had scattered my men!*

I had it all planned.

I had it all laid out.

Yet, I stood feet away from the house of God. Committing sin on sacred ground, decorating the manicured lawn and its statues in red and sinful rain.

I had it sealed, perfected, or so I had thought.

Now we were outnumbered, and our men who traveled were most likely stuck in a fabricated disturbance, delaying their arrival and machinery.

Arlo made it next to me. Sergio followed him as he helped Rana walk into the shelter. Rana dropped to the floor, eyes shut in agony as his thigh bled in rapid gushes. A puddle quickly grew, and his sweaty face was tinted in ash.

"Get your belt!" I ordered.

Sergio quickly removed his belt. I fastened it high on Rana's thigh in hopes of reducing his bleeding.

"It's no use," he muttered.

"Shut up," I spat.

"We are on our own, Lucca," Arlo mumbled, locking his phone back and tucking it in his pocket.

"Where's Viktor?" I asked for the brother I still hadn't seen.

I met his clashing irises, hooded. Adam's apple bobbed as his head shook. "I don't know."

My attention was drawn by a gripping fist. It was weak, and yet, my eyes fell on the man who desperately needed me. If it hadn't been for the color draining out of his face and the trembles that shook against my chest as he hung onto my shirt, I would've killed him on the spot.

I was too consumed by red to see past reasoning, too lost in ire and bloodthirst.

Too out of control.

"Boss." His breath quivered. "Please, Milly. I was all she had left."

*Was.*

"Don't let her get sent to a home." His eyelids grew heavy. "Please," he begged.

*Milly.*

The bright, talkative child whose mother died at birth. The five-year-old that ran through the church pews as if God's house was her own jungle gym. The little girl who spent most of her time in the bakery, covered in flour and stained in chocolate. This was when Rana roamed the streets doing his capo's, Sergio's, bidding. But it was *my bidding*. My orders.

No mother. No grandparents. No aunts or uncles.

Milly only had Rana.

"Please." His hand fell, his will faded, but his eyes waited, holding for one more second.

Holding on for peace.

Hoping while his spirit bled away with the red.

I held on to his eyes as they dimmed. Dark maroon watered down as if ice melted them from the inside, taking their color, their life, the pain.

"I won't," I promised, and he let go.

*No father.*

An orphan.

A girl alone in a ruthless world.

My heart plummeted. I had taken the only life that mattered to a child, and while I'd taken many, it hadn't been Milly's.

What a cruel, unfair world.

"We need to move."

The need to lay my eyes on Katia was a current I couldn't fight against. A tiring battle in vain, doomed with every stroke. Seeing Rana's vacant eyes and his daughter's name slipping past his lips as his last words was enough to succumb to the current.

"You're hurt," Arlo voiced.

"And Rana is dead. Viktor is gone, *and my fucking woman is not by my side!*" I roared. "We need to get moving, Arlo, or we will face the same fate as Rana!"

I turned to Sergio. "Where are the others?"

He whistled.

Rio, Casper, and Fer rushed through the fire and three more followed.

"The others were spread around the outside of the church, posted in corners," Sergio added when I waited for more to appear.

"How low are you?"

Ammo.

"We are on the last clip, boss." Casper's bald head shone with glistening raindrops.

"Okay." I thought about our numbers. "We will go on three. Arlo, Sergio, and I will be the last. Pick up any loaded guns you find. Ready?"

"*Yes, boss,*" echoed, and lawless gazes turned toward the door.

"Be quiet. We don't know what's waiting inside," Arlo cautioned.

I discarded the empty gun to the side, picked up the heavy weapon on my back, and pulled the lever back.

"Ready," Arlo uttered.

Here we go.

I closed my eyes and breathed in deeply.

"One," he whispered.

Controlling my breathing, I aimed.

"Two."

Zeroed in, sight clear.

"Three." His shot wasn't clear.

My target's head was easy to keep secure. A mop of long wavy hair drifted with the storm in black drapes of filth, late twenties with an addiction. From the twitch he couldn't suppress to the persistent hand that itched his nose, he was too high to take cover.

Too high to realize he was about to take the last hit.

"Go."

I exhaled.

*Pop, pop.*

Six bodies tumbled under gravity.

All six of us hit our targets, and when the gunfire returned in our direction, we had new targets to expire.

The next three went, and I'd killed five men in mere minutes. Together and in sequence, our system worked better than the wasted ammunition of loose bullets.

"I think we can take these out, Lucca," Arlo's low tone murmured.

I believed so too, but my need to get Katia overruled logic. In the end, my reeling emotions had no power over the lives of others. No power when these feelings were too *raw*, *rare*, and *new* for my mind.

"No loose ends," I whispered back.

Sergio slipped his last magazine and readied.

We pointed and finished the job until no more rounds were heard or trained at us.

Blood rushed from my head, and I steadied my feet, falling back onto the wall. I closed my eyes for a brief second while my hand crossed to my side as the burning increased. But until I could dig out the piece of lead from inside my body, the damage would continue.

"Boss?" Sergio questioned.

"I need to find Katia." I launched forward, taking a look at Arlo's calculating gaze. I didn't care. My demon screamed to find her. "You coming?"

"Let's go." Arlo turned, and we followed his silent trail.

Alert and searching for a threat, I picked up a gun from the floor just feet away from the door. Quickly I released the magazine and stared at the four bullets left before Arlo and I slipped inside the door with Sergio in tow.

It was a trap.

And the reason we weren't caught on the floor dead was Fer. He sat with his finger over his mouth beneath the shadow cast by the rail. Next to him, a body faced the ground with its head bent unnaturally to the side.

We moved away from the door, hiding from the light.

"Ilias took our men upstairs. Borelli has every inch covered from the top." Fer's hushed whisper carried only into our ears. "Ilias's plan was to slip behind them, spread away, and take them all at the same time."

My head shook.

It was either the worst fucking plan I'd ever heard of, or the greatest if achieved.

"We have the numbers inside the church. But it's bad." His eyes slid away from me. "Most of ours carry empty guns, and…"

And what?

Why couldn't he look at me?

*Fucking face me!*

"*Speak*," I gritted.

"It's bad, boss. They've captured many, and…"

The current pulled me beneath. Stealing my breath. Burning my lungs. Poisoning me in salt as open wounds torched in pain. Every gasp for air was replaced by suffocating blades slicing through my airway, flooding me with fear.

"Katia?" I whispered her name, obtaining the response I sought out of him.

Fer's eyes lowered, and his head turned to the rail opening. Katia was through there.

She couldn't be.

*Breathe.*

It was shallow. Useless.

Katia.

I took a step, and a hand stopped me.

"Wait, Lucca. You must think it through," Arlo rushed out.

*Think it through?*

All I did was fucking think! I was a prisoner of the future, pondering for a time when I wished to be God. As if every piece I moved didn't cause a chain reaction. As if I felt anything but anger. *All the time.*

Anger for my mother.

Anger for the boy I once was.

Anger for who I'd become.

Anger because *I enjoyed it.*

Just anger.

*Until her.*

I pushed him back against the wall with my arm over his collarbone.

"Look at what it's gotten me."

"Don't lose control. *Not now.*"

Not now...

My lips curled with a snarl.

"What control?" I pushed off his body and turned.

"You hear that, sweetheart?" Old croaks rasped, and I was paralyzed. Feet rooted, soles embedded to the ground by *his* voice. "Silence. Either he's dead or inside." He chuckled. "Oh, Lucc-aaa!" Borelli sang loudly.

His voice carried through the Pipe organ, echoing throughout the church. One of the hardest instruments to learn and master, yet his voice produced a sinister-driven melody as his vocals filtered in pressured air up its windpipes with my name. A repetition bounced into the high ceilings of the church, and the storm that roared outside the web-stained windows played the acoustics.

A full-crafted tune.

*I wasn't ready for what I will be encountering. Because the scene in my head was far from the nightmare I would soon witness.*

My feet pushed forward into the light, strong footfalls that carried me into dismay and fright.

Blond hair, kneeling with a gun to his head.

*Viktor.*

*Fratello.* My stomach turned with rattling bile as his deep blues were straight ahead by the threat that touched his skull.

To his left, Enzo mimicked the same position. On the floor, a body lay face down, beaten into deep sleep, perhaps even death.

Leo.

*Katia.*

It's true, they never made it to safety.

My eyes flew above to the guns drawn and pointed at me, but everywhere I turned, Katia was nowhere to be found.

"Borelli!"

"You just couldn't be dead, could you?" My head snapped, and my fingers trembled in rage upon seeing her.

Katia.

*My Katia.*

Walking backward, Borelli dragged Katia with an arm wrapped around her neck like a noose. Bruising and suffocating, with a silver Colt on her head. A barrel begging to be used, a trigger twitching to be pulled.

The bottom of her dress cracked with the top layer of dried muck. A trail of raindrops plopped onto the floor from its soaking ends, and the rest was a scarlet tie-dye.

A cherry watercolor.

The corner of her lip bled. Her wrists and arms were sharp violet. A whole sleeve hung in crying lace by a thread, and her eyes popped with ruby vessels that blanketed over its white.

I met her dull olives. They were dry, tired, but they latched on and clung to me even as she struggled to match his pace. Fabric trapped her feet, causing him to drag her tighter into his arm's chokehold.

I took a step, and guns cocked all around.

Borelli pressed his Colt harder on her. "*Tsk, tsk,*" his tongue warned.

I didn't take another.

"Let her go," I seethed.

Calm washed me, but it was the calm that promised cruelty. Ill wishes and acid torment. The kind of calm that masked evil.

"Did you really think it would be that easy?" Gray disheveled hair and dark circles colored his puffy eyes. He'd lost weight since the last time I saw him. His sickness took a toll on him. But it wasn't a natural sickness. It was a sickness he'd created with his mind and deranged retribution.

What started as a broken vow turned into war to gain respect. Instead, he had lost because of his own delusions.

And now, I stood before the most dangerous type of man. The kind who had nothing to lose.

Power stripped.

His only child, dead by my hands.

And it was too late for a countermove. Because as I saw his unhinged aura, all he had left was his madness.

Seeing it, witnessing it with him wrapped around her, I felt my heart cracking. A bursting layer that shattered into dust. A black powder that once coated in smoke exploded in sulfur and carbon, like gunpowder. Leaving me open, raw, *feeling*.

Emeralds.

Cherries.

Admiration.

My heart screamed in broken pumps.

Love.

It had been there, offered. Now that it could be taken, I found my biggest remorse. And it was flung before my eyes, threatened, beaten.

The woman who weakened me.

The woman who resurrected my heart into a stupor.

The woman I'd fallen savagely for.

Katia.

*Hold on,* my eyes begged hers.

Trembles furiously shook inside, awakening my pitiless soul, wrecking my demon into homicide, and taking what was ours. To hold her, possess her, and keep her for an eternity.

"What is it that you want?"

Fuck, I would kneel. I would ridicule myself in front of my man. I would disrespect and give my crown away. My seat.

Anything I once thought mattered.

But a rule without Katia was now meaningless.

No legacy, no fight left.

I had just been too proud to see it.

"I thought I'd made it clear, now drop your gun," Crazed black eyes spoke.

I didn't.

He drove the gun harder, causing her head to crane to her shoulder. Her teeth shone with pain, brows deepened with closed eyes.

I tossed it.

"Now kick it!"

I watched how her eyes slowly opened, and I kicked forward.

She was so far away. Closer to the front door than to the altar facing my back.

"I mean, how many young girls had to die for you to hand her over? How selfish could you be to allow bullets meant for her into others?" Borelli wanted to be heard. He wanted to toy with guns drawn at me. My family and the Vitellis on my left with guns pointed at them, and *his* to her. He finally spoke openly. "I thought maybe you would see it my way. You would understand that vows were meant to be kept. But no, you figured you were above me. You thought you deserved her more than I did. You thought your arrangement was superior to mine. *All you had to do was hand her to me!*"

Katia didn't blink for too long, and when she did, it was three quick flutters. She was trying to tell me something. She wanted our eyes to speak.

But what?

"I didn't break it, Borelli." I had to keep him talking.

Buy us all time.

For Ilias and Arlo to take over.

For my men to arrive.

To decipher what Katia wanted to translate.

"But you didn't honor it!" Spit flew from his lips, and his face colored in flushed red.

Katia's right hand twitched. My eyes fell to her fist. It concealed something with curled fingers. I caught the blade's quick glimmer resting up against the inside of her arm, tucked close to her dress and hip for no one to find.

I snapped my gaze to her with straining lungs.

*No.* My head barely moved.

*No.* My eyes thundered louder than the skies.

It hadn't been a question. Katia gave me a heads-up. Nothing more.

A quick five-second head start.

*Not yet!*

Her wrist flicked, and the handle spun in her palm. She pushed her left shoulder down with a jerk, and her hand flew. Crossing up over her chest and driving straight just east of his heart.

Katia stabbed her target, and everything changed.

Above, struggles were loud.

To my left, a brawl broke. A struggle for power.

I ran, then slid my knees across the floor, swiping the gun I had kicked away. I cocked it while gliding to a stop and raised it from below, but his hands were wrapped around hers. Possessing the knife beneath her grip, he pulled it out with a scream. Katia's eyes widened in shock. Startled by how he'd captured the will of her hands and surprised to see the blade out in the open again.

Madness had no limit.

I had no clear target as their bodies erratically moved. One fought for freedom, the other to gain control. I couldn't shoot without the possibility of striking the wrong head.

It all moved too quickly.

It all moved too slowly.

And his hand overpowered hers once again, and my heart emptied as he drove his fists into her abdomen. The blade slipped and hid past her shrieking scream until all was left to see was the handle flush with her flesh. Stabbed by her own friend and the enemy.

Mouth parted, shocked, tortured emeralds cried out.

I, too, felt it. The piercing agony of hearing her pain, slicing and butchering my heart.

"No!"

My hand hit the ground as I lifted myself to reach her.

But instead, I kicked my feet at the sight of him pulling it out, and blood *poured.*

Borelli took the knife from her hand and placed its tip on her neck.

"Stay down!" he threatened, taking one step back.

*Taking her farther away from me!*

My muscles jumped.

He nicked her skin.

"I said. Stay. Down."

I did, and my eyes followed my soul as it was towed farther away. An alone tear marked her cheek, running silently as her hand stretched out for me.

And I broke.

I was powerless as Borelli continued to threaten her with the knife against her delicate neck. He continued to walk farther away as her stained dress swept in fresh red.

Powerless as he slipped through the door, taking her away from me.

Gone were her cherry lips, her golden skin, and her spirited emeralds.

I screamed out in painful rage in the middle of a church. Under God's eyes. The one who gave her to me and took her from me. In his home!

I yelled in blots, ruined and torn in misery as I watched the empty spot where she once stood.

One beat.

Two beats.

Three beats.

I turned.

The odds had spun.

*They were at our mercy.*

My eyes rose to the cross above.

And a silent prayer tumbled from my lips as I whirled back to the front doors, walking.

Mind blank.

Heart soaring.

*Find Katia,* my demon ordered.

"Kill them all."


### *TO BE CONTINUED...*

*"Breathe. Come on, breathe!"*

**COMING SOON**

**A Kingdom Before Us**
(The Moretti Crime Family Book 3)
Lucca & Katia : PART 2

Add *A Kingdom Before Us* to your Goodreads TBR.
*https://bit.ly/AKBUgoodreads*

# NOTE FROM AUTHOR

My father taught me the game of chess as a child.

My mother taught me how to play like a lady.

With time I learned chess is similar to life, filled with moves we decide. Some paths are one shift closer to your goal, while others draw you back.

Life is an open board. It's filled with joy, victories, losses, and stumbles. A mind game. So play it like a lady. A queen, a king, or a knight; head held high and one move at a time.

We are meant to stumble and learn.

We are meant to laugh and feel joy.

We are meant to win.

We are meant to lose.

So cry, feel, scream, giggle. Believe in you and don't allow your crown to tumble.

You are the main piece of your board.

If you enjoyed Katia & Lucca's story, don't be shy, leave a review or a rating. I would be thrilled to read your thoughts and emotions you've experienced while reading their love story.

Stay dangerous, gorgeous.

Hugs,
K Dosal

# ACKNOWLEDGMENTS

My past two years have been a whirlwind of emotions, and if it weren't for the love and support of a few I need to thank, A War Around Us wouldn't exist.

My readers. You push me forward. You push me, and I give. Our tug-of-war game is something I love. Thank you for always giving me motivation to keep writing and pouring pieces of myself into my writing.

Nicole, thank you. For always, ALWAYS being there for me. For calming me when I'm a mess. For believing in me, sometimes more than I believed in myself. For the number of times you have paused your writing, the calls, your time listening to my book rants, and just overall being the best damn friend anyone could have. I love you, Niks.

Justin, Jay & Roy, I adore you. Thank you three for always reminding me to smile. To take a deep breath. For always helping me in seeing the bigger picture. For your unconditional love and cheering.

Smile, breathe, see, love.

To my ARC Team, thank you for your patience, your understanding. For the chance you've taken on Lucca & Katia. For signing up and giving me the chance. Please know that every comment, every reaction, direct message, email, and reply I hold each dearly. You hype me and my words for others to give me that same chance.

Mama, gracias por todo tu amor. Por siempre darme las fuerzas para seguir adelante. Por darme paz que siempre puedo contar contigo. Te amo, madre.

Mitch, thank you for taking my jumbled vision and transforming those ideas into a hauntingly beautiful cover. Your artwork amazes me and I am beyond grateful to have you in this Moretti world.

Love,

K.

# ABOUT THE AUTHOR

K. Dosal is a hopeless romance author, with work ranging from Contemporary, Young Adult, to Mafia. She lives on the Gulf Coast with her Amazing husband, who is always supportive of her wild dreams, and their two energetic boys. When she's not writing or reading, you can find her at the beach with her family, going on boat rides, binge watching, or daydreaming her next book with a coconut Redbull in hand.

K started writing on a spiral notebook after reading a book that made her ask herself, *why not me?* After falling in love with the first pages she wrote, she continued until there was no paper left, then switched to her laptop. Since then, she has been making her dreams come true and living on the *why not me?*

Music lover, kitchen dancer, poker player, and beach lover, K is always looking forward to book-talk and watching where her mind will take her with the stories that inhabit within.

I love to hear from readers.
Feel free to contact me on social media:
@kdosalbooks

## K . DOSAL
SWEET & DANGEROUS ROMANCE